Telegraph Avenue

Telegraph Avenue

A Novel

Michael Chabon

HARPER

An Imprint of HarperCollins*Publishers*

Designed by Leah Carlson-Stanisic
Photograph by Malik Johnson

ISBN 978-1-62490-139-3

To Ayelet, from the drop of the needle to the innermost groove

Call me Ishmael.

—Ishmael Reed, probably.

Dream *of* Cream

A white boy rode flatfoot on a skateboard, towed along, hand to shoulder, by a black boy pedaling a brakeless fixed-gear bike. Dark August morning, deep in the Flatlands. Hiss of tires. Granular unraveling of skateboard wheels against asphalt. Summertime Berkeley giving off her old-lady smell, nine different styles of jasmine and a squirt of he-cat.

The black boy raised up, let go of the handlebars. The white boy uncoupled the cars of their little train. Crossing his arms, the black boy gripped his T-shirt at the hem and scissored it over his head. He lingered inside the shirt, in no kind of hurry, as they rolled toward the next pool of ebbing streetlight. In a moment, maybe, the black boy would tug the T-shirt the rest of the way off and fly it like a banner from his back pocket. The white boy would kick, push, and reach out, feeling for the spark of bare brown skin against his palm. But for now the kid on the skateboard just coasted along behind the blind daredevil, drafting.

⊙   ⊙   ⊙

Moonfaced, mountainous, moderately stoned, Archy Stallings manned the front counter of Brokeland Records, holding a random baby, wearing a tan corduroy suit over a pumpkin-bright turtleneck that reinforced his noted yet not disadvantageous resemblance to Gamera, the giant mutant flying tortoise of Japanese cinema. He had the kid tucked up under his left arm as, with his free right hand, he worked through the eighth of fifteen crates from the Benezra estate, the records in crate number 8 favoring, like Archy, the belly meat of jazz, salty and well marbled with funk. *Electric Byrd* (Blue Note, 1970). Johnny Hammond.

Melvin Sparks's first two solo albums. Charles Kynard, *Wa-Tu-Wa-Zui* (Prestige, 1971). As he inventoried the lot, Archy listened, at times screwing up his eyes, to the dead man's minty quadrophonic pressing of Airto's *Fingers* (CTI, 1972) played through the store's trusty Quadaptor, a sweet gizmo that had been hand-dived from a Dumpster by Nat Jaffe and refurbished by Archy, a former army helicopter electrician holding 37.5 percent—last time he'd bothered to check—of a bachelor's in electrical engineering from SF State.

The science of cataloging one-handed: Pluck a record from the crate, tease the paper sleeve out of the jacket. Sneak your fingers into the sleeve. Waiter the platter out with your fingertips touching nothing but label. Angle the disc to the morning light pouring through the plate window. That all-revealing, even-toned East Bay light, keen and forgiving, always ready to tell you the truth about a record's condition. (Though Nat Jaffe claimed it was not the light but the window, a big solid plate of Pittsburgh glass vaccinated against all forms of bullshit during the period of sixty-odd years when the space currently housing Brokeland Records had been known as Spencer's Barbershop.)

Archy swayed, eyes closed, grooving on the heft of the baby, on the smell of grease coming off of Ringo Thielmann's bass line, on the memory of the upraised eyes of Elsabet Getachew as she gave him head yesterday in the private dining room of the Queen of Sheba Ethiopian restaurant. Recollecting the catenary arch of her upper lip, the tip of her tongue going *addis ababa* along the E string of his dick. Swaying, grooving, feeling on that Saturday morning, just before the boots of the neighborhood tracked bad news through his front door, like he could carry on that way all day, forever.

"Poor Bob Benezra," Archy said to the random baby. "I did not know him, but I feel sorry for him, leaving all these beautiful records. That's how come I have to be an atheist, right there, Rolando, seeing all this fine vinyl the poor man had to leave behind." The baby not too young to start knowing the ledge, the cold truth, the life-and-death facts of it all. "What kind of heaven is that, you can't have your records?"

The baby, understanding perhaps that it was purely rhetorical, made no attempt to answer this question.

⊙   ⊙   ⊙

Nat Jaffe showed up for work under a cloud, like he did maybe five times out of eleven or, be generous, call it four out of every nine. His bad mood a space helmet lowered over his head, poor Nat trapped inside with no way to know whether the atmosphere was breathable, no gauge to tell him when his air supply would run out. He rolled back the deadbolt, keys banging against door, working one-handed himself, because of a crate of records he had crooked up under his left arm. Nat bulled in with his head down, humming low to himself; humming the interesting chord changes to an otherwise lame-ass contemporary pop song; humming an angry letter to the slovenly landlord of the nail salon two blocks up, or to the editor of the *Oakland Tribune* whose letters page his anger often adorned; humming the first fragments of a new theory of the interrelationship between the bossa nova and the *nouvelle vague*; humming even when he wasn't making a sound, even when he was asleep, some wire deep in the bones of Nathaniel Jaffe always resounding.

He closed the door, locked it from the inside, set the crate on the counter, and hung his gray-on-charcoal pin-striped fedora from one of nine double-branched steel hooks that also dated from the days of Spencer's Barbershop. He ran a finger through his dark hair, kinked tighter than Archy's, thinning at the hairline. He turned, straightening his necktie—hepcat-wide, black with silver flecks—taking note of the state of box 8. Working his head around on the neck joints a few times as if in that creak of bones and tension lay hope of release from whatever was causing him to hum.

He walked to the back of the store and disappeared through the beaded curtain, laboriously painted by Nat's son, Julie, with the image of Miles Davis done up as a Mexican saint, St. Miles's suffering heart exposed, tangled with a razor wire of thorns. Not a perfect likeness, to be sure, looking to Archy more like Mookie Wilson, but it could not be easy to paint a portrait of somebody across a thousand half-inch beads, and few besides Julius Jaffe would ever contemplate doing it, let alone give it a try. A minute later Archy heard the toilet flush, followed by a spasm of angry coughing, and then Julie's father came back out to the front of the store, ready to burn another day.

"Whose baby is that?" he said.

"What baby?" said Archy.

Nat unbolted the front door and spun the sign to inform the world that Brokeland was open for business. He gave his skull another tour of the top of his spinal column, hummed some more, coughed again. Turned to his partner, looking almost radiant with malice. "We're totally fucked," he said.

"Statistically, that's indeed likely," Archy said. "In this case, how so?"

"I just came from Singletary."

Their landlord, Mr. Garnet Singletary, the King of Bling, sold grilles and gold finger rings, rope by the yard, three doors up from Brokeland. He owned the whole block, plus a dozen or more other properties spread across West Oakland. Retail, commercial. Singletary was an information whale, plying his migratory route through the neighborhood, taking in all the gossip, straining it for nutrients through his tireless baleen. He had never once turned loose a dollar to frolic among the record bins at Brokeland, but he was a regular customer nonetheless, stopping by every couple of days just to audit. To monitor the balance of truth and bullshit in the local flow.

"Yeah?" Archy said. "What'd Singletary have to say?"

"He said we're fucked. Seriously, why are you holding a baby?"

Archy looked down at Rolando English, a rusty young man with a sweet mouth and soft brown ringlety curls all sweaty and stuck to the side of his head, stuffed into a blue onesie, then wrapped in a yellow cotton blanket. Archy hefted Rolando English and heard a satisfying slosh from inside. Rolando English's mother, Aisha, was a daughter of the King of Bling. Archy had offered to take Rolando off Aisha's hands for the morning, maybe pick up a few items the baby required, and so forth. Archy's wife was expecting their first child, and it was Archy's notion that, given the imminence of paternity, he might get in some practice before the first of October, their due date, maybe ease the shock of finding himself, at the age of thirty-six, a practicing father. So he and Rolando had made an excursion up to Walgreens, Archy not at all minding the walk on such a fine August morning. Archy dropped thirty dollars of Aisha's money on diapers, wipes, formula, bottles, and a package of Nuk nipples—Aisha gave him a list—then sat down right there on the bus bench in front of the Walgreens, where he and Rolando English changed themselves some foul-smelling diaper, had a little snack, Archy working his way through a bag of glazed holes from the United Federation of Donuts, Rolando English obliged to content himself with a pony of Gerber Good Start.

"This here's Rolando," Archy said. "I borrowed him from Aisha English. So far he doesn't do too much, but he's cute. Now, Nat, I gather from one or two of your previous statements that we are fucked in some manner."

"I ran into Singletary."

"And he gave you some insight."

Nat spun the crate of records he had carried in with him, maybe thirty-five, forty discs in a Chiquita crate, started idly flipping through them. At first Archy assumed Nat was bringing them in from home, items from his own collection he wanted to sell, or records he had taken home for closer study, the boundaries among the owners' respective private stocks and the store's inventory being maintained with a careless exactitude. Archy saw that it was all just volunteers. A Juice Newton record, a bad, late Commodores record, a Care Bears Christmas record. Trash, curb fruit, the bitter residue of a yard sale. Orphaned record libraries called out constantly to the partners from wherever fate had abandoned them, emitting a distress signal only Nat and Archy could hear. "The man could go to Antarctica," Aviva Roth-Jaffe once said of her husband, "and come back with a box of wax 78s ." Now, hopeless and hopeful, Nat sifted through this latest find, each disc potentially something great, though the chances of that outcome diminished by a factor of ten with each decrease in the randomness of the bad taste of whoever had tossed them out.

" 'Andy Gibb,' " Nat said, not even bothering to freight the words with contempt, just slipping ghosts of quotation marks around the name as if it were a known alias. He pulled out a copy of *After Dark* (RSO, 1980) and held it up for Rolando English's inspection. "You like Andy Gibb, Rolando?"

Rolando English seemed to regard the last album released by the youngest Gibb brother with greater open-mindedness than his interlocutor.

"I'll go along with you on the cuteness," Nat said, his tone implying that he would go no further than that, like he and Archy had been having an argument, which, as far as Archy could remember, they had not. "Give him."

Archy passed the baby to Nat, feeling the cramp in his shoulder only after he had let go. Nat encircled the baby under the arms with both hands and lifted him, going face-to-face, Rolando English doing a fine job of keeping his head up, meeting Nat's gaze with that same air of willingness to cut people a break, Andy Gibb, Nat Jaffe, whomever. Nat's humming turned soft and lullaby-like as the two considered each other. Baby Rolando had a nice, solid feel to him, a bunch of rolled socks stuffed inside one big sock, dense and sleepy, not one of those scrawny flapping-chicken babies one ran across from time to time.

"I used to have a baby," Nat recalled, sounding elegiac.

"I remember." That was back around the time he first met Nat, playing a wedding at that Naturfreunde club up on Joaquin Miller. Archy, just back from the Gulf, came in at the last minute, filling in for Nat's regular bassist at the time. Now the former Baby Julius was fifteen and, to Archy at least, more or less the same sweet freakazoid as always. Hearing secret harmonies, writing poetry in Klingon, painting his fingernails with Jack Skellington faces. Used to go off to nursery school in a leotard and a tutu, come home, watch *Color Me Barbra*. Even at three, four years old, prone like his father to holding forth. Telling you how french fries didn't come from France or German chocolate from Germany. Same tendency to get caught up in the niceties of a question. Lately, though, he seemed to spend a lot of time transmitting in some secret teenager code, decipherable only by parents, designed to drive them out of their minds.

"Babies are cool," Nat said. "They can do Eskimo kisses." Nat and Rolando went at it, nose to nose, the baby hanging there, putting up with it. "Yeah, Rolando's all right."

"That's what I thought."

"Got good head control."

"Doesn't he, though?" Archy said.

"That's why they call him Head-Control Harry. Right? Sure it is. Head-Control Harry. You want to eat him."

"I guess. I don't really eat babies all that much."

Nat studied Archy the way Archy had studied the A-side of the late Bob Benezra's copy of *Kulu Sé Mama* (Impulse!, 1967), looking for reasons to grade it down.

"So, what, you practicing? That the idea?"

"That was the idea."

"And how's it working out?"

Archy shrugged, giving it that air of modest heroism, the way you might shrug after you had been asked how in God's name you managed to save a hundred orphans trapped in a flaming cargo plane from collision with an asteroid. As he played it off to Nat, Archy knew—felt, like the baby-shaped ache in his left arm—that neither his ability nor his willingness to care for Rolando English for an hour, a day, a week, had anything whatsoever to do with his willingness or ability to be a father to the forthcoming child now putting the finishing touches on its respiratory and endocrine systems in the dark laboratory of his wife's womb.

Wiping a butt, squeezing some Carnation through a nipple, mopping up the milk puke with a dishrag, all that was mere tasks and procedures, a series of steps, the same as the rest of life. Duties to pull, slow parts to get through, shifts to endure. Put your thought processes to work on teasing out a tricky time signature from *On the Corner* (Columbia, 1972) or one of the more obscure passages from *The Meditations* (Archy was currently reading Marcus Aurelius for the ninety-third time), sort your way one-handed through a box of interesting records, and before you knew it, nap time had arrived, Mommy had come home, and you were free to go about your business again. It was like the army: Be careful, find a cool dry place to stash your mind, and hang on until it was over. Except, of course (he realized, experiencing the full-court press of a panic that had been flirting with him for months, mostly at three o'clock in the morning when his wife's restless pregnant tossing disturbed his sleep, a panic that the practice session with Rolando

English had been intended, vainly, he saw, to alleviate), it never would be over. You never would get through to the end of being a father, no matter where you stored your mind or how many steps in the series you followed. Not even if you died. Alive or dead or a thousand miles distant, you were always going to be on the hook for work that was neither a procedure nor a series of steps but, rather, something that demanded your full, constant attention without necessarily calling on you to do, perform, or say anything at all. Archy's own father had walked out on him and his mother when Archy was not much older than Rolando English, and even though, for a few years afterward, as his star briefly ascended, Luther Stallings still came around, paid his child support on time, took Archy to A's games, to Marriott's Great America and whatnot, there was something further required of old Luther that never materialized, some part of him that never showed up, even when he was standing right beside Archy. Fathering imposed an obligation that was more than your money, your body, or your time, a presence neither physical nor measurable by clocks: open-ended, eternal, and invisible, like the commitment of gravity to the stars.

"Yeah," Nat said. For a second the wire in him went slack. "Babies are cute. Then they grow up, stop taking showers, and beat off into their socks."

There was a shadow in the door glass, and in walked S. S. Mirchandani, looking mournful. And the man had a face that was built for mourning, sag-eyed, sag-jowled, lamentation pooling in the spilt-ink splash of his beard.

"You gentlemen," he said, always something elegiac and proper in his way of speaking the Queen's English, some remembrance of a better, more civilized time, "are fucked."

"I keep hearing that," Archy said. "What happened?"

"Dogpile," Mr. Mirchandani said.

"Fucking Dogpile," Nat agreed, humming again.

"They are breaking ground in one month's time."

"One month?" Archy said.

"Next month! This is what I am hearing. Our friend Mr. Singletary was speaking to the grandmother of Mr. Gibson Goode."

Nat said, "Fucking Gibson Goode."

Six months prior to this morning, at a press conference with the mayor at his side, Gibson "G Bad" Goode, former All-Pro quarterback for the Pittsburgh Steelers, president and chairman of Dogpile Recordings, Dogpile Films, head of the Goode Foundation, and the fifth richest black man in America, had flown up to Oakland in a customized black-and-red airship, brimming over with plans to open a second Dogpile "Thang" on the long-abandoned Telegraph Avenue site of the old Golden State market, two blocks south of Brokeland Records. Even larger than its giant predecessor near Culver City, the Oakland Thang would comprise a ten-screen cineplex, a food court, a gaming arcade, and a twenty-unit retail galleria anchored by a three-story Dogpile media store, one floor each for music, video, and other (books, mostly). Like the Fox Hills Dogpile store, the Oakland flagship would carry a solid general-interest selection of media but specialize in African-American culture, "in all," as Goode put it at the press conference, "its many riches." Goode's pockets were deep, and his imperial longings were married to a sense of social purpose; the main idea of a Thang was not to make money but to restore, at a stroke, the commercial heart of a black neighborhood cut out during the glory days of freeway construction in California. Unstated during the press conference, though inferable from the way things worked at the L.A. Thang, were the intentions of the media store not only to sell CDs at a deep discount but also to carry a full selection of used and rare merchandise, such as vintage vinyl recordings of jazz, funk, blues, and soul.

"He doesn't have the permits and whatnot," Archy pointed out. "My boy Chan Flowers has him all tangled up in environmental impacts, traffic studies, all that shit."

The owner and director of Flowers & Sons funeral home, directly across Telegraph from the proposed Dogpile site, was also their Oakland city councilman. Unlike Singletary, Councilman Chandler B. Flowers was a record collector, a free-spending fiend, and without fully comprehending the reasons for his stated opposition to the Dogpile plan, the partners had been counting on it, clinging to the ongoing promise of it.

"Evidently something has changed the Councilman's mind," said S. S. Mirchandani, using his best James Mason tone: arch and weary, hold the vermouth.

"Huh," Archy said.

There was nobody in West Oakland more hard-ass or better juiced than Chandler Flowers, and the something that evidently had changed his mind was not likely to have been intimidation.

"I don't know, Mr. Mirchandani. Brother has an election coming," Archy said. "Barely came through the primary. Maybe he's trying to stir up the base, get them a little pumped. Energize the community. Catch some star power off Gibson Goode."

"Certainly," said Mr. Mirchandani, his eyes saying *no way*. "I am sure there is an innocent explanation."

Kickbacks, he was implying. A payoff. Anybody who managed, as Mr. Mirchandani did, to keep a steady stream of cousins and nieces flowing in from the Punjab to make beds in his motels and wash cars at his gas stations without running afoul of the authorities at either end, was likely to find his thoughts running along those lines. It was almost as hard for Archy to imagine Flowers—that stiff-necked, soft-spoken, and everlastingly *correct* man, a hero in the neighborhood since Lionel Wilson days—taking kickbacks from some showboating ex-QB, but then Archy tended to make up for his hypercritical attitude toward the condition of vinyl records by going too easy on human beings.

"Anyways, it's too late, right?" Archy said. "Deal already fell through. The bank got cold feet. Goode lost his financing, something like that?"

"I don't really understand American football," said S. S. Mirchandani. "But I am told that when he was a player, Gibson Goode was quite famous for something called 'having a scramble.' "

"The option play," Nat said. "For a while there, he was pretty much impossible to sack."

Archy took the baby back from Nat Jaffe. "G Bad was a slippery motherfucker," he agreed.

⊙   ⊙   ⊙

Mr. Nostalgia, forty-four, walrus mustache, granny glasses, double-extra-large Reyn Spooner (palm trees, saw grass, woodies wearing surfboards), stood behind the Day-Glo patchwork of his five-hundred-dollar exhibitor's table, across a polished concrete aisle and three tables down from the signing area, under an eight-foot vinyl banner that read MR. NOSTALGIA'S NEIGHBORHOOD, chewing on a Swedish fish, unable to believe his fucking eyes.

"Yo!" he called out as the goon squad neared his table: two beefy white security guys in blue poly blazers and a behemoth of a black dude, Gibson Goode's private muscle, whose arms in their circumference were a sore trial to the sleeves of his black T-shirt. "A little respect, please!"

"Damn right," said the man they were escorting from the hall, and as they came nearer, Mr. Nostalgia saw that it really was him. Thirty years too old, twenty pounds too light, forty watts too dim, maybe: but him. Red tracksuit a size too small, baring his ankles and wrists. Jacket waistband riding up in back under a screened logo in yellow, a pair of upraised fists circled by the words BRUCE LEE INSTITUTE, OAKLAND, CA. Long and broad-shouldered, with that spring in his gait, coiling and uncoiling. Making a show of dignity that struck Mr. Nostalgia as poignant if not successful. Everybody staring at the guy, all the men with potbellies and back hair and doughy white faces, heads balding, autumn leaves falling in their hearts. Looking up from the bins full of back issues of *Inside Sports*, the framed Terrible Towels with their bronze plaques identifying the nubbly signature in black Sharpie on yellow terry cloth as that of Rocky Bleier or Lynn Swann. Lifting their heads from the tables ranged with rookie cards of their youthful idols (Pete Maravich, Robin Yount, Bobby Orr), with canceled checks drawn on long-vanished bank accounts of Ted Williams or Joe Namath; unopened cello packs of '71 Topps baseball cards, their fragile black borders pristine as memory, and of '86 Fleer basketball cards, every one holding a potential rookie Jordan. Watching this big gray-haired black man they half-remembered, a face out of their youth, get the bum's rush. *That's the dude from the signing line. Was talking to Gibson Goode, got kind of loud. Hey, yeah, that's what's-his-face.* Give him credit, the poor bastard managed to keep his chin up. The chin—him, all right—with the Kirk Douglas dimple. The light eyes. The hands, Jesus, like two up-rooted trees.

"Consider yourselves fortunate, gentlemen," Mr. Nostalgia called as they swept past his table. "That man could kill you with one finger if he wanted to."

"Awesome," said the younger of the goons, head shaved clean as a porn star's testicle. "Long as he buys a ticket first."

Mr. Nostalgia was not a troublemaker. He liked to smoke prescription indica, watch television programs about World War II, eat Swedish fish, and listen to the Grateful Dead, in any combination or grouping thereof. Undoubtedly, sure, he had issues with authority, his father a survivor of two camps, his mother a marcher on Washington, Mr. Nostalgia unfit to hold down any job requiring him to answer to a boss. Great as he might be in circumference, however, Mr. Nostalgia was only five-six, almost, in his huaraches, and not quite in fighting trim. His one reliable move, if you hoped to base a style of kung fu on it, you would probably have to go with Pill Bug. Mr. Nostalgia avoided beefs, quarrels, bar fights, and showdowns foreign and domestic. He deplored violence, except in 1944, in black and white, on television. He was a merchant of good reputation and long standing who had forked over a hefty fee to the organizers of the East Bay Sports and Card Show, some of which money had gone to pay for the protection, the peace of mind, that these goons in their blue blazers would, at least in theory, provide. And peace of mind, face it, was not merely a beautiful phrase; it was a worthy ambition, the aim of religions, the promise of underwriters. But Mr. Nostalgia, as he would afterward explain to his wife (who would sooner eat a bowl of mashed Ebola than attend another card show), was deeply outraged by the rough treatment to which a hero of his youth was being subjected, for no reason other than his having managed to ninja himself onto the floor of the Convention Center without a ticket. And so, on that Saturday morning in the Kaiser Center, Mr. Nostalgia surprised himself.

He came out from behind the ramparts of his neighborhood—replete as a Vegas buffet with choice offerings in the nonsports line that he had made his specialty and métier, among them a complete set of the 1971

Bobby Sherman *Getting Together* cards, including the very tough number 54. Mr. Nostalgia moved with a stately glide that had led at least one uncharitable observer over the years to remark, seeing him go by in one of his floral numbers, that the Pasadena Rose Parade appeared to be missing a float.

"Wait up, let me get the man a ticket," he called after the retreating security escort.

Gibson Goode's bodyguard glanced over his shoulder for half a second, like he was verifying that he hadn't just stepped in dog shit. The goons in the blue blazers kept walking.

"Hey, yo!" Mr. Nostalgia said. "Come on! Hey, come on, you guys! That's Luther Stallings."

It was Stallings who came to a stop first, digging in, bucking his captors, turning to confront his redeemer. The familiar smile—its charm gapped and stained by drugs or prison dentistry or maybe only by the kind of poverty that would lead you to try to skirt an eight-dollar admission fee—put an ache behind Mr. Nostalgia's breastbone.

"Thank you, my good man," Stallings said. Ostentatious, showing up the goons. "My dear friend . . ."

Mr. Nostalgia supplied his actual last name, which was long, Jewish, and comical, a name for a type of cheese or sour bread. Stallings repeated it flawlessly and without the hint of mockery that it typically inspired.

"My friend here," Stallings explained, shouldering free of the goons like an escape artist shrugging out of a straitjacket, "has kindly offered to float me the price of admission."

A slight rise in intonation at the end, almost putting a question mark there. Making sure he had his facts right.

"Absolutely," Mr. Nostalgia said. He remembered sinking deep into a greasy Herculon seat at the Carson Twin cinema, a Saturday afternoon thirty years ago, an elephant of joy sitting on his chest, watching a movie with a mostly black cast—it was a mostly black audience—called *Night Man*. In love with every single thing about that movie. The girl in her silver Afro. The hand-to-hand fighting. The funky soundtrack. A chase involving a green 1972 Saab Sonett driven at top speed through streets that were recognizably those of Carson, California. The gear, tackle, and explosives carried by the bank robbers. Above all, the movie's star, loose-limbed, still, and taciturn like a McQueen hero and with the same willingness to look silly, which was another way of saying charm. And—indisputably, in 1973—a Master of Kung Fu. "It's truly an honor."

The goons zoomed in on Mr. Nostalgia, training their scopes, scanning the green two-day exhibitor's pass hanging from a lanyard around his neck. Faces going dull, losing some of their bored swagger as they tried to remember if there was anything about this type of situation in the official goon manual.

"He was harassing Mr. Goode," said Goode's bodyguard, stepping in to shore up morale in the muscle department. "You buy him a ticket," he told Mr. Nostalgia, "he just going to harass him some more."

"Harassing?" Luther Stalling said, wild with incredulity. Innocent of every crime of which he ever had or ever would be accused for all time. "How I'm harassing that man? I just want to get with him, have my thirty seconds at his feet, standing on line like everybody else. Get my autograph off him, go about my way."

"Straight autograph from Mr. Goode going to cost you forty-five dollars," the bodyguard pointed out. For all his girth, height, and general monstrousness, his voice was gentle, patient, the man paid, basically, to suffer fools. Maintain a fool-free perimeter around G Bad without making his employer look like a dick. "How you going to pay that, you ain't even have eight?"

"Buddy, hey, yo," Stallings said, then got the name right again with another painful flash—painful to Mr. Nostalgia, at any rate—of that scrimshaw smile. Whatever the man had been doing, apart from simply getting old, to have so brutally pared himself down, hollowed himself out, since his glory days, it didn't seem to affect his memory; or maybe he wasn't doing it anymore. "I hope, I, uh, wonder," going all in with the question mark this time, "if maybe I could persuade you to help me out?"

Mr. Nostalgia stepped back, an involuntary move ingrained by years of tangling with the hustlers, operators, schnorrers, and short-change artists who flecked the world of card shows like weevils in flour. Thinking there was a difference of more than thirty-seven dollars between offering to pick up the price of admission, a gesture of respect, and springing for the man to buy himself, of all things, a Gibson Goode autograph. Mr. Nostalgia tried to remember if he had ever seen or even heard of a celebrity (however well forgotten) who was prepared to stand in line to pay cash for another celebrity's signature. Why did Stallings want it? Where was he going to have G Bad *put* it? He did not appear to be carrying any obvious signables, book, photograph, jersey, not even a program, a napkin, a Post-it. *I just want to* get *with him.* To what end? Mr. Nostalgia never could have flourished in his trade without maintaining a keen ear for the slick lines of grifters and bullshit artists, and Luther Stallings was definitely setting off Klaxons, up to something, working some angle. Had already blown his play, in fact, until Mr. Nostalgia for some reason had felt it necessary to leave the safety of his neighborhood and stick his nose where it didn't belong. Mr. Nostalgia could hear his wife passing the sole necessary judgment on the matter, another in the string of endless variations on her single theme, *What in God's name were you thinking?* But Mr. Nostalgia's title was not a mere honorific; his d/b/a was his DNA. Remembering the weight of that elephant of happiness upon him, on that Saturday afternoon at the Carson Twin in 1974, he chose to believe in the truth of Luther Stallings. A man could want things far stranger and less likely than a quarterback's signature on a scrap of cash register tape or a torn paper bag.

"Maybe I can do better than that," Mr. Nostalgia said.

He reached into the back pocket of his denim shorts and took out a folded, sweat-dampened manila envelope. Inside it were the other two green badges on lanyards to which, at his level of participation, he was entitled. He fished out one badge and pushed his way through the screen of goons. Luther Stallings bowed his head, revealing an incipient Nelson Mandela bald spot, and Mr. Nostalgia bestowed the badge on him, Oz emboldening the Lion.

"Mr. Stallings is working for me today," he said.

"That's right," Stallings said at once, sounding not just sincere but impatient, like he had been looking forward for days to helping out in

Mr. Nostalgia's booth. His eyes had flicked, barely, across the badge as Mr. Nostalgia hung it on him; he said, not missing a trick, "In Mr. Nostalgia's Neighborhood."

"Working how?" said the older of the two goons.

"He's doing a signing at my booth," Mr. Nostalgia said. "I got a complete and a partial set, no Bruce Lee, of the *Masters of Kung Fu* series, I got a few other things Mr. Stallings has kindly consented to sign. A lobby card from *Black Eye*, I'm pretty sure."

" '*Masters of Kung Fu*,' " Stallings repeated, barely managing to avoid sounding like he had absolutely no idea what Mr. Nostalgia was talking about.

"Donruss, 1976, it's a tough set."

Four clueless looks sought enlightenment at the hands of Mr. Nostalgia.

"Uh, guys?" Mr. Nostalgia said with a circular sweep of his hands, taking in the echoing space all around them. "Trading cards? Little rectangles of cardboard? Stained with bubble gum? Pop one in the spokes of your bicycle, make it sound like a Harley-Davidson?"

"Damn, seriously?" Stallings could not keep it back. "*Masters of Kung Fu*. They got a Luther Stallings in there?"

"Naturally," Mr. Nostalgia said.

"Luther Stallings." The older of the two blue blazers, lank dark hair, the flowerpot skull and triangle chin of a Russian or a Pole, about Mr. Nostalgia's age, tried out the name. Scrunching up one side of his face like he was screwing a loupe into his eye socket. "Okay, yeah. What's it? *Strutter*. Seriously, that's you?"

"My first part," Stallings said, seizing upon this unexpected opportunity to preen. Loving it. Putting one of those massive antler hands on Mr. Nostalgia to let him know he was loving it: doing what he must do best. Restoring the goon squad to their proper roles as members of the Luther Stalling Irregulars. "Year after I won the title."

"Title in what? Kung fu?"

"Wasn't one at that time. Was in karate. In Manila. World champion."

"World champion, bullshit," said Goode's bodyguard. "I give you that."

Stallings flat ignored the big man. Mr. Nostalgia, feeling fairly balls-out pleased with himself, tried to do the same.

"We all done here, gentlemen?" Stallings asked the blue blazers.

The security guys in the blue blazers checked in with the bodyguard, who shook his head, disgusted.

"I tell you what, Luther," the bodyguard said. "You even flick a boogie in Mr. Goode's general *vicinity*, I will come down on you, motherfucker. And I will show no mercy."

The man turned and, with a forbearing hitch in his walk, rolled back to the signing table where his boss, head shaved to stubble, wearing a black polo shirt with a red paw print where the alligator would have gone, armed with nothing but a liquid-silver marker and a high-priced smile, sat fighting his way through an impressively long line of autograph seekers. Game-worn jerseys, game-used footballs, cards, ball caps, he was going to clear nine, ten thousand today.

"Yeah, whatever," Stallings said, as if he could not care less about Gibson Goode.

Working up a surprising amount of swagger, he followed Mr. Nostalgia to the booth. You would have thought the man had just saved himself from being tossed out of the building by the goon squad. Mr. Nostalgia recognized objectively that he ought to be annoyed, but somehow it made him feel sorrier for Stallings.

"Wow, check this shit out."

Stallings worked his gaze along the table, taking in the sealed wax packs of *Garbage Pail Kids* and *Saturday Night Fever*, the unopened box of Fleer *Dune* cards, the *Daktari* and *Gentle Ben* and *Mork & Mindy* board games, the talking Batman alarm clock, the Aurora model kits of the *Spindrift* and *Seaview* in their original shrink-wrap.

"They even got cards for that *ALF*, huh?" he said.

His voice as he made this observation, like his expression as he took it all in, sounded unhappy to Mr. Nostalgia, even forlorn. Not the disdain that Mr. Nostalgia's wife always showed for his stock-in-trade but something more like disappointment.

"Used to be pretty standard for a hit show," Mr. Nostalgia said, wondering when Stallings would get around to hitting him up for the forty-five dollars. "Nothing much of interest in that set."

Though Mr. Nostalgia loved the things he sold, he had no illusion that they held any intrinsic value. They were worth only what you would pay for them; what small piece of everything you had ever lost that, you might come to believe, they would restore to you. Their value was indexed only to the sense of personal completeness, perfection of the soul, that would flood you when, at last, you filled the last gap on your checklist. But Mr. Nostalgia had never seen his nonsports cards so sharply disappoint a man.

"*ALF*, yeah, I remember that one," Stallings said. "That's real nice. *Growing Pains*, *Mork & Mindy*, uh-huh. Where the *Masters of Kung Fu* at?"

Mr. Nostalgia went around to a bin he had tucked under the table that morning after setting up and dug around inside of it. After a minute of moving things around in the bin, he came out with the partial set, the one that was missing the Lee and the Norris cards. "Fifty-two cards in the set," he said. "You're number, I don't know, twelve, I think it is."

Stallings shuffled through the cards, whose imagery depicted, bordered by cartoon bamboo, labeled with takeout-menu-style fake Chinese lettering, a fairly indiscriminate mixture of real and fictitious practitioners (Takayuki Kubota, Shang-Chi) of a dozen forms of martial arts in addition to the eponymous one, including bartitsu (Sherlock Holmes) and savate (Count Baruzy). At last Stallings came up with his card. Stared at the picture, made a sound like a snort through his nose. The card featured a color still from one of his movies, poorly reproduced. A young Luther Stallings, in red kung fu pajamas, flew across the frame toward a line of Chinese swordsmen, feet first, almost horizontal.

"Damn," Stallings said. "I don't even remember what that's from."

"Take it," Mr. Nostalgia said. "Take the whole set. It's a present, from me to you, for all the pleasure your work has given me over the years."

"How much you get for it?"

"Well, the set, like I said, it's pretty tough. I'm asking five, but I'd probably take three. Might go for seven-fifty with the Bruce Lee, the Chuck Norris."

"Chuck Norris? Yeah, I went up against the motherfucker. Three times."

"No joke."

"Kicked his ass all over Taipei."

Mr. Nostalgia figured he could look it up later if he wanted to break some small, previously unbroken place in his own leaf-buried heart. "Go on," he said. "It's yours."

"Yeah, hey, thanks. That's really nice. But, uh, no offense, I'm already so, like, *overburdened*, you know what I'm saying, with stuff out of the past I'm carrying around."

"Oh, no, sure—"

"I just hate to add to the pile."

"I totally understand."

"Got to keep mobile."

"Of course."

"Travel light."

"Right-o."

"How much," Luther Stallings said, lowering his voice to a near-whisper. Swallowing, starting over, louder the second time. "How much you get for my card by itself."

"Oh, uh," Mr. Nostalgia said, understanding a microsecond or two too late to pull off the lie that he was going to have to tell it. "A hundred. Ninety, a hundred bucks."

"No shit."

"Like around ninety."

"Uh-huh. Tell you what. You give me this one card, Luther Stallings in . . . I'm going to make a wild guess and say it was *Enter the Panther*."

"Has to be." Mr. Nostalgia felt the play begin again, the game that Luther Stallings was trying to run on him and, somehow, on Gibson Goode.

"And I'm a sign it, okay?" Here it came. "Then I'm a trade it back to you for forty-five bucks."

"Okay," Mr. Nostalgia said, feeling unaccountably saddened, crushed, by the pachyderm weight of a grief that encompassed him and Stallings and every man plying his lonely way in this hall through the molder and dust of the bins. The world of card shows had always felt like a kind of true fellowship to Mr. Nostalgia, a league of solitary men united in their pursuit of the lost glories of a vanished world. Now that vision struck him as pie in the sky at best and as falsehood at the very worst. The past was irretrievable, the league of lonely men a fiction, the pursuit of the past a doomed attempt to run a hustle on mortality.

"If that's how you want it," Mr. Nostalgia said. He was not averse, in principle, to raising the five-dollar value of the Stallings card by a factor of three or four. But as he handed Stallings the gold-filled Cross pen, a bar mitzvah gift from his grandparents that he liked to use when he was getting something signed for his own collection, he wished that he had never come out from behind the table, had let the security guards sweep Luther Stallings past Mr. Nostalgia's Neighborhood and clear on out of the Kaiser Center.

Over the course of the next half hour, he checked on Stallings a couple of times as the man made his way to the end of the signing line for Gibson Goode, then inched his way to the front one lonely man at a time. In the middle of selling a 1936 Wolverine gum card, "The Fight with the Shark," for $550 to a dentist from Danville, Mr. Nostalgia happened to glance over and see that Luther Stallings had regained his place at the front. The bodyguard got to his feet looking ready, as promised, to suspend mercy, but after a brownout of his smile, Gibson Goode reached for the bodyguard and gently stiff-armed him, palm to the big man's chest, and the big man, with a mighty headshake, stepped off. Words passed between Goode and Stallings—quietly, without agitation. To Mr. Nostalgia, reading lips and gestures, sometimes able to pick up a word, a phrase, the conversation seemed to boil down to Gibson Goode saying no repeatedly, with blank politesse, while Luther Stallings tried to come up with new ways of getting Goode to say yes.

There was only so much of this that the people in line behind Luther Stallings were willing to put up with. A rumor of Stallings's earlier outburst, his near-ejection, began to circulate among them. There was a certain amount of moaning and kvetching. Somebody gave voice to the collective desire for Stallings to *Come on!*

Stallings ignored it all. "You asked him?" he said, raising his voice as he had done an hour ago, when the blue blazers came to see how he might like to try getting himself tossed. "You asked him about *Popcorn*?" Talking loudly enough for Mr. Nostalgia and everybody in the neighborhood to hear. "Then I got the man for you. Hooked him. You know I did."

The expressions of impatience, general down the line, rose to outright jeering. Stallings turned on the crowd, trying to scowl them into silence, snapping at a man in a Hawaiian shirt standing two guys behind him. The man said, "No, fuck *you*!"

Wading into the signing area, arms windmilling to reach for Stallings in a kind of freestyle of aggression, came the two blue blazers, Shaved Ball and the Soviet. They took brusque hold of Stallings's arms, faces compressed as if to resist a stink, and jerked his arms back and toward his spine.

Two seconds later, no more, Shaved Ball and the Soviet were lying flat on their backs on the painted cement floor of the hall. Mr. Nostalgia could not have said for certain which of them had taken the kick to the head, which the punch to the abdomen, or if Luther Stallings had even moved very much at all. As they'd gone tumbling backward, the line of autograph seekers had shuddered, rippled. Human turbulence troubled all the surrounding lines, people waiting for Chris Mullin, Shawn Green.

"Bitch," Stallings said, turning back to Gibson Goode, in his polo shirt, with his sockless loafers. "I want my twenty-five grand!"

Gibson Goode, being Gibson Goode, Mr. Nostalgia supposed, might have had no choice in the matter: He kept, as his legend said he must, his cool. The same quiet, restraining hand against his bodyguard's chest. Unintimidated. Still smiling. He took out his wallet, opened it, and counted out ten bills, rapid-fire. Slid them across the signing table. Luther Stallings studied them, head down, chest rising and falling. The money lay there, exciting comment in the line, ten duplicate cards from the highly collectable Dead Presidents series. Luther shook his head once. Then he reached down and took the money. Resigned—long since resigned, Mr. Nostalgia thought—to doing things he knew he was going to regret. When he went past Mr. Nostalgia's table, without so much as a thank-you, he had not managed to get his chin up again.

It was only later, as a voice on the PA was chasing stragglers from the hall and the lights went out over the signing area, that Mr. Nostalgia noticed Luther Stallings had walked off with his gold pen.

⊙   ⊙   ⊙

On a Saturday night in August 1973, outside the Bit o' Honey Lounge, a crocodile-green '70 Toronado sat purring its crocodile purr. Its chrome grin stretched beguiling and wide as the western horizon.

"Define 'toronado,' " said the man riding shotgun.

Behind his heavy-rimmed glasses, he had sleepy eyes, but he scorned sleep and frowned upon the somnolence of others. In defiance of political fashion, he greased his long hair, and its undulant luster was clear-coat deep. His name was Chandler Bankwell Flowers III. His grandfather, father, and uncles were all morticians, men of sobriety and pomp, and he inhabited a floating yet permanent zone of rebellion against them. Nineteen months aboard the *Bon Homme Richard* had left Chan Flowers with an amphetamine habit and a tattoo of Tuffy the Ghost on the inside of his left forearm. The shotgun, holstered in a plastic trash bag alongside his right leg, was a pump-action Mossberg 500.

" 'Define' it?" said the driver, Luther Stallings, not giving the matter his full attention. His eyes, green flecked with gold, kept finding excuses to visit the rearview mirror. "It's the name of a car."

"But what does it *mean*? What is the definition of the word 'toronado.' Tell me that."

"You tell me," Luther said, more wary now.

"It's a question."

"Yeah, but what are you really asking?"

"Toro-*nah*-do." Chan strumming the "R" like a string of Ricky Ricardo's guitar. "You're driving it. Talking about it. In *love* with it. Don't even know what it means."

Luther massaged the leather cover on the steering wheel as if feeling for a cyst. He took another glance in the mirror, then leaned forward to look past Chan at the Bit o' Honey's front door. Where Chan ran to dark and stocky, Luther Stallings was long and light-skinned, with an astronaut chin. He had served one tour in the U.S. Army, most of it spent splintering planks with his feet for a hand-to-hand combat demonstration team. He was dressed as for dancing, tight plaid bell-bottom slacks, a short-sleeved terry pullover. His hair rose freshly stoked into a momentous Afro.

"I believe it is Spanish," Luther said. "A common expression, can be loosely translated to 'suck my dick.' "

"Vulgar language," Chan said, drawing on his rich patrimony of improving maxims. That stiff mortuary grammar, hand-beaten into him by his old man, had always embarrassed him when they were youngsters. In this hoodlum revolutionary phase he was going through, Chan flaunted the properness of his speech, a lily in the lapel of a black leather car coat. "Always the first and last refuge of the man with nothing to say."

Luther broke free of the mirror to look at Chan. *"Toronado,"* he said, employing the imperative.

"You don't know, do you?" Chan said. "Just admit. You are driving around, you paid three thousand dollars for this vehicle, cash, for all you know, a toronado's, what, might be some kind of brush you use for cleaning a Mexican toilet bowl."

"I don't care what it—"

"Juanita, quick, get the toronado, I have diarrhea—"

"It means a *bullfighter!*" Luther said, rising to the bait despite long experience, despite needing to keep one eye on the rearview and one on the diamond-tufted vinyl door of the lounge, in spite of wanting to be a hundred years and a thousand miles away from this place and this night. "A fighter of bulls."

"In *Spanish,*" Chan suggested in a mock-helpful tone.

Luther shrugged. When Chan was nervous, he got bored, and when he got bored, he would start trouble, any kind of trouble, just to break the tedium. But there was more to this line of questioning. Chan was mad at Luther and trying to hide it. Had been trying for days to hold his anger close, like the Spartan boy with the fox in his shirt, let it feast on his intestines rather than cop to hiding it.

" 'Bullfighter,' " Chan said with bitter precision, "is *torero*."

He bent down to scoop a handful of twelve-gauge cartridges from a box between his feet and pocketed them at the hip of his tweed blazer. His hair, heavy with pomade, gave off a dismaying odor of flowers left too long in a vase, putrid as envy itself.

"Then uh, 'tornado,' " Luther tried.

This was such a contemptible suggestion that Chan, who generally never lacked for verbal expressions of contempt, could dignify it only with a smirking shake of his head. Luther was about to point out that it was he, the ignorant one, who'd just laid down thirty-two hundred-dollar bills for the beautiful car with the mysterious name, while Professor Flowers remained a frequent denizen of the buses.

"Chan, you captious motherfucker—" he began, but then stopped.

From another pocket of his tweed blazer, patches on the elbows, Chan drew a pair of sateen gloves, dark purplish blue. Shoddy things, busted at the seams, tricked out with pointy fish fins. Last Halloween, Chan's little brother, Marcel, out trick-or-treating in a Batman suit, had been hit by a car and killed. Drunken negroes in a Rambler American, boy stepping off the curb with his face too small to really fit the eyeholes of the mask. Chan had some tiny hands, but even so, the gloves were a tight fit, and as he pulled them on, they split some more.

When Luther saw Chan wearing Marcel's purple crime-fighting gloves, he didn't know what to say. He threw another glance at the rear-view: Telegraph Avenue nocturne, a submarine wobble of light and shadow. Chan reached into the garbage bag, came out with a bat-eared mask stamped from flimsy plastic. He slipped the elastic string over the back of his head, parked the borrowed face at the top of his forehead.

"Okay," Luther said at last, the second smartest boy in the room every day of his life from 1955 to the day in 1971 that had Chan shipped out, "tell me what it means."

A girl, at key points also constructed like the car along a beguiling x axis, came out of the Bit o' Honey Lounge. She wore tight white jeans whose flared legs bellied like sails. Her hair was tied back shiny against her head to emerge aft in a big puffball. Her feet rode the howdahs of swaying platform sandals. As she sauntered past the car, she pulled the tails of her short-sleeved madras shirt from the waist of her jeans, knotting them together under her breasts.

"That's it," Luther said. He pressed down on the clutch and readied his hand on the gearshift. "Go if you're going."

Chan lowered the mask over his face, and Luther saw that it had been painted top to bottom, matte black paint effacing the line that marked the bottom edge of Batman's cowl, paint sprayed over the heroic molded chin dimple, the affable molded smile. Behind the mask, Chan's eyes glistened like organs exposed by two incisions.

"Jungle action," Chan said behind the baffle of the mask. "Oh, and by the way." He shouldered open the passenger door and sprang out of the car. The shotgun in the garbage bag hung by his side like a workaday implement. " 'Toronado' doesn't mean shit."

Chan's right arm snaked into the mouth of the garbage bag as, with his left hand, he grabbed hold of the brass handle of the upholstered front door of the club. He yanked the door open, flinging his right arm out to the side. The garbage bag flew off, revealing the riot gun that Chan had checked out that afternoon from the basement arsenal of a Panther safe house in East Oakland. There was a gust of horns, palaver, and thump, and then the door breathed shut behind Chan. The garbage bag caught on a thermal hook and spun in the air, teased and tugged by unseen hands.

Luther lowered the volume on the in-dash eight-track. City silence, the sigh of a distant bus, the tide of the interstate, Grover Washington, Jr., setting faint, intricate fires up and down the length of "Trouble Man." Beyond that, nothing. Luther felt his attention beginning not so much to wander as to migrate, seeking opportunity elsewhere. Far down the coast highway, at the wheel of his beautiful green muscle car, he made his way to Los Angeles, capital of the rest of his life. In a helicopter shot, he watched himself rolling across an arcaded bridge with the ocean and the dawn and the last of the night spread out all around him.

He heard the stuttering crack of a number of firearms discharging at once. The door of the Bit o' Honey banged open again, spraying horns and shouts. Chan came out at a running walk. He got into the car and slammed the door. Blood streaked his left shoe like a bright feather. The shotgun gave off its sweet, hellish smell, electricity and sizzling fatback.

Luther shifted into first gear, standing on the gas pedal, balanced on it, and on the moment like the trumpeter angel you saw from the Warren Freeway, perched at the tip of the Mormon temple, riding the wild spin of the world itself. Everything Detroit could muster in the way of snarling poured from the 450 engine. They parlayed a dizzying string of green lights all the way to Claremont Avenue. It had been a case of love at first sight for Luther and the Toronado two days before, at a used-car lot down on Broadway. Now, as they tore up Telegraph, something slid coiling through his belly, more like a qualm of lust. Chan tossed his brother's Halloween mask out of the open window, slid the gun under the seat. He peeled away the gloves and started to throw them out, too, but in the end seemed to want to hold on to them, the right one bloody and powder-burned, a while longer. He sat there clutching them in one fist like a duelist looking for someone to slap.

At the Claremont intersection, with no one after them and no sign of the law, Luther eased the car into a red light. Just an ordinary motorist, window down, elbow hooked over the door, grooving on the passage of another summer evening. Somewhere in the vicinity, he had once been told, covered over by time and concrete, lay the founding patch of human business in this corner of the world. Miwok Indians dreaming the dream, living fat as bears, piling up their oyster shells, oblivious to history with its oncoming parade of motherfuckers.

"What happened?" Luther said to Chan, affecting lightness. Only then, in the wake of posing this awful question, did he begin to feel something like dread. Chan just turned up the volume on the music. "Chan, you did it?"

Luther could see Chan struggling to frame the story of what had transpired inside the Bit o' Honey Lounge in some way that did not infuriate him. One thing Chandler Flowers hated more than being underestimated for his intelligence was giving evidence of any lack thereof. The light turned green. Luther steered, for mysterious reasons and in the absence of counterinstruction from his companion, toward the image in his mind of that westernmost angel blowing that apocalyptic horn. A minute went by which Joe Beck and his guitar organized according to their own notions of time and its fuzztone passage. At last Flowers emitted, as through a tight aperture, four words.

"Shot off his hand."

"Left or right?"

"The right hand."

"He a righty or a lefty?"

"Why?"

"Is Popcorn a righty or a lefty?"

"You are suggesting, if Popcorn Hughes turns out to be right-handed, maybe I messed this job up a little less. Because at least now Popcorn only has the hand he doesn't use."

Luther reflected as they rumbled up Tunnel Road toward the spot where, invisibly as a decision turning bad, it became the Warren Freeway. "No," he conceded at last.

After this, they did not speak at all. Luther went on reflecting. At seven in the morning, Monday, he was expected to report to a rented soundstage down in Studio City to film his first scenes for *Strutter*, a low-budget action movie in whose lead he had recently been cast. He was driving around tonight in the up-front money from that job. There was ten grand yet to come, and after that, anything: sequels, endorsements, television work, the parts that Jim Brown was too busy to take, a costarring role with Burt Reynolds. Now, through some damned interlocking of bravado, loyalty, and the existential heedlessness that had helped him to become the 1972 middleweight karate champion of the world, Luther had knotted his pleasantly indistinct future like a sackful of kittens to the plunging stone of Chan Flowers.

Tonight had gone wrong, but even if Popcorn, as planned, had caught a fatal chestful of lead shot and pumped out his life in a puddle under a table by the stage, the situation would have been no better. True, the seed of Panther legend that Chan Flowers hoped to cultivate as Chan "the Undertaker" Flowers, killer of men—a real one, not some make-believe hard-ass in a low-budget grind-house feature—would have been planted. True, the ongoing mental distress caused to Huey Newton by the continued existence of Popcorn Hughes might have been assuaged. But there still would have been no benefit whatsoever to Luther Stallings. Success of the mission would have been another kind of failure, even deeper shit than Luther was in now.

Luther had no politics, no particular feelings toward drug dealers like Popcorn or toward the Black Panthers who had targeted them. He did not care who controlled the city of Oakland or its ghetto streets. He had seen Huey Newton once in his life, black leather jacket, easy smile, talking some shit about disalienation at a house party in the Berkeley flatlands, and had marked him right away as just another stylist of gangster self-love. Luther Stallings, future star of blaxploitation and beyond, had no call to be here, no interest in the outcome either way. Chan asked him to drive, so Luther drove. Now, instead of a murder in his rearview mirror, there was the bloody trail of a fuckup. Meanwhile, the image of the golden angel of the Mormons soloing atop his spire worked its strange allure on Luther's imagination.

"Take a left," Chan said as they rolled off the freeway at the Park Avenue exit.

Luther was about to protest that a left turn would lead them away from the temple when he realized that he had no real reason to want to go to that place. The vague longing to bear some kind of witness to the glory of the angel Moroni winked out inside him, crumbled like ash. Luther aimed the Toronado up Joaquin Miller Road.

"Where we going?" he said.

"I need to think," said the smartest boy in the room. He stared out at the night that streamed like a downpour across the windshield. Then, "Shut up."

"I didn't say nothing," Luther said, though he most definitely had been tossing around some combination of words along the lines of *Ain't it a little late for that now?*

⊙   ⊙   ⊙

"Yeah, I was in that Dogpile one time," Moby was saying. "Down in L.A.?"

Moby was one of the noontime regulars. He was a lawyer, none too unusual a career path for a three-hundred-dollar-a-month abuser of polyvinyl chloride, except that Moby's clients were all cetaceans. His real name was Mike Oberstein. He was notably—given the moniker—white and size 2XL. Wore his longish hair parted down the center and slicked back over his ears in twin flukes. Moby worked for a foundation out of an office in the same building as Archy's wife, bringing action against SeaWorld on behalf of Shamu's brother-in-law, suing the navy for making humpbacks go deaf. He was a passionate and free-spending accruer of fifties and sixties jazz sides.

"It was pretty tight," Moby added.

"Was it?" Nat said. Giving a bottle to Rolando English, who sat fastened safely into an infant carrier, propped up on the counter by the cash register. Nat kept his gaze fixed on the baby so that, Archy understood, he would not have to kill Mike Oberstein with gamma rays shot out of his eyeballs. "Was it *bangin*?"

Archy knew—could not help knowing all the man's rants and treatises on the subject—how it bothered Nat that Moby tried so hard (to be honest, probably wasn't even trying anymore) to sound like he was from the 'hood, from *round the way*, as Moby would have put it, even though he was a sweet-natured white guy from Indiana, someplace.

"It was straight-*up* bangin," Moby said, so well armored in his sweetness and his imaginary Super Fly fur coat that he was impervious if not oblivious to the eyeball lightning Nat was always forking in his direction. "No joke. Found me this crazy side called, Nat, get this, *Jimmy Smith Live in Israel*. Thought it was a myth. I been looking for that for, like, years."

Nat nodded, watching the formula steadily disappear from the bottle, while in his imagination, as Archy could infer by the knot of Nat's shoulders, he took a pristine pressing of *Jimmy Smith Live in Israel* (Isradisc, 1973) out of its sleeve and snapped it over his knee. Twice, into quarters. Then handed it back to Moby without a word, not even needing to say, *Man*, fuck *Dogpile. And the motherfucking Dogpile blimp.*

"Part I don't understand, all due respect, is why y'all act like it some kind of *invasion*," said the King of Bling. "Dogpile coming into this neighborhood."

Garnet Singletary, Baby Rolando's grandfather, was sitting beside Moby at the glass display counter that ran nearly half the length of the south wall of the store, at the end farthest from the window, in order to preserve a certain distance between himself and the parrot. Fifty-Eight, the African grey, sat perched on the shoulder of Cochise Jones, who occupied his usual stool tucked into the corner by the window, Mr. Jones with that inveterate hunch to his spine from fifty years conducting experiments at the keyboard of a Hammond B-3. Decades of avian companionship had raised a fuzz of claw marks at the shoulders of Mr. Jones's green leisure suit, tussocks on the padded polyester lawn. Restless as a radio telescope, the parrot's head with its staring eye plowed the universe for invisible signs and messages. Every so often Fifty-Eight, whose public utterances tended to be musical, would counterfeit the steely vibrato of his owner's B-3, break out into a riff, a stray middle eight, the bird programming its musical selections with an apparent randomness in which Singletary, who feared and admired the bird, claimed to find evidence of calculation and ironical intent.

"Gibson Goode was born here," Singletary continued when no explanation was forthcoming from either partner.

Singletary was in his mid-fifties but looked thirty. Hair sprang carefully from his head in micro-dreads no thicker than his grandson's fingers. His smile easy and warm, his eyes as cold as pennies at the bottom of a well. Like Fifty-Eight's, those eyes missed nothing, cloaking in a universal fog of conversation the ceaseless void of his surveillance. Archy wondered if the man's unease around the bird arose from recognition of a rival or a peer.

Singletary said, "Man grew up down in L.A., but his granny still living over in Rumford Plaza. Y'all was operating in Atlanta, New York, and this dude showed up in his great big black blimp, I might understand how you could feel some resentfulness. But Gibson Goode is a semi-local product. Like"—the eyes teaming up with the smile to give notice that he was about to mess with Nat—"if you was to put you and Archy together. Half local, half out of town."

"Half and half," Nat said, humming to himself, pouring the formula into Rolando English. The boy definitely had an appetite; they had run through the bottles of Good Start by eleven this morning and were working on a can of Enfamil powder mixed with water at Brokeland's bathroom sink, the Enfamil provided by S. S. Mirchandani from a deep, remote, and spidery shelf over at Temescal Liquor, which he owned. The infant carrier came courtesy of the King of Bling.

"Look at him go." Cochise Jones watched the baby formula work its way like mercury in a falling thermometer down the graduations. Intent, pleased, doubtful, as if he had money riding on the outcome. He winked at Archy. Mr. and the late Mrs. Jones never had children of their own. "Boy making me thirsty."

"Yes, I am feeling quite thirsty myself," said Mr. Mirchandani, and Archy felt a flutter of anticipatory dread. "You know, Nat, you really should put in an espresso machine or other form of beverage service."

Archy plunged himself deeper into the mysteries of crate number 8. The theoretical espresso machine was a sore subject, the most recent of many arguments between the co-owners of Brokeland having begun over the question of whether, as Archy had been hinting with increasing heavy-handedness for a couple of years, the time had come to offer more at the counter than unlimited supplies of music and bullshit on tap. Because the truth was, they were *already* fucked, with or without Gibson Goode and his Dogpile empire. They were behind on the rent to Singletary. Their inventory was dwindling as their ability to purchase the better collections ran afoul of cash flow problems. Probably if you looked at the matter coolly and rationally, an activity in which neither partner could be said to excel, they were on their last legs. So many of the other used-record kings of the East Bay had already gone under, hung it up, or turned themselves into Internet-only operations, closing their doors, letting the taps of bullshit go dry. Brokeland Records was nearly the last of its kind, Ishi, Chingachgook, Martha the passenger pigeon.

Every time Archy broached the subject of trying some new angle, branching out, beefing up their website, even, yes, selling coffee drinks and pastries and chai, he ran into heavy resistance from Nat. Not just resistance; the man would shut down the conversation, shut himself down, with that infuriating, self-righteous Abraham the Patriarch way he had sometimes, acting as if he and Archy were not a couple of secondary-market retailers trying to stay afloat but guardians of some ancient greatness that must never be tainted or altered. When really (like any religion, Archy supposed), it was a compound of OCD and existential panic, a displaced fear of change. Reroutings of familiar traffic patterns, new watermarks and doodads on the national currency, revised rules for the bundling of recyclables, such things were anathema to Nat Jaffe. Fresh starts, clean slates, reboots: anathema. He stood against them like an island in the flow, a snag of branches.

"You want a fucking macchiato?" he had said a couple of days earlier, throwing a record album at Archy, nothing too valuable, just a copy of *Stan Getz and J. J. Johnson at the Opera House* (Verve, 1957), Getz sitting in with Johnson, Oscar Peterson, Ray Brown, and Connie Kay. "Here's your fucking macchiato!"

Meaning, sweet light froth of a white guy on top of a dense dark bottom of black. The shot had gone wide, but damn, a flying record, the thing could have sliced Archy's head off. Archy found himself annoyed just thinking about it now. It annoyed him as well that Mr. Mirchandani had mentioned the espresso machine, even though he knew that Mr. Mirchandani was only trying to help out, take up the cause, join the chorus of those who did not want to see Brokeland die. There was no mistaking the fact that Nat was on high simmer today, perhaps two bubbles away from a full-on roll.

"Gentlemen."

It was a mild voice, the voice of a man trained to extol the highest in men and women while seeing them at their lowest. Trained to seemliness, to keeping itself soft and low under the pall of remembrance and grief that forever hung over Flowers & Sons. At the sound of that funereal voice, its head cocked in Singletary's direction, the African grey parrot began to give out, note-perfect, Cochise Jones's reading of the old Mahalia Jackson spiritual "Trouble of the World," found on Mr. Jones's only album as a bandleader, *Redbonin'* (CTI, 1973).

"Look out," Mr. Jones said, but as usual, Fifty-Eight was way ahead of him.

⊙   ⊙   ⊙

In the shade of a wide-brimmed black hat whose vibe wavered between crime boss and Henry Fonda in *Once upon a Time in the West*, pin-striped gray-on-charcoal three-piece, black wing tips shined till they shed a perceptible halo, Chan Flowers came into the store. Slid himself through the front door, ineluctable as a final notice from the county. Straight-backed, barrel-chested, bowlegged. A model of probity, a steady hand to reassure the grieving, a sober man—a *grave* man—solid as the pillar of a tomb. A good dose of gangster to the hat to let you know the councilman played his politics old-school, with a shovel in the dark of the moon. Plus that touch of Tombstone, of Gothic western undertaker, like maybe sometimes when the moon was full and Flowers & Sons stood empty and dark but for the vigil lights, Chan Flowers might up and straddle a coffin, ride it like a bronco.

"Looks like we have ourselves the hard *core* here today," he said, quickly tallying the faces at the counter before settling on Archy, a question in his eyes, something he wanted to know. "Wait out here," he told his nephews.

The two Flowers nephews stayed out on the sidewalk. Like all of Mr. Flowers's younger crop of nephews, they seemed not to be wearing their ill-fitting black suits so much as to be squatting inside them until some less embarrassing habitation came along. They had the solemn faces of practical jokers waiting to spring a gag. One of them took out a book of Japanese math puzzles and started working them with a stub of pencil.

"Mr. Jones!" Flowers said, starting in, with that politician resolve, to fill the boxes of this human sudoku.

"Your Honor," said Cochise Jones.

Flowers reached for Mr. Jones's octave-and-a-half hand, its nails like chips of piano ivory.

"The honor is indeed mine," Flowers said, "as always, to bask in the reflected luster of the legacy you represent. Inventor of the musical styling known as Brokeland Creole." Mr. Jones was also, as far as Archy knew, the first person to use the term *Brokeland* to describe this neighborhood, the ragged fault where the urban plates of Berkeley and Oakland subducted. "Hello, Fifty-Eight."

There was a silence. The bird regarded Flowers.

"Say hello," Mr. Jones said.

"Say *hello*, you little jive-ass motherfucker," Fifty-Eight said.

The voice was that of Cochise Jones, the unmistakable smoker's croak, but way more irritable than Archy had ever heard Mr. Jones become. Everybody laughed except Chan Flowers. His eyes kept aloof from the smile on his lips.

"Keep it up," Flowers told Fifty-Eight. "You know I have a deluxe cherrywood pet casket sitting on my stockroom shelf right now, waiting to house your remains."

This was true; Cochise Jones had made funeral arrangements of Egyptian exactitude for himself and his partner in solitude.

"Brother Singletary." Flowers pointed a slender finger. "The King of Bling, how are you, sir?"

"Councilman," Singletary said, looking at Flowers the same way he looked at Fifty-Eight, with a mix of curiosity and distaste, as if touching his tongue to something bitter at the corner of his mouth.

The two of them, Singletary and Flowers, had beefed often and openly over the years, always in a civilized way. Lawsuits, real estate, a long cold war fought against a backdrop of redevelopment money using proxies and attorneys. West Oakland rumor traced the source of beef to the late 1970s, tendering the story that Singletary had married his wife out from under a preexisting condition of Chan Flowers. Rumor further added the dubious yet somehow creditable information that her reason for choosing Singletary over Flowers came down to an ineradicable odor of putrefaction on the undertaker's hands. "I'm all right, 'less you here to tell me otherwise."

"Now, you know," Flowers said, half addressing the room, the voice modulated, genial, but not, in spite of the rhetoric, orotund. Cool and dispassionate, as ready to express disappointment as flattery. "Back in the Bible, only a *king* could even wear the *bling*. They did not call it that, of course, did they, Mr. Oberstein? King Solomon, in his book of Ecclesiastes, do you know the vernacular he employed to allude to that which we now style 'bling'?"

Moby guessed, "Frankincense and myrrh?"

"He called it *vanity*," said the King of Bling. "And I got no argument against that."

"Well, that's fine, because I did not come in here looking for an argument," Flowers said. "Mr. S. S. Mirchandani, a latecomer to these shores, but wasting no time."

"Councilman Flowers."

"Good for you, sir. And Mr. Oberstein . . ."

Flowers frowned at the whale attorney, plainly searching for the kind of fitting summary he liked to bestow on people, an epitaph for every headstone.

" 'Keepin it real,' " Nat suggested.

"No doubt," said Moby, beaming. "True dat."

"Mr. Jaffe," Flowers concluded. He pressed his lips very thin.

"Councilman."

A silence followed, deeper and more awkward than it might have been because Archy had forgotten to turn over the record on the turntable. It was rare, very rare, to see Flowers at a loss for words. Was there guilt on his conscience over changing his mind about the Dogpile deal? Had he come in, this lunchtime, manned up to break the bad news himself? Or was he so caught up in running his own big-time playbook, in setting up his line to defend against the scramble, that he'd forgotten he might run into some resistance at the front counter of Brokeland?

"Archy Stallings," Flowers said, and Archy, confused, knowing he probably should play it cold and hostile with Chan Flowers but in the lifelong habit of looking up to the man, gave himself up to a dap and a bro hug with the councilman.

"Your dad around?" Flowers said, not quite whispering but nearly so.

Archy drew back, but before he could do anything more than squint and look puzzled, Flowers had his answer and was moving on.

"I seem to remember," he said, letting go of Archy, "somebody telling me you had left a message for me, Mr. Jaffe. At my office, not very long ago. Thought I would stop in and inquire as to what it might have been regarding."

"Probably did," Nat said, still without looking up. At times his protean hum took the form of an earful poured into the councilman's office answering machine or, when possible, directly into the ear of one of his nephews, assistants, office managers, press secretaries, Nat complaining about this, that, or the other thing, trash pickup, panhandlers, somebody going around doing stickups in broad daylight. "Huh." He feigned an effort to remember the reason for his most recent call, feigned giving up. "Can't help you."

"Huh," the councilman repeated, and there was another silence. *Awkward turtle,* Julie Jaffe would have declared if he had been present, making a turtle out of his stacked hands, paddling with his thumbs.

"Now, hold on! Look here!" Flowers noted the baby, who had fallen asleep on the bottle. His eyes went to Archy with unfeigned warmth but flawed mathematics. "Is that the little Stallings?"

Flowers reached out his hand for a standard shake, and Archy took it with a sense of dread, as if this really were his baby and all his impotencies and unfitnesses would stand revealed.

"I know it might seem impossible," said Flowers, holding on to Archy's hand, still working the room, "but I remember when *you* were that size." Everybody laughed dutifully but sincerely at the idea of Archy's ever having been so small. "Child looks just like you, too."

"Oh, no," Archy said. "No, that is Aisha English's baby. Rolando. Mr. Singletary's grandson. My wife and I got like a month to go. Nah, I'm just babysitting."

"Archy is practicing," Mr. Mirchandani said.

"It is never too early to start," Flowers said. Though well provided with nephews and nieces, little shorties all the way up to grown men who had played football with Archy in high school, Flowers was a bachelor and, like Mr. Jones, had no children of his own. "It can definitely sneak up on a man."

"Maybe I should start practicing being dead," Nat said too loudly, though whether the excess volume was deliberate or involuntary, Archy could not have said. Before any of them had the chance to fully ponder the import of this remark, Nat added, "Oh, yeah. I do remember why I called, Councilman. It was to ask you to come on by and slit my throat."

Flowers turned, taken mildly aback. Smiled, shook his head. "Brother Nat, I will never tire of your sparkling repartee," he said. "What a treat it is."

"Also, I have that Sun Ra you were looking for," Nat said, banking the anger, using his smile like a valve to feed it nourishing jets of air. "I don't know, maybe you want to wait and pick it up at that new Dogpile store of yours. I hear their used-wax department is going to be straight-up *bangin.*"

"Nat," Archy said.

"Duly noted," Nat replied without missing a beat. "Warn me again in twenty seconds, okay?"

"I can certainly understand your distress at the possibility of the level of competition you are going to be facing, Brother Nat," Flowers said with perfect sympathy. "But come on, man. Show some faith in your partner and yourself! What's with the defeatist attitude? Maybe you want to consider the possibility your anxiety might be premature."

"I have never actually experienced anxiety that turned out to be premature," Nat said, always happy to keep punching in the clinch. "It usually shows up right on time, in my experience."

"Just this once, then," Flowers suggested. Itching to get out, tugging at the lapels of his jacket. "Premature."

"Are you saying that Gibson Goode, the fifth richest— What is it?" Nat turned with an audible creak of his neck bones to Garnet Singletary, who drew back, tight smile noncommittal; in no way, shape, or form interested, not being a fool, in openly taking up against his favorite enemy from way back in the day. "Fifth—?"

"I believe I read in *Black Enterprise* that he is currently the fifth most richest African-American," Singletary said carefully. "I didn't see my own name anywheres on the list."

Again all the men in the store laughed, happy to let Singletary break up the tension, all the same feeling sympathy for Nat, Archy was certain. The place was part of their lives, including the life of Chan Flowers, who had for years come every week to get his hair cut by Eddie Spencer and afterward never lost the habit of stopping by.

"Are you saying, Councilman, that Gibson Goode does not have an open field ahead of him, thanks to you, to start putting in this *Thang* two blocks down from here, thus effectively cutting not only my throat but the throat of this great big ex-baby of whom you are so very fond? Because what we heard, and I believe we even heard it from your lips, was that Mr. Goode was having serious trouble with some of your friends on the zoning commission, and that because of that, *in this climate*, was the term I believe you employed, the banks were giving him a hard time."

"If I told you that," Flowers said, "I was only reporting what I knew to be the case."

"So what changed? Or let me rephrase that, how much *change* did it take?"

"Nat, here's that warning," Archy said.

"How much *cheese*. Right, Moby?"

"I—What am I agreeing to?" Moby said.

"Jesus, Nat," Archy said.

"You had better watch what you say, Mr. Jaffe," Flowers suggested. He was looking at Archy when he said it. Not quite in appeal, not quite making some kind of threat. Inquiry widening his eyes when he looked at Archy, something that he would have liked to know. Archy wondered if this question Flowers did not feel comfortable asking in front of a crowd, and not Nat's call about a Sun Ra record, lay behind today's visit from the councilman.

"I checked out Dogpile," Nat said. He smiled at Moby. "Last summer Archy and I went down to play that wedding in Fox Hills. It was, truly, extremely *bangin*. They had a sweet *Nubian Lady*, Roy Meriwether. The pricing was more than competitive. What's more, I got into a very interesting discussion, forty, forty-five minutes, with the manager of the used-vinyl department. Young guy, college guy, black, good-looking, very passionate about Ornette Coleman. Making a case that Coleman basically rediscovered the original tone of the New Orleans cornet players, basically *thought* his way back to it like Einstein thinking about passing trains. And that closed the circuit. The story ended. That was the end of jazz as we know it. Kind of an ouroboros thing, the snake swallowing its own tail. I don't know if I completely agree, but it was an interesting argument. Oh, I also picked up a really decent *Out There*."

"I don't go in for the hyperbole the way my partner does, Councilman," Archy said. "You know that. And I apologize on his behalf for the disrespect, which you won't hear any more of, or I'm going to kick his ass from here to the Carquinez Bridge. Right, Nat? But look here, if you come through for Gibson Goode, after all this time you been such a good customer to us, not to mention, you know, blessing us with the example of your coming in here and meeting some of your music needs from time to time, then with respect, excuse me, but you really did turn your back on us. Seems like."

Flowers's gaze slid over to the sleeping baby. He seemed to be seeing little Archy himself lying there, hearing some wah-wah echo of 1968.

"I sincerely hope that is not true," he said, returning to the present. "I would miss this place, I truly, truly would. But a Dogpile Thang is going to be a real boon to the community."

"The community."

Ho, shit, Archy thought.

"The community!" Nat repeated.

"Be cool, Nat," Archy said.

"Oh, sure, I'll be cool. I'll be really fucking *cool* when I'm down the street selling my blood plasma!"

"Nat . . ."

Having to sell his blood plasma was always Nat's worst-case scenario, the example he gave to his son, his wife, his partner, anyone he needed to persuade of the dire expedients and financial ruin that loomed before him.

"You know, Councilman, I don't know why, but I was under the impression that this place right . . . here"—and Nat pounded the counter, *Right! Here!*—"was a community! But I guess I was wrong."

Nat reached under the counter and pulled out a copy of *The Soul Vibrations of Man* (Saturn Research, 1976) and hurled it across the room. You could hear it crack, a snapping like wood in a fire. Along with fretting about having recourse to selling his blood plasma, Nat liked to throw record albums, usually the slag. Alas, this one was rare and valuable.

"You can ask Gibson Goode and the community to find you a sealed original mono copy of *The Soul Vibrations of Man*. Because we're closing. Right now. As of this moment. Why delay it? Why draw out the suffering? We are closing this store today. You can all leave, thank you very much for your support all these years. Goodbye, gentlemen."

Flowers started to say something, to remonstrate with Nat, reproach him for the destruction of that beautiful disk. Thought better of it. Fixed those searching peepers on Archy one last time, seeming to see some kind of answer in Archy's blankness.

"Well, then." Flowers touched his fingers to the brim of his hat, bowed to the men at the counter. He walked out of the store, and the nephews took up their places on either side of him. "Enjoy your day. Mr. Jones, Mr. Singletary."

"Gentlemen, goodbye," Nat said.

The customers turned, looking dazed, Mr. Mirchandani and Moby appealing to Archy. Archy shrugged. "Sorry, fellas," he said.

Archy picked up Rolando, snoozing in his caddy, and made a formal transfer of custody to the grandfather, England turning over Hong Kong, mournful trumpets of farewell, a weird ache in Archy's heart like the forerunner or possibly the distant memory of tears. The men slipped from their stools and trooped out.

Mr. Jones stopped in the doorway, unhunched himself from the perpetual ghostly keyboard, and turned back. He shot a look at Nat in which sympathy and scorn contended. Fished his pipe and tobacco out of his hip pocket. Then, gesturing with the stem of the pipe toward Rolando as the King carried out the baby, Mr. Jones nodded to Archy. "You keep on practicing, Turtle," he said. "You going to get it."

"I hope I do, Mr. Jones."

"You got the good heart. Underneath all the other stuff. Good heart is eighty-five percent of everything in life."

Tears ran burning along the gutters of Archy's eyes. Generally, he tried, following the example of Marcus Aurelius, to avoid self-pity, but Archy had not experienced a great deal of appreciation in his life for his good qualities, for his potential as a man. His mother had died when he was young, his father had bounced early on. The aunts who raised him died with their ignorance of his good qualities perfectly preserved. His wife, though no doubt she loved him, was the latest in a long line of experts and connoisseurs, reaching back through the army and high school to his aunties, to underrate the rarity and condition of Archy's soul. Only Mr. Jones had always stopped to drop a needle in the long inward spiraling groove that encoded Archy, and listen to the vibrations. Even in the days when Mr. Jones's wife was alive and he was sought after in the clubs and recording studios, halfway famous, he always seemed to have time for Turtle Stallings.

"Thanks, Mr. Jones," Archy said.

"What is the other fifteen percent?" Nat said. "Just out of curiosity?"

"Politeness," Mr. Jones said without hesitation. "And keeping a level head."

Nat blushed and failed to meet Mr. Jones's watery gaze.

"We got that gig tomorrow," Mr. Jones said. "I'm a need my Leslie, boy."

"And you will have it," Archy said.

"Said it would be ready Sunday."

"It will be."

After the parrot had piloted Mr. Jones out of the store, Nat shut the door behind them. He bolted it, turned the sign so that it read CLOSED. "The 'community,' " he muttered. He stood with his hand on the bolt, humming. Then he slid it back, pulled the door open, and ran out onto the sidewalk, shouting in the direction that Councilman Flowers had taken: "The community hasn't made a decent record since 1989!"

Nat came back in—stomped, really—and repeated the business with the deadbolt. He went back around the counter and stood, breathing in and out, making an effort to calm himself, the pounding of his heart visible in his temples. He stopped in front of Archy and fixed him with a level stare.

"See, Archy, this is why I hate everyone and the world," he said, as if there were some connection between these words and what had just happened, some sequence of events like a theory of Ornette Coleman and the lost horn men of Storyville. "This is why I hate my sad-ass little life."

He snatched his hat from the hook, pulled it down tight over his head, and went out. Archy tried and failed to decide whether to take seriously any, some portion, or none of the things that Nat had said. He reached for the Penguin *Meditations* stashed at the ready in his hip pocket, but he knew without consulting it what Marcus was unlikely to suggest: the kind of solace a man could find in the heat and spice of Ethiopia, a rank sweet sauce on the fingertips.

⊙   ⊙   ⊙

Gwen Shanks was headed north on Telegraph Avenue, on her way to work a home birth in the Berkeley hills, when she found herself blown off course by an unbearable craving into the cumin-scented gloom of the Queen of Sheba. Steeled by a lifetime of training in the arts of repression, like Spock battling the septenary mating madness of the *pon farr*, Gwen had resisted the urges and surges of estrogen and progesterone for each of the first thirty-four weeks of her pregnancy, denying all cravings, battened down tight against hormonal gusts. In her patients, Gwen uniformly and with tenderness indulged the rages, transports, and panics, the crying jags and cupcake benders, but she was not in the habit of indulging herself. Though she was a midwife by profession, her life's work was self-control. Two weeks earlier, however, without explanation, her husband had dropped by the offices of Berkeley Birth Partners bearing, satanically, a fateful Styrofoam cup filled with something called *suff*. Since that day Gwen had been plagued by an almost daily hankering for this chilled infusion of sesame seeds, its flavor bittersweet as regret. A black belt in Wing Chun–style kung fu, Gwen had spent the morning in the dojo of the Bruce Lee Institute, working out for over two hours with her master, Irene Jew. Making a conscious effort not only to sharpen her practical edge against the loss of focus, strength, and quickness that pregnancy had brought but, more important, to regain some measure of discipline over herself. Wasted time. Parking in a yellow zone, risking lateness, Gwen abandoned herself to her thirst.

She was standing by the cash register, waiting for her change, and had taken her first painful and blessed sip when she noticed her darling husband sitting in a booth halfway back along the south wall, behind a tan-and-brown curtain of beaded strands that managed, in its sparsity, to leave nothing and everything to the imagination. Archy Stallings, dog of dogs, his thick Mingus fingers all up in a sticky compound of injera and the business of a long-headed rust-brown young bitch with the wondrous huge eyes of some nocturnal mammal. Elsabet Getachew, the Queen of Sheba, coiled on her side of the table like a soft and sinister intention. Across from her, Archy took off his horn-rims, polished their lenses with a soft cloth. That was all she saw; though it did not quite qualify as innocent, it was, in all fairness, not much. Afterward she could not be sure how or why she conceived the idea of marching back to the curtained booth and dumping a nice cold Styrofoam cupful of frothy regret onto her darling husband's head. "Idea" was not even the right word; she seemed at that instant to define herself as the woman who was going to do that thing, to be the sea in which that action was the one and only fish.

Throughout her pregnancy, attacks of fatigue had alternated with bouts of bodily exaltation, but as she marched, rolling with the weight of the baby well distributed along the engineering of her bones, over to the fifth booth from the back, Gwen felt positively indomitable. She flung aside the beaded strands with a left hand that could splinter pine planks and reduce cinder block to gray dust. Strings snapped. Hundreds of brown and tan beads rattled down, darting and pinging and scattering in whorls, mapping, like particles in a cloud chamber, the flow of qigong from her black-belt hand.

In fact, Gwen disbelieved in qi and in 97 percent of the claims that people in the kung fu world made about it, those stories of people who could lift Acuras and avert bullets and bust the heads of mighty armies by virtue of their ability to control the magic flow. Ninety-seven percent was more or less the degree to which Gwen disbelieved in everything that people represented, attested to, or tried to put over on you. And despite midwives' latter-day reputation as a bunch of New Age witches, with their crystals and their alpha-state gong CDs and their tinctures of black and blue cohosh root, most midwives were skeptical by training, Gwen more skeptical than most. Nonetheless, she felt something coursing through her and around her, mapped by the flying beads. She glowered down at the bastard who had somehow managed to conceal his bulk behind her 3 percent blind spot and sneak into her life.

As soon as Gwen appeared alongside the booth, Archy seemed to cotton all at once on to the whole scenario—wife, discovery, beads, size-large *suff*—with the instantaneous understanding common to unfaithful men. In the space of that instant, his eyes widened, apologizing, protesting, as wooden beads rained around him and eighteen ounces of ice-cold Ethiopian beverage were upended onto his head.

"Damn," he said as the milk-white stuff streamed down his glasses and alongside his nose into his collar. He did not lose his temper, raise his voice, jump out of the way, or even shake himself like the dog he was. He just sat there dripping, suffering the punishment, as if doing so were a form of uxorious indulgence, the price that must be paid for having a wife who was not merely pregnant but, apparently, out of her mind. "I was only talking to the girl."

"Excuse me," said Elsabet Getachew with her husky accent, attempting with head lowered to slide out of the booth. Her hair was a glory of tendrils for the snaring of husbands. She smelled violently of the kitchen, of nuts and oils and crushed handfuls of orange spice. Gwen interposed herself between the woman and freedom, glad to be huge and impassable. She waited until the young woman looked up, daring her to meet the wifely gaze: a wall, a dam, the arm of a government. The girl looked up. In those ibex eyes, Gwen saw guilt and mockery; but above all: contempt.

All at once the lights came on inside of Gwen. She looked down at her belly, at her pilled and distended stretch top, at the saggy knees of her CP Shades pants, at the ragged black espadrilles into which she stuffed her feet. And under all that! the preposterous bra, the geriatric panties!

"No excuse for you," Gwen said feebly, and stepped aside.

Elsabet Getachew slipped past her and disappeared through another fringe of beads into the kitchen. Apart from the happy couple, there were now nine other human beings in the dining room, and all of them appeared to be enjoying the ongoing spectacle of Gwen.

"So, what?" Archy wanted to know. "Now I'm not allowed to interact with my fellow neighborhood merchants? Maintain the dialogue? How we supposed to keep a lid on crime, we don't exchange tips and information, tell me that?"

" 'Tips and information,' " she quoted. "Uh-huh. I see."

"Always have to assume the worst-case scenario." He grabbed up some napkins and tenderly patted his pate, dabbed at his streaming cheeks. He shook his head.

"I just go with the odds, Archy," Gwen said. "I'm looking at the numbers."

Yes, she conceded as he followed her out the front door of the restaurant and down Telegraph to her black 1999 BMW convertible, Archy and Elsabet had appeared to be *just talking*, and if they were *just talking*, then it was completely and without question unreasonable for her to have bugged out on him the way she had. Given the innocence of the observed encounter, it was wrong to have gone and drenched his beautiful pumpkin sweater and tweeds in a soft drink from the Horn of Africa. Yes, she knew perfectly well that Archy ate lunch at Queen of Sheba all the time. She knew that Elsabet Getachew worked at the restaurant and that she was the niece of the owner, who was a nice guy. And no, she did not expect him to be rude to a friend and fellow member of the Temescal Merchants Association.

"It's the indignity of it," she heard herself telling him, invoking a key concept of her mother's code of morality with such stone likeness that it chilled her, spiders walked on the back of her neck, you might as well swing the camera around and show Rod Serling standing there behind a potted banana tree in an eerie cloud of cigarette smoke.

She got right up in his face so she could make her speech without raising her voice. "I have been doing this for thirty-six weeks," she began. "I am tired, I am large, I am hormonal. And I am hot. I am so hot and so large, I have to wear a culotte slip to keep my thighs from rubbing together when I walk. So, I admit, yes, I lost it. Maybe I ought not have poured my drink on your head. But I don't know"—was this the prompting of estrogen or logic? could she tell the difference anymore?—"maybe I ought. Because even if you are 'just talking' to some astonishingly beautiful girl, Archy, it's *humiliating*. I'm sick of it. I have to walk around my city, the place where I live, and wonder if next time I stop in, wherever, I don't know, the drugstore to pick up a jar of Tucks medicated pads, I'm going to see my husband macking on the *pharmacist*." This was not a hypothetical example. "It's embarrassing. I have more pride than that." She placed a hand against her sternum then, feeling the next words coming like a mighty belch. She lowered her voice to a whisper, as if being obliged to invoke the memory of her immensely dignified mother, only the second female African-American graduate of Harvard Medical School, were the greatest humiliation of all. "I have too much self-respect."

"Way too much," Archy agreed.

"Swear to me, Archy," she said. "Raise your right hand and swear to me, on the soul of your mother, you aren't getting up to anything with that girl, Chewbacca or whatever her name is."

"I swear," Archy said, but there was appended no oath that might require the damnation of his late mother. No raised hand.

"Raise it up," Gwen said.

Archy lifted his right hand, a flag of surrender.

"Swear. On the soul of your mother, who raised you to be a better man than that."

Before forming the words required, Archy hesitated, and in that half-second he was lost. All Gwen's protestations of dignity and invocations of self-respect were scattered like deck chairs on the promenade of a heaving ship. She glanced up and down the street, casing it for witnesses, then plunged her hand down into the front of his pants. The upper serif of his belt buckle, a gold Ferragamo F, scraped her wrist. Her fingers found the heavy coil of hose cupped in the bag of his boxers. Her fingertips were briefly snagged by a film of bodily adhesive as weak as the glue on a Post-it. She tugged her sticky fingers loose, brought them to her nose, and took a quick but practiced sniff. Market stalls, smoking braziers, panniers of lentils. All the spice and stink of Ethiopia: turmeric, scorched butter, the salt of the Red Sea.

"Mother*fucker*," Gwen said, turning on itself, like a cell going cancerous, the oath that Archy would not swear. It was only the third time in her life that she had used the word, and the first time without quotation marks demurely implied, and after it there was nothing more to say. Gwen went around to the driver's side of the car, ignoring a parking citation in an acid-green envelope that had been poked, during her absence, under her left wiper. She guided herself into the space between seat and steering wheel. Then she and her battered dignity drove off, with the parking ticket flapping against the windshield and with the want of a cup of *suff*—for one more caramel sip of which she just then would have endured any affront to her self-esteem or stain upon her pride—doomed to burn on inside her, unassuaged, for many days.

⊙   ⊙   ⊙

The house on Stonewall Road was one of those California canyon houses put up in the late sixties with a Jet Propulsion Laboratory arrogance toward gravity, a set of angles on skinny poles engineered out into the green void. From the street, all you could see of it was its mailbox and carport, with the house concealed downslope as if it planned to spring an ambush on a passerby. In the middle of the driveway, over an eternal attendant puddle of leaking motor oil, sat Aviva Roth-Jaffe's car, a Volvo station wagon whose age could be reckoned in decades. It had gold-on-blue vanity plates that read HEK8. At some point it had been condemned by a hundred-dollar Earl Scheib paint job to approximate the color of a squirt of fluoride Crest.

Gwen leaned against the trunk of her car, took a long slow breath. Shook off as much of the memory of the past half hour as would shake loose, and tamped down everything else. She had work to do, and when this job was over, her husband would still be there, and he would still be a dog, and the smell of another woman's pussy would still be on him. She hoisted her black gym bag over her shoulder—the bag held clean bed linens, gloves, meds and syringes, forceps, a portable Doppler—and hefted it and herself down the twisting stairway from the street to the front door. The slope behind her was overgrown with morning glory. Tendrils of jasmine fingered the wooden stairs. A huge trumpet vine with its disappointed yellow mouths threatened to engulf the wooden house clear to the peak of the steep shed roof. The air on Stonewall Road smelled of cedar bark, eucalyptus, fir logs burning in a woodstove. From the lowest limb of a Meyer lemon, a wind chime searched without urgency for a melody to play. An adhesive sticker pasted to the sidelight beside the front door told prospective firefighters how many cats (three) to risk their lives in rescuing. From inside the house came the forlorn and piteous bellowing of an animal in pain.

"Hello?" Gwen called, letting herself in the front door. A small black Buddha greeted her from a low table by the front door, where it kept company with a photograph of Lydia Frankenthaler, the producer of an Oscar-winning documentary film about the neglected plight of lesbians in Nazi Germany; Lydia's partner, Garth; and Lydia's daughter from her first marriage, a child whose father was black and whose name Gwen had forgotten. It was a Chinese Buddha, the kind that was supposed to pull in money and luck, jolly, baby-faced, and potbellied, reminding Gwen of her darling husband apart from the signal difference that you could rub the continental expanse of Archy Stallings's abdomen for a very long time without attracting any flow of money in your direction. "Somebody having a baby around here?"

"In here, Gwen," Aviva said.

Lydia and Garth, a lawyer for the poor, were having their baby in their living room. It was a large room with a vaulted ceiling and nothing between it and the canyon but a wall of solid glass. The girl—Arabia, Alabama, she had a geographical name—sat marveling blankly at the spectacle of her naked mother reposed like an abstract chunk of marble sculpture in the center of the room. Against her legs the girl held a rectangle of cardstock to which she had pasted the three pages of her mother's birth plan, decorating the borders in four colors of marker with flowers and vines and a happy-looking fetus labeled BELLA. Two low sofas had been pushed to the sides of the room to make space for a wide flat sandwich crafted from a tatami mat, a slab of egg-carton foam rubber, and a shower curtain decorated with a giant self-portrait of Frida Kahlo. Garth, a small-boned, thin-shanked man with a red beard and red stubble on his head, lay sleeping on the improvised bed.

"I'm at nine!" said Lydia by way of greeting, adding whatever comment was provided by her spread, furry-ish butt cheeks and the backs of her legs as she bent over in the downward-facing-dog position to grab two handfuls of floor. "A hundred percent effaced."

"I've been trying to persuade her to try a little push," said Aviva. She tilted back on her haunches, down on the floor beside Lydia, studying the looming pale elderly secundigravida. Disapproving of the woman, but only Gwen would have caught it, the lips pursed to the left as if withholding a kiss. Barefoot in a loose cotton shift over black ripstop pedal pushers, the roiling surf of her black hair, with its silver eddies, pulled back and tied in a sloppy bun. Stubble showing blue against her luminous shins. Toenails painted a deep cocoa red like the skin of Archy's Queen of Sheba. "But all Mom wants to do is goof around like that."

"I don't want to push," Lydia said. A string of pain drew and cinched her voice, a yogic voice, inverted and tied carefully to the rhythm of her breathing. "Is it okay, Gwen? Can't I just stay this way for a little while longer? It feels a lot better."

If Aviva said it was time to try a little push, then it was, in Gwen's view, time to try a little push. You did not get to be the Alice Waters of Midwives by leaving your gratins in the oven too long.

"Well, you've got gravity working for you," Gwen tried, less inclined than her partner to patience or politeness but good for at least one go-round with an upside-down naked lady in labor. "But if anybody ever pushed out a baby in that jackknife thing you've got working right there, Lydia, then I never heard about it."

"It could be interesting," Aviva said. "Now that you mention it. Maybe you should give it a try." The words were humorous, but her tone continued to be critical, at least to Gwen's ear.

"Let me just wash my hands and whatnot, and then I'll fire up my Doppler and see what's happening in there," Gwen said, dropping her bag on a black leather armchair. "Hi, honey." *Arcadia.* "What do you think of all this, Miss Arcadia?"

The girl shrugged, eyes wide and teary but not despairing. Without cant or reference to the threefold moon goddess or other such nonsense, it was a deep and solemn business that they were about in this room, and nobody was going to feel that, in all its fathomlessness, like a kid. Certainly not old Garth over there, sacked out with one toe poking out of his left sock and sleep working the bellows of his skinny frame.

"Kind of gross," the girl said, hoisting the birth plan higher as if to shield herself from the grossness of it. Article Seven requested that the umbilical cord not be cut until the placenta had ceased to pump. Article Twelve was some kind of nonsense about the use of artificial light. Gwen was not one to disrespect a well-made birth plan, but there were always wishful thinking and juju involved, and when things went the way they were going to go, as they must, many plans took on a retrospective air of foolishness. "No offense, Mom."

"You don't." The string cinching tighter. "Have to. Watch it, baby. I told you—"

"I want to stay."

"Gross can be interesting," Gwen said. "Huh?"

Arcadia nodded.

Lydia lowered her hips and sank to her knees, giving way like a sand castle, and on all fours she rested, head hung, eyes closed, as if about to pantomime some animal behavior. "I'm going to push now," she announced. In the same stewardessy voice, she added, "Everyone please shut up."

Her tone was wrong and startling, like a struck wineglass with a secret flaw, and at once Garth sat up and gaped at Gwen, blinking, wiping his lips with his sleeve. "What's wrong?" he said. His eyes came unstuck from Gwen's, and he looked around, kicking up from the deep-sea trench of a dream, looking for his new baby, finding his wife, who was seeing nothing at all.

"Everything's fine, sweetie," Aviva said. "Only we're going to need Frida Kahlo."

Gwen went into the kitchen to drink a glass of water and, in the name of asepsis if not pride, eradicate every last whiff of Elsabet Getachew from her hands. *No excuse for you*—that was sterling dialogue. She strangled the renascent memory of her shame with a pair of latex-free gloves. When she came back into the living room, she saw that Frida Kahlo had been veiled with an orange bath towel. Lydia lay on her back, propped up on an old plaid bolster, pale abdomen shot like an eyeball with capillaries, making a new kind of low growling sound that built slowly to an energetic whoop and flowered in a burst of foul language that made everybody laugh.

"Good one," Aviva said. "Good one."

Though Aviva had caught a thousand babies with hands that were steady and adept, now that it was time, she deferred to her partner, to the virtuoso hands of Gwen Shanks, freaky-big, fluid as a couple of tide-pool dwellers, cabled like the Golden Gate Bridge.

As Aviva gave way to Gwen, she tried by means of her powerfully signifying eyebrows to communicate that she felt something in this situation to be amiss, something not provided for in the birth plan, which lay sagging and looped onto itself under the little girl's chair. Aviva's apparent psychic ability to know in advance when something might go wrong, especially in the context of a birth, was not merely the statistical fruit of an abiding pessimism. Skeptic that she was, Gwen had seen Aviva make unlikely but correct predictions of disaster too many times to discount. Gwen frowned, trying to see or feel what Aviva had detected, coming up short. By the time she turned to Lydia, every trace of the frown had been blown away.

"Okay," she said, "let's see what little old Miss Bella is up to."

Gwen lowered herself by inches and prayers to the floor and, when she arrived, saw that the inner labia of Lydia Frankenthaler had conformed themselves into a fiery circle. A smear of fluid and hair presented its credentials at this checkpoint, advance man for the imminently arriving ambassadress from afar.

"You're working fast now," Gwen said. "You're crowning. Here we go. Oh my goodness."

"Lydia, honey, remember how you said you really didn't want to push," Aviva said, climbing in alongside Gwen, "well, now I would actually like you to stop. Stop pushing. Just let her—"

"Coming fast," Gwen said. "Look out."

There was a ripple of liquid and skin, then with a vaginal sigh, the little girl squirted faceup into Gwen's wide hands. The small eyes were open, nebular, and dull, but in the instant before she cried out, they ignited, and the child seemed to regard Gwen Shanks. The air was filled with a hot smell between sex and butchery. The father said "*oh*" and pressed in beside Gwen to take the sticky baby as she passed it to him. Arcadia hung back, aghast and thrilling to the redness of the birth and the life kindling in her father's hands. They wrapped the baby loosely in a candy-striped blanket, and as Aviva stroked Lydia's hair and helped to raise her head, Garth and Arcadia made the necessary introductions of mother and baby and breast. That left Gwen, crouched at the other end of the silvery umbilicus, to observe the heavy flow of blood that seeped from Lydia's vagina in a slow pulsation, like water from a saturated sponge.

It required all of Gwen's training and innate gift for minimization of disaster not to pronounce the fatal syllables "*Ho, shit.*" But Aviva caught something in her face or shoulders, and when Gwen looked up from the pulsing blood that had begun to pool in a red half-dollar on the shower curtain, her partner was already on her way around to have a look. Aviva hunched down behind Gwen, an umpire leaning in on a catcher's shoulder to get a better look at the ball as it came down the pike. She smelled of lemon peel and armpit in a way that barely registered with Gwen by now except as a steadying presence. They settled in to wait for the placenta. The soft click-click of the baby's nursing marked the passing of several minutes. Aviva reached down and gave a gentle tug on the umbilical cord. She frowned. She made a humming sound deep in her throat and then said, "Hmm."

Her tone pierced the bubble of family happiness up by Lydia's head. Garth looked up sharply. "Is it all right?"

"It's fine."

Gwen ripped back the Velcro straps of her hypodermic kit, unrolled it, and felt around with her left hand for the vial of Pitocin.

"Right now," Aviva said, "the placenta is feeling a little shy, so we just all want to really encourage the uterus to do some contracting for us. Lydia, you just keep right on nursing her, that's the very best thing you can do. How's that coming?"

"She went right on!" Lydia cried. Everything was wonderful in the world where she had taken up residence. "Great latch. Sucking away."

"Good," Gwen said, practicing the business of syringe and vial in a mindful series of ritual taps, sinking the vial onto the shaft of the needle, reading the tale of liquid and graduation. "Keep it up. And just to make sure it all gets nice and tight and contracted in there, we're going to give you a little Pitocin."

"What's the deal?" said Garth. He craned forward to see what was happening between his wife's legs. There was not, say, an ocean of blood, but there was more than enough to shock an innocent new father awash in a postpartum hormonal bath of trust in the world's goodness. "Oh, goddammit. Did you guys fuck something up?"

He swore stiffly but with a sincere fury that took Gwen by surprise. She had pegged him as the gently feckless type of Berkeley white guy, drawstring pants and Teva sandals worn over hiking socks, sworn to a life of uxorial supportiveness the way some monks were sworn to the work of silence. Gwen didn't know that Garth and Lydia had quarreled repeatedly over the idea of home birth, that Garth had viewed Lydia's insistence on having their baby at home as the latest in a string of reckless and unnecessarily showy acts of counterconventionality that included refusing, to date, three separate proposals of marriage from Garth. Garth believed in hospitals and vaccines and government-sanctioned monogamy and had absorbed from his poor black and Latino clients powerful notions of the sovereignty of bad luck and death. He had suffered no ill fortune throughout the length of a tranquil, comfortable, and fulfilling life and so at any moment anticipated—even felt that he deserved—the swift equalizing backhand of universal misfortune.

"It's okay, Dad," Gwen said. "It's going to be okay."

"Yeah?"

"Oh, yeah." She laid it on, but only because she could do so in good conscience. This kind of hemorrhaging was not unusual; the Pitocin would kick in momentarily, the uterus would contract, the mysterious bundle of the placenta, that doomed and transient organ, would complete its brief sojourn, and that would be that.

"I mean, well," Garth said. He appeared to consider and decide against speaking the words that had entered his mind, so as not to cause alarm, then said them anyway: "It's just that it looks kind of bad."

Gwen's eyes snapped onto the little girl, but Arcadia seemed to have decided not to know anything except the baby sucking at her mother's left breast and the feel of her mother's hand in hers.

"That's mostly just lochia," Gwen said. "Lining, mucus, all that good stuff. It's normal."

"Mostly," Garth repeated, his tone both flat and accusatory.

"How about you run get us some towels, Dad," Aviva suggested. "And lots of them."

"Towels," Garth repeated, clinging to the rope of his desire to be useful.

"Definitely," Gwen said. "Go on, honey. Go on and get us like every damn towel you got. Also, yeah, some sanitary pads."

Gwen had a more than adequate supply of pads in her bag, but she wanted to give him a concrete mystery to grow entangled in, hoping that might keep him busy for a few minutes. Whenever she asked Archy to bring her a Tampax, he always got this look on his face, somewhere between intimidation, as by an advanced concept of cosmic theory, and dread, as if mere contact with a tampon might cause him spontaneously to grow a vagina.

Garth went away muttering, "Towels and sanitary pads."

Aviva called Aryeh Bernstein. "Sorry to bother you," she said. She gave him the essentials, then listened to what their backup OB had to say about Lydia Frankenthaler's placenta. "We did. Yep. Okay. All right, thanks, Aryeh. I hope I won't have to."

"What did he say?"

"He said more Pitocin and massage."

"On it," Gwen said.

As Aviva prepped another push, Gwen laid her hands on Lydia's belly and felt, blindly and surely, for the hard shuddering uterus. She sank her fingers into the crepey flesh of Lydia's abdomen and kneaded with dispassion and no more tenderness than a baker. She disbelieved in the mystical power of visualization according to strictures of her 97 percent rule, but that did not prevent her from imagining with every flexion of her fingers that Lydia's womb was clenching, sealing itself up, condensing like a lump of coal in Superman's fist to a hard bright healthy diamond.

They heard cabinets slamming in a bathroom somewhere with a panicked air of comedy, and then a glass broke, and the girl jumped. It was not impossible that Gwen jumped, too. Aviva held steady, guiding the second needle into Lydia's vein.

"Hey, there, Arcadia," Gwen said. "How you doing?"

"Good."

"You got a nice strong grip on your mom's hand, there?" The girl nodded, slow and watchful. Gwen winced at the false tone of cheeriness she could hear creeping into her voice. "Know what I'm doing? I'm massaging your mom's uterus. Now, I know you know what a uterus is."

"Yes."

"Duh. Of course you do, smart as you are."

"Oh, uh, Gwen, um," Lydia said, and she sank back deeper against the plaid bolster, her head lolling like a flower on a broken stem. Her left arm with the baby curled in its crook subsided, and there was a loud smack as the small mouth popped loose. "Oh, man, you guys, I don't know."

"Any change?" Aviva said.

"Some."

Gwen tried not to look at her partner as Aviva went over to her flight bag, a gaudy pleather thing blazoned with the obscurely ironic legend SULACO, and broke out the bags, barbs, and tubing of an IV kit. Gwen crouched, up to her elbows in the dough of the woman's life, knowing that everything was going to be all right, that it was a matter of hormones and massage and a husband judiciously sent to find Kotex and bath towels. She also knew that she suffered from or had been blessed with a kind of reverse clairvoyance, the natural counterpart to her partner's predictive pessimism. Gwen was resistant to if not proof against clear signs of danger or failure. Not because she was an optimist (not at all) but because she took failure, any failure, whether her own or the universe's, so personally. If a bridge gave way outside of Bangalore, India, and a bus full of children plunged to their deaths, Gwen felt an atom-sized but detectable blip of culpability. She had been taught firmly that you could not take credit for success if you were unprepared to accept blame for failure, and one useful expedient she had evolved over the years for avoiding having to do the latter was to refuse—not consciously so much as through a reflexive stubbornness—to acknowledge even the possibility of failure. And that was what she would have to accept if she looked up from her wildly bread-making hands and saw Aviva, with that grim measuring gaze of hers, holding up the bag of intravenous saline to catch the sunshine, her mouth drawn into a thin defeated line.

"Don't fall asleep, Mommy," Arcadia said. "Here comes Daddy with the towels."

⊙   ⊙   ⊙

Gwen hurried along the corridor, bleeding from a fresh cut on her left cheek, trussing her belly with one arm, trying to keep up with Aviva, who was trying to keep up with the single-masted gurney on which Lydia Frankenthaler was being sailed toward one of the emergency-room ORs by a crew of two nurses and the EMT who had accidentally slammed the ambulance door on Gwen's face. The EMT hit the doors ass-first and banged on through, and the nurse who was not steering the IV pole turned and faced down the midwives as the doors swung shut behind her. She was about Gwen's age, mid-thirties, a skinny ash-eyed blonde with her hair in a rubber-band ponytail, wearing scrubs patterned with the logo of the Oakland A's. "I'm really sorry," she said. She looked very faintly sorry. "You'll have to wait out here."

This was a sentence being passed on them, a condemnation and a banishment, but at first Aviva seemed not to catch on, or rather, she pretended not to catch on. As the Alice Waters of Midwives, she had been contending successfully and in frustration with hospitals for a long time, and though, by nature, she was one of the most candid and forthright people Gwen had ever known, if you sent her into battle with another nurse, an intake clerk, or most of all an OB, she revealed herself to be skilled in every manner of wheedlings and wiles. It was a skill that was called upon to one degree or another almost every time they went up against hospitals and insurance companies, and Gwen relied upon and was grateful to Aviva for shouldering the politics of the job so ably. She envied the way it seemed to cost Aviva nothing to eat shit, kiss up, make nice. Catching babies was the only thing Aviva cared about, and she would surrender anything except her spotless record for catching them safe and sound. She had, Gwen felt, that luxury.

"No, no, of course, we'll wait," Aviva said in a chipper voice. She made a great show of gazing down at herself, at her white shirt with its chart of blood islands, at the chipped polish on her big toenail. With the same partly feigned air of disapproval, she surveyed Gwen's cheek, her played-out saggy-kneed CP Shades. Then Aviva nodded, granting with a smile the whole vibe of dirt and disorder that the partners were giving off. "But after we clean up and scrub in, right? then it's no problem, right"—leaning in to read the nurse's badge—"Kirsten? If you want to check with Dr. Bernstein, I'm sure . . ."

Gwen could see the nurse trying to determine whose responsibility it was in this situation to be the Asshole, which was of course the purpose of Aviva's gambit. Sometimes that awful responsibility turned out to be endlessly deferrable, and other times you got lucky and ended up in the hands of someone too tired or busy to give a damn.

"Bernstein's stuck in traffic," Kirsten said. "The attending's Dr. Lazar. I'll check with him. In the meantime, why don't you two ladies go ahead and have a seat." She told Gwen, "You're going to want to have a seat."

You have a seat, bitch. That's my patient maybe bleeding to death in there.

"No, thank you," Gwen said. "I prefer to stand."

Her relations toward authority, toward its wielders and tools, were—had to be—more complicated than her partner's. She could not as blithely subordinate her pride and self-respect to the dictates of hospital politics, distill her practice of midwifery, the way Aviva did, to the fundamental business of the Catch. But Gwen knew, the way a violinist knew tonewood, how to work it. She had grown up in a family of doctors, lawyers, teachers, cops. For many years her father was an assistant district attorney for the city of Washington, D.C., and then a lawyer for the Justice Department. Both of her mother's sisters were nurses. Her uncle Louis had been a D.C. patrolman and plainclothesman and was now the chief of security for Howard University, and her brother, Ernest, ran a lab at George Mason. To the extent that Gwen had been hassled in her life by representatives of the white establishment, she had been trained to get the better of the situation without compromising herself, sometimes by dropping a name, sometimes by showing a respect that she genuinely felt or could at least remember how to simulate. Mostly by letting the doc or the officer feel that she understood how it was to be on the job.

"But truly, thank you, Kirsten," Gwen added, reaching for chipper like a note that was just beyond her range. "We really appreciate your taking the time. We know how busy you are." She smiled. "And maybe I will sit down a minute, at that."

As though doing Kirsten a favor, Gwen lowered herself into one of the plastic chairs bolted to a nearby wall.

"Definitely want to have somebody look at that cheek," the nurse said, her brittle tone expressing solicitude for the cheek less, Gwen thought, than for her own worn-out, urban-population-serving self.

"Oh, thank you so much for your concern," Gwen said. Struggling a little harder, knowing from the way Aviva was looking at her, that she was starting, in Aviva's phrase, to *leak*. "Now, please, honey, go ask the doc when we can see our patient."

It must have been the "honey."

Kirsten said, "She's not your patient anymore."

This was not technically true. As a result of years of hard work, steady and sound practice, slowly evolving cultural attitudes in the medical profession, and long, unrelenting effort begun by its founder and senior practitioner, by the summer of 2004, Berkeley Birth Partners enjoyed full privileges at Chimes General Hospital, with every right to assist in and attend to the care of Lydia Frankenthaler, who would remain a patient until such time as Lydia herself decided otherwise. But Aviva and Gwen had come this evening in an ambulance, giving off a whiff of trouble, with an unnecessary police escort they had managed to acquire along the way. Like a pair of shit-caked work boots, they were being left outside on the porch.

"We'll wait here." Aviva stepped in with the perfect mixture of unctuous sweetness and professional concern, spiking it lightly, like a furtive elbow to the ribs, with a warning to Gwen to seal all leaks or else shut the hell up. "As soon as you talk to the attending, you come find us, okay, Kirsten?"

Gwen followed Aviva into the bathroom, fighting the urge to apologize, wanting to point out that if you were white, eating shit was a choice you could make if you wanted; for a black woman, the only valid choice was not to.

In silence at separate sinks, they washed their hands and faces and rued the ruination of their shirts. The reverberation of water against porcelain intensified the silence. In the mirror, Gwen saw her partner staring at the bloodstains with an emotion between horror and hollowness, looking every one of her forty-seven years. Then their eyes met in the reflection, and the defeated look was gone in an instant, smuggled off, hooded and manacled, to the internal detention facility where Aviva Roth-Jaffe sent such feelings to die.

"I know," Gwen said. "I was leaking."

"Literally," Aviva said, coming in to get a look at the damage the ambulance door had done to Gwen's cheek. It had stopped bleeding, but when Aviva touched it, a fresh droplet formed a bead on the cut's lower lip. The cut was about the size of a grain of pomegranate, pink and ugly. It would leave a scar, and Gwen was prone to keloids, and so forever after, she thought, she would have something special to remind her of this wonderful day. In her mind, she replayed her stumble, the optic flash as her face struck the steel corner.

"You need a stitch," Aviva said. She leaned in to look at Gwen's cut. "Maybe two."

They went out to the ER and, after a few minutes of further genial self-abasement by Aviva, found themselves shown into an examination room with needle, suturing thread, and a hemostat. When it came time for novocaine, Gwen sat on her hands and told Aviva to go ahead and sew it up. "One stitch I can handle straight," she said.

"Better call it two."

"Two, then."

"Aren't you fucking macho."

"I'm liable to start crying anyways, might as well give me a reason." Gwen gasped as the needle bit. "Ow, Aviva, ouch."

Aviva tugged the thread with a severe gentleness, breath whistling in her nostrils. Gwen focused her attention on the pendant that hung from a leather thong around Aviva's throat. It had been made by Julie Jaffe in a flame-work class at the Crucible, lovely and enigmatic, a small glass planet, a teardrop of blue alien seas and green continents and polar caps tinted ice blue. For as long as Gwen had known him, Julie had been a mapper of worlds, on newsprint and graph paper and in the phosphor of a computer screen. Gwen recalled having asked him where he found the inspiration for the tiny glass world he had presented her as a Christmas present last year, and she tried to take comfort or at least find shelter from the pain of the suture needle in the memory of his reply: *By living there*. Then Aviva sank the barb a second time, and that was when Gwen started to cry, no big show or anything, they were both a couple of cool customers, your Berkeley Birth Partners. No sobbing. No whoops of grief. Just tears welling up and spilling over, stinging in the fresh seam of the wound. To be honest, it felt pretty good.

She permitted the tears to flow only as long as it took Aviva to snip the thread from the second stitch, lay down the hemostat, peel off her gloves, and hand Gwen a tissue. Gwen dabbed her eyes and then used the tissue to blow her nose, a nice big honking blast.

"They aren't going to let us in," Gwen said bitterly.

"I guess not."

"Where's Bernstein?"

"He was in the city. He's coming."

"We need to be *in* there. They're going to want to do a hysterectomy, I know it. When all they need to do is just *wait* a little. Lazar. Who's Lazar?"

"Don't know him."

"Tell me she's going to be all right."

"She will be all right."

"I should have noticed it sooner."

"There was nothing to notice until you noticed it. You noticed it right away."

Gwen nodded, ducking her head, balling the tissue in her fist. She stood up and paced the room, stopped, hugged herself, notching her arms into the groove over the swell of her abdomen. She sat down, stood up, blew her nose again, and paced the room some more. She knew perfectly well there was nothing anyone could have done, but somehow that only made it feel more imperative to blame herself. It implied no kind of self-exoneration if she felt compelled to blame some other people, too.

"I can't believe they aren't letting us in there!"

"Take it easy," Aviva said in a hushed voice that was meant, Gwen knew, to communicate the fact that she was talking too loudly. But Gwen could tell that she was rattling Aviva, and for some reason, it pleased her to see it. For the second time that day, she had a sense of trespassing on some internal quarantine, crossing a forbidden zone into the *pon farr*; amok time. It would not be right for Aviva to make her go there alone.

"I've had enough of this," Gwen said. "Aviva, no, seriously. Listen to me."

"I can hear you loud and clear, Gwen."

"Come on. You have worked too hard. We have both earned the right to be treated better than this."

There was the squeak of a sneaker on tiled floor. The partners turned, startled, to the door of the examining room, where a young pink-faced doctor appeared, his head shaved almost to the scalp, leaving only a ghostly chevron of pattern baldness. Dead-eyed, already tired of listening to them before they ever opened their mouths.

"I'm Dr. Lazar," he said. "I was able to do a manual removal of the placenta. Mrs. Frankenthaler is stable, uterine tonicity looks good. We stopped the bleeding. She'll be fine."

The partners stood, perfectly still, tasting the news like thirsty people trying to decide if they had just felt a drop of rain. Then they fell on each other and hung on tight, Gwen half stupid with relief, drunk on it, clinging to Aviva as if to keep the room from spinning.

Dr. Lazar studied the celebration with his flounder eyes and a mean smile like a card cheat with a winning hand. "Do you think," he said after an interval not quite long enough to pass for decent, "uh, I don't know, do either of you ladies think maybe you could explain to me how you managed to screw up this birth quite so badly?"

"Excuse me?" Gwen said, letting go of Aviva as the dizziness abruptly passed.

"Ten more minutes of sage-burning or whatever voodoo you were working, and that mom—"

"Voodoo?" Gwen said.

Instead of wincing at this clear instance of having said something he was bound to regret, Dr. Lazar turned gelid, immobile. But he flushed to the tips of his ears. "You know what?" he said. "Whatever."

He turned and walked out of the room, and Gwen noticed a purple Skittle adhering to the seat of his surgical scrub trousers. For some reason, the sight of the smashed piece of candy stuck on the doctor's ass inspired a minute compassion for the fish-eyed and weary young man with his burden of alopecia, and this, in turn, sent her over the edge.

"Gwen!" Aviva said, but it was too late, and anyway, the hell with her.

⊙   ⊙   ⊙

An hour ago, when they had blown in on a gust of urgency from the ambulance bay, EMT yelling instructions, calling for a stretcher, Garth looking modestly wild-eyed, dancing like a man who had to pee, holding the baby who needed to be fed, Aviva breaking out a bottle of Enfamil from her backpack and cracking it with a sigh and that formula smell of vitamins and cheese, the wonderful avid baby needing every ounce of it—Gwen had failed to remark just how busy it was tonight at the emergency room of Chimes General Hospital.

Every room seemed to be occupied. Her pursuit of Dr. Lazar was haunted at its edges by glimpses of a pale hairy shin slashed with red. A forlorn teenager in a volleyball uniform clutching her arm at a surrealist angle. A young man with baby dreadlocks gripping either side of a sink as if about to vomit. The whole scene scored with a discordant soundtrack of televisions and woe, the nattering of SpongeBob, an old man's ursine expectorations, a pretty Asian woman cursing like a sailor as something nasty was extracted from the meat of her hand, the horrific shrieking of a toddler being held down by its father while a phlebotomist probed its arm for a vein. Outside the last examination room before the waiting area, a young Hispanic man lolled in a chair, holding a bloody ice pack to his face, while from inside the room, a doctor yelled cheerfully in English at his bleeding companion as if the man were deaf and retarded.

"I am a nurse," Gwen said, managing to sound calmer than she felt, catching up with Lazar. "Please tell me that I did not just hear you employ the term 'voodoo' in reference to my licensed and certified practice of midwifery."

Lazar stopped at the threshold of the waiting area, where he planned, she assumed, to tell Garth and Arcadia that Lydia would be okay, business that was definitely more important, as Gwen knew perfectly well in some cool, quiet corner of her being, than whatever point she was attempting to make. The doctor turned to confront her with an air of resigned willingness to go along, an obedient soldier saddling up for the ride into the valley of death.

"I know you were burning something," he said. "I could smell it on her."

"It was ylang-ylang," Aviva said, hurrying up behind them, taking a step toward Gwen as if to interpose her body between Gwen and the doctor. "Her husband was burning it during the first part of her labor. She likes the smell."

"That woman," Gwen said, "Lydia. The placenta was retained. There was stage zero hemorrhage, borderline stage one. Uterine atonicity. And she went into a hypovolemic shock."

"Correct," the doctor said, impatient.

"Even though we had her on a course of supplements and immediately began to administer oxytocin and do uterine massage. Exactly like you or any doctor would have done. Is that not correct?"

He blinked, not wanting to give up anything to her.

"So tell me this, Doctor, how many accretas, how many postpartum hemorrhages, have you guys had here this month? Like, what, I'm going to say six?"

"I wouldn't know."

"Ten?"

"I don't know the answer to that, Ms. Shanks, but see, the thing is, when those things happen here, okay? When they happen here? When there's some hemorrhaging? Which does occur, of course. Then the patient's *already in the damn hospital*. Where she ought to be."

Gwen looked over at the young man with the ice pack, his visible eye dull and maddened, his knuckles swollen like berries on the point of rot.

"You know what?" Aviva said, and out came the pointing finger so feared by all who loved her, Gwen among them, as the Berkeley faded and the Brooklyn broke through, and all at once Aviva's proximity no longer buffered but menaced the doctor. "In fifteen years, my practice has never lost a single mother. And not one single baby. Can this place make that claim? No, I happen to know very well it can't, and so do you."

"Who would ever want to have a baby *here*?" Gwen observed, half to herself, a hand settling on her belly like an amulet or shield.

"It's a *birth*," the doctor said. "You know, call me crazy, but maybe in the end that's one of those things you just don't want to try at home. It's not like conking your hair."

Somebody gasped out in the waiting room. An arch, eager female voice went *Awwwwww shit.*

"You racist," Gwen began, "misogynist—"

"Oh, come on, don't start that crap."

Lazar turned his back on her and went into the waiting room. Throwing up his hands, shaking his head: all the bad acting people tended to engage in when they were most sincere. Gwen stayed right with him. Everyone in the waiting room raised their head, face blank and attentive, prepared if not hoping for further entertainment.

"Don't you bait me," Gwen said, feeling an internal string, years in the winding, snap with a delicious and terrible twang. "Don't you ever try to bait me, you baldheaded, Pee-wee Herman–looking, C-sectioning, PPO hatchet man."

*Ho! Uh-*uh*! Go, Mommy!*

Gwen was right up against him, her body, her belly, the pert cupola of her protruding navel flirting through the fabric of her blouse with actual physical contact. He backed off, betraying the faintest hint of fear.

Garth stood up, holding the baby stiffly, forlornly, as if it were a rare musical instrument, some kind of obscure assemblage of reeds and bladders that he would now be called upon to play. His blue eyes looked frightened, bewildered, and when she saw him, Gwen felt ashamed.

Arcadia, curled in on herself in a plastic armchair, woke up and started to cry.

"Mr. Frankenthaler?" the doctor said.

"Garth, she's fine," Aviva said. She hurried over to Garth, rubbed his shoulder. "She's fine, she's going to be fine."

"Why don't you come with me, Mr. Frankenthaler? I'll take you to see your wife," Lazar said.

"She isn't my wife," Garth said, dazed. "My last name is Newgrange."

Lazar crouched down in front of Arcadia and spoke, in a tender voice, words that only she could hear. She nodded and sniffled, and he moved a thick coil of her dark hair, damp at the end with tears, out of her eyes, painting a shining trail across her cheek. Suddenly, the man was the kindest doctor in the universe. He stood up, and Arcadia took hold of the hem of her father's windbreaker, and they followed Lazar back into the ER. Two seconds later, Lazar reappeared and pointed his finger at Gwen in a parody, perhaps unconscious, of Aviva's recent performance.

"I'm writing this up," he told Gwen, who stood there, shoulders heaving, all the righteousness emptied out of her, the last bright tank-ful burned off in that final heavenward blast. "Count on that."

"Did you hear the way he spoke to me?" she said to Aviva, to the room, a note of uncertainty in the question as if seeking confirmation that she had not in fact imagined it. " 'Voodoo.' 'It's not like having your hair conked.' Did you hear? I know everybody in this room heard the man."

Aviva was back to the hushed voice, gently taking hold of Gwen's elbow. "I heard," she said, "I know."

"You *know*? I don't think you do."

"Oh, come on," Aviva said with an unfortunate echo of Lazar in her tone. "For God's sake, Gwen. I'm on your side."

"No, Aviva, *I'm* on my side. I didn't hear him say one damn word to *you*."

Gwen pulled her arm free of Aviva's grasp and trudged out of the waiting room, through the covered entranceway to the ER, and out to the driveway, where Hekate the Volvo still sat, her hazard lights faithfully blinking. The late-summer-afternoon breeze carried a smell of the ocean.

Gwen shivered, a spasm that started in her arms and shoulders but soon convulsed everything. She had barely eaten all day, which was horrible, reprehensible, two months from delivery and already a Bad Mother. Now she felt like she was starving and at the same time like she might throw up. The stitches burned in her cheek. There was a reek of butts and ashes, out here beyond the doors, and a live thread of fresh smoke. She turned to see a pair of women whom she recognized from the waiting room, young and wide-eyed with matching taffy curls, cousins or possibly sisters, one of them even more hugely pregnant than Gwen, sharing a Kool with an air of exuberant impatience as if, when they finished it, something good was going to happen to one or both of them.

"Hello," Gwen said, and they laughed as if she had said something stupid or as if she herself were stupid regardless of what she might say. They were among those who had cheered and taken great pleasure in Gwen's public argument with Dr. Lazar. The pregnant one smoked, inhaling in that strange impatient way, and studied Gwen as if the sight of her confirmed some long-held theory.

"You a midwife?" the pregnant woman said.

Gwen nodded, trying to look proud and competent, a credit to her profession and her people. The pregnant woman dropped the burning cigarette and stepped on it, and then she and her companion turned to walk back to the emergency room, the pregnant woman's flip-flops scraping and slapping against the soles of her feet.

"See, now," she told her companion, "don't want to be messing with that country shit."

⊙   ⊙   ⊙   .

Around the time when Baby Frankenthaler was bundled from her mother's belly red and headlong into the world, Archy came rolling out of his front door for the second time that day and stood on the topmost step of his porch, freshly showered, toweled, and eau-de-cologned, dressed in a crisp shirt of seafoam-green linen and a linen suit of dulce-de-leche brown. Only to his pride did there still cling, perhaps, the faintest whiff of sesame. He reached up and out with both arms to shoot his cuffs, and for an instant he might have served to illustrate the crucial step in a manual on the seizing of days. He had already seized this particular day once, but he was prepared, if need be, to go ahead and seize the motherfucker all over again.

It was a pretty day for seizing, that much was certain: the prettiest that Oakland, California, had to offer. The fog had burned off, leaving only a softness, as tender as a memory from childhood, to blur the sunlight that warmed the sprawl of rosemary and purple salvia along the fragrant sidewalk and fell in shifting shafts through the branches of the monkey-puzzle tree. This whimsical evergreen, mammoth and spiky, dominated the front yard of Archy and Gwen's sagging 1918 bungalow, formerly the home of a mean old Portuguese man named Oliveira. Reputed, when Archy was a kid, to contain an extensive collection of shrunken heads gathered during Mr. Oliveira's career as a merchant seaman, the house had been a reliable source of neighborhood legend, especially at Halloween, and the mythic memory of those leering heads gave Archy pause sometimes when he came home on an autumn evening, a ring-and-run thrill. He had to this day never forgotten the strange horror of glimpsing one of Mr. Oliveira's many tattoos, like something out of Nathaniel Hawthorne, consisting of a ragged rectangle, a bar of black ink scrawled across the cordovan hide of the old sailor's upper arm in order to blot out, like the pen of a censor, some underlying name or image whose memory, for mysterious reasons, was abhorrent.

Archy patted the hip pocket of his jacket, checking for *The Meditations*, coming down the front steps with his sense of resignation stiffened, in best Stoic fashion, to a kind of resolve. Knowing he had done wrong, prepared to make amends, settle his business. Determined to return to Brokeland, open the doors wide to the angel of retail death, and run the place into the ground all by himself, if that was what it took—but to fail calmly, to fail with style, to fail above all with that true dignity, unknown to his wife or his partner, which lay in never tripping out, never showing offense or hurt to those who had offended or hurt you.

He heard the grumbling of a vintage Detroit engine, inadequately muffled, and watched with dull foreboding as a 1970 Oldsmobile Toronado, recurrent as a bad dream, turned onto Sixty-first Street. The vehicle was in awful shape: formerly green and bleached to a glaucous white, rusted in long streaks and patches so that the side visible resembled a strip of rancid bacon.

Archy was a compulsive admirer of American muscle cars from the ten-year period following his birth in 1968, a period which, in his view—a view often and with countless instances, oral footnotes, and neologisms expounded at the counter of Brokeland Records—corresponded precisely with the most muscular moment in the history of black music in America. His own car, parked in the driveway, was a 1974 El Camino, butterscotch flake, maintained with love and connoisseurship by himself and Sixto "Eddie" Cantor, Stallings Professor of Elcaminology at Motor City Auto Repair and Custom Jobs. Archy was the author of the as yet unwritten *Field Guide to Whips of the Funk Era*, and thus, even if he had not grown up as the virtual older brother of this particular Toronado, he would have been able, by its GT hood badge and dual exhaust, to identify the model year of the low-fallen specimen rolling up to his house. Of the chrome trim only the white plastic underclips remained, and the hood was held shut by a frayed knot of nylon rope looped through the grille, several vanes of which had fallen out, leaving the unfortunate car with a gap-toothed and goofy Leon Spinks grin. In the backseat he thought he glimpsed the blue plastic Samsonite suitcase his grandmother used to take with her on the Fun Train up to Reno. From the right rear window protruded a deco-style halogen floor lamp of the type that caught Lionel Hampton on fire.

"Nuh-uh," Archy said, seeing that this was to be one of those days when it was best to remember, following the cue of Marcus Aurelius or possibly Willie Hutch, that the things of the body are as a river, and the things of the soul as a dream and a vapor; and life is a warfare and a pilgrim's sojourn, and fame after death is only forgetfulness. "Y'all can just continue on your way."

He could see that it was not Luther at the wheel. Any one of a number of interstellar fuckups and freakazoids might be at the helm of this broke-down starship of the seventies, but Archy's thoughts leaped with a bitter instinct to Valletta Moore.

Sure enough. A lamentable lamentation of the door hinges, sounding like the gate on a crypt filled with vengeful dead folks being thrown open, and Valletta Moore got out of the car. Big-boned, shapely, on the fatal side of fifty, high-waisted, high-breasted, face a feline triangle. Beer-bottle-brown eyes, skin luminous and butterscotch, as if she herself had come fresh from the spray gun of Sixto Cantor. Ten, eleven years since the last time Archy had seen her, at least.

"Uh-oh. Look out."

"I know you remember me," she said.

"I remember you didn't used to be quite as fine as you are now."

" 'Look out,' " Valletta quoted back at him, shaking her head, lowering over her amber eyes a pair of bulbous sunglasses with white plastic frames. "I guess I know where you learned that shit."

Looking at her, already smelling her perfume, Archy's memory dealt him a rapid hand of images, of which the ace was unquestionably the grand soft spectacle of Valletta Moore, 1978, shaving her legs at his father's apartment in El Cerrito, glimpsed through the five-inch crack of the open bathroom door. Slender right foot planted on the floor, other foot arched on the shining lip of the bathtub, Valletta bent like a watchmaker over the work of painting a brown razor stripe up the white lathered inside of her long left leg, hair wrapped in a towel but her strong body naked and bold as a flag. The architecture of her ass was something deeper than a memory to Archy, something almost beyond remembrance, an archetype, the pattern of all asses forever after, wired into the structure of reality itself.

"Valletta," he said, thinking she still looked good, then abandoning all wisdom and ignoring his Spidey sense long enough to let her take him in her arms, the skin of her bare shoulder in a halter top cool against his shoulder, the lady most definitely giving off that heavy 1978 Spencer's smell of love candles and sandalwood incense but, laid over top of it, the stink of cigarette, the instant-potatoes smell you might find in the interior of a beat-to-shit Toronado. "Damn."

It was only when she let go of Archy that he saw the tight line of her lips. She looked left, right. She was worried, hiding, running: running to Archy. In the pit of his sensitive belly, neurotransmitters registered with a flutter of dread whatever kind of trouble his father was currently getting himself into. Already thinking it might have something to do with Chandler Flowers, his father's best friend, back in the day. How Flowers had come into the store today, asking, of all things, *Your dad around?* Luther reported to have been down in West Hollywood someplace, last Archy heard, not that he ever sought the least news or information of Luther's who-, what-, where-, when- or whyabouts.

"Well, it sure has been a long time, Valletta," he said cheerfully, deciding to pretend that he believed she had been driving Luther's car down Sixty-first Street, happened to see him on his front porch, and decided to stop and say hello. As if she could have stared clean through 175 pounds and thirty years to recognize the teenager in whose dreams she briefly but intensely featured. "I do have to be running, because I got to, you know, get to the store, but, hey—"

"Archy, no, no, wait, hold up—"

"You have a good day, now. All right? No, really. I'm sorry. But you have a *positive* day."

Back when he was a boy, there used to be a gentleman named Joseph Charles, man would stand out every day at the corner of Oregon and Grove wearing a pair of dazzling yellow gloves. Waving to every car that passed him, extending to its driver, regardless of race, creed, or receptivity, one (1) genuine, heartfelt greeting. Mr. Charles's manner bold and cheerful but a touch formal, hinting, though not in any unkind way, at the impersonal. No intention of greeting you in particular; simply reminding you that, like all humans, you partook in the noble human capacity for being greeted. It was Mr. Charles's manner that Archy tended to adopt around women when he sensed they might be about to pose him some kind of problem. He gave Valletta's shoulder a fond squeeze, started away. In his heart, he already knew that he was not going to get anywhere; not yet. Like many abandoned sons, he was conscious of owing a mysterious, unrepayable debt toward the man of whom, in truth, he was the eternal creditor.

"Archy, it's your dad," she said, tendering that unpayable IOU, "it's Luther."

She raised the sunglasses at him and hit him straight on with twin blasts of yellow-brown fire, with the shock of the bitter work of time and corruption. Cakes of mascara cobwebbed her lashes.

"Yeah?"

Valletta checked out the shadows and rustlings up and down both ends of the street one more time, ran the broom of her paranoia up the quiet little pond of a street built around a pocket playground that some unknown amateur of children had tucked, like an Easter egg, onto an island of grass in the midst of Sixty-first Street. Archy wondered if Valletta might not be high, cashed out on something that was making her go all Pynchonesque. The last time he found himself unable to prevent hearing news of Luther, it was a tale, grand and heartwarming, of cleanness, sobriety, redemption. Luther had drawn a judge down south who remembered *Strutter* and, never having been the man's son, was willing to take a chance on Luther Stallings, divert him to a drug court. Luther went around after that, supposedly, making amends to 17,512 people on two continents. That was at least a year ago, and the amends that Archy consented to allow his father to make to him at the time had consisted, in full, of a sober, clean telephone promise to leave Archy the fuck alone from now until the end of time.

"Can we go in?" she wanted to know, sighing, impatient, maybe, he thought desperately, only needing to pee. "Inside your house?"

"Huh-uh," Archy said, not trying to charm or work her anymore, the deep 1978 El Cerrito–apartment sullenness starting to seep out of him as he remembered how Luther and Valletta used to leave him there all night by himself, nothing on the television but Wolfman Jack and some movie where a shark-toothed devil doll was biting Karen Black on the ankles. Only thing he wanted to know now: what kind of bullshit trouble Luther Stallings was trying to get Archy into this go-round and how much it was going to cost in blood and treasure. "Just say what you came to say. No joke, Valletta, I really do have to go."

"Mm-hmm, yeah, you ain't changed," she said, lighting up icy diodes at the heart of those eyes that, in the summer of 1977, had stared not only into Archy's soul but into the soul of young black America from the covers of *Jet* and *Sepia* and from the feathers-fur-and-leather kung fu splendors of her role as Candygirl Clark in one of the last blaxploitation films of that era, *Strutter at Large*, in which she costarred with a lean, wiry, and beautiful Luther Stallings in his most famous part. "Still walking around all pinch-up and pouty-face, giving everybody a fish-eye, most of all your father or his friend."

"Y'all are still friends, then."

"We took up with each other again. Third time, you know what they say."

Archy had contrived to miss the second near-fatal intersection of Luther and Valletta by cleverly timing his service in the United States Army to coincide with the geopolitical hard-on of Saddam Hussein.

"He back in town, then?"

She stared him down, challenging him, not wanting to give up anything if he was going to make her stand out on the damn sidewalk to say it.

"And now you come around here. Saying Luther sent you, is that right? Come around here hoping to find out what, exactly?"

"Luther don't know nothing about it. Man knew I was here . . ." She chewed on the earpiece of her sunglasses, seeming to rehearse Luther's anger in her mind. "He knows how you feel, he wants to respect that."

"So you don't want money."

"Truly," she said, "I do. I'll take whatever you can spare me. We need to get far away from here and stay there."

It did not take a lot of effort for Archy to harden his heart against his father; that clay was well fired, long and slow. Anger, resentment, scorn, disgust, Luther's son kept these handy in the pocket of his soul as surely as the copy of *Meditations* at his hip. So it must testify to something, some abiding foolishness peculiar to the sons of broken fathers, that it took any effort at all. Thirty-six years of this shit, and Archy was still willing to let the man disappoint him.

"I'm not going to ask why," Archy said. "Because if you don't tell me, then I won't know."

"Archy, I can't get into it out here."

"I am so fine with that, Valletta."

"Your daddy . . . Luther . . ." She tried for a couple of seconds, pursing her lips, tapping them pensively with her right fist, to put it into words. Then she gave up. "He been clean and sober thirteen months now."

"Uh-huh. Good for him."

"And, like, now he got some irons in the fire."

"I bet he does," Archy said, thinking that was the perfect expression to describe the future as it stood in permanent relation to Luther Stallings: a big pile of irons glowing red-hot, to be snatched from the fire only at the cost of singed flesh. "Investment opportunities, that right?"

She fell back once more on her optic beams, but either this time Archy was ready or the effect had begun to dull. She lowered the sunglasses again.

"Let me guess," Archy said. "Because I am experiencing premonitions."

⊙   ⊙   ⊙

Chan and Luther unhooked a heavy chain between two pillars, left the Toronado tucked into a fold of midnight at the back of a gravel parking lot. Crunched up a hillside through fumes of eucalyptus, Chan carrying the shotgun, to a lookout they at one time favored for planning their conquests of the world. At their spot Chan turned and swung the gun, let it fly. It helicoptered out into the night and came whipping down with a clang of pipe somewhere in the woods behind them. Then they sat on their bench, perched side by side on the high shoulder of Oakland. Looked out at streets and bridges and highways embroidered, stitched out, in lights onto dark panels of water and sky.

In the interest of furthering his stone-cold pistolero legend, of which purity was to form a key component, the Undertaker never drank and rarely smoked. Luther passed him a package of Kools, and the Undertaker took one and lit it. Luther fished a fifth of Rumple Minze from his jacket pocket. The Undertaker surrendered the last fragment of his stillborn legend to the possibility of solace offered by the bottle of schnapps.

"He grabbed hold of his wrist, sat there looking at it," Chan said, wiping his lips. "Meat and blood. A stump. All calm and collected, cuff of his jacket shot up to threads. Just a rag where his hand used to be, looking at it."

"Popcorn Hughes," Luther said admiringly.

"I need to hide myself, Luther."

"Where at?" Dread inflated a taut balloon in Luther's rib cage. He could barely muster breath to get out the next syllables: "L.A.?"

For that was the obvious solution: Swing by Luther's mother's house and pick up the canvas suitcase and the three Berkeley Farms crates, packed and ready to go. Hit L.A. by morning, Chan could buy what he needed when they got there. Track down some shitbox safe house where Chan could hole up. Wave goodbye then. Engage in the theater of turning their separate ways, meeting their respective fates, until the next of his friend's schemes went wrong, the next time Chan found himself confronting the truth that his faith in himself was misplaced, his intelligence fated to go unrewarded because it was no substitute for luck, no proof against the world's massive, even hostile, indifference to the productions of a black man's intellect. Like the Party he had joined too late, too young, Chan was a lost claim check, a series of time-lapse photos of a promise as it broke. He was a king of finite space, bound in a nutshell. And Luther was sick of it. He rued all the time he had wasted since the call came from his agent, feeling guilty, feeling sorry for Chan.

"Or," he said, trying to be helpful, "uh, lot of Panthers in Chicago, right?"

Chan didn't say anything.

"Morocco, then. Or Spain."

"Spain," Chan said. Luther could hear the hard little smile creasing his face. "Good thinking. Go to Spain. Become a toronado."

"Why not? All the revolutionary Negroes been skipping to Morocco, Spain. Paris. You were doing their business. They got to take care of you."

"Who?"

"The Party."

"Luther, if I had the kind of clout, get myself that far away from here? I wouldn't have needed to impress anybody in the first place with the fool thing I just tried to do."

Somewhere right around here, Luther remembered, if you went farther up the path behind the picnic tables, you would stumble across a pyramid of built-up stones left behind by some crazy old beard-faced poet back when Oakland was nothing but a slough and a stables and a cowboy hotel. In school they came here on field trips, checking out the poet's little white farmhouse, a big lumpy statue of him riding on a Mongoloid-looking horse. A pyramid of stone and, farther back, a stone platform the man had built, intending it to be used for his funeral pyre. Out here in the hot sun, day after day, the man piling up rocks like lines in one of his boring poems. Dreaming, the whole time he was stacking those rocks, about how all those olden-time gangsters of Oakland, those whoring, robbing, land-grabbing Indian killers, opium addicts and loot seekers down there in the flatlands, how some fine night they were going to look up here at this green slope and marvel at the spectacle of a burning poet. Nothing ever came of that plan, far as Luther could recall. But then that was the general tendency of plans.

"If you're a fool," Luther said, "what's that make me?"

This was a question that could never be answered, and Luther carried swiftly on to the next.

"Why'd I want to go and mess up my good thing driving your murder taxi around West Oakland?" he said. "Tell me that? So the Marxist gangsters can roll over the running-dog capitalist gangsters, take over their drugs and cash flow?"

"Leave, then," Chan said. "You're not in this. You go on and get."

Before Luther could begin to feign that he was not entertaining this generous suggestion, there was a flicker of moonlight, like the bright quick of a fingernail, at the corner of his eye. Chan was pondering a handgun. Taken like the shotgun, no doubt, from the Party arsenal that it was Chan's official duty to keep inventoried, secret, and in fighting shape. A .45, a handsome piece, probably brand-new. Luther's heart misgave at the way Chan was balancing it on both palms, weighing it like a heavy book that held a heavy answer.

"What you going to do with that?" Luther said.

"Try again," Chan said at last. "Find out what hospital they took Popcorn to." He found a solid grip on the pistol. "Get it right the second time."

"Maybe you ought to talk to somebody first. Maybe Huey be satisfied with what you already did to fuck Popcorn up for him."

A fog began to blur the prospect of Oakland spread beneath them. Silence gathered around the friends until it felt like something profound. The coals of their cigarettes flared and crackled. The fog hissed like carbonation in a drink.

"You remember what your uncle Oogie used to do on your birthday, at Christmas?" Chan said finally. "All 'Yeah, uh, listen, I was going to get you a air rifle.' " His imitation of Oogie's mumbly drawl was flawless. "Expecting you to be as grateful as if he did give it to you. Now I'm supposed to say, 'Uh, yeah, Huey, I was going to kill Popcorn Hughes for you, but, uh . . .'?"

"Why not?"

" 'Why not?' " Chan said, making it come out high and childish. "Easy for you to say. Tell me this. You get down there on that movie set, are you going to forget your lines? Tell the director, 'Uh, yeah, I meant to memorize that shit, but, uh . . .'?"

"No."

"Are you?"

"No!"

"Then why do you want me to do it?"

"Come on, then," Luther said. "Let's go."

"Go where?"

"Let's, uh, let's get out of here. You come with me. Down to L.A. Hide out down there. San Pedro. Long Beach." Trying to summon or feign enthusiasm for his proposal. "Yeah, Ensenada."

It was too dark for Chan to see what was not in Luther's eyes and too dark for Luther to see him missing it.

Chan stood up and dropped the .45 into his hip pocket. It rattled against the extra shotgun rounds. "I woke up this morning," he said, "had all kinds of beautiful intentions. Prove myself to the Supreme Servant of the People, take a major annoyance off his hands. Move in, move up, maybe in a year I'm running the Oakland chapter. Then I get my eye on the account books. See what kind of holes might be in them, waste and whatnot. Bring a little more structure, a little more discipline. Now, no. Nuh-uh. Now I just have to make it *right*. You go on, though. Go on, Luther, and get your good thing."

His voice broke, and from the crack in it emerged the voice of the boy he recently was. Fiercely shy and bookish, absorbing without saturation, on behalf of his sisters and his baby brother, the endless seep of the elder Flowers's venom. At the memory of that vanished boy, Luther regretted, without entirely renouncing, his earlier disloyal thoughts. He put his arm around the professorial shoulders of his friend. "It's already too wrong, Chan," he said. "No way you can make it right."

"That is probably true."

"You got to leave. Come on. Come to L.A., hole up. Ride it out."

"I appreciate the gesture, Luther," Chan said. "I already troubled you sufficiently."

"Then go somewhere else."

"Where?"

"Anywheres that a bus could take you."

"Maybe I will," Chan said, to end the conversation.

When the peppermint brandy was drunk, they got up and left behind them the spot where a forgotten dreamer of the California dream had planned to have his glory notarized by fire. Turned and hiked, sliding, back down to the car. After a silent drive to the bottom of the city, the blue dome of the Greyhound station loomed before them like a promise of adventure. There was an OPD cruiser parked at the curb when they pulled up, but before they could consider bailing on the bus station plan, a cop came strolling out of the station, got back into the car, and drove away.

Luther had three hundred dollars in his wallet, all that was left of his up-front money. He handed it over to Chan, " 'Kay, then," he said.

They stood facing each other at the back of the Toronado. Its taillights were slits as narrow as the eyes in the Batman mask, a skeptical squint regarding them. The friends exchanged a couple of palm slaps. Each clasped the other briefly to his chest. Chan offered up some parting bullshit about catching a northbound up to Alaska, or maybe head south, work those shrimp boats down in the Gulf of Mexico. It was all smoke. Chan had never been a boy to leave food on a plate, a math problem without a solution, an open pussy unfucked. He wasn't going to go into the bus station, get on a bus for North Nowhere. Soon as Luther left, he would get busy finishing, for the sake of finishing, the trouble he had started.

"Seriously," Luther said. "What you going to do?"

"You don't need to know, Luther. Tell you this, though, whatever it is? When I'm done, I'm going to be able to hold my head up high."

"I know that's true."

"See you do the same down there. Comport your ass with dignity. Do what you have to do."

"Yeah."

"Promise?"

"Yeah."

Luther tried not to show his impatience, his eagerness to get quit of Chandler Bankwell Flowers III and his cup of clabbered ambition. To get quit of Oakland and Berkeley and all the local fools. The broken promises, the pyres that never got lit.

"You are having good luck right now," Chan said. "Good luck is good. But that's all it is, you dig? Not any kind of a substitute for doing what you have to do."

Luther nodded, said, "No doubt, no doubt," thinking about the ads you used to see in the pages of *Ebony* and *Esquire* selling the long, low, smiling crocodile of 1970, the slogan across the top of the page: WOULDN'T IT BE NICE TO HAVE AN ESCAPE MACHINE?

"I know what it means," Luther said.

"Huh?" Chan said. "What—"

"I can define 'toronado.' "

Chan frowned, remembered, frowned more deeply. "Do it, then," he said.

Luther shook his head. "You don't need to know," he said.

Then he strapped himself into his escape machine, and headed for the Nimitz Freeway, San Jose, Los Angeles: the world and the fortune that awaited him.

Popcorn Hughes, Luther heard afterward, was shot to death early that morning in his bed at Summit Hospital. The only suspect was the unknown, unidentified black male who had been described, by witnesses to the first attack at the Bit o' Honey Lounge, as wearing a mask that was meant, it was generally agreed, to resemble the one worn in Marvel comics by the Black Panther, the first black superhero.

The killer was never apprehended. The Toronado overheated in the Grapevine just north of Lebec and had to be towed across the L.A. County line.

⊙   ⊙   ⊙

"He's looking for investors," Archy guessed.

Valletta affected to study some scene or detail in the distance, beyond the playground, beyond Berkeley, beyond Mount Lassen, saying nothing, infinitesimally shaking her head, mouth down-twisted in a way that might have been disapproving of Archy, Luther, herself, or some combination thereof, arms crossed furiously under her breasts: unable to believe, finally, that she was party to this latest bullshit scheme of Luther's, or that Archy declined to be party to it, or perhaps that the world did not and never would appreciate the genius of Luther Stallings.

"He still talking about that damn movie?"

"What d'you think?"

She rummaged around in her bag and took out what appeared to be a boxed set of three DVDs entitled *The Strutter Trilogy*. Its cover featured a handsome close-up shot of the long-jawed, Roman-nosed, Afro-haloed, 1973-vintage Luther Stallings as master thief Willie Strutter, and it promised restored or digital versions of three films: *Strutter*, *Strutter at Large*, and *Strutter Kicks It Old-School*. But it was an empty hunk of packaging with no disks inside, and on closer inspection, it proved to have been painstakingly crafted from the cardboard case to a *Complete Back to the Future* box set over whose panels had been pasted vivid but crudely executed cut-and-paste computer artwork, a minor but necessary bit of imposture, since, as far as Archy knew—and he knew far; too far—there was no such movie as *Strutter Kicks It Old-School*.

"*Strutter 3*. Is that right? Going to write and direct and star! Triple threat! Going to make it fast, cheap, and badass, like they used to do back in the day. Old-school. And you're going to be his leading lady. That the story he sent you here to tell me, Valletta?"

Out of gentlemanly impulses and, worse, feeling sorry for this woman, one of a string he had auditioned during his childhood for the role of Archy's New Mother, Archy struggled to keep a tone of derision from creeping into his voice as he offered this bit of informed speculation as to Luther's line—phrases such as "triple threat" and "fast, cheap, and badass" having formed part of his father's formulary of bullshit over the years. He did not entirely succeed. The only thing lamer than the piece-of-shit plan Luther had come up with for peeling money loose from Archy, for a film that he had not the least intention of making, was the idea that Luther thought his son would give him anything ever again.

"He's going to put in a nice big part for you. That right, Valletta? Maybe somehow it turns out Candygirl wasn't dead all along?"

He detected a ripple along the muscles of her cheek. She held on to her silence, watching as Tibetan flags strung from the front porch of the Sandersons' house across the park bade their random prayers farewell.

"We're in preproduction," she said at last. Defiant, lying the lie.

"So you, what, you have a script?"

"Nah, but your dad, he has the story all figured out. Told me the whole thing, every character, every shot, every minute of screen time, told it ten different ways five hundred times. Archy, it's gonna be *good.*"

"Kind of a, what, Strutter comes out of retirement, one last job, gets his revenge type of thing?"

"You want to hear how it goes?"

Archy closed his eyes, anticipating the tedious madness of the scenario that he was about to be pitched, some kind of incoherent mashup of *Ocean's Eleven*, *The Matrix*, and *Death Wish*, his father's favorite movie, interlarded with a thick ribbon drawn from the saga of whatever kind of bullshit landlord trouble or IRS trouble or dental trouble his father and the lady had gotten themselves into. But Valletta fell silent again, and he opened his eyes to find a lone tear lingering on her cheek, a tiny solitary pool of outrage or shame. He felt his heart sink and drew another draft on his endless reserve of misplaced guilt. He took out his billfold and conducted a sorry inventory therein.

"Nah," she said, pushing away from her the bills that emerged, four crisp twenties, a faded five, and two soft, crumpled ones. "Nah, never mind. Keep your money. I didn't come here to bother you for money. I know you don't believe that—"

"Sure, I—"

"And I did not come here to bother you with that motherfucking movie you and I both know ain't *ever* going to get made."

"Okay."

"I know if I told you your dad was in trouble because of the drugs, you wouldn't feel inclined to help him in any way, shape, or form, and since I got with the program, fourteen months and nine days clean and sober, I respect that position, and so does he. What I want to ask you is, what if we was in some other kind of trouble, didn't have nothing to do with using? Would you possibly be willing to help him out then?"

"What did he do?"

Again the careful study of the street, the neighboring trees and houses. "I don't really know," she said. "But hypothetical."

"Hypothetical? Hypothetical, if that man's hair was on fire, I would not piss on his head to put it out."

She put her sunglasses back on.

"That's just a theory, though," Archy said. "We don't need to test it."

She nodded, chewing her lip, and he saw that under the lipstick, it was already ragged with chewing.

"Go on, Valletta," he said, pressing the money on her. "If you promise not to tell me where he's living at, or what he's doing, or how bad he looks, or give me any information at all, that's worth eighty-seven to me right there."

She considered it. Her tongue emerged from her lips and ran around her mouth once hungrily. Then she knitted up the money in her long fingers and made it vanish so quickly and completely that she might have been alluding to the length of time it was likely to spend in her pocket. She would not take the empty DVD box.

"Nah, y'all keep that, anyway. He got five more just like it."

"All right."

He took the box, Jack with a handful of beans, already awash in eighty-seven dollars' worth of regret over his own stupidity.

"Maybe I should come back next week," Valletta said, and a smile lacking one lower bicuspid made a brave appearance along the lowermost regions of her face. "Come up with a few more things about him you don't want to hear, see what that gets me."

"Funny," Archy said.

"Don't worry, you won't see me again."

"Valletta—"

She'd started for the Toronado, but he called her back.

"Come on," he told her. "You got to say it."

During the summer of 1978, Valletta's summer, the T-shirt shops of urban America had offered for sale an iron-on transfer that depicted Valletta Moore in a bell-bottom zebra-print pantsuit, surrounded by the glitter-balloon letters of the catchphrase with which she would forever be associated, first spoken in *Strutter at Large*. The iron-ons were produced by Roach, kings of the rubber transfer, who had divided all the profits, presumably considerable, with retailers and the movie's distributors.

"You want me to say it?" she said, doubtful, pleased.

"I think eighty-seven dollars buys me that," Archy said.

She sighed, pumped her fist once, like it was the head of a very heavy hammer, and said, "Do what you got to do." The fist burst apart in slow motion, fingers blooming. "And stay fly."

She wrestled with the steel of the car door, resuscitated the engine by patience and finesse, and rolled, shocks creaking, away.

"Stay fly, Valletta," Archy said.

⊙   ⊙   ⊙

Julius Jaffe was rereading his memoir in progress, working-titled *Confessions of a Secret Master of the Multiverse*. He had begun to write it two months earlier in a six-inch Moleskine, in a fever of boredom, drugsick on H. P. Lovecraft, intending to produce an epic monument to his loneliness and to the appalling tedium he induced in himself. That first night he had cranked out thirty-two unruled pages. Page one started thus:

This record of sorrow is being penned in human blood on parchment made from the hides of drowned sailors. Its unhappy author—O pity me, friend, wherever you lie at your ease!—perches by the high window of a lightning-blasted tower, on a beetling skull-rock beside the roaring madness of a polar sea. Chained at the ankle to an iron bedstead, gnawing on the drumstick of a roasted rat. Scribbling with tattered quill on an overturned tub, his sole illumination a greasy flame guttering in a blubber lamp. A prisoner of ill fortune, a toy of destiny, a wretched cat's-paw for gods of malice who find sport in plucking the wings from the golden butterfly of human happiness! Thus shorn of liberty and burdened with the doubtful gift of time do I propose to ease the leaden hours in setting down this faithful record, the memoir of a king in ruins.

The night after he penned these words, Titus Joyner had appeared on the scarp of Julie's solitude, swinging his grappling hook. Since then Julie had not added a word to his chronicle of boredom. He closed the Moleskine, fitted his memoirs with the little elastic strap, his own heart cinched with a tender compassion for their boy author in that distant age.

The front door slammed and the secret master of the multiverse said, "Shit."

"Titus," Julie said. "It's my dad. Get up."

Titus Joyner lay on his back with a pillow mashed down over his face, held in place by the hook of an arm. That was how he slept: shielded. Titus from Tyler, in Julie's imagination a sunblasted and horizonless patch of infinite Texas, a necromantic Dia de los Muertos city of prisoners and roses, where Titus had been raised by a forbidding grandmother known as Shy. In Julie's imagination, Shy was all in black, lit by lightning. Dead now, and Titus cast to his fate, claimed like a lost hat by an auntie from Oakland, a stranger from a house of strangers.

"Dude!" Julie said in a whisper. "T!"

Julie reached for the portable eight-track cassette player Archy had picked up for him at the Alameda swap meet. It was tank-corps green, styled like a field radio, and it had a webbed strap so that a Soldier of Funk, Julie supposed, could march his groove around. He popped out

Innervisions (Motown, 1973), one of the few among the small stock of eight-track cassettes he had managed to scrounge that Titus would consent to listen to, and shoved in, with a meaty thunk, *Point of Know Return* (Kirshner, 1977), aware of how it would irritate his father.

"Julie? You up there?"

Enigmatic white midwesterners of the 1970s aired curious ideas about the role of the violin and the organ in a rock-and-roll context. Titus dragged the pillow from his head and sat up. Awake, looking right at Julie; then, before Julie was quite aware of it, scrambling up out of the bed. Buck-naked, as Titus called it. Titus crumpled his clothes into an armload, went to the window, spun around, and confronted an art deco chifforobe that had belonged to Julie's great-grandmother. It opened with a great-grandmotherly creak, and Titus climbed inside.

Julie accepted this move without considering whether it was necessary or desirable.

He knew. He knew more than me or you. You can tell by the pictures he drew.

"Hide the hookah," his father said. "I'm coming up."

With a solemn intake of breath, Julie activated his secret master training. He would use his Field of Silence, he thought, in combination with his Scowl of Resounding Finality. The door swung open and his father looked in, eyes bright and sunken, cheek nicked by the razor, in one of his old-time hepcat suits. He had that shifty-eyed look he got whenever he had just done something he probably ought not to have done. This might not be a bad time, Julie saw, to confess or at least allude to his own most recent instance of bad behavior. Yet there was something he loved about the way Titus had entered into conspiracy with the chifforobe.

His father covered the fact that he was sniffing the air of the room for the molecular residue of burnt cannabis by making a show of sniffing the air of the room. "You just sitting around?" he said.

Julius Lovecraft Jaffe (though on his passport the middle name, by one of those metaphysical clerical errors forever being committed by reality on the true nature of his being, read *Lawrence*), gazed calmly back at his father. He sat on his bed, cross-legged in his tie-dyed long johns. Not the tie-dyed long johns with the infinite Escher stairway silk-screened across the chest but the ones with the space galleon setting sail for Tau Ceti across a sea of stars, which he had purchased last spring in the women's section at Shark's, where they had been labeled with a handwritten tag on which was printed, in an architect hand and in terms guaranteed to finger the deepest chords of his soul, COOL 70S SPACE KITSCH. The Field of Silence pulsed steady and thick as a stream of annihilating syrup. The Scowl burned shimmering hot pathways in the air between Julie and his father.

"What *is* that?"

His father's face seized up around the eyes, and his cheeks went hollow. He looked like a man with inner ear problems, halfway between disoriented and about to vomit.

"My God," he said. "Please tell me you aren't listening to *Kansas*."

There was a small prog bin at Brokeland, but it spurned the pinnacles and palisades in favor of the dense British thickets, swarms of German umlauts. Wander into Brokeland hoping to sell a copy of *Point of Know Return* or, say, *Brain Salad Surgery* (Manticore, 1973), they would need a Shop-Vac to hose up your ashes.

Julie took his wallet from the back pocket of his cutoff denim shorts. It was a yellow plastic wallet printed with a scratched image of Johnny Depp sporting hair of the eighties and the words 21 JUMP STREET in fake-wildstyle lettering. He unsnapped the wallet's coin purse, in which he rotated a selection from the variety of business cards he had printed up for himself at Kinko's at the beginning of the summer, just before he met Titus. A well-chosen card had served him well a number of times since then as a substitute for conversation, particularly with his parents. This time he chose one that read:

JULIUS L. JAFFE

curator

"I have to admit," his father said, sounding like the admission was not a costly one, "I'm getting pretty fucking sick of these fucking cards." He passed it back to Julie, who returned it to his wallet and put Johnny Depp back in the pocket of his shorts. "What's with the enormous shoes?"

They were size-fifteen Air Jordans, white on white on white. They looked like a couple of scale-model Imperial destroyers docked neatly on a deck of the Death Star. Julie considered making this claim. He saw that he would have to collapse the Field of Silence, at least temporarily, and throw up a Snare of Deceit. "It's that art project," he said. "The one I told you about." This strategy—Julie's mother called it "gaslighting"—could be surprisingly effective on his father, who spent so much time lost in his own humming that he sometimes missed out on real-world events.

"Huh," his father said.

There was no good reason to lie; on some level, Julie knew that. His parents had to figure-slash-understand that Julie was semi-bicurious, or maybe even gay, or what have you. Twenty-five minutes to gay o'clock. But the confession felt like too much work; Titus was too hard to explain. He was, for example, straight-up-noon straight, both hands on the twelve, though that had not prevented him from accepting every last note and coin of Julie's virginity over the past two weeks. There was so much more to it than sex, gender, race, and all that piddly shit. Julie felt that his life had suddenly, like amino acids in the primordial soup, begun to knot and pattern and complicate itself. How to confess that he had sneaked out with his skateboard every night to hook up with Titus, in slang but also quite literally joining himself by the hand to Titus's shoulder as they rolled through the nighttime summer streets of South Berkeley and West Oakland, through the wildly ramifying multiverse of their mutual imagination? Titus preferred the street to the roof and walls within which a hard fate and a ninety-year-old batshit auntie had obliged him to shelter, and Julie preferred nothing to the feeling of Titus's shoulder bone and muscle against his hand, preferred nothing to the grind of his wheels, each tree, parked car, and lamppost a whisper as they passed.

"It's that thing at Habitot," Julie added for verisimilitude. "I have to decorate them."

His father nodded knowledgeably. There was no other way that he knew how to nod. "So what *are* you doing?" he said. "Playing MTO?"

As a matter of fact, before Titus nodded off, they had been taking turns at Julie's laptop, logged on to Marvel Team-Up Online. Leveling up their latest characters, Dezire and the Black Answer, running them in their capes and energy auroras through the teeming streets of Hammer Bay, on the island of Genosha.

Julie said, "Filing my teeth."

"Uh-huh. Not smoking dope."

"Just crack. And a little opium. Just, like, this much." He pinched an imaginary pellet between his fingertips. "Fuck, Dad."

"Because you know it would be all right if you did."

"Yes, Dad."

"Not all right, but I mean, if you were getting high, I would want you to tell me about it, right?"

"Right."

"Not feel like you have to hide it or anything."

"I get it."

"Because that's when you start to drift into stupid."

Julie said that he planned to continue his lifelong policy of avoiding stupid at every opportunity.

"So," his father said. "Just sitting here, what, feeling sorry for yourself?"

"I don't need anybody's pity," Julie replied, seeing the words scrawl themselves across the page of his imagination in the florid hand he had affected when writing in his Moleskine with his fountain pen. "Least of all my own."

That raised a smile on his father's face.

"Why are you even here in the middle of the day?" Julie said.

"I, uh, came home," his father said. "I guess I should probably go back."

The shorter his father's stories got, the more unwise or embarrassing his behavior turned out to have been. His father's eyes wandered unseeing for the one thousand and seventh time across the artwork that Julie had drawn and pinned to the lath ceiling, the portraits of cybernetic pimp assassins and blind albino half-Jotun swordsmen and one cherished sketch of Dr. Strange produced with Crayolas and a Flair pen when Julie was five or six. A *Nausicaä* poster, the Israeli one-sheet for *Pulp Fiction*. The gatefold inner sleeve of a record called *Close to the Edge* (Atlantic, 1972), with its world of cool, enigmatic waterfalls that endlessly poured their green-blueness into infinity. His father seeing nothing, understanding nothing, searching for the line, the signal, the telling bit of repartee. Recently and unexpectedly, the fiber-optic cable between the continents of Father and Son had been severed by the barb of some mysterious dragging anchor. His father stood there in the attic doorway with his hands in the jump-jive pockets of his suit jacket, loving Julie with a glancing half-sly caution that the boy could feel and yet be certain of the uselessness thereof, that love occupying as it did only one small unproductive zone of the Greater Uselessness that seemed to pervade his father's life from pole to pole.

"Did something happen with Archy?" Julie said.

"With Archy?"

"Something at the store."

"At the store?"

"Question with a question."

"Sorry."

"What did you do?"

"Nothing, I didn't, I just kind of blew my stack."

"Oh, Dad."

"At Chan Flowers. Councilman Flowers."

"Whoa."

"Yep."

"Is that guy kind of, like, scary?"

"I have always thought so, yes."

"Kind of a creeper?"

"At times he gives off that vibe."

"But he buys a lot of records."

"An all too common conjunction of behaviors."

"And you *yelled* at him?"

"Threw him out, actually," Nat said. "Then I threw out every other shmegegge in the joint."

"Oh, fuck, Dad—"

"Then I closed the store for good. How do you like that?"

"You what? For good?"

"As in out of business."

"You closed the store?"

"I really felt I had no choice."

"For good?"

"Question with a question," his father said. "Look, I'm fine. I got over myself. Now I'm going to go back, say I'm sorry to Arch. I'll apologize to Flowers, Moby, everybody else who needs it. Apologies are cheap, Julie, and effective all out of proportion to their cost. My father used to say, 'Carry 'em like a roll of bills in your hip pocket, pass 'em out freely.' Remember that."

"Cool, okay."

"Used to say, 'They are good for business, and they make the world a better place.' "

Clearly, his dad was cycling high today, getting that Groucho Marx quality to his delivery. For years he had been on and off various medications whose names sounded like the code names of sorceresses or ninja assassins. Disastrous from the first dose or disappointing in the long run, each wore out its welcome in his father's bloodstream without ever managing to lay an insulating glove on the glowing wire inside him. His moods had little in the way of pattern or regular rotation apart from a possible intensification in Septembers and Februarys, but if Julie had over time learned to live unshaken by his father's unpredictable temblors of mania, he had grown inured as well to their completely predictable aftermaths, however heartfelt, of apology and remorse.

"Say sorry," Nat said. "Then open the store back up like I was, you know, on a little mental lunch break. False alarm. Everybody go about your business."

"Except Gibson Goode, right?"

"Whatever," his father said. "Man has a right to sell what he wants, where he wants. Bring him on. Meanwhile, you. Cheer up. You got two more weeks of summer to get through."

With a wan crackle, the Field of Silence fluttered back to life between them.

And he tried. But before he could tell us he died.

His father closed the door. Julie listened for the creak of his passage down the twisting stair.

The narrow, mirrored door of the old art deco chifforobe swung open, betraying the folded articulate span, half dressed in pressed blue jeans, of Titus Joyner.

"Yo yo yo," Titus said. Bit by careful bit, he took himself out of the chifforobe and reassembled himself on the floor of Julie's bedroom, a hit man snapping together the pieces of his rifle. He looked tired. He smelled like the locker room at the Y. "Five more minutes," he said.

He unrolled himself along the floor of Julie's room, on the coiled braids of a rag rug, and stretched out. He closed his eyes; his breathing turned solemn and slowed the rise and fall of his chest. He was a prodigy of furtive and impromptu sleep. The nightly bed that fate had furnished him was a zone of danger and dark insomnia. If you closed your eyes in that unsafe house, they would rifle your nightmares and violate your dreams.

"Titus," Julie said. "Yo, T."

Nothing; gone. Julie pulled the quilt from his bed and laid it over Titus. It was an antique of the '80s, Michael Jackson in a tacky spacesuit with a motley crew of robots and aliens. Julie stared at the boy on his floor, a mystery boy fallen from the sky like the Wold Newton meteorite, apparently inert and yet invisibly seething with the mutagenic information of distant galaxies and exploding stars.

Julie was in love.

⊙   ⊙   ⊙

The title of the course, offered through the summer evening enrichment program of the city of Berkeley's Southside Senior Center, was

"Sampling as Revenge: Source and Allusion in *Kill Bill*." It was scheduled to meet every Monday for ten weeks through August, amid the folding furniture of a beige multipurpose room where, in the past, Julie had taken classes in puppet making, clay sculpture, and ikebana. Always the youngest in the room by decades, half centuries, and happier there among the elderly than ever seemed possible in the company of his so-called peers.

That first Monday in June, a week after his graduation from Willard, Julie had taken his seat in the front row of five chairs at the exact center of the room, midway between the video projector and Peter Van Eder, whom Julie had always imagined, from his irritated tone in the *Berkeley Daily Bugle*, to be this one pudgy bald gentleman with aviator glasses and a square-tipped knit tie whom he would see from time to time at the California, glumly suffering the opening night of *Planet of the Apes* (perhaps the greatest disappointment in the movie life of Julie Jaffe, a mad Tim Burton fan) or *Steamboy* (another tragic dud). But Van Eder turned out to be a bony young guy not far past college age. Big Adam's apple, big wrist bones, one shirttail untucked, his hair long and stringy and flecked with dandruff or ash from his cigarettes or both. On his chin, a hasty pencil sketch of a goatee.

Julie took a glue stick and a bright orange notebook, quadrille-ruled, out of a Pan Am flight bag. Neatly, he folded and glued to the inside front cover the syllabus of films that Peter Van Eder proposed to screen and discuss:

Lady Snowblood (1973) d Toshiya Fujita
The Doll Squad (1973) d Ted V. Mikels
The Good, the Bad and the Ugly (1966) d Sergio Leone
Female Convict Scorpion: Jailhouse 41 (1972) d Shunya Ito
Ghetto Hitman (1974) d Larry Cohen
The Tale of Zatoichi (1962) Kenji Misumi
The Band Wagon (1953) d Vincente Minnelli
A Clockwork Orange (1971) d Stanley Kubrick
36th Chamber of Shaolin (1978) d Gordon Liu
Coffy (1973) d Jack Hill

Julie studied the syllabus as Van Eder waited for the last two names on his roster, one of them, Julie was interested to learn, being Randall Jones. Mr. Jones had both given and attended classes at the Southside Senior Center, and it was through him, a few years ago, that Julie had learned of the puppet-making class. Mr. Jones, whose taste in film ran strongly to violent western and crime, was a regular attendee of Peter Van Eder's film series at the Southside.

Julie found himself dizzied by his ignorance of Van Eder's choices, only two of which, the Sergio Leone and *The Band Wagon*, he had seen. Unless, as seemed likely, there was another movie called *The Band Wagon*, because *The Band Wagon* that Julie had watched with his maternal grandparents one Christmas in Coconut Creek, Florida, was a delicious musical with Fred Astaire and Cyd Charisse, whose thighs stirred ancient and somewhat distressing longings in Grandpa Roth. A couple of the other titles and directors were familiar. *Zatoichi*. Kubrick, duh.

Somebody said, "Look at the *bird*!"

Cochise Jones, wearing a leisure suit with a faded houndstooth check, stepped into the multipurpose room with Fifty-Eight manning the poop deck of his left shoulder, trailing a kid, perhaps a grandson, about Julie's age, light-skinned, light-eyed, broad at the shoulder, and slender at the hips. Though as far as Julie knew, Mr. Jones didn't have any family apart from the bird. When he noticed Julie, he frowned, looking thoughtful, hesitating, as if trying to make up his mind about bringing over the kid to meet Julie.

"He a friend of Fifty-Eight," Mr. Jones explained straight-faced, apparently deciding that no harm could come of the introduction. "Also a fan of Mr. Tarantino." Only he pronounced the name as if it rhymed with "Tipitina."

"Hey," said Julie, twisting a finger in the tattered selvage of his denim cutoffs until the blood ceased to circulate in his fingertip. His index finger in its noose of cotton thread swelled and pulsed and throbbed and in general served as symbol or synecdoche for its owner and his fourteen-year-old heart, for that all-encompassing, all-expanding disturbance in his skinny little chest that was the love of Tarantino, the world, or all mankind. "I like him, too."

Titus Joyner nodded, mildly amused (if that) by the spectacle of Julie in his cutoffs and sleeveless T, his portable eight-track on the floor by his feet in their clear white jellies, with his bright blue flight bag like one of the moon stewardesses in *2001*. He didn't say anything. A slender, loose- and long-limbed kid, skin the color of a Peet's soy latte. Hair worn in a neat, modest Afro with an air of studied retroism. Eyes wary, derisive, cold apart from that ghost of amusement, or maybe it was a flicker of recognition, as if he thought he knew how best to label Julie. Cleft chin. Clothes neat and spotless: dark jeans, short-sleeved, button-down oxford-cloth shirt. Nothing fancy, but somehow the crisp white shirt and the sharp creases ironed into the front of his trouser legs gave him an air of formality. On his feet he wore those imperial star-destroyer kicks.

"What's up?" he said.

Julie took a card, newly printed, from his wallet, and passed it to the kid, one that read:

JULIUS L. JAFFE
Ronin ·HIRED BLADE

The look of mockery was still on the kid's face as he studied the card, but he studied it. Slipped it into a pocket of his jeans. Then went to the back of the room to scatter his limbs across an upholstered armchair tucked into a corner.

"I'M SORRY, SIR." It was one of the other students, a man in a wheelchair, speaking through a robo-box. Julie had seen the guy racing around Temescal, in the neighborhood of Brokeland, his body a toy in the paws of some brutal ailment. His voice came sparking through its Hawking box. "SIR? I'M SORRY, BUT I HAVE A BIRD ALLERGY."

"A *bird* allergy," Mr. Jones said, looking blank, failing to see how this assertion could pertain to him. "I'm sorry to hear that."

"Maybe you could— Can he wait outside?" said Peter Van Eder. "Or . . . ?"

Fifty-Eight browsed politely through the silvery down at its breast, appearing to find no offense in the turn things had taken, but Mr. Jones, either because he had been looking forward to this series, or maybe on Fifty-Eight's account, appeared to be heartbroken.

"IT'S QUITE SEVERE," said the man in the wheelchair, the torsion of his neck giving him, no doubt unfairly, a sidelong and mendacious look as he said it, like maybe he was really just afraid of parrots or had something against Fifty-Eight personally. "I'M SO SORRY."

Mr. Jones sighed. Even if he and Fifty-Eight had not been inseparable, there was no way you could leave a rare and costly bird sitting out in a hallway somewhere. He turned to the kid at the back of the room and raised a sheepish eyebrow. The kid stared at the dude in the wheelchair with open and admiring horror.

"You can get a bus?" Mr. Jones said. The kid knit up his limbs and gave a fractional nod, about to be left alone in this roomful of cripples and old people.

"Bye, Fifty-Eight," Julie said. "Bye, Mr. Jones."

"I FEEL TERRIBLE," said the man in the wheelchair, but in the tonelessness of his voice-o-tron, it was hard to be sure whether he was referring to his remorse at the ejection of Fifty-Eight or the onset of anaphylaxis.

"Come on, fool," Mr. Jones said to the bird.

Van Eder passed a syllabus to Titus Joyner, who thanked him softly, with an automatic "sir." Then the kid's eyes locked on the syllabus, scanned it. He frowned. Something written on the page dismayed him, filled him with outrage and confusion. He squirmed with it, deep in the armchair, until he was obliged to speak up.

"*The* Band *Wagon?*" he said.

His disdainful drawl intoned the title of the seventh film on the syllabus with a contempt so all-encompassing that it led one of the fearsome-looking, old, ex-nun-style, Communist, lesbian retired piano teachers who principally made up the enrollment of "Sampling as Revenge" to get up and start passing out oxygen masks and air tanks, so that all the other old people and Julie could go on breathing and not have the air sucked out of their lungs by the whooshing vacuum that followed this sally from the back of the room.

Peter Van Eder blinked and looked mildly amused. "Do you have a problem with *The Band Wagon?*" he said.

"It's a *musical,*" Titus said. "It has, like, Sid Caesar."

"Cyd Charisse," said Peter Van Eder harshly, flatly, the way Julie's old fencing teacher Mr. DiBlasio had been wont to correct Julie's form with an impatient flat of the blade on the buttocks.

The kid nodded as if satisfied with this correction. He picked up his copy of the syllabus and held it at arm's length in a display of nearsightedness that Julie took for mocking. "Gordon Liu," he said slowly with a skeptic squint, pronouncing the Chinese name to rhyme with "shoe." "Stanley Kubrick. *Cyd Charisse.*"

The old ladies—there were seven of them, all white—and the three old gents (one of them an Asian-American in an Oakland A's cap) and the wheelchair guy apparently saw nothing at all droll or absurd in the presence of a Fred Astaire–Cyd Charisse film on that inventory of mayhem and martial arts action. On the contrary, they appeared shocked, even mildly disgusted, by the kid's show of disrespect, either because they were old or because they were white or both. Julie was certainly shocked.

"Tarantino himself has often argued that his movies should be situated in the context of the big-screen musical, with the outbursts of violence serving the same structural narrative function as the musical numbers," Peter Van Eder said. "Like a lot of Minnelli, *The Band Wagon* exhibits a strong female character of the kind that has come to be foregrounded in Tarantino's work. More important—I'm getting ahead of myself, but whatever—the self-enclosed, self-reflexive world of actors and dancers it portrays prefigures exactly the hermetic, empty universe of physical artistry that we find in *Kill Bill*. It also showcases the technical virtuosity of Minnelli that is an acknowledged influence not only on Tarantino but on Martin Scorsese as well. In other words . . ."

Van Eder smiled, a stiff, genuine smile made more horrible somehow by its genuineness, in which were intermingled an ingratiating familiarity and a desire to put this kid in his place.

". . . gots to be hip to Minnelli, my man."

Julie wanted to die of his own whiteness, to be drowned in the tide of his embarrassment on behalf of all uncool white people everywhere when they tried to be cool. Titus Joyner glowered at Van Eder. He pursed his lips, easing them pensively back and forth, wavering perhaps between giving Van Eder his due for wisdom imparted and taking offense at that horrible "my man."

"*Lady Snowblood,*" Van Eder went on.

He addressed the class for ten minutes, reading from a set of four-by-six index cards in a soft, stupefied, increasingly breathless tone like an astronaut pleading with a mad supercomputer to open an airlock, the voice that, for unknown reasons, Van Eder relied on for the imparting of information. He touched on the ambivalent place of women in the postwar Japanese economy, feudal history and Western values, the popularity in Japan of comic books like the original *Snowbird*, the Japanese literature of revenge, the tension between the needs of the individual and the norms of the community, et cetera. Then Van Eder switched on the video projector, pulled down the screen, and put out the lights.

Taking advantage of the sudden darkness, Julie turned to look back at Titus Joyner. The kid reached into his shirt pocket and pulled out a set of massive spectacles, at once square and rounded, a style somewhere between early Spike Lee and Miles Davis on the cover of *Get Up with It.* In the flickering light from the projector lens, the kid saw Julie looking at him, and a smirk drew a fishhook at the corner of his mouth. Then he turned to the screen, and the disc spun inside the Panasonic projector, and the fan whirred, and the soundtrack scratched, and the cymbals clanged, and Julie dreamed for two hours with his eyes open.

It was a dream *Kill Bill*, angelic and ghastly, more beautiful, more simplistic, bleaker. More, he tried, *existential.* At least the Bride, Beatrix Kiddo, had known love and happiness, companionship, hope for the future. Even at her lowest, even comatose and raped by crackers, she carried the memory inside her, in the place vacated by the baby she had lost. Her revenge was haunted by the ghost of happiness. From birth, Yuki Kashima—Meiko Kaji, so delicate, so badass!—had never known anything but the curse of her bloody and useless use. And the swordplay! Criminals and rogues, masters and pupils, slashing and hacking, fatal parasols. And the blood! Severed limbs flying, blood on fresh fallen snow, curtains and cataracts of blood!

When the lights came up at the end, Julie's reptile brain was dimly aware of Van Eder apologizing for having exceeded the time allotted for class, the rustle of papers, and the scrape of chair legs. The biomass designated as Julie Jaffe stood up, and its autonomic systems took over and propelled it toward a beige corridor, along beige linoleum tiles, through a beige world, while in another universe, his traveler soul honed its katana and ate rice with chopsticks by a fire and tied a thick topknot in its wild black mane. Julie was halfway to the snowy courtyard where the existentially absurd and beautiful combat between Yuki and her final enemy was appointed—halfway to the glass doors of the Southside Senior Center, which opened onto a cement plaza with a sculpture fountain—when he heard a strange howl behind him, canine and low at first, then rising to articulate a screech of mock Japanese challenge.

Julie whirled just in time to see the kid, Titus, coming at him, glasses returned to his shirt pocket, eyes twisted up with homicidal glee, kick-flying through the air while whirling an imaginary blade over his head.

"Hi-yah!" he cried, alighting only inches away and bringing his sword down as if to cleave Julie from cranium to coccyx. Julie drew and parried in a single swift motion, then stepped back in a shower of sparks and let the other kid's crazy momentum carry him forward with an ungainly lurch. As the kid went past, Julie jabbed downward with his left elbow (stopping just short of striking the small of his back).

"Yah!"

The other kid regained his feet and swung around, and they exchanged a quick series of attacks and parries, simulating with their mouths the clash and clang of steel on steel as Titus backed out of the glass doors of the Southside Senior Center and into the summer night.

Yah!

Hah!

Hah-YAH!

As the ladies and the geezers in their ball caps shuffled past, Julie and his opponent hacked and ducked, slashed, feinted, thrust. They dashed around the wide floodlit plaza with its random scattering of concrete oblongs, hopping up and off, circling the fountain at the center. Julie, with two disappointing years of fencing lessons in his recent past, had the advantage of knowing what you could do with a sword if you actually held one, while Titus had the advantage that he always would have: The whole thing was his idea. He was the one causing things to happen, driving them, taking them seriously long enough and intensely enough—and in public—to make them somehow *be*. Julie chased him, and Titus ran, laughing. He leaped up onto the broad lip of the fountain and took a deep breath. Three concrete-jacketed light fixtures led like stepping-stones across the water to the sculpture, a big mutant hand of steel entitled *Dancing Group II* that grasped at the night sky from the center of the fountain. With the tip of his tongue protruding from the corner of his mouth, Titus island-hopped the lights along to the sculpture. He scrambled up onto the steel palm of the open hand and stood there, beaming at Julie. Way down along Fourth Street, the train for Sacramento mourned its own passage. The air smelled of chlorine from the fountain, of cut grass from the soccer field on the other side of the Southside Senior Center.

"Dude, what's your name again?" Julie called, though he knew it was breaking the spell. "Are you— Is Mr. Jones your, like, grandpa or something?"

For answer, Titus leaped from the sculpture into the air, out over the turbid pool water and the scattered wishes of pennies and dimes, helicoptering his blade over his head, legs outstretched fore and aft like a hurdler's, clearing a gap of six horizontal and four vertical feet to land with a dainty stutter step on the lip of the fountain. Julie stopped breathing.

"Titus Joyner from Tyler, Texas," he said. "And I am here to dismember your pink bicycle–riding, plastic shoe–wearing, Jethro Tull–singing, faggoty Mr. Spock ass."

Julie's heart seized, and then a strange fizz of wonder seemed to engulf him, as if he had been dropped like an ice cube into a glass of sparkling water. The previous evening, he and his parents had gone to Archy and Gwen's for fish tacos, a specialty of the house. After a while, Julie had grown restless with the trend of conversation at the table and had wandered outside with his eight-track player to kill some time. On the little grass island where the neighborhood children were wont to abandon their toys, Julie had come upon a girl's bicycle, pink with white handlebar grips and white rubber tires. Wearing a blue science-section *Star Trek* T-shirt with a black collar and the little flying "A" over the left breast, from which he had cut away the sleeves, Julie rode the pink bike around and around the cul-de-sac, singing along with the eight-track at the top of his lungs about how a bungle in the jungle was all right with him. He had not been aware that even then he was being observed by a cold intelligence from another world. Now he gaped up at Titus Joyner as the other boy brought down his weapon hard, and Julie, deeply interested and intensely embarrassed, allowed himself to be killed. He died.

⊙　⊙　⊙

"I can stay here?"

Julie jumped. Titus lay motionless under the shelter of the comforter, eyes closed, somniloquent.

"Uh, okay, yeah," Julie said. "My dad went back down to the store, he probably won't be home for a while. I think my mom's at a birth, so she's probably gone all day. You can shower. And I could, I have to do some laundry. I could wash your clothes."

Julie, under the guise of a sudden blossoming of self-reliance and a desire to help around the house, had been washing Titus's clothes secretly along with his own for the past two weeks. Titus had only three pairs of pants, three shirts, and five pairs apiece of socks and briefs, but he was obsessive about keeping himself neat and clean. He had a horror of bad breath that approached the pathological, and he spent an aggregate hour a day, at least, in the maintenance of his modest little 'fro.

"Nah, nah," Titus said. "I mean can I stay here."

"You mean—What? You mean, like, can you move *in*?"

From the time of his arrival in June on a flight out of Dallas, Titus had been cribbing, as he put it, in West Oakland, in an undisclosed location; at any rate, he would not disclose its location to Julie. Mr. Jones and Fifty-Eight were neighbors, that was all Julie knew. The house held nine people in three bedrooms, cousins and unrelated relations, all living under the furious, disregarded administration of Titus's ancient auntie, who was actually a great- or maybe even a great-great-aunt. No one in that house, which—in Julie's imagination—teemed at every window like a cartoon asylum with madmen and psychotics, knew or cared if Titus came or went, if he dressed and fed and cleaned himself, if he lived or died, smoked crack, or built himself a suitcase bomb in the basement. And yet every day, more or less, he appeared before Julie in crisp jeans and a bright white T-shirt, with the white oxford or one of two plaid short-sleeve button-downs, a blue-black and a green-black, worn unbuttoned over the tee. And the starship shoes, scrupulously tended. Julie was obscurely moved by this scrupulousness, so helping Titus maintain it felt not like a chore but an honor. An offering of love.

The eight-track cassette punched to the next program with a loud clunk, and Titus sat up, wild-eyed and startled. He reached into his pocket for his glasses, and Julie noticed for the first time the coiled plug of black electrician's tape holding together, at the nosepiece, the right and left halves of his big Spike Lees. Titus had seemed weird last night when they first rendezvoused in Frog Park, but it was too dark then for Julie to spot the evidence of trouble.

"What happened?" Julie said. "Did you get in a fight? Did somebody— Did they say you had to leave?"

Titus appeared to be awake, blinking, swallowing, wiping his mouth on the back of his hand, but it took a long time for a reply to emerge.

"I don't want to talk about it," he finally managed, his voice little more than a whisper. Then he shook it off. "Shake it off," he told himself.

He got up and came over to Julie's bed, staring down through his lenses, and his expression was mocking, of himself, of Julie for his solicitude.

"I've seen things," he said, looming over Julie, close enough for Julie to smell the orange and cloves of his own brand of underarm deodorant, smeared somehow across Titus as they had grappled that morning in the dark. "Attack ships on fire off the shoulder of Orion."

"C-beams in the dark near the Tannhauser gate. You can't stay here."

"Just tell them I'm your imaginary friend," Titus said. "A only child, come on, you got to have a imaginary friend."

"I did when I was little."

"Yeah? What was his name?"

"His name was Cherokee."

"*Cherokee*. He still live here?"

Before he could quite dismiss the question as the joke it was intended to be, Julie had a quick look around the attic. When he was four or five years old and sleeping in the room next to his parents', he used to come up here to hide and conspire with his imaginary playmate. Now there was nothing left of Cherokee but the dry cool pulse of Indian fingers against his palm.

"Second, okay, that's first, but second, you promised me, T."

"What I say?" Titus gave the question an offhand spin and turned to examine, in a dish on the dresser, the orrery of small glass planets that Julie had made over the years at the Crucible. Trying to play it off, to persuade Julie that whatever rash thing he might have said was a joke, insincere, forgotten. "Only thing I promised you," he continued, "is that when I'm a A-list Hollywood auteur, you get to help me out on the screenplays. I remember promising you that. Isn't any other promise I remember."

"You said you would . . . you know." Julie felt his voice get very quiet. "If I came with you."

Like Galactus, like some giant, timeless celestial older than the stars, Titus scooped up a handful of planets, tumbled them between his fingers, let them splash chiming back into the dish. "True," he said. "But check it out, man." He laughed, bitter laughter, contemptuous. "I'm afraid of *her*. I heard her one time kind of like whispering to him from the porch when he dropped a garbage bag all over the sidewalk. Reminded me of this principal I had back in Texas, had that same quiet way of getting angry, talking all soft and reasonable, then suspend your ass for three days 'cause you threw a pencil."

"Yeah," Julie agreed. "She gets all Eastwood." Then, "How often do you go by there?"

"I followed him home a couple times."

"Just, what, stalking him or something?"

"Just looking."

Julie envisioned Titus pedaling past Archy and Gwen's house at twi-light, the sagging porch with its freight of bougainvillea, the life in which Titus was not permitted or could not bring himself to share pass-ing back and forth like a movie to be memorized shot for shot across the screen of the big bay window. Then Titus turned around, and Julie was shocked to see that he had tears in his eyes.

"I am not going back to my auntie's, tell you that," Titus said, and a flat, genuine twang of Texas crept into his voice. He took off his glasses to wipe away the tears with the back of his arm, and the two halves fell apart, the wad of black tape giving way, the sections of broken frame rattling against the plywood subfloor of the attic. "No way I'm ever go-ing back to that house."

They stood there with six inches and an adamantine membrane of the multiverse between them. Julie longed to put his arms around Ti-tus, to console him, but he could not be sure that Titus would welcome such a touch. Indeed, he suspected Titus would reject it. Julie could only guess, the intuition guided if not shaped entirely by the dubious and histrionic hand of ghetto melodramas, cop shows, and the brutal lyrics of rap songs, at the latest trauma that Titus had undergone.

Julie knelt and picked up the pieces, then carried them over to the bare pine table, its surface an action painting of Testors paint, scorched black in patches by the glue guns and the glowing elements of solder-ing irons, inscribed with an illegible cuneiform of X-ACTO-blade scars, where he had been wont, in the limitless trances of his loneliness, to as-semble his scale models of AT-ATs and Gundam Wing fighters, and to ornament his little metal armies of orcs and paladins, and to invest the unspent and endlessly compounding principle of his inner and only life. There were three neat plastic racks of screw and nail drawers, and he rummaged among them until he came up with a tube of superglue, the crusted tip of its nozzle forever pierced, like some allegorical wound in a story of King Arthur, by its tiny red-capped pin. He squeezed out two drops and then eased the acrylonitrile halves of Titus's glasses together with the practiced touch of a modeler until they held and there was not even a fissure visible. Then he handed them back to Titus, who gingerly tested the join. Without his frames, his face looked vulnerable, raw.

"Anyway, they just glass," he said.

"Seriously?"

"I got like twenty-ten. I just wear them to, uh, make me look smart." He put them on again, and something armored, sealed off, unassailable resumed its dominion over the features of his face.

"You could stay here tonight," Julie told him, and as he said the words, he felt a pang of regret for them, intuiting the valediction they contained. If Titus accepted the terms with which Julie was about to present him, the period of their secret friendship would come to an end. After today, the world would know about Titus Joyner, and knowing that, would begin to know, or believe that it knew, Julius Jaffe, too. Yet he felt so far from being ready to know himself or contend with the world and its definitions. "After that, I don't know, we'll see."

"Cool," Titus said. "Damn, thank you."

"Okay, it's on one condition."

"I'm not eating any more of that tempeh. Shit is nasty."

"We don't actually eat that much tempeh," Julie said, feeling himself blushing at the thought of the hopeless Berkeletude of himself and his family. "I don't know why it was even in our fridge. And no, that's not it."

"What, then?"

"You know."

"No," Titus said. "No way. I'm not—"

"You have to. I mean, even if my parents let you stay, and I don't *even* want to think how I'm going to explain it all to them, I just have to, like, rely on the fact that they are going to get off on the idea that I have a troubled young African-American friend they can, like, help out or whatever. But you can't just keep riding your bike past his house all the time. That is just sad."

Julie went down to the bathroom to brush his teeth and, strangely modest, change into his clothes. When he came out of the bathroom, he found Titus sitting on the bottom attic step, fully dressed, upright, hands on his knees, as if awaiting a court date.

"What if he doesn't like me?" he said.

Julie thought about squeezing in next to Titus, between him and the wall of the stairwell. Put his arm around the boy, lay his head against his shoulder, hold his hand. If he were Titus's girlfriend, it would be the easiest thing in the world.

"I wish I were your girlfriend," he said.

"Shut up, faggot," Titus said gently.

"Hate speech," said Julie. He sat down on the other side of Titus, where there was room for them to share the stair without touching. "Just do what I tell you. It's going to be fine."

Titus wiped his cheek with the back of one hand and snuffled once. Julie offered him a Kleenex. Titus waved it off.

"Tears in the motherfuckin' rain," he said.

$$\odot \quad \odot \quad \odot$$

On his way back to throw open the doors of Brokeland to the winds of doom, Archy decided to take a detour, drive past the site of the former Golden State market, corner of Forty-first and Telegraph, from whose shelves, as a pup, he had shoplifted all kinds of tasty and desirable items. The Golden State chain, small and local to the Bay Area, had suffered some kind of implosion while Archy was over in the Gulf. The site at Forty-first was sown with the salt of failure, and since then no enterprise had taken root at the cursed spot. Not the plastic-plant nursery. Not the store that sold novelty floor coverings, the kind you usually saw for sale draped over hurricane fences along vacant corner lots, shagrug portraits of Malcolm X and shag-rug Aztec warriors cradling dead Aztec ladies in the deep nylon pile of their arms.

Archy parked and got out of the El Camino. In the same spirit of research that made him borrow Rolando (he hadn't gotten the chance to tell Gwen about that, to show her he was capable, willing, and at this point, telling her would be like dropping a penny in a parking meter), Archy applied himself to the study of this slab of failure hewn from the greater zone of vicissitude that was his hometown. He tried to see it the way a successful businessman and top-ranked rich person like Gibson Goode was seeing it: as something that, unlike a plastic houseplant, could be made to grow. He studied the boarded-up plate windows, the rusting iron barrier around the empty cart corral. The mysteriously virginal circle of white concrete where, at the nexus of all earthly desire, there had stood a coin-operated peewee carousel with fiberglass horses, grinding around their tiny orbit in a way that only a kid could have found magical. As he ambled toward the back of the building to the shuttered and chained loading dock, he saw a pudgy man wearing a turquoise tracksuit and sneakers like a pair of tropical birds, murmuring into a cell phone. Big sunglasses made of turquoise plastic concealed the upper part of the man's face, but the lower part gathered itself into a troubled pout. The man said softly, "Hey."

"Tsup," Archy said, fixating his connoisseurial attention on the completely featureless and uninteresting cinder-block backside of the building. He stroked his chin and nodded as if confirming some rumor about the building's construction, as if noting that the ratio between the width and height of the cinder blocks echoed information that had been hidden by God in the works of Pythagoras, in the radio pulsing of the stars. Slowly, he walked on without giving the man in the bright kicks a second glance, heading down Forty-first Street toward Highway 24 like he had some proper business to attend to.

Forty-first was all sky and wires and broken rooflines and, like a lot of streets that had been cut in two by the construction of the Grove-Shafter Freeway, after all these years it still had a dazed feel, a man who had taken a blow to the head staggering hatless down from Telegraph, face-planting at the overpass. Archy felt a balloon of failure inflating in his rib cage. Between the days of peewee carousels and hectic stolen packages of Ding Dongs and this afternoon in the wasteland of the Golden State parking lot, there seemed to lie an unbridgeable gulf. As if his history were not his own but the history of someone more worthy of it, someone who had not betrayed it. He felt, not for the first time today, that he had not made a good decision in his personal or professional life since 1989, when he had accepted an impromptu one-night invitation to play a Funkadelic show at the Warfield (Archy was, at the time, a member of a P-Funk tribute band called Bop Gun) after Boogie Mosson was laid up with a case of food poisoning. That was no decision at all, since a request from George Clinton was an incontrovertible voice from the top of a very high mountain. Archy was tired of Nat, and he was tired of Gwen and of her pregnancy with all the unsuspected depths of his insufficiency that it threatened to reveal. He was tired of Brokeland, and of black people, and of white people, and of all their schemes and grudges, their frontings, hustles, and corruptions. Most of all, he was tired of being a holdout, a sole survivor, the last coconut hanging on the last palm tree on the last little atoll in the path of the great wave of late-modern capitalism, waiting to be hammered flat.

He followed Forty-first as it bent around to run into Forty-second, then turned right and found himself, speaking of sole survivors and the fatal path of the tsunami, in front of Neldam's bakery. A lint-bearded geezer of the type known in Archy's childhood as a wino sat on an over-turned milk crate just beyond the entrance, making his way with evident contentment through a sack of Swedish rolls.

"Pretty good rolls," Archy remembered.

The wino stopped chewing and looked at Archy, his expression bleary but somehow astute, most likely trying to decide whether Archy was trying to menace or cadge a roll off him.

"This here my lunch," he said apologetically. "Breakfas', too."

"I have no intention to molest your lunch, brother," Archy said. "I was always a Dream of Cream man myself."

When he was a boy, a Dream of Cream from Neldam's—crumbly chocolate cake interglaciating floes and tundras of whipped cream, the outside armored in a jagged tectonics of wide chocolate shavings—was a prodigy, a work of wonder, five dollars no one could spare spent annually by stingy but cake-loving ladies to celebrate the coming into the world of a fatherless and motherless fatboy.

"Well, then, go on in and get yourself one," the wino said. "Look like you might could need it."

"Maybe I could," Archy allowed.

He entered the bakery, with its curvy display cases and its pallid eighties palette of gray and pink. He breathed very deep, and the smell of the place, the olfactory ghosts of Pine-Sol and caramel and long-vanished dreams of cream, filled him with a sense of loss so powerful that it almost knocked him down. The cakes and cookies at Neldam's were not first-rate, but they had an old-fashioned sincerity, a humble brand of fabulousness, that touched Archy in this time when everything good in life was either synthesized in transgenic cyborg vats or shade-grown in small batches by a Buddhist collective of blind ex-Carmelite Wiccans. And now word was that Neldam's, too, was slated to close its doors.

"I need a Dream of Cream," he told the woman working the counter.

She was a hard-eyed little Filipina lady with no time or patience for his sorrow. "Big one or small?" she said.

Archy said, "Are those my only choices?"

He ate half the enormous cake in the car, using a spork from Vik's Chaat, stained yellow with turmeric, that he exhumed from the deepest stratum of his glove compartment. He shoveled freely, emitting bearish sighs and exclamations, and found that the Dream of Cream was, like so few things in this world, almost as good as he remembered. This discovery, along with the anticipated charms of sugar, fat, and chocolate, buoyed his spirits and steeled him sufficiently to confront with customary heedlessness his melancholy retail fate. He left the half a cake not yet required in its pink cardboard containment unit, under a stack of newspapers on the passenger seat, and wiped his mouth on the back of a parking ticket that had, like the fate of Brokeland Records, fallen victim to the Stallings moral code of studied negligence.

"Whatever," he told himself.

⊙   ⊙   ⊙

The open-closed sign hanging from the door of Brokeland was spun for the third time that day. Archy went back behind the counter and prepared to resume his lonely inventory of the musical remains of the late Benezra. He was aware, as he did so, of a poignant air of tragic dedication in all his actions, the dutiful routines of a doomed picket manning his lonely watch as, beyond the next range of hills, the barbarian horde mounted its conquering ponies. Then the shop door banged open, and those toucan-bill Adidas came walking right into Brokeland, their occupant lagging, as always, a fraction of a second behind and listing three degrees to the right.

"Damn, Turtle," said the cantilevered man with a show of bitterness. "You hurt my feelings."

Archy had been present, throughout the late 1970s, as that gait was first propounded and then painstakingly crafted to serve as a pedestrian variation on the Gangster Lean as specified by William DeVaughn, in his song "Be Thankful for What You Got" (Roxbury, 1974), as a necessary precondition for Digging the Scene. "Rubbing that Velcro you got stuck onto your chin. Acting all 'Heavens, what a interesting example of commercial urban vernacular, I must consult my notes.' Like you didn't *even* see me there."

"Kung Fu!" Archy said, coming around the counter to exchange a fist bump and a hug with Walter Bankwell, his best friend from kindergarten all the way through senior year at Oakland Tech, ten pounds heavier and four square inches balder than the last time Archy had seen him. Walter Bankwell was a nephew of Chan Flowers, had put in his time among the cadavers back in the day. Bombing around in the hearses, carrying a pager in case of a corpse, with that smell coming off of him like the water in a vase of old flowers. Somehow the boy managed to slip free of his uncle. Got into the music business, repping for a string of indie hip-hop labels that all folded. Managed a string of modestly gifted rappers, one of whom had almost blown up, sort of, in the greater L.A. area. Meanwhile, constantly in and out of trouble with the police, the IRS, lawyers, record executives, mothers of the young girls his clients liked to fuck. Walter always, lifelong, working that 51/49 smart-to-stupid ratio. A few years back, he had fucked up in a way that invited a severe beatdown from some Long Beach kingpin, put him in the hospital, rehab, physical therapy, Walter's 49 percent ultimately costing him the sight in one eye. "What's *up*, boy?"

"Aw, you know."

"Working?"

Walter stepped back from Archy, his tracksuit dazzling and sickly green as a glow stick, a long, slow, mocking smile inching up his face at either side.

"What?" Archy said.

"Just like old times, Turtle Stallings, sneaking round the Golden State market. Expect you to have a sixty-four-ounce Orange Crush stuffed down your pants, and two packs of Now and Laters."

Saying it " 'nihilators," the way they used to.

"Huh," Archy said.

"Checking out the competition, I suppose. Got that Thang moving in, going to have a used-vinyl department twice the size of what y'all got going on here."

"Nobody knows that. Anyway, it's apples and oranges."

"Then when you see me coming out the door, it's like, 'Ho, shit.' Run, Turtle."

"Fuck you, Walter. Last time I ran from something was in 1991, in Kuwait, and it was a bat with rabies."

"I'm just playing with you. Check it out."

Walter's hand crept into one of the zip pockets of his warm-up jacket and emerged palming a case for business cards, a nice vintage-looking brass one mounted with a big white stone that wanted you to think it was a diamond. Walter took out a card and handed it to Archy. It was printed in black and red ink, with a familiar logo of a paw print in half-tone behind the text.

" 'Community Relations,' " Archy read. " 'Dogpile Entertainment Group.' Since when?"

Walter shrugged.

"Since *before* your uncle changed his mind . . . ?" Even before he saw the smirk pushing out Walter's lower lip, Archy knew it was a stupid question. "Oh, okay," he said. "It's like that."

"Quit pro crow," Walter said. "As they say. One hand scratching the other."

"Chan's little Walter," Archy said. "I begin to understand."

A pudgy boy, soft-faced, asthmatic, given to fevers, often hospitalized, supposedly a dead ringer for Chan Flowers's only brother who had died, Walter was always Chan's favorite, could always worm his way out of whatever trouble the other nephews got into. All due respect to cynicism itself and to Mr. Mirchandani its prophet, it was hard for Archy to believe that Flowers would sell out Brokeland for a simple payoff. The councilman didn't give off the smell of that particular kind of corruption. But to reach out a hand to his nephew, the boy not a boy anymore, scuffling around for the past ten years, had only one eye. Maybe that was something Archy could begin to understand.

" 'Community relations,' " Archy said. "Mr. Gibson Goode."

"Working for G Bad."

"G Bad know you have a congenital condition in which you were sadly born full of shit?"

"Paid vacation. Corporate retreats in Hawaii. Health benefits."

Walter trying to sound like it was all due and proper, Archy knowing him too well to miss the almost desperate wonder lighting up his face. Something like that coming along, a hook on a helicopter, snatching him out of the churn and froth and icy water. A paycheck, benefits. Archy imagined coming home with such things in his backpack, how it would be if he could meet Gwen's reproachful look with news like that, the 50 percent gain in domestic peace that would result if he could move from being shiftless and cheating to merely the latter. A stack of quarters to feed the meter, move the needle out of the red, way over to the right.

"Yeah, that sounds real nice, Walter," Archy said. "And I wish you the best. Now get the fuck out of here."

"Turtle—"

"Are you serious? This is my house, you come in here, working for that corporate expansionist retail bullshit—"

"All right, chill, Turtle, damn. I get it. I know how much love you got for this old ex-barbershop, have so many spiderwebs, dust in here, all Roger Corman and shit." Walter took in the faded sleeves tacked in Plexiglas frames, the old NyQuil-colored clamshell iBook they used for inventory, the bins that Archy and Nat had built themselves, mounting them on rollers so they could be pushed aside to make room for the famous Brokeland rent parties they rarely put on anymore. The arcologies of spiders. "But I tell you what. Dogpile is a one-hundred-percent black-owned enterprise. A hundred percent."

As if summoned like a genie by this allusion, Nat walked into the store. He was carrying a box of donuts from the Federation next door, and he wore a soul patch of powdered sugar. He took in the spectacle of Walter's tracksuit and shoes, then seemed to recognize Archy's old friend with a vague nod.

"Oh, yeah, uh, Nat, this here, you remember Walter Bankwell? Old running buddy of mine? Walter, this is my partner, Nat Jaffe. Walter was, he's in town on business, and, uh—"

"How you doing?" Nat said. He reached out to shake hands, but Walter raised his arms like a pair of crazy aerials at weird angles to his body. He flattened his hands into a pair of shovel blades and crouched low, sweeping the floor behind him in an arc with the toe of one foot. Some kind of Crane-style move, Archy thought.

Walter straightened up. "Later," he told Archy without another glance at Nat. His shoes walked out of the store, followed shortly thereafter by Walter, gangster-leaning now a little to the left.

"We used to call him Kung Fu," Archy explained.

"Just stopping by?"

"That's all."

"Old times' sake."

"We for sure used to get into some crazy shit, me and him. Right about when I was Julie's age."

"You *still* aren't Julie's age," Nat said. "Julius Jaffe was born older than you are now."

"I don't know about that, boss," Archy said.

Standing across the avenue, right in front of the funeral home, was Speak of the Devil, stepping his skateboard up into his hand, fidgeting alongside a solemn-faced youngster on a bicycle, nobody Archy knew. Casing the joint—Archy felt it deep in the mischief center of his brain— for some kind of metaphysical stickup.

Nat turned to see what Archy was seeing. "You know that other kid?" he asked.

He looked perturbed; recently, Archy gathered, Julie had begun to wobble on his axle. Until now it had been hard for Archy to imagine the boy getting into any kind of trouble that could not be ameliorated by rolling a handful of twenty-sided dice.

"Huh-uh," he said. "From here, he looks like my little cousin Trevor, but no. That ain't Trevor."

"From here, you know who he looks like?"

"What are they doing, just standing there?"

"Maybe they're planning to hold us up."

"Huh," Archy said, feeling, at this echo of his own offhand first reaction, a vague anxiety at the sight of Salt and Pepper over there, waiting to get spilled. "That why *you* came back?"

"No, Archy," Nat said. "That's not why I came back."

⊙   ⊙   ⊙

Useless, by James Joyce. That was Nat's father's joke, passing sentence on himself when he spaced on the dry cleaning, when the phone bill went past due and service got cut, when he could not start a fire or turn over an engine, when he ran another candy store or newsstand into the ground. A man with a talent for nothing but tipping weary waitresses, slipping lollipops to babies when their mothers' backs were turned. Saddled with the especial uselessness of the third-generation socialist, one of the lonely grandsons of Eugene V. Debs, stood up by Utopia, stranded with a payroll to make. Fatherhood among the Jaffes afforded a history of uselessness, with Nat only the latest chapter: luftmenschen, ineptitudes, and bankrupts going all the way back to Minsk Guberniya. Standing there like an ass in the doorway to Julie's room—*fucking useless!*—serving up the traditional blend of banter and bluster, an old family recipe. Seeing misadventure, doubt, confusion in his son's eyes and having not a clue what to do about it. Knowing that as the boy got older, every such moment might turn out to be the last of its kind. Something to be seized upon and savored, not allowed to slip away in hints and smart remarks.

Carpe diem. Was there ever a more useless piece of advice?

Nat remembered how, when he went back for his father's funeral, a few weeks after he and Aviva started sleeping together, he found the old man's copy of *Ulysses* in a box of ten-inch records, mainly classical, mostly Shostakovich. That chunky softcover from the late fifties or early sixties, fat "U," slender "L," swaybacked, edges sueded, pages yellow as the filter of a smoked cigarette. Tucked into his father's favorite passage—the hungry cat giving its morning oration—Nat had found a clipping from the *Times-Dispatch*. NEWSSTAND OWNER FOILS ROBBERY. A Sunday morning in 1968 in Shockoe Bottom. Suspect, a Negro male in his early twenties, asked for a copy of *Bird Fancier* on a shelf behind the counter, then rifled the cash register when the owner's back was turned. Pistol-whipped a customer who tried to intervene. Store owner Julius Jaffe, forty, then struck the assailant with a (*Times-Dispatch*) newspaper weight. Alertly flagged a passing police car. Almost certainly averted further violence, the suspect having served time at Powhatan for attempted murder and assault with a deadly weapon. Julius the First was not the type to save clippings, never one to stand back and admire himself—the fifteen-year-old story came as news to Nat, who could only conclude that, though his father never spoke of it, the incident had meant a great deal to him. A high point in a life lived at sea level, prone to flooding.

At the time, when he was in the midst of mourning his father, the discovery of the clipping had made Nat smile. Three weeks earlier, walking home from the Telegraph Repertory where he worked as an usher, Nat had interrupted a mugger in the act of taking a wallet, a watch, and a silver Tibetan barrette off a young woman whom Nat recognized as a regular patron of the theater, particularly fond, it seemed, of the work of Elliott Gould, to whom Nat had always fancied he bore a resemblance. Nat acted without reflection, plan, or reservation and was rewarded for his courage with a blow to the stomach and a night in the arms of the young woman, whose name was Aviva Roth. As he read the old clipping—teary at the thought that the incident had meant so much to Julius that he kept a record of it between the favorite pages of his favorite book—it did not occur to Nat, not for an instant, that the day would come when he, too, would look back on a moment's thoughtless heroism, almost twenty years before, as the only useful thing he had ever done.

"First thing, I came to apologize," he told Archy. "I'm sorry. I fucked up."

"I see."

Archy was going to delay acceptance for a while, Nat knew. Apologies were the flip side of Nat's huffing and puffing, and they flowed so freely from his lips that the people in his life had learned to hold out against them as stoutly as against the tantrums that necessitated them. Hunker down in the house of bricks, wait and see if Nat planned to come all the way down the chimney. He always did.

"That's why the donuts," he said.

"They are appreciated," Archy said. He opened the box, surveyed its contents like he was taking a first look at a crate of fresh inventory, there being, of course, as Archy often explained to Nat, a profound spiritual analogy, hole and all, between donuts and vinyl records.

"So, I'm sorry. I was a total ass. That's first. Sorry, sorry, sorry. I will apologize to everyone personally. Mr. Jones, Moby. All of them."

In the last paragraph of that clipping from the *Times-Dispatch*, it had been reported, with a certain editorial bemusement, that after foiling the robbery, storekeeper Jaffe had been heard to apologize to the would-be robber for having beaned him with a lead ingot.

"Okay, okay," Archy said, wigwagging his hand impatiently. "I got it. Apology accepted. What's the second thing?"

"The second thing is," Nat said, and as he prepared to adumbrate the second item on his agenda, it did him the great favor of occurring to him: a sentence that his father, rest his soul, had never quite managed to articulate aloud, at least in Nat's hearing. "I am not going to lose this motherfucking store."

"Well, all right."

"Because I don't know about you, but I feel like, Archy, if I don't have this place? I'm not sure I really *have* a place."

"I hear you."

"You think it's melodramatic."

"You? No way."

"Because I'm totally serious," Nat said. "Look at me. What else am I fit for, you know? The ice melts, where do you put the penguin?"

"A valid question."

"Where else am I going to *be*."

"In the spiritual sense, you mean."

"Exactly."

"Besides," Archy said, his eyebrows saying, *Brace yourself, you are about to get fucked with*, "like, in your house. With your *family*."

"Archy, I love my wife, and I love my son. You know that."

"I do."

"You'll attest to that."

"I will."

"But this store is my world. These are my *records*. You know?"

"I do know, Nat." For all of Archy's teasing, the tongue-in-cheek approbations, Nat had felt his words landing, sticking, here and there, like snow on ready ground. When you chose to pledge your share of labor and your worldly assets to partnership with a man who liked to get up on his high horse, make speeches, let it rip, it was probably because you knew that somebody had to do that from time to time, and it wasn't going to be you. "This store is *our* world."

"You get that."

"I do."

"So that's why I'm not just going to stand around being useless," Nat said, having worked it all out: the feeling of being caught under the wheels of the Dogpile juggernaut that Mirchandani's news had first engendered. The bitterness of his talk with Julie. The memories of his father's bookmark life. "I'm going to fight them."

"Gibson Goode?"

"Gibson Goode. Chan Flowers. All those motherfuckers."

Archy smiled, neither mocking nor quite pleased. The smile you gave something, good or bad, when it showed up right on time.

"You'll help me, right, Arch? If I promise I won't do anything stupid, lose my temper? If I keep it constructive and positive? You're going to help me fight?"

Before he could get an answer out of Archy—not that, when you came right down to it, he really needed one—a pattern of percussion intruded from outside the store, getting itself all tangled up with the thing Jack DeJohnette was laying down on the store's turntable; the door banged open; and the boys came in, Julie and that kid, Julie giving off strong waves of something heavily plated with Moog and in a tricky time signature, sounded like Return to Forever. The boy never went anywhere without that fucking eight-track now, bopping all over town with his woeful Isro and his bell-bottom jeans, some kind of little Jewish soul elf. All of Nat's regret and retrospective longing to connect to his son seemed to turn at once to irritation. He reached for the eight-track's dial, and the volume dropped to zero.

"Who's this?" Nat turned to the other boy. "Who are you?"

"Okay," Julie said. "So. Dad."

From the time he went verbal—two, three years old—Julie had made it a point to appear before the bench with his arguments scrubbed and tidied. Business plan all formatted and punctuated. Scheming, deep scheming, but letting you see that he was scheming, that your consciousness of his machination was a part, maybe the key element, of his scheme.

"This is Titus Joyner. He and I met in my film class, you know, 'Sampling as Revenge,' the Tarantino thing, which by the way is awesome, this week we get to watch *Clockwork Orange*, which is possibly not as great as *2001* or *The Shining* but is maybe number three, as I think you will agree."

Nat signaled that he was willing at least to argue this—he was not personally interested in any top three that did not include *Barry Lyndon*—but something had come over Archy. He stared at Titus Joyner, unblinking, breathing through his mouth. A kind of exploratory alarm, Nat would have said, as if he'd just realized he had left his wallet in a taxicab in a city far away and was trying to remember how much money it contained.

"Yeah," Julie said. "So, moving along, Titus, say hi, Titus."

"Hi."

"So, what can I tell you? Titus just moved to Oakland, not, what, not even two months ago, from Texas. He is fourteen years old, extremely intelligent, and well behaved. Really good at MTO. Has excellent habits of personal hygiene, as you can see."

Indeed, the kid's pleats, seams, and hemlines were all crisp and tidy. His nails were flawless seashells.

"He was living with his granny Shy in Texas, but Shy died, and now he is living at his old, crazy, like, senile auntie's house, where there were already—what was it—fourteen?"

He turned to his friend, who was staring blindly up at Art Kane's famous photograph of that great day in Harlem, looking like his ears were full of hornets that he was trying not to anger or disturb.

"Nine," he said softly.

"*Nine!*" Julie cried, as if this were a number even greater and more outrageous than fourteen. "He's living in unsafe, unhealthy, and unsanitary conditions, and don't get all wiggy on me, okay, Dad, but I told him that, pending an intense family discussion between you and Mom, he might be able, we might consider, seeing as how he is such an awesome, nice, smart person with so many startling creative ideas and what I might be tempted to call a truly fresh cinematic vision—"

"Resist the temptation," Nat said. "I beg you."

"I was hoping he could stay with us. Unless maybe—"

Julie turned to Archy. Hitherto, he had been carried away on a gust of his own enthusiasm, but his nerve or his blarney seemed to fail him as he saw the look in Archy's eyes, which Nat felt he would have to describe, trying to avoid exaggeration, as *raw panic*. The surname Joyner belatedly played a chord in Nat's memory, a mu major, something a little off about its beauty. Jamila Joyner, a girl Archy had been stuck on, stuck to, the summer when he and Nat first met. Right after he came home from Kuwait. A girl who stayed around enough to wear Archy out, then went on home to Oklahoma. Or possibly, come to think of it, to Texas.

"Well," Nat said. "I guess congratulations are in order."

⊙   ⊙   ⊙

Archy stood in the front bay window of his house like a doomed captain on the bridge of a starship, pondering, as if it were a devourer of planets, the approach of his wife's black BMW. Stroking his chin, using intricate mental tables of cosines and angles to decide whether the intensity of Gwen's response to the business with Elsabet Getachew would be squared or full-on cubed by the news that his child had appeared out of nowhere, or rather out of some nowhere known only, it seemed, to Julie Jaffe. The results of Archy's calculations were sobering.

The BMW pulled up to the house and then sat, lights lit, engine heat troubling the atmosphere above its hood, windshield a glossy gray-blue blank of reflected sky. Daylight was taking its sweet time fading into dusk, and the street at suppertime seemed to be holding its breath, torn into patches of deep shadow and sunshine, motionless but for the little white moths stitching their loopy crewelwork in the honeysuckle. In the sandpit of the tiny playground, dozens of toy vehicles and appliances lay bleached and upended, primary-colored plastic ruins as of some toddler cataclysm.

The door on the driver's side swung open. Gwen took hold of the doorframe with her left hand and the door itself with her right and, jaw set, head lowered as to a thankless task, simultaneously heaved and thrust herself, belly first, out of the car and onto her feet. For a few seconds she wavered there like the evening itself. Then she reached into the back of the car and came out not with the assault rifle, rocket launcher, or perhaps flying guillotine that Archy feared but rather an aluminum water bottle and the shoulder strap of her birthing bag. She tried to yank the bag by its strap through the space between the back of the driver's seat and the doorframe, but it got wedged. She jerked hard and then stumbled as something—the strap, probably—gave way. When she went to unlatch the seat back, she dropped her car keys. They bounced once and skittered under the car. She let the broken strap dangle and fell back against the side of the car with a show of quiet despair.

Over the past hour, Archy had envisioned Gwen's return according to a number of scenarios, incorporating into these fantasies of anger, reproach, and reconciliation elements derived from Italian opera, pornographic films of the mid-eighties, and footage of tornadoes vandalizing Kansas with lightning and wind. Gwen lost her temper so rarely, and with such a lasting sense of self-betrayal, that it was difficult for Archy to imagine with any accuracy how far beyond the unprecedented events of that morning she was capable of going. But it had never occurred to Archy that Gwen would come home to him covered in defeat.

She stood there leaning against the car, looking at the broken strap of her birthing bag as if its frayed ends encoded the general intentions of the universe toward her. Archy padded down the front walk of his house, his step light and cautious, the pavement warm against his bare feet. He assumed that the sorrow, the weariness of spirit attested to by the slump of Gwen's shoulders, by her bowed head, by the whole pregnant-lady version of *The End of the Trail* she had going, that all this served to express the cost to her of returning to his cheating embrace.

"I'm sorry," he said, all his planned speeches and formulas forgotten. "Gwen, I just—*Ho*." He came around to face her square-on and saw the blood on her shirt. The antennae of two sutures on her cheek. "Damn, girl, what the fuck?" An iron bar, cold as a flagpole in winter, plunged into his chest. "Are you—?"

"It's not my blood," Gwen said in a bitter tone, as if to suggest that by rights it ought to be. She raised her head and tried to meet his gaze but could not seem to manage it. "I—" Now she looked at him. She had those beautiful Seminole eyes, mysterious and hooded, their color between tea and molasses. They filled rapidly with tears as if through the sudden breach of some inner dam. "I messed up, Archy."

She let go of the broken strap, fell against him. Smell of a hospital in her hair, smell of hard work and failure rising off her body, and somewhere in the midst of it, a miscellaneous note of incense. She went completely boneless on him, expecting him to hold her up, all one hundred and sixty-odd pounds of her, bloodstains and belly, arms thrown around his shoulders. He resolved to do it. He belted her to him with his arms like her chute had failed and they were plummeting earthward a hundred miles an hour at the mercy of wind, cable, and rippling silk. He resolved on the spot to be equal to the challenge of bearing up. He was a husband who could be true. He was Superman grabbing hold of the train engine as it plunged from the bridge.

"It's going to be okay," he said.

As soon as the words were out of his mouth, he regretted them. This breakdown or whatnot, he saw, had nothing to do with him or with their marriage. Gwen had sacrificed her dignity to return home not for his sake but for her own, because she needed to fall apart, and that was something she would permit herself to do only at home. So here she was, bloody and wrung out and ragged, and Archy had no motherfucking way of knowing whether it was going to be okay.

"Did somebody die?" he said. "Gwen. Honey. A baby?" She shook her head. "A *mom*?"

"Nobody," she said. "Nobody died. The baby, the mom's fine."

"You're fine, too?"

She nodded. He laid a hand on her belly, and as always, the contact stirred him sexually. Something fructuous about the swell of her, asking to be opened.

"The baby?"

She stopped crying abruptly, with a sputtering finality, like the last frame of film running out on a reel. "The baby is fine."

"Aw, then," he said, fighting down the hard-on, even more inappropriately timed than usual, that had begun to unfurl in his boxers.

"No, Archy, listen, I can't—I'm not—Oh, Archy, I messed up so-ho-ho *bad*."

She sank to the ground, and Archy sank with her, the Man of Steel dragged along by the plummeting train. His arms ached, his knees trembled. Gwen seemed by the second to gain pounds and babies and fluids in her amnion.

"Come on inside. Yeah. Stand up. It's okay."

He hoisted her and she stood up, her legs going back about their business, but that was all she could seem to manage. She laid her head against his chest and rested. He was thinking, *I can stay here like this all night until my arms break off and fall on the ground in a million pieces*, failing to notice at first how intently Gwen was pressing her face against the front of his shirt, pressing it right up to the skin at his collar, now the hollow of his throat, taking deep inquisitorial breaths.

"Why do you smell like candles?" she said.

She drew back, watching him. She pulled a wad of paper napkins from the pocket of her bloodstained shirt and blew her nose.

"Long story," he said, "Now tell me what happened."

She shook her head. "I don't want to talk about it. I lost my temper. Now we're going to have our privileges revoked at Chimes, and Aviva's pissed off at me, and we'll probably have to close down our practice, and . . . and . . ."

Titus Joyner, riding his brakeless bicycle, rounded the corner by the Island of Lost Toys, the surface of his bare chest lustrous as motor oil. Wearing his T-shirt with the neck hole encircling his head and the rest hanging down behind like a burnoose. Archy's heart tipped and fell from its shelf. He had persuaded Nat and the boys to go no farther for now, to say nothing to Aviva or anyone else, least of all Gwen. He did not deny or even seriously question the boy's claim on his paternity. He remembered having heard about Jamila getting pregnant with a child he half assumed to be his, a half assumption that did not prompt him to protest or take any action at all when she went off to Arkansas or wherever to have it. Whenever he heard one of the popular songs of the era, which had provided a soundtrack, as it were, to the blind flailing of his spermatozoa through the inner darkness of Jamila Joyner, he might spare a nano-momentary thought for that child. But until this afternoon Titus had remained an eternal fat, stolid toddler dressed in the world's tiniest tuxedo, as in the one photo of him that Archy had seen, years ago, sent by the Texas grandmother along with news of Jamila's death in a car crash. No other comment, no request for the check—in the amount of $375.00—that Archy had provided, uniquely, in return for the photo and the tragic news. He had kept his distance with the boy in the store today, but he was careful not to be cold or unfriendly. The embrace they had exchanged was perfunctory and all but imperceptible to Archy behind the turmoil of his emotions. Now the boy pedaled past, eyes forward, expression blank, looking at neither Archy nor Gwen, neither left nor right, wearing his T-shirt do-rag. He was, like Gibson Goode and the impending fat, stolid toddler in Gwen's belly, going to ruin everything.

"Who's that?" Gwen said, watching Archy intently as he watched the kid ride past. There must have been some kind of slackening of Archy's jaw or widening of his eyes. "Archy, what's wrong?"

"Nothing," said Archy. At the last possible instant the kid folded. His eyes slid toward Archy, flicked at him before returning front. "I'm— Nothing. No."

He watched the kid ride off, then turned to face the ruination of his wife, trying to think what he could do. "Wait here," he said. He walked over to the El Camino in the driveway and opened its passenger door, then slid out the enormous pink aircraft carrier of the cake box from Neldam's.

"What," Gwen said, taking a deep shuddering breath, her face wary but brightening visibly, at least to Archy's trained eye. "In God's name. Is that."

"Dream of Cream," Archy said.

The Church *of* Vinyl

Can't play a Hammond through no apology," said Mr. Randall "Cochise" Jones. " 'Less you got some new type a patch cord I don't know about."

Making it a joke, wanting to hide his irritation. Up all night, spinning five thoughts in his head: *Gig tomorrow. Brown and gold plaid. Bird need his arthritis drops. Gas up the van. Get the Leslie.* Gig, plaid, bird, van, Leslie; needle in a locked groove endlessly circling the spindle of his mind. Mr. Jones felt ashamed of that scanty midnight track list. When he was a younger man, his insomnia used to play it all. Sex, race, law, politics, Bach, Marx, Gurdjieff. All kinds of wild and lawless thinking, free-format, heavy, deep, and wide. Now, shit. Fit it all onto a pissant five-track EP going around and around.

"Said, be here Saturday," Mr. Jones said.

"I know I did."

"Black man my age, that could be asking a lot."

"But here you are," Archy said.

"Here I am."

Here he was, sixty-six and still, in fact, lean and strong. The brown and gold plaid giving off that good casino-lobby smell of leisure suit fresh from the cleaners. Bird on his shoulder freely dosed with dandelion tablets mashed into a dish of Quaker grits. Van gassed up to the tune of fifty dollars, backed into the boy's driveway. It was a white '83 Econoline, odometer rolled over twice, napped with gray dust. Sitting there, rear doors open, empty as a promise. Boy had told him last week he was finished with the job.

"Mr. Jones, damn, I'm sorry, what else can I say?" Archy said. "It's been a lot going on."

"Told me it was finished."

"Yeah, it pretty much was, but then, huh, turned out your treble driver went bad. I had to go all the way to this dude up in Suisun, pick up another one."

Archy dialed the padlock on the garage door, unhooked the clasp. Stooped to grab hold of the door handle. Nine o'clock in the morning, boy in his pajamas. Slept in some kind of kung fu getup, satiny red with BRUCE LEE INSTITUTE stitched in white silk across the back.

"It really is almost done. Two, three hours, tops. Definitely for sure in time for the gig. When they expecting us?"

"You don't know that, how you know you be ready in time?"

Archy shot a look at the bird, a roll of the eyes to say, *Can you believe this man, waking me up at 8:57 in the goddamn morning to bust my balls with feats of logic?* Archy Stallings to this day the only person besides Fernanda ever tried to engage the bird in conversation about Mr. Jones. Mr. Jones remembered the way Fernanda used to do it, how she would slam a bottle of pills down on the kitchen table, maybe, turn to the bird on its perch by the window, say something like *You want to make sure he takes his medication, Fifty-Eight. Day he dies, I'm selling you to KFC.*

"Nah, but seriously, Mr. Jones. I just need to put it back together, then you ready to go."

"Young man," Mr. Jones said, "I need to play it *before* the gig. See it works, how it sounds."

The garage door swung upward on its hinges with a ringing of springs. The bird, a pound of warmth and steady respiration on Mr. Jones's shoulder, greeted the Leslie speaker by reproducing the whir of its treble rotor when it powered up. But the Leslie, gutted, said nothing. Its cabinet was even emptier than the van, which at least had some furniture blankets piled into it, a tangle of rope and bungee cords, the dollies. All of the Leslie's motors, wheels, drivers, rotating horns, and drum, its amplifier like a Kremlin of vacuum tubes, lay ranked in an orderly grid across the workbench at the back of the garage. Mr. Jones could see that everything had been cleaned and oiled and looked correct.

That gravitation toward correctness was something Mr. Jones had always liked about Archy Stallings. Even when Archy was a boy of five or six, kept his fingernails clean and square, never an escaped shirt-tail. Wrapped his schoolbooks in cut-up grocery bags. When he got older, fifteen, sixteen, boy started working those old-school hipster suits, the hat and a tie, styling himself somewhere between Malcolm and Mingus. Always reading some Penguin paperback, translated from the Latin, Greek; penguin the most correct of all birds, made even the fastidious Fifty-Eight look like a feather duster.

"I've been distracted," Archy said. "And I dropped the ball. Between this thing with Dogpile, you know? And some other things . . ."

"You got to maintain focus," Mr. Jones said, though the sound of his words made him wince. He recalled with perfect clarity the irrelevance of old men's maxims to him when he was young. Rain against an umbrella, a young man all but sworn to the task of keeping dry. Archy was not so young anymore, and Mr. Jones had been raining down the pointless counsel on him for a good long time. No more able to restrain himself than a heavy-bellied cloud. "You made a commitment."

"Oh, no doubt," Archy said, shaking out his umbrella. "No doubt. Tell you what. You don't have somewhere you need to be, I can put the whole thing together right now. That work for you? Take me, like, seriously, an hour. Then we can go over to your place, plug the Hammond into it, test out the whole rig. Thing needs adjustments, I make them right there. Then I help you load everything up into the van." He straightened, tightened the string of his kung fu robe. "And you're one. Ready for tonight. Okay? Sound like a plan?"

Using the placating tone he took with Mr. Jones, understanding like no one living, apart from one feathered savant, that Cochise Jones was in secret an angry man, prone to impatience, outrage, injury of the feelings. In the liner notes of *Redbonin'*, Leonard Feather called him "the unflappable Mr. Jones," and at the time, in the chaotic midst of the seventies, that was the rap on Cochise, laid-back and taciturn like some movie Indian, Jeff Chandler in *Broken Arrow*. Nowadays people took him for this harmless, smiling, quiet old parrot-loving gentle-man who, from time to time, at the keyboards of a Hammond, adopted the surprising identity of a soul-jazz Zorro, fingertips fencing with the drawbars and keys. Mr. Jones felt as trapped inside that nice old gentleman, smiling, chuckling, as he had inside the wooden-Indian cool of his youth.

"Day I need help moving that thing," Mr. Jones said, "is the day I give it up for good."

The Hammond B-3 was diesel-heavy, coffin-awkward, clock-fragile. To gig with one, a man needed to be strong-limbed or willing to impose on his friends. From the day in 1971 when he bought it off Rudy Van Gelder, Mr. Jones had always gone with the former course.

"Find me a chair, then," he said. "And maybe someplace I can put this damn bird."

Archy went into the house, came back with two mugs of black coffee, a computer chair, and a broomstick that he rigged with a C-clamp for Fifty-Eight to perch on. He spread one of the furniture blankets from the back of the van on the floor of the garage. Turned out to be Count Basie's birthday: KCSM was playing the Lambert, Hendricks & Ross version of "Li'l Darlin'," the Count himself taking a rare spin at the keys of a B-3, holding on to the mournful churchliness that the instrument had carried over coming, right around that time, into jazz.

Mr. Jones got out his pipe and his pouch of tobacco and settled in to observe the boy work. He found it satisfying to watch Archy's meaty Jazzmaster fingers take up one by one the Leslie's unlikely components, items could have been scrounged from a kitchen drawer, a toy box, and a U-boat, then oblige them, one by one, to cohabit inside the cabinet. His pipe, an angular modernist briar, a gift from Archie Shepp, seemed to draw particularly well today. Alongside the driveway, bees lazed among the honeysuckle bells, and a hummingbird sounded its mysterious ping. Fifty-Eight rummaged idly with its black bill in its dappled breast. The Leslie would be fixed, and they would play their gig tonight up in the Berkeley hills. Everything was manifestly all right. And yet something continued to rankle at Mr. Jones, like a sour finger of acid in the windpipe, a failure that loomed ahead of or lay behind both Archy and himself.

"What 'other things'?" Mr. Jones said.

Fifty-Eight pinged like a hummingbird.

"Huh?" Archy had the treble assembly mounted in the uppermost of the cabinet's three stories, belted to the AC motor. He crouched, peering in, listening to the well-oiled silence as the disk with the two horns, the real horn and its dummy brother, whirled on the bearing tube. Blades of a propeller on a cartoon beanie. "What other things *what?*"

"You distracted by."

Archy switched off the power, and the treble rotor came to rest with an audible sigh. He swung around to face Mr. Jones, laborious and purposeful as a bus turning a tight corner. Rocked back on his haunches, contemplating. Breathing through his nose. Making up his mind whether or not he wanted to start in on it.

"Turns out I got a son," he said. "Fourteen years old. Showed up at the store yesterday out of the motherfucking blue. Turns out he's been living right here in Oakland since June."

Enough time went by for Archy to fairly conclude that Mr. Jones might have nothing to say. Even though Mr. Jones had suspected, even hoped, that Titus might be the "distraction," the word "son" had caught him off-guard, which in turn left him nonplussed on a deeper level, irritated that the word should still, after all these years, reverberate. At one time you could drop it like a tray of dishes on a tile floor, cut off every conversation taking place inside of Mr. Jones. Now it played only with a soft tremolo of regret, more or less like any other regret that might be audible to the heart of a man of sixty-six. Mr. Jones sat there, confounded by grief, turning Archy's information this way and that, a paperweight, something small and heavy cut with a lot of facets. Wanting to say something to this fine and talented young man, something lasting and useful about sons, loss, and regrets. The longer the silence stretched between them, the more irritated Mr. Jones became. Archy swung back to the Leslie. Unplugged it, picked up the bass rotor, and slid it into place, tightened the mounting nuts.

"You know your wife how long?" Mr. Jones said.

"Ten years."

"Uh-huh."

The pipe was dead, and Mr. Jones passed it to the bird. The bird nipped onto the pipe stem with a click of its beak, then flew off the perch and into the morning. Knock-knocking it against the sidewalk.

Probably dropping its mess while it was out there, bird better house-broken than a child of five. A few seconds later, the bird came fluster-ing back to light on Mr. Jones's shoulder. Passed back the pipe with its freshly emptied bowl. Fifty-Eight had come equipped with that trick by some owner before Mr. Jones, before Marcus Stubbs, who had lost the bird to Mr. Jones in a poker game and who did not smoke a pipe and who furthermore could not have trained a shark to favor steak. Mr. Jones took the pipe, and the bird hopped back up onto the makeshift perch.

"I didn't tell my wife yet, by the way," Archy said. "Case you were wondering."

"You didn't know you had a son before now?"

"I knew, but I mean, we never had, like, contact. Boy was off in Texas somewheres, uh, Tyler, I think it is."

"I know it." Gigging at some corrugated-shack crossroads bar and grill, the night dense and humid and haunted by a smell of roses. Idris Muhammad on the drums back when he was a kid named Leo Morris. Going on half a century ago.

"Boy had his granny, the mom's mom, living there," Archy said. "The old lady sent me a picture one time."

"Uh-huh."

Mr. Jones poked another hank of his favorite perique into the bowl of his pipe, tamped it down with a finger.

"Nobody ever asked me to be a daddy to the boy," Archy said. "And I didn't . . . you know. Volunteer."

"Uh-huh."

"Yesterday, boy shows up in my store, and I still don't really under-stand why, but. He's with Julie, you know."

"Julie?

"Julie Jaffe."

"I didn't know that boy had any friends."

"Julie got a full-on crush on the motherfucker."

"Oh," Mr. Jones said. "So he's like that?"

"I do believe that he is," Archy said.

Nothing in that to disturb Mr. Jones. When it came to lifestyles and behaviors, Mr. Jones played it strictly live and let live. Gays, Wiccans, people who wanted to punch a metal grommet in their earflaps. But somehow it made Mr. Jones sad, without surprising him, to learn that Julie Jaffe had come out a homosexual. That felt to him like something too complicated, too heavy, for a boy so young to lay on himself. He did not disapprove, but he could not see any reward in it. "Boy that age," he said, shaking his head. "Smart, too."

The bird beeped like Mr. Jones's microwave, four times. Popcorn, popped. Then, following its own inscrutable logic, it began to articulate Groove Holmes's version of the chorus to "American Pie." A ghostly rotor whirring in its throat.

"Said they met up at some film class," Archy said, setting the woofer drum into place in the lower story of the Leslie. "Over at the Southside Senior Center."

"Is that right?" Mr. Jones said, staring at the parrot as if to warn it to hold his tongue about that evening in June.

"It's a Quentin Tarantino class. I don't know, I guess they're studying *Kill Bill* or some shit, watching a bunch of kung fu movies, B movies. Surprised you didn't sign up for it, loving that *Pulp Fiction* like you do."

"Only I did sign up for it," said Mr. Jones. "Sounds like you got to be talking about my boy Titus. No shit, that's your son?"

Archy raised up slow and careful. Came around on Mr. Jones a little at a time, like he expected to find himself looking down the barrel of a gun. "You know him?"

Whenever Mr. Jones, again in the characteristic style of useless old men, wished to contemplate the brokenness of the world, or at least that part of the world bounded by the Grove-Shafter Freeway and Telegraph Avenue on Forty-second Street, he had only to look across and up two doors to the home of his neighbor Mrs. Wiggins. The woman already seemed old when he and Francesca first moved in with Francesca's mother back in 1967. But Mrs. Wiggins was strong then, furious and churchgoing, pleased to be known for and to advertise her own iron rule over the tribes of loose children who flowed like migrants through her door—the late Jamila Joyner among them—taking what she could pay them in love and beatdowns, in clean clothes, food on the table. Years, decades, Mrs. Wiggins went on and on, like one of those

Japanese soldiers who kept fighting in the Solomon Islands or wherever, nobody ever showing up to reinforce her, tell the poor woman to
surrender. But time, crime, and misery in all its many morphologies
had at last ground old Mrs. Wiggins down. Though she lived still, she
was a gibbering ghost of herself. You had to pity any child who found
himself consigned by the high court of bad luck to her care. When Mr.
Jones was growing up in Oklahoma City, he had been taken to a carnival
whose sideshow featured a man purported to be John C. Frémont and
a hundred and twenty-odd years old. Bone hands, a mat of hair, and a
pair of filmy eyes peering out from a heap of blankets, shivering. All
around the staring thing, in the shadowed tent, stirred the freaks and
bodily horrors, sly, embittered, and cavorting. That was how Mr. Jones
thought of old Mrs. Wiggins now, in that little house across the street.

"I might be the cause of this particular distraction coming your way,"
Mr. Jones said. "Titus stays with Mrs. Wiggins. You know that house
across the street from me?"

"Yeah, okay. She was Jamila's, like, auntie."

"I see the boy come out the house one day, something about him
seemed familiar, you know? Boy had on a little sweater vest. Hair in order, crease in his jeans."

"He does present a neat appearance, I will give you that."

"We started talking."

In those three words, Mr. Jones condensed a two-week history of
passing nods. The boy coming and going on his bicycle at any given
time of the day or night, Mr. Jones looking for signs of creeping doom
on the child but observing, day after day, nothing of note except a small
and fiercely maintained repertoire of button-downs and blazing white
tees. Then, all at once, a blast of conversation, Titus drawn in by a burst
of eerie parrot zitherings coming through Mr. Jones's kitchen window,
KQED having shown *The Third Man* the night before.

"Boy told me he wants to be a movie director," Mr. Jones said. "Talking about Walter Hill, Sam Peckinpah, Stanley Kubrick. I'm thinking,
well, all *right*."

"He has taste."

"Then he mentions how he likes Tarantino. So I told him about the class. Only when we got there, this one dude in a wheelchair." Mr. Jones broke off, pressed his lips together. Took a deep breath, shaking his head in furious sorrow. "Says he has a *bird allergy.*"

According to Dr. Hanselius at the Niebyl-Proctor Marxist Library, bird allergies were, quote, extremely uncommon, unquote, and something in the lingering sting of humiliation that Mr. Jones had felt that night, a sense that he and the bird had been the victims of some esoteric form of bigotry, fed the anger that had been mounting in him since finding out that the Leslie wasn't ready for tonight's gig; since being thrown out of the Tarantino class; since the assassination of Marcus Foster or Dr. King; since 1953, 1938.

"Son of a bitch probably sleeps on a feather pillow every motherfucking night," Mr. Jones said.

He looked at the bird, feathers giving off that faint parrot smell of scorched newspaper, in whom all his loneliness and outrage were distilled. Fifty-Eight screamed like a slide whistle.

"So I had to leave," Mr. Jones said, aware that his explanation of his role in bringing Archy his son had fallen somewhat off track. "Titus stayed. And Nat's boy was, like, sitting right there."

"In the front row, right by the teacher?"

"Right down front and center. Guess the two of them, they must have hit it off. I thought maybe it could happen, boy might find his way to you sooner or later."

"You mean you knew?"

"Not for sure."

"But, I mean, Mr. Jones, how come you didn't just *tell* me?"

Mr. Jones squirmed at the question. "Figured I already played my part. Might be y'all's turn next. You and him."

"Wow," Archy said. "Huh. You are a cryptic old motherfucker sometimes, Mr. Jones."

"I can't disagree."

"You move in mysterious ways. Did you tell *them*?"

Maybe that was when Mr. Jones began to realize that he felt offended.

"Think I would say something to them, not you?"

"Must of taken some serious figuring between them, find their way to my doorstep."

"That where Titus is now, your doorstep?"

"Figurative doorstep."

"Not living with you?"

"From, like, one day to the next? Uh, yeah, 'Hi, I'm your son,' 'Great, okay, you can move in'?"

Mr. Jones tried to find the flaw in this scenario. He loved Archy Stallings and had always tried to see the best in him. He was struggling to understand what would keep a man from taking hold of the unexpected blessing of a live boy, good-looking and correct, with commendable taste in film directors.

"I don't move that fast, Mr. Jones, you know that. And like I told you, I didn't say nothing about it yet to Gwen. I'm already number one on her shit parade due to certain lapses in judgment."

"But you didn't leave him with Mrs. Wiggins?"

"Nah, he's staying with Nat and them for right now. Figured, make Julie happy. Have himself a little slumber party up in the attic."

"That ain't what you figured," Mr. Jones said.

"No," Archy agreed. "No, you're right. It's just, with the baby coming, and the Dogpile thing . . ."

"Distractions."

"Yeah."

"Getting you off your main focus."

"That's right."

"Which is what, again?"

"Huh," Archy said. "Hey, Mr. Jones? What's wrong?"

Mr. Jones was up and out of his chair. He reached out a hand to Fifty-Eight, and the bird sidled up the gangplank to its inveterate perch.

"Mr. Jones, what did I say? Why you leaving? I'm not quite done, but I'm almost."

"Just bring it to the gig," Mr. Jones said. "It don't work, fuck it."

He started toward the back of the van, wanting—or feeling that at the very least he ought—to tell Archy about Lasalle, born and died April 14, 1966. Tell him about the two hours and seventeen minutes' worth of the pride and the joy that Archy had been squandering for fourteen years. He went to the Econoline, slammed the doors on the empty cargo bay. Mr. Jones helped the bird onto the headrest of the driver's seat, where he liked to ride, clutching the shoulder belt with one claw to keep its balance.

"Maybe you need to start trying to focus on the distractions instead," Mr. Jones said. "Maybe then they wouldn't be so distracting."

"Mr. Jones! Hey, come on, now. What'd I say?"

Mr. Jones got into the van, started the engine. Even over the slobbering of its three-hundred-horsepower V8 Windsor, he could hear Archy repeating uselessly, "Mr. Jones, I'm sorry."

⊙   ⊙   ⊙

"Pulling a Band-Aid," Gwen said.

"Not even," Aviva said.

"You promise?"

"I promise. Be brave."

Aviva was flying the bravery flag. Feet planted side by side, flat on the gray Berber wall-to-wall. New sandals with straps that crisscrossed in epic-movie-style up past her ankles, toenails freshly painted plum. Suntanned legs shaved, shins shining like bells in a horn section. Gray linen skirt and white linen blouse, not new but tailored with severity and maintained with care. Blouse buttoned to a professional altitude and yet at the collar managing to betray a fetching freckled wedge of clavicle and suprasternal notch. On her lap, an abstruse tome entitled *Acupuncture: Points and Meridians*.

" 'Be brave,' " Gwen said. She tugged at the hem of the overworked black maternity skirt she had pressed into service for this exercise in ritual humiliation. Her shirt, though crisp and clean, was originally her husband's and Hawaiian. But her hair was looking all right. Clean, springy, baby locks freshly twisted. Her hair was definitely equal to this morning's ordeal, and in that Gwen found a modicum of comfort if not, perhaps dangerously, defiance. She cleared her throat. "If I was brave, Aviva, I wouldn't be sitting here."

"I mean long-term brave," Aviva said. "Big-picture brave."

"The cowardly kind of brave."

"Right," Aviva said. "As opposed to the stupid kind."

This distinction accorded with Gwen's experience and, to a lesser extent, her beliefs; and yet making it did not comfort her at all. "You swear," she said, seeking this guarantee for the third time that morning. "Aviva, you swear to me."

"It does not mean a thing," Aviva said.

"Because, I have to tell you, it feels so meaningful that I kind of want to vomit."

"You going to be sick?" said the Saturday receptionist, looking over from her monitor to study Gwen, her tone saying, *Don't you* throw *up in my office.* She had a vibrant head of sister curls, and Gwen recognized her as a fellow disciple of Tyneece at Glama. They had crossed paths a few times, pilgrims to the shrine. Something about the woman had always bothered Gwen, and now she knew what it was: an invisible, pervasive miasma of Lazar.

"You know, I might?" Gwen said. She lowered her voice to the peculiarly audible whisper common among the women of her family; peculiar not in its audibleness but in the disingenuous way that, like God handing down His commandments to a bunch of folks He knew perfectly well were going to break all of them repeatedly for all time, it bothered to be a whisper at all. A Shanks woman with a practiced embouchure could not only modulate the dynamics of her whisper but send it through closed doors, around corners, across time itself to echo everlastingly, for example, in the reprobate ears of a granddaughter married to a no-account man. "Having to eat you-know-what will do that to you."

Aviva lowered her face to her textbook, not quite in time to conceal a smile. The receptionist, for her part, did not appear to find Gwen amusing. Her long fingernails resumed their furious clacking against the keys of her computer, a sound that had been annoying Gwen, she realized, since they sat down. Gwen shifted in one of the vinyl-upholstered steel chairs that furnished the waiting room, tipping herself first onto her left buttock and then onto the right. Whenever she leaned one way or the other, her thighs peeled away from each other with a sigh, like lovers reluctant to part. The muscles at the small of her back had gathered themselves into an aggrieved fist. Baby's head was jammed up against the left side of her rib cage, just under her heart, right at the spot where Gwen ordinarily felt premonitions of disaster.

"What I need," she said, in the same Shanks whisper, audible to the dermatologist in the office next door, "is something to wash it down with." Thinking of a cup of creamy white *suff*, which she would never again permit herself to enjoy. "Something to get rid of the taste of—"

"Shush," Aviva said. She reached down for her handbag, unzipped an inner pocket, and took out a miniature airplane bottle of Tabasco sauce. "Put a few drops of that on it."

Gwen took the bottle and shook it a few times, thinking, *Squeeze a few drops into Lazar's bathroom soap dispenser. Massage the stuff right into his stubbly pink head. Work it right on down to the pores.*

As she pictured herself, oddly satisfied, performing this bit of revenge grooming, the door between the waiting room and the examination area swung open and Dr. A. Paul Lazar, FCOG, came out. He appeared to be in a transitional state between the delivery room and the seat of his bicycle, green scrub top worn over slick black Lycra shorts and a pair of Nike bike shoes. In this hybrid getup, he looked perfectly suited to his waiting room, which conformed to the general aesthetic of Berkeley doctors' offices by freely mixing elements of a secondhand furniture showroom, a real estate title company, and the Ministry of Truth from *1984*. Lazar was better-looking and not as young as Gwen remembered him, not quite so pallid and dead-eyed. But there was still something fish-faced about the man.

"Ladies," he said inauspiciously. He held out his hand for them to shake it, with an air of portent but also a hint of mischief, as if they had gathered to sign a treaty that would permit him to occupy their country in the guise of defending it. "Come on in."

Aviva slid the acupuncture atlas into a canvas KPFA tote bag and stood up. Gwen leaned on Aviva's arm for help getting to her feet. Lazar watched her rise with a bright diagnostic eye. Dread or the skull of her baby seemed to wedge itself deeper between the bones of Gwen's rib cage as she followed Aviva into the office. It was a dull tank—black steel shelves, artwork by Pfizer, view of the parking lot—enlivened only by the disorder of Lazar's medical texts and by a framed photograph of him sharing the sun atop some gray-green mountain with a horse-toothed young woman and two Italian bicycles. Lazar and his wife or girlfriend were smiling with an air of dutiful rapture, the way you did when some total stranger agreed to snap a photo of you. Gwen fanned the flicker of pity that lit within her at the sight of Lazar's office, sensing that the light of its flame offered her sole hope of finding a path out of the mess she had gotten the Birth Partners into. Pity and pity alone could mask the bitter taste of shit.

"So," Lazar said. "Here you are."

"Here we are," Gwen agreed, trying to stand up to his blue eyes as they further annotated her case. Edema, melasma.

"I know I have you two over a barrel," he said. "I appreciate the gesture nevertheless."

He smiled insincerely to show them that he was pretending to be kidding. The flame of Gwen's pity was snuffed out. She screened a brief martial arts sequence in her imagination, perhaps a hundred frames in all, ending with a different *gesture*, one that would introduce her foot to the knob of Lazar's larynx. She retained control of herself and resisted the urge to share this scenario with him. Still, his remark proved difficult for either of the partners to rally back over the net.

"I—" Gwen glanced at Aviva. "I spoke to Lydia this morning. She sounds good. I don't know if you—"

"She'll pull through just fine," Lazar said. *No thanks to you*, said his eyes.

No, no, Gwen was only being paranoid. She had been out of line yesterday. Allowed her emotions to overcome her judgment, which was not at all like her, by nature and fiat, by habit and preference. Powerful as her emotions could be, she had known since she was seven years old that they were good for very little, and that by contrast, her judgment was uniquely reliable. It was all that, and the long, bloody unraveling of the birth yesterday, and then the hormones rolling like a thunderhead across the prairie of her third trimester, that had led Gwen to betray her principles. From a medical point of view, Dr. Lazar had performed flawlessly. Gwen had no clinical beef with him, none worth jeopardizing their standing at the hospital, which, like that of all nurse-midwives who had privileges at Chimes, was always mysteriously fragile. Now, thanks to an intervention by Aryeh Bernstein, all that Gwen needed to do was speak the two most meaningless words in the English language to Paul Lazar, and she would be forgiven. An apology, what did Nat always say, supposedly quoting his dad: It was a beautiful thing, no, a miracle of language. Cost you nothing and returned so richly. Easy for Nat to say.

"Yesterday was long and confusing," she began, knowing this would not do, that the logical conclusion of the line, were she to follow to it, must be that fault lay not with Gwen or bad luck but with poor, long, confusing yesterday afternoon. "Normally, Doc, I am way too proud ever to put myself in the kind of position that I put myself into yesterday when I lost my cool."

Aviva sneaked a glance at her partner and, somewhere in the profoundly dark recesses of her deep-set eyes, sent up an arcing flare of warning. Gwen had not come to discuss with Paul Lazar, MD, the flow and vagaries of her pride or her cool.

"And so," Gwen tried.

She became aware of a flat, fetid taste building up at the back of her tongue. In coming here, she saw, she had been instructed not only to swallow her pride, apologize to this man who had insulted her with a racial slur, but also to put up with his smugness, and his bike shorts, and worst of all, the equine grin of his woman in the photograph, which no longer struck Gwen as pitiably friendless so much as self-satisfied, boastful, the smile of someone who felt that she most belonged on the tops of mountains. Or, no, maybe the bike shorts were the worst thing of all.

"And so," she resumed, "looking back over my conduct. And taking into consideration the strong recommendation of my partner. Who has spent her whole professional life standing up to doctors, hospitals, in-surance company bean counters . . ."

"Gwen, darling," Aviva said, mixing forward the Brooklyn, either to ironize the term of endearment or else by way of genuine warning.

". . . so that you can be sure she knows, the way I know, that just like we have to be twice as competent, twice as careful, twice as prepared, twice as sensitive, and twice as cool under fire—"

"Are we talking about midwives or Jackie Robinson?"

"—as some Lance Armstrong wannabe doctor with a diploma from—" she checked the med school sheepskin—"Loma Linda—"

"Whoa," Lazar said. "Excuse me?"

"—just like she knows we have to be twice as good at everything as you all—"

"For God's sake, Gwen—"

"—you can be sure that Aviva knows, because she's the one who told me, and because God knows I've seen her do it enough times herself, that we also have to eat *twice as much shit.*"

Aviva fell back in her chair.

"So that's what I'm here to do. In two bites. Two little words. Not the two words I might choose to say if I had any choice in the matter, but I don't."

Gwen stood up with what felt to her like remarkable alacrity and even, for the first time in many weeks, a kind of grace. The sight of Aviva slumped and fuming in her chair, the glitter in Lazar's eyes—he would move to have their privileges pulled, no doubt about it—stirred no answer of remorse or regret. She went to the door, and put her hand on the knob, and turned back to Dr. Lazar, and, not quite as if she were telling him to go fuck himself, not quite as if she were suggesting that he con-duct an experiment to see how far up his ass he could fit the saddle of his three-thousand-dollar Pinarello, but rather with the full force of the pity to which lately she had pinned her hopes of slipping through this ordeal without ruining everything that she and Aviva had both worked so hard to accomplish, found two little words to sum up her feelings toward this narrow-assed, C-sectioning, insurance-company-obeying excuse for a doctor, toward his entire so-called profession, toward the world that regarded everything that was human and messy, prone in equal measure to failure and joy, as a process to be streamlined and standardized and portion-controlled:

"I'm sorry."

Feeling as if she were kicking her way across a swimming pool, free of mass, momentum, inertia, Gwen went through the outer office to the door. Aviva caught up to her at the elevator, change jangling against a key ring in her tote bag.

"I'm sorry," Gwen said again, and this time it was not an expression of regret for the things she had said or done but rather the opposite: Her apology was, as apologies so often are, fighting words. She was sorry only that she was not sorry at all.

⊙   ⊙   ⊙

She rolled to a stop in front of the house, footsore, craving a shower, each soft part of her body affixed with an epoxy of hormones and sweat to at least one other part. Nauseated by the tide of jasmine that surged down the front porch across the yard to beat against the slat fence in a spiky spray of blossoms whose color and smell reminded her of the flesh of spoiled bananas. Irritated by the insect buzz of a harpsichord on KDFC (which she obliged herself to tune in to for the supposed relaxing properties of baroque music, despite its always having struck her as the auditory equivalent of trying to fold origami in your mind). Preoccupied not by the proper strategy for facing the inevitable board to which, after her latest self-righteous outburst, she and Aviva must now submit themselves but instead by trying to cook up some plausible excuse to bail on tonight's childbirth class. She cut the engine. The door to the garage, irremediably cluttered, swung open on its hinges, irreparably creaky. And here came Archy, dressed in his three-piece Funky Suit—ten yards of purple satin—backing a massive wooden chunk of gig equipment along the driveway toward the bed of his El Camino, apparently in no need at all, as usual, of any excuse to forget about Lamaze.

The class was held Saturday evenings in the community center of a Baptist church on Telegraph. Gwen had selected it, from among the dozens that weekly rehearsed the expectant of Berkeley and Oakland in techniques of breathing and relaxation, because she had heard that it drew young black couples. She hoped not only that she and Archy might thus (so ran the fantasy) befriend the nice 60/40 boho-to-bougie-ratio mommy and daddy of some future nubby-headed little playmate for their baby but also, by an unhappy mathematics, to reduce the possibility that she would bump into one of her patients among the circled yoga mats. As it turned out, the only other black people attending the underenrolled session that convened each week beneath the humming fluorescent tubes of the recreation hall, with its lingering fug of feet and armpits from the capoeira class that preceded it, were a pair of single mothers having only their own mothers to coach them, and the husband halves of two biracial couples, one Asian wife, one white. The instructor, Ms. Pease, also taught in the church's religious school, and she had a Sunday school manner at once saccharine and condemnatory. In any case, there was nothing for Gwen to learn: Apart from whatever marital and parental unity it might symbolize, their attendance was manifestly, even blatantly, for the benefit of Archy. Yet every week he forgot about class until Gwen reminded him, then he tried to pretend that he hadn't forgotten, then he spent the entire class wearing a look so earnest, so engaged, so eager to absorb the parturient wisdom of that bitter and treacly old windbag Charmayne Pease that there was no way—and Gwen had tried—to credit it as genuine.

This facial expression, too patient, too forbearing, too sincere to be anything but mocking, had begun to occupy the space between his chin and forehead sometime early in her pregnancy. It was a kind of précis, for Gwen, of her husband's whole attitude toward impending fatherhood as its duties and obligations had so far been revealed to him. He could take the business seriously, it seemed to her, only to the extent that he knew enough, most of the time, to pretend to take it seriously. Even then she had to push his nose in it to get him to pay attention, forcing on him articles and Web links related to spina bifida, dorsal sleeping and SIDS, the pros and cons of pacifiers. Reading aloud to him from pregnancy books that she bought and feigned to study, bored and perpetually quarreling in her mind with the authors, only so that Archy would be obliged, lying beside her in bed at night, to listen to her reading aloud. It was like one of those Piaget experiments on babies: The prospect of being a father, when you removed it from his immediate view, ceased, in his mind, to exist. And the reappearance, whenever Gwen reminded him, was more painful to her than the vanishing.

So she arrived home that night, having spent the afternoon listening like some Zen apprentice to the sound of Aviva not saying anything about the meeting with Lazar—the silence more painful than any reproach, Gwen's life furnished perhaps too amply with people who wore you *out* with paradox—feeling that smooth cranium of dread lodged against her rib cage, prepared to let her lying, cheating, no-good Darling Husband off the hook tonight—and look at the fool! Saving her the trouble. Messing around with his bungee cords and his moving-van blankets. Big and purple as the cause of all her problems, the ridiculous splendor of his platform saddle shoes measuring in lofty inches the distance between him and any world that might construe itself in terms of duty and obligation.

Though only a few minutes earlier, she had been trying out on herself various backhanded or gently sarcastic ways of telling Archy that she wanted only to spend tonight tangled on the couch with him, eating Fentons Swiss milk chocolate from a half-gallon carton and watching whatever program he felt like watching, now she perceived that she would rather let him fuck every woman in Ethiopia and Eritrea, in twos and threes, than let him miss out on the company of Ms. Pease.

Then she caught sight of the play of muscle across the back of his jacket, glints like the naps of knife blades, as, in a single effortless arc, he hoisted the big wooden cube of the amplifier—old Mr. Jones's precious Leslie, on whose repair Archy had lavished their final weeks of childless freedom—into the back of his car. Hoisting that great big thing as if it were a carton full of packing peanuts. Gwen let out a sound that slipped unintentionally from the intended *hmmph* of disapproval to a bass thrum like the loosing of some inner string.

"Uh-oh," he said, turning. "You got your hand on your hip, that way."

"I know you must be *unloading*," Gwen said. "Even though it looks like you're putting stuff *in*."

"Yeah, no, uh, we got a gig tonight. A good one. Kind of political fund-raiser, up by Kensington. Cragmont, someplace, off the Arlington or—" He saw that she was not interested in details of North Berkeley geography. "Oh, shit. It's Saturday."

"Are you sure?"

"Okay," he said, "here's the thing. They really don't need me. It's Nat and Boom and Mr. Jones, and long as I get him the Leslie, that man with just his one left foot can do anything that I could offer on bass with two hands. Seriously." He consulted his watch. "We run it up there, drop it off, grab you something to eat, raise that blood sugar up to a useful level, we can make it back down for the birthing class right on time. Sound like a plan?"

"Yes, as a matter of fact, that does sound like a plan," Gwen said. "But not *your* plan. Your plan, let me guess: Toss the rest of that stuff in there." She gestured to the J Bass in its case, the bass amp and preamp, stacked beside the right front fender of the El Camino. "Head on up to North Berkeley, not even give a second thought to the only important thing you have going on in your life right now. I bet you didn't even write me a damn *note*."

At this grave charge, Archy started to register a protest, prepared to make his objections known, feeling his way into it like a man backing down a hallway in the dark, as if hoping that when he reached the far end, he would discover, with a cry of vindication and triumph, that indeed, au contraire, he had written a note and simply, in the interval, forgotten. But no; the hope of this died in his eyes. Then he got himself an idea. Held up a finger. Patted his pocket. Nodded. Overplaying the whole thing with an air of comic pantomime, trying to defuse her by acting cute, a tactic with a decent record of success over the years, though failures were numberless and spectacular. He reached into the breast pocket of the Funky Suit jacket, took out a black Sharpie and a scrap of paper that proved to be an unpaid city of Emeryville parking ticket issued two years earlier, scrawled a few words on the back of it, and passed it to her with a ceremonious lack of ceremony. Gwen folded it in half without reading it, wondered why on that June afternoon two years previous his El Camino had been parked in front of 1133 Sixty-second Street, concluded that it was either a woman or a basement full of some dead man's records, folded it a second time, and poked it back into his hand.

"I am going to take a shower," she said. "Go to La Calaca Loca right now, and get me one of those *elotes* they have, light on the chile, and a fish taco, two fish tacos, the batter kind. And a bottle of that *tamarindo*, and have it back here and waiting for me when I come down."

"Yes, ma'am," Archy said.

A funny look passed across his face, like the flicker of a television during a brownout, and his eyes darted from right to left, tracking the cicada whirr of a bicycle. She turned to see the back of a long-limbed boy on a bicycle, maybe a neighborhood kid, nobody she could place, and when she looked back at Archy, he was swinging the rest of his gear into the El Camino, saying,"*Elote*, huh, yeah, that sounds good. I could eat Mexican every day." He turned back to her. "I love Mexico." He wiped his forehead with the back of one satined arm. "Baby, let's go to Mexico. Like, tonight. Come on. Let's do it. Let's *move* to Mexico."

"Ha ha."

"I'm serious." He made his face all serious, or maybe it really did fall out that way for once. "I am being totally sincere."

"And I am totally, sincerely, about to have a baby, Archy. How am I going to go to Mexico?"

Even as the words burst from her lips, she regretted them, realizing, probably before Archy did, that when he went to Mexico, he need not take her along. Archy could go to Mexico, flat out move there, any damn time he wanted to. He could leave tonight.

Archy took off his sunglasses to wipe the lenses on the end of his necktie. Barefaced, he gazed at her, expression ironic, just kidding, for now.

"Fish tacos," he said. "For days."

⊙   ⊙   ⊙

The valet parkers in matched tan coveralls stood shoulder to shoulder like convicts chained at the ankle, heads back, chins pointed at the

sky. Something up there causing them to ponder. Archy nosed the El
Camino up the hill toward them and the venue: round tower of butterscotch stucco with a Juliet window, blue-tiled arch in a butterscotch
gate. Creeping up the street as it traced the switchback course of some
old arroyo, neighborhood cars shouldering in from both sides to leave
clearance just sufficient for his wide-track choogling slab of lost Detroit. Archy already feeling crowded enough by the marital silence that
at present filled the vehicle, knowing perfectly well, with all the alma-
nack sagacity the word "husband" implied, that the present silence was
more portent than aftermath. A formulating stillness. That pressure
drop, brooding and birdless, right before the touchdown of a tornado.

They passed Nat's Saab, rolling up to the valet stand where the four
parkers in their Carhartt zip-ups stood gawping at the sky, Hispanic
kids as varied in size and girth as sample popcorn servings ranged
along a movie theater snack bar. Gwen poked her head out the window
on her side of the El Camino, saw what they saw, slumped back against
the bench seat. Fitted her folded arms between her breasts and belly.
Spoke for the first time in approximately eighteen minutes, or at any
rate laid down an utterance, troubling to pack it beforehand, like a ji-
hadi packing an IED, with shards of irony, nails of bitterness, jagged
chips of bleak wonder.

"*Huh,*" she said.

Archy got out of the car. For a second or two, his eyes were diverted
by the great canvas of city, bay, and bridges stretched across the frame
of eucalyptus trees beyond the terra-cotta roof tiles of the venue. Paint
laid on with brushes fat and fine, washes of fog and winking sun on
window grids, the foundered wreck of Alcatraz, the iron giant jubilat-
ing up there on Twin Peaks. And then there it was, against the curve of
August sky.

As long as his forearm, as fat around, humming to itself like Nat Jaffe
evolving a theory about the profound effect on world history if Hank
Crawford had not stood up Creed Taylor for the sessions that became
the first album by Grover Washington, Jr., the Dogpile blimp slid by.
All black from nose to fins, emblazoned on its flank with a red paw print
and the Dogpile name in bold red slab-serif type. A taunt implied in the

sloth of its passage, lazy and deliberate as a Benz-load of bangers rolling by your door with their windows down.

"We're not staying," Archy told the valets as he went around the back of the El Camino to unstrap the Leslie in its swaddling clothes.

"How about you just leave the suit, then," one of the parkers said. "Because my flashlight is dead."

Archy might have liked to offer the young man, if not a return critique of the brown bag he was standing stuffed into like a furtive forty-ounce, at least an anatomical storage suggestion with regard to the putative flashlight. But like all pure stylists, Archy had long since learned that in handling those who could not dig, the only proper course was to carry on confusing them. *Light 'em up, blow 'em out like candles.* The intended effect of his withering stare was diminished to a degree by the snort of laughter that came out of Gwen.

"Flashlight," said his betrayer. "I love it."

The musicians had been asked to set up out-of-doors, beside a goldfish pond at the far end of a slate-flagged courtyard strung with chilipepper lights and paper lanterns: pink concertinas, green pagodas. Archy came huffing and heaving through the French doors, moving fast under a hundred pounds of Leslie, harried along by a calmly panicking little Asian chick with a clipboard over which her pen hovered, ready to inventory every ding or scrape Archy might be inclined to put into a wall or doorway.

"Thank you for coming, by the way," she said. "At such short no—oh. Oh my God, please be careful."

"I am known for my carefulness," Archy assured her. "I would say thank you for letting us play, but the truth is, I'm doing you a favor, 'cause we are way better than that weak shit that canceled on you, fully three of those guys are dentists."

"Oh, well, thanks," said the girl from the campaign.

Nat, wearing his red Jazzmaster slung low across his narrow hips, raised an index finger and the opposite eyebrow, signaling to Archy. Warning him not to interrupt or spoil the effect of the display of ferocious swearing being mounted by Stanley "El Boom" Ellerbe, hunched over the leg bracket of his floor tom, fiddling at it with a plastic table knife. El Boom was a bus driver, as notorious for jinxed equipment as he was for letting out, in long and enthusiastic skeins, the choice words he bit back and stored up all day long in serving the public and the whims of traffic behind the wheel of the 51. Cool as a cup of crushed ice on the drums, though, El Boom kept time like an atom clock.

No sign yet of Mr. Jones or his Hammond, a circumstance guaranteed to complicate Archy's own marital timing since A) he could not in good conscience drop off the Leslie without first verifying that it worked all right for Mr. Jones, B) the old man, despite his pride or vanity, would need help getting the Hammond down all those stairs, and C) Archy liked the way Mr. Jones always seemed to dig it when he swung the Leslie around, taking the pleasure an older man sometimes took in the exertions of a younger one. Flashing all those little Krugerrands he kept salted away up inside his mouth there, saying, "Look out! Comin' through!," getting his whole bony self into it the way he might snuffle up the breeze off a snifter of Hennessy, a plate of fried catfish, or something else forbidden by his doctor. Tears in the man's eyes when Archy first offered to repair the Leslie; Archy wished Gwen could have seen that. No need, of course, to mention that Mr. Jones had those pearly oyster eyes, always a certain film of moisture. Or, for that matter, what a grouch he was that morning, something mysteriously offensive to him in talk of Titus Joyner.

"Y'all go on, do what you have to do," Archy told the clipboard girl, who was glancing toward the ever darkening cloud of blue air over El Boom Ellerbe as if trying to decide whether it presented a security threat. "I need help with this, I'll be sure to call you." His eyes went to her name tag so he could give proper emphasis to the dismissal and there read, with a smile, LESLIE.

El Boom left off questioning the maternal purity of his drum kit and stood up to greet the amplifier, venerable and pedigreed, a Model 122 known to have been owned at one time by Rudy Van Gelder, in whose Englewood Cliffs studio it was employed by Johnny "Hammond" Smith and Charles Earland before passing into the possession of Mr. Jones, on whose *Redbonin'* it could be heard to everlasting glorious effect. Cleaned, oiled, restored, and rewired. Archy had been grateful for the chance to climb inside of history like that, walnut-paneled, belt-driven, analog history with all its parts spinning, however many hours of his spare time the job had required. What kind of insensitive, disrespectful, superficial person with the necessary skill set would ever turn his back on an opportunity like that? Not to mention the chance to help out a lonely old gentleman living off his Social Security, nothing but that and a small royalty on the co-credit (with a white record producer whose label kept the rights to every other song Cochise Jones ever wrote) for "Cold Cold Sunday," a minor 1969 hit on the soul charts for Wilson Pickett that had been used in the late eighties in an ad campaign for Dreyer's ice cream? Thus arguing on with the Gwen who lived inside his head, Archy eased the Leslie—the wooden one—down onto the flagstones and rumbled it, stately as a hearse, across the patio.

"Deep purple!" said El Boom, taking stock of Archy in his Funky Suit. Across the beeswax-buffed surface of the Leslie, the drummer ran the varnished walnut of his big-hitting right hand.

"Yeah, Boom, what up. How you doing?" Palm slap, finger tangle, shake, the older man's hand dry and cool. "I got some tools in the car, you need pliers, a socket wrench, anything like that." Archy fought down somewhere around 92 percent of the smile that tried to break loose on his face. "Blowtorch."

"She-it," said El Boom, reduced by helpless despair to this monosyllable, though he sustained it. "Thing's a brand-new secondhand Ludwig."

Archy shook his head in sham sympathy and turned to Nat, letting fly the smile. Nat played a lick on his unplugged guitar, a comic snippet of Carl Stalling's cartoon jazz. With Mr. Jones sitting in at the organ, and with the original contractor for this evening's musical entertainment laid up at home with some chronic alphabet letter of hepatitis, being a (soporific, in Archy's opinion) guitarist, Nat had come armed with his Jazzmaster and a finicky old Epiphone to which he was attached for sentimental reasons, guitar being his second best instrument after piano. Guitar, organ, drums, they would be fine without Archy. He tried to work some of that reassurance into his eyes, then drew back a step and inclined his head in a way meant to signify the need for confidential communication with his partner. Nat fitted the Fender into its stand and picked his way among the cables to join Archy beside a man-high cactus in a Talavera pot, where only the goldfish would be able to overhear. Ugly things, technically koi, Archy supposed, freaky mutant motherfuckers all dappled and pop-eyed and tangled up in the shimmery scarves of themselves.

"Mr. Jones running late?"

Everything would be fine, Archy thought, at least until Nat looked up at the sky, got an eyeful of that big black visual pun on centuries of white male anatomical anxiety.

"Generally speaking," Nat said. "Did you call him?"

"I saw him this morning. He was on it, giving me shit about being on time."

"I find you have to tell him to come half an hour before you actually need him to be there. Now, not unlike you, he's"—checking his watch, a Swiss-railroad number Nat kept set, out of habit from long-ago days tending bar, seven minutes ahead—"twenty-three minutes late."

Something—pre-gig jitters, the last-minute-sub nature of the booking, the high caliber of the venue and clientele, for all Archy knew the politics behind the event itself, the candidate for president whose campaign the event would benefit not doing as well as might be hoped at this juncture—was bringing an edge to Nat's voice. He had on a black sharkskin suit, by design too short at the cuffs of trousers and jacket and too snug across the chest. Black cowboy shirt snapped all the way up to its collar button. A bolo tie whose cinch was adorned with a miniature black-and-white portrait of Richard Nixon. Any one of these items of apparel might contribute to the increase of Nat's native tight-assedness. Archy elected to forestall for another second or two having to tell Nat that, Leslie delivered, he would be blowing off the chance to expose the Wakanda Philharmonic to a mansionful of deep-pocket East Bay tastemakers any number of whom could be counted on in the near future to get married, turn fifty, or bar mitzvah their children, in order to go sit around, instead, on a rubber mat in a foot-stanky church rec room, learning a set of procedures and techniques without which, for fifty, sixty thousand years, fathers had managed to do all right. Even though it was becoming more difficult to imagine that Gwen would in any way welcome his feckless presence at the birth. Archy all stumbling and dropping shit around the castle like Eyegore in *Young Frankenstein* while Gwen plunged two-handed and full-tilt into the thunder and the lightning (life! *life!*) of the business, the job that she knew better than anyone with the possible exception of Aviva Roth-Jaffe, who for that matter was going to be there, too, rendering Archy more useless than he already felt.

"Is that how you do?" he said. "Tell people to come half an hour early just because you anticipate they going to be half an hour late?"

"Black people, yeah," Nat said. "Thirty-seven minutes."

"So, including me, you routinely—"

"You I cheat at least forty-five. And somehow, go figure, you're *still* twenty minutes late." He gave the back of his head a puzzled scratch. "I don't claim to understand the math of it."

"Yeah, look here," Archy said, running a confidential finger alongside his nose. "I got Gwen in the car, and uh . . ."

"She okay?"

"Yeah, no, she's fine. She uh, she just, I forgot—"

"I heard she's been, I don't know"—Nat pretended to search for the right word, though Archy could see it unboxed, unwrapped, plugged in, sitting there in the man's mind all ready to go—"a little *irrational* past couple days. Stuff with the birth and the . . . incident. With the doctor. Guy sounds like a royal turd, but the way things work around that place—"

"Yeah, I don't know, she—"

"You tell her about Titus yet?"

It was like dropping into a manhole, hearing that name. Every motherfucking time. Walking down the street, sun on your sunglasses, beats in your earbuds, rolling with your own particular roll along the pavement, and then *fwoop!* Not even the puff of smoke or patch of ashes that a thunderbolt might leave behind. Gwen was always accusing Archy of not thinking or caring about, not preparing for, the baby who was on its way. Which only showed how little she knew him or, to be fair, how parsimonious he could be in sharing with a woman, with anyone, the almost constant state of anxiety in which he was living. Anxiety that, for example, had led him to volunteer to keep an eye on little Rolando yesterday, to see how he could manage the whole diapers-and-formula routine. But this boy. *Titus*. His son, half grown and staring him down from the far side of all that resentfulness and abandonment. If Gwen knew about Titus Joyner—and sooner or later, she was going to find out—then there would be justice in her charge of obliviousness, lack of consideration. Because since yesterday Archy had been trying to resume his former state of happy ignorance and think as little as possible about the child he already had.

"That revelation is still, uh, forthcoming," he said.

"Maybe you should try it out on her now," Nat suggested. "Holistic approach. Cure it with poison. Fire with fire. Drive her insane from a totally different direction, she comes out at zero."

"Yeah," Archy said without enthusiasm. "Right now we're at week thirty-six, I don't think I have too much influence over the situation inside her head anymore." Nat inclined his head, pursed his lips, nodding, having nothing to offer in the way of argument. "How's he comporting himself round your house? Titus."

"Oh, uh, fine. I don't know. He's okay. Funny kid."

"Funny."

"Solemn little motherfucker."

"Solemn as in?"

"Solemn as in somewhat restrained in his emotional palette."

"Fronting? Being hard?"

"Maybe some of that. But it seems like he and Julie—"

Before Nat could continue, he saw something that made both his eyebrows shoot up. His face went blank, like the screen of an Etch A Sketch, in a single shake.

"Hey, lady," he said.

⊙   ⊙   ⊙

El Boom said, "Look out."

Look out, here came Gwen, through the French doors that connected the patio to the living room with its arcing vaults and folk-art Virgins.

She had checked a vintage bowling shirt out of Archy's library, pink on black, originally sported, according to the inscriptions in silkscreen and embroidery thread, by an inferably large gentleman named Stan, bowling in the service of Alameda Wire and Pipe. She was bearing straight for Archy, endowed by pregnancy with that locomotive chug. No chance that she was coming to tell him he was off the hook, forgiven his sins, large or small. Gwen had never in her life arrived at forgiveness in the physical absence of its needful object. Not, at least, without the intervention of some external force: the advice of her father, for example, or of Dr. Nickens, the pastor of her childhood church, or, under certain conditions, some trumping piece of bad news. Said absence affording too convenient a vessel for the laying in of refined counterarguments, further supporting examples, freshly recalled instances of past infractions, etc.

"Hello, Nat," she said. "Arch. Um. Okay. Listen here."

Level and cool, she looked from Nat to Archy and back, and with an interior lurch, Archy concluded that Gwen had descended from the El Camino to issue an ultimatum in the presence of Nat Jaffe and the world, and whatever it was or however she phrased it, he would have to tell her about Titus, and that would be that, adieu and later to the second great partnership of his life, not because he *had* a son on the side, which, all right, was maybe no big thing, but because he had never mentioned the fact to Gwen, ever, neither in passing nor in detail. Because in ten years or more, Archy had never *thought* of the boy, not once, a habit of oblivion that continued even now, with the kid back and smacking up against the outside of their life like a moth banging against a lampshade. Stashed there, up in the Jaffes' attic.

Archy knew an instant of pure panic. Nothing caused him greater revulsion than signs of weakness in a man, keenest of all in himself; and there was no one in this world weaker than someone trying to keep something secret, unless it be someone obliged to confess.

"I can't stay, Nat," he said, deciding to throw the littlest confession overboard first, see where that got him. "I'm really sorry. Gwen and I have birth class tonight, and when I said I could play, I just fucking forgot."

"No," said Nat and Gwen at the same time. *Jinx, lock, you owe me a soda.* And then Nat, without waiting for anyone to speak his name and release him, said, measuring the words, always happy to take the opportunity to educate, "Please, no, I totally get it. That shit is important, Arch. They've done all kinds of studies. You're on *your* game, things are going to go a lot easier for Gwen and whoever that is in there." He pointed a furry finger at Gwen's belly. "Y'all go on and go."

"No," Gwen repeated. "Guys, I— Archy, your phone rang, in the car. I answered it."

The mainspring of Archy's panic tightened farther, his thoughts, like Nat's watch, running seven minutes ahead of themselves. Ransacking all the files, thinking what girl, bitch, or lady, what mess did he leave lying around.

"It was Garnet Singletary," Gwen was saying. "Archy, Mr. Jones. He, oh, Archy, he died. He's dead."

"He . . . what?" Archy said, feeling the words first as a surge of blood to his cheeks. "No, I saw him this morning."

"I guess—I guess the neighbor lady, uh, Mrs. Wiggins, across the street. She's the one who called the ambulance."

Archy not all the way there yet, enough presence to notice how Gwen seemed rattled, shaky. *This is* true, he thought.

"I talked to him two *hours* ago!" Nat said, as if he thought these words could disprove, discredit, the nonsense Gwen was talking. He ran his fingers through his steely Brillo. Fished his phone out of the hip pocket of his jacket. "Yeah, hey, Garnet," he said. "Nat Jaffe. What the fuck?"

He spun away across the patio, his back to Gwen and Archy, skeptical to a fault, doubting every story he heard on principle until he got independent confirmation, anything at all remarkable that anyone felt like putting out there an "urban legend," a "misnomer," a "popular delusion," a "false etymology." One of the man's balls there to question the testimony of the other, both of them doubting what his dick had to say. Probably hoping Garnet would help him get hold of Mrs. Wiggins, the police report, the coroner's statement.

Oblivious, El Boom woke up the kick drum, divvied out sixteenth notes between the hi-hat and snare, then began to lean heavily on the one, working up a half-drunk second-line crab-step rhythm that stumbled somehow into the break from "Funky Drummer" (King, 1970). Mr. Jones always claimed James Brown as a cousin on his mother's side (offering no evidence that would satisfy Nat Jaffe beyond an unsupported mention in the liner notes for *Redbonin'*). Archy remembering the way Mr. Jones one time got down off his stool at Brokeland to execute a tricky Mashed Potato across the tile floor, studying his bitty bird feet with a dazed smile as if they were a couple of miracles.

"Oh, no," Gwen said. "Archy, please don't start that."

She wiped at her own cheek with a forearm. She came over and did her best to get herself around him. He was too high and she too deep. So she pulled him over to a chair, one of those Mexican affairs made out of pigskin and sticks. She fell onto his lap, panicking the chair. In her arms, Archy let go of himself for a minute. The smell of Gwen's hair, cool against his cheek, clean, flowery.

"It's okay," she said. "I know."

All at once—just like that—he could feel her forgive him. Somewhere in the midst of the continent of shock and grief that was Archy Stallings, a minor principality rejoiced.

"Closest thing I had to a father," he said.

"That's what you always said."

She meant it to sound sweet, he knew, but it came out sounding like reproof as much as eulogy. Gwen got along with Mr. Jones, but to her he was a sweet-natured, emotionally vague, and reticent man whose greatest steadfastness, away from the keys of his organ, was loyalty to his parrot and to leisure wear of the 1970s, nothing at all like a father in any important way. Archy did not disagree with that assessment. He was okay with coming in second to Fifty-Eight, parrot was like some kind of prodigy, a Mozart of the birds.

"He was loading the Hammond," Nat said, slipping his phone back into his pocket. "I guess he didn't have the straps right on the dolly. The Hammond fell on top of him."

Day I need help moving that thing is the day I give it up for good. Archy had let him go, let him walk out of the garage. Angry, stirred up about something that Archy would never understand. Careless, distracted, nobody to help him lift that heavy, heavy thing.

"Oh, uh, hi," said Leslie the clipboard girl, peering out from behind Gwen, the one they sent in with a stick to poke the wrestling bear. "So, people are starting to show up? Robin and David were thinking you might want to, uh. Start?"

"We're ready," Nat said. "Just, uh, I'm going to have to make a little adjustment in the fee for you all, a reduction, I mean, because my bass player has a birthing class, and it turns out, wow, tragic thing, my organ player, he, uh, he just *died*."

"Oh, no," Leslie said, blinking. She glanced down at the clipboard, looking for a little help from the campaign on how to proceed in the event of a dead musician. "I'm *so* sorry."

"So I only have a two-piece for you tonight. Guitar and drums. But we can—"

Two of the valet parkers came out onto the patio. One had Archy's Jazz Bass in its soft gig jacket, the other coming right behind him with Archy's tubes and wires. The lead parker handed Gwen a claim ticket for the car, and Gwen nodded them toward Archy.

"You got a trio," she said to Leslie. "Plus one pregnant lady in a bowling shirt."

⊙   ⊙   ⊙

Just before his hostess for the evening, who held the patent on a gene that coded for a protein to prevent the rejection of a transplanted kidney, directed everyone to gather under the carved and stenciled fir beams of her living room, and sent the young woman from the campaign out to tell the band to knock it off for ten minutes so that the state senator, Obama of Illinois, could address his fellow guests, each of whom had contributed at least one thousand dollars to attend this event, an address in which he would attempt by measured words and a calm demeanor to reassure them (vainly and mistakenly, as it would turn out) that their candidate for the presidency of the United States would not go down to inglorious defeat in November, Obama stopped in the doorway that opened onto the flagstone patio to listen for a minute to the hired band. They were cooking their way with evident seriousness of intent through an instrumental cover of "Higher Ground."

The rhythm section consisted of a gray-haired older man in a white turtleneck, who had that deceptive stillness of the rock-solid drummer, whaling away and at the same time immobile as a gecko on a rock. A big dude in a preposterous suit, a younger man, played bass through a huge old wooden organ amplifier that was the size of an oven. Its acoustics lent a fat, muddy, molasses-black grandeur to the bass line. Off to one side, a grim-countenanced stick figure of a white guy coiled up the notes in high jazzy meringues on top of the heavy, heavy bottom of the tune, a personal favorite of the state senator. He lingered there in the doorway, his hostess getting a tiny bit antsy, Obama tapping his foot, bobbing his close-cropped head.

"Those guys are pretty funky," he observed, directing his remark to a short, extraordinarily pregnant woman in a man's bowling shirt who stood beyond the open patio doors, dark, pretty, her hair worn in a fetching artful anemone of baby dreadlocks. The fingers of her right hand flicked shadow bass notes on her belly. At his remark, the pregnant woman nodded without turning to look at him—there was an elaborate candelabra of a potted cactus behind whose tapered thorns she appeared to be attempting, somewhat punitively, to conceal herself. Obama was running for the United States Senate that summer and had given a wonderful speech last month at the Democratic Convention in Boston. When she did turn to him, her eyes got very wide.

"Friends of yours?" he said.

It was a reasonable inference, given the fact that, in her bowling shirt, she stood out from the other women in attendance, most of them done up in cocktail attire. She was also one of a strikingly few women of color in the room. She nodded again, more stiffly, no longer playing along with the bass, stare going glassy. Feeling big, he supposed, underdressed, and trapped behind a cactus by a celebrated black man in a fancy house full of white folks. He went further out a limb.

"My man on bass?"

The pregnant woman looked sidelong at him, a droll look, and seemed to recover from her initial bout of self-consciousness. "Well, that's the question, now," she said with an asperity that took him aback. "Isn't it?"

"Senator?" said the hostess, looking very handsome in an elaborate thing, all crinkled and structural. "If you're ready? I can ask the band to—"

"Let's let them finish this number," Obama said.

His memory filled in the missing vocal line, the lyrics that somehow managed to be at once hopeful and apocalyptic, perfectly in keeping with the mood of the hour politically, if there were anyone in the crowd to attend, which, frankly, the state senator from the 13th district of Illinois, judging from the bright unrelenting roil of chatter and gloomy expatiation going on, inside the house and out, kind of doubted. He listened awhile longer.

"Shame nobody's dancing," he said.

"I guess it's not that kind of party," said the pregnant woman.

"They seldom are," Obama allowed. "All too seldom. Now, I would ask you to dance, but I don't think my wife would be happy if it got back to her that I was observed dancing with a gorgeous sister in your condition."

"I like the underlying philosophy of that," the pregnant woman said, staring fixedly at the bass player in a way that confirmed, to the senator's satisfaction, his earlier inference. "That's a philosophy I can get behind. Shame it isn't more widespread."

The senator felt compelled to smile. "Brother puts his heart into it, though," he observed. "You can see that. A lot of heart."

The bass man felt his way up and down the fretboard like a blind man reading something passionate in Braille. The senator recalled having caught a few words over the PA earlier tonight, to the effect that the band wanted to dedicate tonight's performance to someone who had died, name of Jones. He watched the man in the purple suit play his kaddish.

"That is quite a suit," Obama said. "Takes a special kind of man to go around wearing a suit like that."

"You know, he isn't even aware of that?" the pregnant woman said. "Man doesn't feel self-conscious, not one little bit embarrassed, walking around in that thing." Scorn and admiration in her tone in about equal measure. "The outside of him matches perfectly with the inside. It's like, I can't even tell you. Not stubborn, I mean, yes, he can be stubborn as hell, stubborn and full of pride, but to walk around looking like that, I mean, a purple suit even a pimp might have doubts about it, and *saddle shoes* . . . you have to have—"

"Dignity."

At the sound of the word, the pregnant woman looked at him. A strange expression passed over her face, as if, he thought, she might be experiencing a contraction.

"He just had a loss," she said.

"I gathered that, something about a man named Jones."

"Yeah, yes, he was supposed to be here, he played the organ. It's Cochise Jones."

"Cochise Jones, okay."

Perhaps the name registered, a shallow footprint tracked in the sand of the senator's memory. But the print might as easily have been left by Elvin or Philly Joe.

"He was supposed to be here, to play. It just happened, he passed this afternoon."

"I am so sorry to hear that."

"He was like a father to my husband."

Somehow, seamlessly, the band morphed into a cover of Bad Medicine's "Trespasser."

"Thank you for telling me that," Obama said. "You know, I could hear it in his playing. Something grieving. But I didn't know what it was."

"Mr. Jones was his own kind of shiftless fool," she said gently. "A musician. He made, I guess he made, all these elaborate plans for his funeral, a marching band, a Cadillac hearse." She shook her head. "The past two weeks, when we could have been getting ready for the baby, enjoying our last time alone together? My husband chose to spend them in the garage, repairing that dusty old dinosaur of an amplifier over there.

Now, with a month to go? He's going to get caught up in all this funeral foolishness. Instead of what he should be focusing on."

"But you know," the senator said, "I, I understand your frustration. We've all heard, we all know how musicians can be. But traveling around, campaigning, at home, around the country, I have seen a lot of people, met a lot of people. The lucky ones are the people like your husband there. The ones who find work that means something to them. That they can really put their heart into, however foolish it might look to other people."

At these words, perhaps, the state senator felt a slight misgiving, a mild Braxton-Hicks spasm of dread, recalling the purpose for which he had been flown up here yesterday, aboard Gibson Goode's private airship, the *Minnie Riperton*, Goode on his way to some kind of memorabilia show, the senator catching a ride.

"And that reminds me."

He turned back to the hostess, her evident impatience with his delay motivated less by some schedule she was sticking to than by her possible desire for reassurance about the upcoming election, which he hoped he would be able to provide.

"All right, Robin," he told her. "Let's do this."

He shook hands with the pregnant woman, who appeared distracted, lost in thought, even surprisingly, given her original discomfiture, uninterested in the rising star from Illinois.

"You're right," she said, and for a second he could not retrieve the thread of conversation that she was following. "I have been wasting my life."

"Oh, don't be too hard on the brother, now," he said, trying, with departure imminent, to keep his tone light.

"I don't mean him," she said. "I mean, I do, but I don't. I mean what you said about work. About putting your heart and soul into something meaningful. Thank you for that."

She shook his hand with a puzzling solemnity.

The band was silenced, the guests assembled, and Barack Obama loped into the living room, at ease and smiling. He stood against a high wall painted cinnamon brown, under a display of *retablos*, battered squares of scrap tin and steel on which credulous souls of Mexico had painted, with painful and touching simplicity of technique, scenes that depicted their woes and expressed in stark terms their gratitude to the Holy Mother of God or various *santos* and *santas* for the granting of relief. The state senator seemed to at least one observer to feel the weight of such wishes upon him. He paused for a couple of seconds before opening his remarks.

"He was the closest thing you had to a father," said the pregnant woman to the man in the big purple suit, filling, at least for those standing nearby, that prolonged silence with her grave whisper, "of course you've got to bury him *properly*."

⊙   ⊙   ⊙

The kid sat at Aviva's kitchen table, wearing the cast-iron dungarees, sweater vest, and short-sleeved plaid shirt in which he had bade her good night the previous evening. If Julie was always a premature *zayde*, born nostalgic, born cranky, born 103 years old, then maybe that was the connection he felt to old man Titus, what to make of him, hunched over a magazine beside a box of Nat's All-Bran in an acrylic sweater vest, sinking his palm into the cheek of his inclined head, so lost in whatever he was reading that he did not look up when Aviva stopped in the doorway, belting her robe more tightly around her waist, and said, "Morning, you."

Titus sat there, perfecting his stillness. She had yet to make up her mind about the kid—she was still collecting evidence—but Aviva liked him for his immobility, his effortless parsimony of movement. He was not a Drummer on All Resonant Surfaces, like Julie, or a Perpetual Hummer of Infinite Tunes, like Nat. She was willing to give Titus credit for that much, at least.

Over the course of the day and two nights of his exile among the Jaffes, Aviva had gotten into the habit of doling out to Titus these modest quanta of credit, none larger or more valuable than, say, a nickel, or a pinto bean. For his neatness, his familiarity with soap and water, his polite manners, his readiness to clear his place after dinner without being told. Behind each of these qualities, she felt the ghostly hard hand of the late Texan grandmother, and it must have been in honor of that lost woman of iron that Aviva was keeping Titus's file open, because from the instant he came limping into the house with that constipated granddaddy walk of his, humping a stained sailor's duffel, bearing, safety-pinned to his soul like a note scrawled in his putative father's hasty hand, an indefinite embargo on sharing the news of his existence with her partner and best friend, Aviva's snap judgment on the kid was: *Trouble.* Trouble for everyone but trouble especially, she guessed, for Julie, who had clearly fallen into some kind of inchoate and disorderly love with Titus Joyner.

Nat agreed (a rare pairing of those words) that on the advent of Titus, all the recent incidents of inexplicable behavior on the part of their son appeared to snap into alignment. Only Aviva's long habit of taking the temperature of her own racism, of her biases and stereotypes about young black males (or about the iron-hard perdurance of their grandmothers) enabled Aviva to set aside, for the time being, her gut reaction—the boy was trouble—and admire Titus's stillness. Here was yet another quality that he did not share with her own ill-washed, ill-mannered, sloppy, and hyperactive offspring.

Then she heard the moist, slow rasp of Titus's breathing: The kid was sleeping. His hair, hitherto maintained with curatorial punctilio in an archival 1973 Afro, was lumps and nap, a topographical globe. He sat propped up and snoozing in the mild gray sunshine that irradiated the morning fog outside the kitchen window, over a copy of—she went over, reached in, and peeled back the front cover of the magazine—*American Cinematographer.*

Out of the self-assembling nanoparticles of her pessimism, in Aviva's imagination, a narrative began to take shape. Titus's nappy head, the unchanged clothes to which there clung an unmistakable if faint smell of Berkeley at night (purple salvia, jasmine, fog, cat spray), the evident depth of his slumber.

Oh, the sneaky little shit!

She backed out of the kitchen so as not to wake him before her theory could be confirmed. Like most people with a suspicious nature, she was gifted at sneakiness herself and inclined to be stealthy in the corroboration of her theories. She crept upstairs to Julie's room and eased open the door, ignoring three separate tacked-up signs warning off a variety of intruders in Klingon, runic, and (presumably) simulated blood. In the dim light, in his IKEA bed, Julie lay curled into a ball so impossibly tiny that she didn't dare look at it, lest nostalgia for the vanished little old man he once had been impede her investigation. On the floor of the attic room, the futon bed, unrolled two nights earlier to accommodate Titus, bore a faint oblong indentation, but it was still made, the covers as tucked and taut as the boy's shirttails and pleats. To Aviva, this suggested or rather confirmed that Titus had lain down on it, fully dressed, until he felt that it was safe to sneak out through the lone attic window, whose lower sash was open as wide as it could go. Under the window, Titus's megalith sneakers lounged at louche angles, suggesting that he had kicked them off as soon as he came tumbling back in from outside.

Aviva went over to stand beside Julie's bed, trying to determine from the visible evidence—the arcing bones of his spine, a tangled sketch of knees and elbows in the bedclothes—whether he, too, had sneaked out of the house last night, then sneaked back in. Using perspicacity as a shield against panic. No telltale shoes, no flung socks.

Aviva went back down to the kitchen and began angrily to cook Titus's stated favorite breakfast, pancakes and bacon. She broke the eggs as if they were the spurious arguments of unworthy adversaries. With the contempt we reserve for those who fail to deliver on arrant boasts, she watched the bacon shrink in its own fat. She peeled the bubbling pancakes from the griddle and flipped them over with a sense of cutting off a pointless discussion. In the batter, buttermilk and baking soda enacted their allegory of her emotional pH. By the time she had, in her view, cashed out the boy's account in silver-dollar pancakes and a sizzling rasher of the Berkeley Bowl's best applewood-smoked, she had worked through and expended most of the outrage that her discovery of his nocturnal adventuring had stirred in her. This was in compliance with Aviva Roth-Jaffe's official policy on outrage, which was that, even when justified, it was an ineffective tool.

"Okay, mister," she said, setting the plate in front of him. "Wake up."

He started, opened his eyes wide, unstuck his cheek from his hand. He looked at her, at the plate, back to Aviva. Putting it together, where he was, what she had made for him, those wide brown eyes going all moist and puppy-dog. Just as Aviva felt the last inch of annoyance drain away, she saw Titus remember what a hard-on he was supposed to be. His gaze iced over. His nostrils flared as if they detected in the steam off the pancakes a distinct whiff of something vile.

"Thank you," he said, neutering his voice of any gratitude, cutting a neat wedge out of the stack of pancakes.

"When did you get in?"

Instead of replying, he hoisted up stratified forkfuls, one after another, as if they were riding a conveyor belt to his mouth.

"You can drop the man-of-few-words routine, dude. I hear you running your mouth to Julie. I know you think you're making a statement about how pointless it is to talk to adults or white people or whatever, but you're just being disrespectful. I haven't done anything to deserve your disrespect. I know your grandmother didn't raise you to be rude."

He chewed the last mouthful, weighing her argument, thinking it through. He swallowed. Took a sip of milk. "Could you please repeat the question?" he said.

"What time did you get in? I know you were out, Titus. Your bed hasn't been slept in. Don't *even* try to lie to me."

"Huh, yeah, well, I don't wear no watch, so. . . ."

The confirmation of her guess did not amaze her—her guesses, rooted in pessimism, were tantamount to Laws of Physics—but neither did it console her. She felt her initial sense of panic begin to return. "Did Julie go out with you?"

"Yeah."

"Oh my God."

Aviva fell into a chair at the table. Sometimes in the event of a shoulder dystocia, after everything else had failed, a doctor would attempt the Zavanelli maneuver, planting his hand on the head of the shoulder-bound baby, pushing it back up into the darkness. Aviva effected a similar maneuver on the sense of panic that was struggling out of her into the light of morning.

"Well," she said. She sat back, trying to come up with something reasonable and authoritative to say. "Where did you go?"

He seemed genuinely to consider attempting to answer her question. Then he picked up a piece of bacon and shrugged. "Everywhere," he said. "Just, like, walking around."

"Walking around?"

"Riding my bike. Him riding his skateboard. Can't do much beside ride it, but he can hook a ride on my bike, I kind of like give him a tow."

She could see it: Julie rolling along behind Titus through the summer darkness of Berkeley, holding on to his friend's shoulder, the way she had seen other pairs of skater boys do.

"I don't want you doing that anymore," she said. "Not while you're a guest in my house. You go to bed, you stay in bed, you wake up in bed in the morning. Do you understand me?"

"Yes, ma'am."

She had to admit that she loved the "sirs" and "ma'ams" that flowed from his lips so readily, drawled out like pats of butter smeared across a biscuit. She remembered hiking in Yosemite with Nat and Julie a few summers back. Climbing to the top of the Mist Trail up a preposterous stairway of stones proposed, cut, hauled, and fixed immovably into place, proof against time and earthquakes, under the auspices of the WPA. She remembered feeling grateful to those long-dead men, the planners and the workers, for their foresight, their labor, the heroic absurdity of that granite stair. That was how she felt, whenever he would "ma'am" her, toward the dead grandmother of this boy.

"When you do that, Titus," she said, softening her tone because she was getting in his face, "when you sneak out of my house like that, you are showing disrespect toward me."

The boy shook his head, face indented with the thumbprint of a smirk, eyes downcast to show his pity for her.

"What?" Aviva said. "You don't agree?"

"I ain't— I'm not saying nothing."

He took up the study of the backsplash behind the sink, tiled in iridescent rust red and cream. Aviva once hated that tile, then for a decade ignored it, and now felt toward those earth tones the same poignant derision she felt toward much of the surviving evidence of the 1970s. The boy might have been staring longingly at some bleak and lonely peak of snow.

"I don't even want to *be* here." His eyes abandoned their scrutiny of the high cold home of his soul long enough to toss a mocking look in her direction. "No disrespect."

"Really?" Aviva said, knowing that she had him on that one, wondering what she hoped to gain from prolonging this conversation, asking herself why she couldn't cut the kid a break. "That isn't what Julie said. He said you begged him to let you stay with us."

"What? Nah, he just—I—nah, no, ma'am."

They were coming more abject and automatic now, those "ma'ams," and she pressed it, channeling an old, dead Texan woman she had never met, getting her thumbs into the seam she had found.

"That's what I heard. Stay with the Jaffes, eat all the tempeh you can hold."

He looked at the plate in front of him with the face of one betrayed. "You put tempeh in the *pancakes*?"

"Only a little," Aviva said. "Kidding. Nobody's going to force you to eat tempeh against your will. So, uh, okay, so where *did* you go?"

He pushed the suspect plate away and started to stand up.

"I didn't excuse you, mister."

Titus nodded; that was indeed the case. He sat back down in the chair and turned to an article in *American Cinematographer*, a man in a white suit gazing at a wedding-cake riverboat that was stuck on a jungle mountain, she forgot the name of that one. An old back issue Julie had picked up somewhere, the Flea Market, the East Bay Depot for Creative Reuse. She got up, rebelted her robe, poured herself a cup of coffee, and sat down across the table from him. *Fitzcarraldo*. She had seen it at the Telegraph Repertory junior year, right around the time she met Nat, who tore tickets there two nights a week. Eighty-four, '85, right toward the bitter end for that stuffy old black box. Not long before the night he came to her rescue. Who knew what might have befallen her if he hadn't come along, with his belated Isro and his unlikely, heart-melting Tidewater accent? Remembering Nat as he was then, the world's most pretentious high school dropout, coming on to her with some complicated

theory about Peter Lorre and a jumbo cup of free popcorn. Simultaneously working at Rather Ripped Records and Pellucidar Books, all long
gone. The man like some exiled Habsburg, bred and schooled to unite
the crowns of kingdoms lost. At one time she had been able to console
herself with his air of heroic obsolescence for the burden, material and
emotional, that being married to him imposed upon her. Now the best
she could hope for most of the time was to shake her head at him with
more amusement than scorn.

"So, okay, you don't want to be here. Where do you want to be? With
your dad?"

The boy appeared to find the article about *Fitzcarraldo* quite fascinat-
ing, or perhaps he had fallen asleep again. Aviva couldn't see his eyes.

"You and Julie have your last class tonight."

"Yes, ma'am."

"Julie says you want to be a movie director."

No answer.

"He said you've written a screenplay."

He dipped the tip of his left forefinger—he was a lefty—into the pool
of maple syrup that remained on his plate. She resisted the urge to slap
his hand, as she would have slapped Julie's. It took him a while to figure
out what he wanted or could permit himself to say.

"That he knows about."

"You've written more than one?"

"Five."

"Tell me the title of one of them."

"May I be excused now?"

"Just another minute of torture."

"*Incident at Al-Qufa Bridge.*"

"Al-Qufa Bridge? Is it—is it a war story?"

"It's a, like, *adaptation* of 'Incident at Owl Creek Bridge.' Only in the
Gulf War, not the Civil," he said, catching her endlessly policed racist
self red-handed. "By Ambrose Bierce, so it's in the public domain, so I
don't got to pay no rights."

"You know, your father, Archy, he served in the Gulf War. In the
army."

No answer.

"Did you know that?"

"Can I go?"

"Go where?" She had a sudden intuition. "Do you know where he lives?"

"Where who lives?"

"*Archy.* You ride by his house, don't you? At night. On your bike."

"I have to use the bathroom."

He looked at her, really looked at her, for the first time all morning. His eyes were filled with pleading, begging her to put him out of his misery.

"Fine," she said, and as he darted around her to get out of the Torque-mada chamber, she touched his shoulder with a right hand that had kept a thousand children from going too far, too fast. "But hear me out. I don't want you getting my son into trouble, staying out all night. And don't you ever lie to me again."

"No, ma'am."

"Don't call me that anymore, please. Aviva will do."

"Got it," the boy said. "Now, please, get your fucking hand off me, Aviva."

She let him go. He started out of the kitchen, then turned back.

"Your boy's a little dick-sucking faggot," he said. "Case you were wondering. And that ain't no lie."

"Way to start," Aviva said. "Way to build that foundation."

⊙   ⊙   ⊙

"Call me Moby."

Gwen clutching her belly as she ran up the front walk of the Nefas-tis Building, a three-story concrete dingbat whose breezeway spawned dust devils of swirling take-out menus and bougainvillea bracts. Miles from the elevator, possibly the slowest elevator in the Western Hemi-sphere, miss it and she would have to wait at least ten minutes. Calling, "Oh, Mr. Oberstein, could you please hold that for me?"

The name on the shingle that Gwen walked past every working day of her life read OBERSTEIN, and she had never met anyone who looked more like an Oberstein, particularly in a three-piece suit. Plus, it always seemed to her that the man's preferred nickname preceded a silent Dick. But the man stuck out a Weejun to keep the elevator doors from closing in her face, and he spent a lot of money every month helping to thin the vinyl herds at Brokeland, so she called him what he wanted her to call him and thanked him for holding the door.

"Thank you, Moby," she said.

She observed that, along with his blue suit and brown loafers, he was wearing white tube socks with a blue stripe. "You're up early," she further observed. Six-thirty in the morning—on Mondays, Berkeley Birth Partners kept early-bird hours, to serve the workingwomen. Moby would be the only life-form in the building besides Gwen and the turtles in Dr. Mendelsohn's terrarium.

"Gots to be in federal court at nine A.M.," Moby said, going into that strange ghetto minstrel routine of his, or maybe trapped inside it permanently, a soft white moth caught in a drop of hip-hop amber. "And I am *not* ready. I'm *trine* to get legal standing for whales, bring suit against the navy on their behalf?"

"Oh, right," Gwen said, only half remembering the story, whales in perdition, baffled by submarine ponging. Still, the man was one-up on her. He was following his heart in his working life, doing what he loved, loving what he did. "Good for you."

They inched skyward. The elevator banged, mooed, and screeched, sounding like Sun Ra and that whole awful Arkestra trapped inside of an MRI machine.

"Low-frequency sonar? Like the navy is testing? That is some bad shit. Fucks with their internal guidance systems, they beach themselves, get brain damage. Every time they test it, you have dead whales washing up in the dozens."

"I have to be honest, Moby," Gwen said, aiming a magician's-assistant *ta-da!* at the surprising feat that was her belly. "I'm not too fond of the word 'whale' these days."

"You due any day, right," Oberstein said. " 'Bout to pop."

"Four weeks."

"Whoa."

"That's what I'm telling you. Truthfully, I'm impressed we both fit in this elevator. Come next week I might need to get an elevator of my own."

"Least in five weeks you ain't gonna be pregnant no more. But I'm a still be fat."

"Oh, let me tell you something." She had not slept well, troubled by the struggling knot in her belly, by the throb of her aching back. By black and red bursts of Lydia Frankenthaler bleeding out, Cochise Jones pinned and gasping under the juggernaut weight of his B-3. By thoughts of Archy and his furtive approach to grief. Holding his sadness close, as if it were a secret, the man always moving from one thing he couldn't talk about to the next, sneaking across the field of his emotions from foxhole to foxhole, head down. She knew it had to be the loss of Mr. Jones, though she couldn't shake a sense that there was something else bothering him. She wondered if maybe he already had something else going on the side; if he was in love with Elsabet Getachew; if he had lied when he said Mr. Jones left money to pay for the funeral, and was secretly bankrupting them to put the old man in the ground in what he termed, worrisomely, fitting style. But mostly, the problem was the throbbing of her back. "I will *always* be pregnant."

"I would like to be done," agreed Gwen's first early bird, Jenny Salzman-House, who shared Gwen's due date but had gained only twenty-eight pounds to the forty-seven that Gwen had managed to pack on. "How about you?"

Jenny was pale pink and long-limbed with a boyish face and blond hair cut in an unflattering Volvo-shaped bob made popular by female tennis stars of the seventies. The swell of a thirty-week child offered little in the way of spectacle, even when she lay back on the examination table and bared her abdomen to the heavens and to the shadowless glare of the fluorescent tubes in the ceiling. She carried her pregnancy like a football tucked into the crook of a fullback's arm, invisibly and with aplomb. Whereas Gwen's belly was like some kind of Einsteinian force, warping the fabric of space-time as she moved through it. She was not, this morning, inclined to sympathize with Jenny and her nineteen-pound shortfall of woe.

"I *am* done," Gwen said. She squeezed a shining coil of ultrasound jelly onto Jenny's modest dome and then settled the business end of the Doppler against it. "Over and done."

"Tell me about it."

Gwen switched on the Doppler, and they listened to the tide of static that flooded the room. Jenny smiled bravely through the usual instant of informationless panic. Then that steady whistling emerged from the void: an interstellar signal, a jet exhaled from the pulsing gill of some denizen of the deep. Rhythmic evidence of life from the bottom of the sea or the farthest rim of the universe. A set of valves and pistons speaking a machine's simple language.

"Hello, baby," Jenny said.

Gwen added the baby's current heart rate to her notes on Jenny's weight, temperature, and abdominal girth. Everything was normal, hardly worth noting at all. Everything was always normal until it wasn't. Until the roar of static endured in the examination room without interruption. Until the arc of the belly measured no greater than it had at the previous visit. Until the typical placenta got stuck in the average uterus, started hemorrhaging, and you ended up rushing in the back of an ambulance through the chicanes of Berkeley, sticky with blood and uterine goo, mouthing off to doctors, trying to save two lives. It was not that there was no point or purpose in notating the normality of Jenny's pregnancy. It was that *nothing* was normal, ever, in midwifery or life; there were only levels of ignorance and denial, of obliviousness to the cetacean looming of disaster. Her marriage was founded on deception and lies. The work that she did meant nothing to the people—her people—to whom she most hoped and desired that it—that she—would matter. In the end, everything was only a ceaseless flow of static, fundamentally no different from silence. The background noise of creation. The implacable flood of time.

"Everything's fine," Gwen told herself, shuddering, switching off the Doppler. "And you're feeling okay."

"Just huge."

"Oh, girl. Don't even."

"Yeah, no, the only problem I'm having right now is that my husband finds pregnant women sexually arousing."

"I am so sorry to hear that."

"Yours?"

"If I would ever let him near me."

In the first third of the second trimester of her pregnancy, Gwen for a time had permitted Archy to indulge in her like a cartoon wolf with a knife and fork, a napkin knotted around his neck. Laid herself out and piled herself high as a Las Vegas buffet and let him keep filling up his plate. From the thirteenth week to the seventeenth, some kind of hormonal messaging crackled along the wires between them, and their bed was lit as by lightning. She could not quite take pleasure in his conventional presence within her, but she discovered, for those strange weeks, an unheard-of appetite for taking him in her ass, some kind of peptide flood that opened her up down there as she had never been opened before. That was over now; she was done with that, too. Sometimes in the night, his leg would arc across her, and she would feel a kind of rage at the contact, an insult to her person, a flicker of fire along her skin. Clearly, in his banishment from her interiors, he had rebelled. He had taken his empty plate and his napkin and gone to Ethiopia to get his fill. Licking his animal chops.

"Would you like me to instruct you not to have sex anymore?" Gwen said.

"Oh, would you?"

"No problem."

Gwen wiped the gel from Jenny's belly and rinsed the Doppler, adrift in a poignant memory of those vanished weeks of fire. Jenny wandered in her conversation as she resumed her suit, blouse, and briefcase, from an account of madness in the Rockridge housing market to a description of something preposterous and beautiful that had been done to figs at Oliveto.

"Can I also tell him you ordered him to make me a root beer float every night for the rest of my pregnancy?" Jenny said as they left the examination room.

An urge to consume root beer, dark, astringent, foaming, and sweet, tore through Gwen's soul.

"Have him call me," she said. She felt demeaned, mocked by her servitude to hormones and to the winds of her moods, powerless in her hugeness as a whale with no attorney, hollow and tired and faking it (as Mike Oberstein, Esq., would have put it) 24/7.

These sensations only increased when she emerged into the waiting room, with its 1980s-modern oak armchairs padded in raspberry wool and its random gallery of foam-core mounted Gauguin posters salvaged from some ancient Roth-Jaffe trip to Denmark, brown-skinned bare-breasted wahines and somber van Gogh potato fields under the arcane legend NY CARLSBERG GLYPTOTEK, and saw the next three early birds stacked up and waiting. A shrink, a real estate agent, and a new patient, another white lady, Coach briefcase at her feet, looking like, of all things, an attorney.

"Goodbye, Jenny," Gwen said, fighting down the obscure, Danish-illiterate discontent that stirred in her every time the words NY CARLSBERG GLYPTOTEK forced themselves into her mind. She turned to the ladies in the raspberry chairs. "Hello, Jenny. Hello, Karen." She considered the new patient, an older mom in a loose black pantsuit, a classic Berkeley cat lady, suit and wearer both adrift in an aureole of dander. "Hello . . ."

"Jenny." The cat lady smiled. "Believe it or not."

"Three Jennys," Gwen said. "How about that."

"This is the second time it's happened since I've worked here," said Kai, the Birth Partners receptionist. Born female but not feeling it too strongly. Hair worn slicked and short, white T-shirts, cuffed jeans, played saxophone in an alternative marching band. They worked street fairs, hipster potlatches, the edges of open-air concerts, showing up flash-mob-style, dressed in yachting hats and frogged military jackets like that Chinese funeral band over in the city, performing skewed Sousa marches, brass-band church music, and Led Zeppelin songs. They called themselves Bomp and Circumstance. "Only the other time it was Carolyn."

Gwen smiled back at the third Jenny and turned with a shameful yet profound and yawning dread to face the second, who gathered her own purse and briefcase and hoisted her baby freight with a lurch, then aimed the whole payload in Gwen's direction.

The door to the office creaked open with its trademark creature-feature spookiness, a sound, impervious to oil can and WD-40 alike, that had in turn haunted the practices of a Jungian analyst, a couples therapist, a specialist in neurolinguistic programming, a hypnotherapist, a shiatsu practitioner, and a life coach before settling in to mock the tenure of the Birth Partners in suite 202. A very young woman with a wide Mayan face looked in and said softly, "Sorry."

Karen, the Jennys, and Gwen all turned to regard the young woman. She was at once tiny and voluminous, at least three inches under five feet tall and call it seven months pregnant, with nowhere to put her unborn child but way, way out in front of herself. Indian features, hair black and glossy as a well-seasoned skillet, yanked to one side of the back of her head and knotted with a sparkly pink scrunchy. Over a pair of black leggings, she wore an extra-large T-shirt that randomly advertised a liquor store and bait shop in Lake Hopatcong, New Jersey. The shirt strained across her belly and gaped at the armholes, where her arms emerged sharp at the elbows and thin at the wrists. As she spoke her tiny sentence, her cheeks flushed in circles so precise they seemed to have been painted on. This might be her fifteenth summer of life.

She took half a step into the waiting room, glancing from the face of one woman to the next, connecting the dots with an expression of mounting regret. Struggling to read the unfamiliar text of this wan and well-worn room, which, for all Gwen knew, looked exactly like the Bureau of Human Vivisection down in Tegucigalpa, or wherever it was the girl had started out.

"Hi!" Gwen said so loudly that the girl started. At the sight of this young woman with her skinny arms, her shadowed eyes, her look of lostness, her shirt on which a largemouth bass leaped joyfully onto the hook that had come to destroy it, Gwen's heart seemed to expand with a kind of dark longing and, like the Grinch's, with a shattering of glass. "Come in! It's okay."

"I think maybe she called yesterday," Kai said. "Was that you? Areceli?"

"Areceli," Gwen said. The girl nodded once, then stopped, narrowing an eye as though she had been warned to expect false blandishments in the grim reception room of the Vivisection Bureau. "Do you speak English?" Areceli gave her head a tentative shake, drawing back toward the door. *"Entre,"* Gwen begged her, her UC Extension Spanish serviceable but bearing inexplicable traces of a Boston accent, *"por favor, entre, puedo verle enseguida."*

"Lo siento mucho, pero tengo un desayuno muy importante a las siete y media," said the next Jenny, *"y no puedo esperar."*

Gwen laid a hand over her chest as though to hold back the heart before it could fly forever out toward the young woman who was going to redeem everything. Reluctantly, but recognizing the need to undertake at least a minimum of patient management—a skill, chore, or art that she generally preferred to leave to Aviva—Gwen turned to the second Jenny.

She said, *"¡Usted habla muy bien español!"*

"He pasado dos años en Guatemala," said Jenny II, *"enseñando al Quiché como manejar una cooperativa del tejer."*

Gwen blinked, picking her way along, getting entangled in *Quiché* and then landing facedown in *tejer.* She had just realized that she did not give a shit where Jenny learned Spanish when she heard the mausoleum creak of the door hinges and the sigh of the door as it closed.

Gwen was paralyzed by a panic that was half outrage, as if she understood from the sudden lurch in her belly that she had been scammed or shortchanged, as if the young pregnant woman were a confidence artist who had lightened Gwen's wallet of a painful and irrecoverable sum.

"Excuse me," she said softly as she chased after Areceli, and once again the demon in the door hinges mocked the possibility of therapy, healing, recovery, of having one's life coached. She ran down the hall, past the offices of the whale attorney, to the elevator. When she jammed her finger against the button, the doors slid open at once. Areceli must have taken the stairs.

This was a barren arrangement of concrete slabs strung on rebar like vertebrae on a spinal cord. Gwen went to the second-story landing and stood listening for the scrape of the girl's descending tread, the telltale bass chiming of the stairway's steel frame. There was nothing, just the steady breeze that came ceaselessly whistling up the stairwell with a Halloween plangency even on the most windless of days.

One by one she took the steps, rocking the whole building as she descended, or so it seemed to her, calling *Areceli!* And then she burst out into the morning, Telegraph Avenue, the chiming rattle of a train of grocery carts being driven across the parking lot of Andronico's, a watery shout echoing from Willard Pool, the urgent sigh of a kneeling bus across the street—a shuffle of folks toward the bus doors, among them a ponytail spray of iron-black hair.

"Wait! Areceli! *Espera!*" Gwen threw up a hand as if to hail the AC Transit bus like a taxicab, and with a heedlessness remarkable even for Gwen, she threw herself into the middle of the avenue. A voice said, "Look *out*," and then she got lost in metal and the smell of metal and the cruel metallic ring of her tailbone against the curb.

"Sorry," said the bicyclist. He had not hit her, she realized; he had pushed her out of the way of an oncoming bus. He was a wiry teenager wearing neat jeans, a hoodie cinched low and shadowy over his face. "You hurt?"

There was a gash in the leg of her pants. She poked a finger into it and discovered a scrape; no other apparent injuries apart from those to her everlasting pride.

"I'm fine," Gwen said, trying to catch her breath. "I'm pretty sure. Thank you."

She waved to the boy, who nodded. Before he climbed back on his bicycle and pedaled off, he seemed to be considering—it would seem to her later—whether or not to offer her, from deep within his Ringwraith hood, some piece of advice or useful information.

"You just aren't a careful person," said a voice, familiar, soft-spoken, a man's. "Are you?"

Garth Newgrange, the dad, behind the wheel of a lettuce-pale Prius. Nosing his way into the driveway that led to the underground structure of the office building that recently went up next door to the Nefastis Building. Jacket, tie, dressed for work, though as far as Gwen could re-

member, Garth worked in downtown Oakland. He must be here bright
and early to see his doctor or dentist.

"How is Lydia?" Gwen said, feeling she lacked the energy to puzzle out
how Garth had meant to engage her with his opening remark; let alone
energy sufficient to engage him in return. But there was something off
about his words, no doubt, something broken in his tight smile.

"How is Lydia? Lydia is very upset, actually. We are all very upset.
The whole thing was traumatic for everyone. It was literally a trauma.
All right?"

He was, and she did not believe she had ever encountered such a
thing before outside the pages of a novel, white with anger.

"Garth—"

"Lydia had a dream, Gwen, and you and Aviva, you guys just— You
fucked it up."

"A dream?"

"Yes."

"Garth, Lydia had a baby."

"I am aware of that," he said. "Yes, Lydia had a baby. She has a baby,
and I have an attorney. His office is, ha, in the building right next door
to you. Funny, right?"

"Are you— You're *suing* us?"

"I plan to," Garth said. "I very much plan to do just that."

"But . . . what? Why? I know it was hard, things could have gone better, but she and the baby are fine."

"Who knows if the baby is fine?" he said. "You don't know. I don't
know."

"Garth, please."

They were already in enough trouble, she wanted to say, without him
piling on some nonsense lawsuit, waste of everyone's time and money.
But if she said that, he would probably go and report it to the attorney
in the next building, and somehow it would end up getting used as evidence against them.

"I hope your lawyer is better at their job than you are," he said, easing
his foot off the brake, punctuating the remark and the interview with

an exclamation mark. The part of the exclamation mark was played with aplomb by Garth's middle finger.

"Nice," she said to the rear end of Garth's Prius as he rolled down the ramp to the underground garage. Then, because it seemed to hold out the promise of expressing everything that she had been feeling that morning—toward her practice, toward her life, toward the world—she gave the finger to Garth, held it up so he could see it in his rearview as he drove away.

"Nice," Aviva agreed, pulling up in front of their building in rattle-trap old Hecate. "Like the Bob's Big Boy sign, only hostile."

⊙   ⊙   ⊙

"Ten years I've known you," Aviva said, down on her haunches, poking around the cabinet beside the sink in examination room 2. The office was closed for lunch; the partners had suite 202 to themselves. "Never once had to give you first aid. Suddenly, it's, like, our little thing we do."

"Uh."

"It's like some kind of not-good date you keep asking me on."

"I'm under stress, Aviva," Gwen said, sounding peevish even to herself. She struggled ankle-deep through a wrack of regret, an unfamiliar ebb-tide stink of remorse. She had badly mishandled the situation with Garth Newgrange, and she knew it. It was time to confess, to acknowledge failure, to submit once again to Aviva's crusty but goodhearted discourse of reproach. "I'm *pregnant*."

"I know that, honey. It's okay. You don't have to explain."

Gwen instructed herself to ease up on the woman, who had made no mistakes, ruined nothing. "That AC Transit had hit me?" she tried. "I would have owed Alameda County a new bus."

"Funny," said Aviva. "Aha." She pivoted from the supply drawer and stood up, holding in each hand a small cardboard box containing an elastic support bandage. She had on an April Cornell dress patterned with morning glories, bought secondhand at Crossroads, knee-length, with a V collar and quarter-length drawstring sleeves. On anyone but Aviva, it would have looked matronly, but Aviva had those wiry arms.

The whole woman was like a wire, all 104 pounds of her. She coiled and uncoiled. The flowered dress was trying to keep up, a bright but inadequate container for her movements. "Which look you want to go with? Caucasian or leper?"

"The beige. I don't know, I guess . . . I guess I was just so excited to see a brown face."

"I guess you must have been."

"It's so pathetic. Chasing after the child. You should have seen me taking those stairs." She laughed, low and rueful. "Don't laugh."

Aviva stopped laughing. "I know why you went after her," she said.

Gwen kept her legs dangling over the edge of the table, the crinkling paper offering its running commentary on her shifting behind as Aviva wrapped her right foot from arch to ankle. It didn't appear to be serious, but Gwen had been on it all morning, and now whenever she put her weight on it, her bones thrummed like wire. The abrasion on her shin Aviva had already cleaned and taped with a Band-Aid. She bound Gwen's ankle with the implacable tenderness of a practiced swaddler. She had that way of not talking; Gwen was powerless against it.

"It was Garth," Gwen said. "That you saw me flipping off when you drove up."

"Huh? You mean Garth Newgrange?"

"Right after the kid on the bike crashed into me, Garth pulled up. Going to see a lawyer next door."

"A lawyer."

"Talking about suing us. Seeing if they have a case."

Aviva rocked back, letting go of Gwen's foot. "Oh, fuck," she said. She pressed the close-trimmed tips of her long fingers against the orbits of her eyes. "What?"

"That's what he told me."

"So you flipped him the *bird*?"

"He flipped me off first."

"Yeah, but see, Gwen, you . . ." She shook off whatever she had been about to say. "Never mind."

"What?"

"Nothing."

"You think it's my fault that he flipped me off. That he's suing us. You think he's in the right. Because we screwed up so bad."

"I— No. No, I don't. Honestly. But I can't help thinking that if we just, you know, *went* to him."

"No."

"And, you know."

"Don't say it."

"Apologized."

"We are not going to do that, Aviva. No. We have nothing to apologize for. We did nothing wrong."

"Yes, okay, I agree with you, Gwen, but he's fucking *lawyering up*."

The door opened; it was Kai, chewing something leafy rolled in a lavash. "In case you wanted to know, can your one o'clock appointment, who showed up early, can she hear it, out in the waiting room, when you guys are having a fight in room two? I have your answer: yes."

"We're fine," Aviva said.

"Really?" Chewing, acting unconcerned, tugging at the collar of her embroidered cowboy shirt.

"Sure, whatever. I'm fine. Gwen's fine. Gwen will be fine for at least another . . ." Aviva looked at her watch, a man's Timex with the face worn on the inside of the right wrist, as if she had everything timed, down to this pending revelation, and was committed to staying on schedule. She frowned, looking disappointed by what her watch told her. "Like, call it five minutes."

Kai frowned, eyebrows knitting Sal Mineo–style, and closed the door behind her softly, as if in reproach.

"What's happening in five minutes?" Gwen said.

"Gwen," Aviva said. Then there was another long Aviva pause, profound and charged. "Gwen, have you talked to Archy?"

Archy has cancer and is hiding it from you, his wife; that was what Aviva's grave expression implied.

Gwen ripped a fistful of sanitary paper away from the sheet beneath her. "What's wrong?" she said, and once again she felt herself caught up in a cyclone of metal and pavement.

"So he didn't say anything."

"What would he say? Is he sick?"

"Oh, God. No. No, he's fine. He, too, is totally fine. For the moment."

"For the next five minutes."

"Call it four now."

"Aviva, what is this?"

"Shit. Okay. You're sitting down. That's good."

"Just a minute," Gwen said. "Hold on. I feel like maybe I want to be standing up."

"Gwen, no, I think you should—"

"Let me put a little weight on it, Aviva."

Aviva fussed at the bandage, found it acceptable, then released the ankle to Gwen.

"Much better," Gwen said. "Thank you so much. Now, what the heck?"

There was a soft knock on the examining room door. Aviva looked at her watch again.

"Aviva, what *is* this?"

The door swung open, and Gwen saw Julie walk in with the kid who had shoved her out of the path of the bus. The kid pushed back the hood of his sweatshirt. He was like a smaller, skinnier edition of Archy's dad, a 45 to Luther's LP. It took less than a second for her to formulate that first wild guess.

"Oh, dear Lord," Gwen said.

The boys stared each in his own all-consuming way at his shoes, at Gwen's ankle, at the floor.

"Titus," Aviva said. "Meet Gwen."

"Hey," said the boy. He looked to be about the same age as Julie, fourteen, fifteen. Gwen undertook the biographical math, syllogized a couple of stray remarks separated by years, guessed at the rest.

"Your last name Joyner?"

The kid looked up sharply but got his playful Luther Stallings smile in place just before meeting her gaze. "Yes, ma'am."

"Okay," Gwen said. And then somebody turned over the record, and *Archy's Cheatin'* came back on, and the first track on side B was called "Jamila." Gwen had never met Jamila Joyner, which, as always, made it so much easier for her to sketch the woman in her mind, with all her wicked contours. "Is she in town?"

The smile winked out like a drop of water on a hot range. "No, ma'am."

"Uh, his mom passed away," said Julie. "A long time ago."

The throb of jealousy subsided, and Gwen's heart, taking its first tentative steps since Aviva had unlocked the office door, went out to Titus, who suddenly looked closer to twelve than fifteen.

"Titus is staying with us," Aviva said. "At the moment."

"*What?* Since when?"

"Since Friday. Gwen, I'm sorry. I was respecting Archy's wishes. God only knows why. He said he was going to tell you. He said he needed a little time to sort things out."

So this, and not his grief over Mr. Jones, or his shame at being caught with the Queen of Sheba, or cancer, was the secret that Archy had been keeping from her, the hollow underlying his physical presence in the room, the delay in replying to her questions. Not that he had a son but that said fruit of his loins was going to be *moving in with them.* Then Gwen would be responsible for three babies instead of the two she had ordered.

"You should have just let that bus hit me," Gwen said. "You should have ridden right on by."

⊙   ⊙   ⊙

Gnat. In his ear, born with it. Hearing the current of his own blood, neural crackle, the omnipresent pulse of the worldwide electro-industrial power and information grid, the unheard music. His head a dish to pull down cosmic background radiation, sines and signals, diminished sevenths coming through the wires of time and space to vibrate secret membranes. Hearing *something.* His moods (unmedicated at the present) prone to act as filters on the input. Melodies on the up days, harmonic structures, polyrhythms, samples and snatches, phrases and hooks, discrete musical ideas. On the down days or in a mixed state, only that rhythmic humming, theorized by one of his many former psychiatrists to be—what else—a dim dull echo of his ma, deceased when

Nat was not yet two. A lullaby in the darkness, a steady soothing pat on the diapered behind. Yeah, whatever. But always, inside, beneath, interlaced with the auditory hallucination du jour, that constant invariant tone, at once low and sharp, infuriating, precious, steady as a handrail. On the menu for this morning, a looping Maceo-style fill, a joyous stab of horn, today shaping up to be an up day, oh, fuck yes, bee-da-lee-dop ba-deeda-la-*dee*!

Also on the menu: fried chicken, Richmond-style. Biscuits. Beans and rice. And most assuredly, greens. Greens the secret weapon, the skeleton key to the soul of a man of Garnet Singletary's age and provenance. Collards the thing to catch the conscience of the King of Bling.

But the kitchen, oy, the kitchen. Ba-deeda-la-*dee*-dop! A fucking disaster area. Nat recalled with a pang how his stepmother, Opal, a bookkeeper in the billing department of Thalhimer's department store, would always stay on top of the disorder, cleaning up after herself in measured intervals, a logic in the steps of her preparations, scraping the trimmed-away ribs and veins of the collards into the garbage while the leaves came to a low simmer in their pot of fatback liquor; the bowl in which the beans had been put to soak the night before washed and sparkling in the wire dish rack as they boiled; the biscuits mixed—the recipe, passed down from the lifelong employer of Opal's mother, a Mrs. Portman, calling for both yeast and baking soda—then left all night to rise under a damp towel in the refrigerator, nothing to be done but roll them out and cut them, put them in the oven ten minutes before you rang the dinner bell. Opal Starrett, *aleha hasholem*, rendered justice with her Scotch Brite pad to every pot, pan, and dish along the way, wiping down every surface to a laboratory shine, leaving herself to contend at the end only with the baking sheets, the big cast-iron skillet, and the blast radius of spat fat on the stovetop.

As with so many other things about her, Nat admired the orderly progression of his stepmother's kitchen, but he could never hope to emulate it. He came wired, like Julius the First, to do everything all at once. Puffs of flour escaping from the requisite brown paper bag in which, with cracked black pepper, cayenne, and salt, he shook the pieces of chicken—legs and thighs, as today's clientele required. A whole weather system, storm fronts of flour moving across the kitchen from west to east. A scatter of dried beans underfoot, their comrades steeped for an hour in boiling water in lieu of the overnight soak rendered impossible by his impulsive play for the King of Bling's support. The lard—another secret weapon in the battle for the soul of Garnet Singletary—starting to mutter and pop in the skillet. It was Opal's skillet, inherited along with her Panzer-plate baking sheets on which half the projected three dozen biscuits lay in domino-spot arrangements, and the big gray Magnalite pot that held Nat's simmering collards, their trimmings piled on the counter alongside peeled onion wrappers, a cut-away strap of fatback rind, the arctic landscape of Nat's uncompleted biscuit rolling. Better not to think about the rice, Christ, the rice, some of it duly sucked up into the belly of the dead-battery DustBuster that was lying abandoned on the floor in the middle of all the unsucked rest of it. All that rice, raining down when he yanked the bag from the pantry shelf, someone, likely Nat, having put it back with its wire tie very loosely twisted. Though it was kind of remarkable the way the sound of raining rice seemed to lay itself down so sweetly over the horn riff in his head, a shimmer of steel brushes on a hi-hat.

At 9:45 A.M. the first batch of chicken parts sank, to the sound of applause, into the pig fat. The fat set about its great work, coaxing that beautiful Maillard reaction out of the seasoned flour, the smell of golden brownness mingling with the warm, dense, bay-leafy, somehow bodily funk of the beans, and with the summertime sourness of the greens like the memory of white Keds stained at the toes with fresh-cut grass, Nat stepped through the time portal that opened within the ring of seasoned iron. Riding the kitchen time machine. Turning the pieces of chicken with a pair of tongs, his hum, which he did not even know he was emitting, like the steady press of massaging fingers at the back of his neck, he remembered Opal standing at the ancient Hotpoint on East Broad Street in high heels and a Marimekko apron patterned with big coral poppies, cursing out Julius the First, furious over some fresh piece of poor judgment, some dud of a snack cake, that Monument Liquor and News was now stuck for to the tune of ten cases, some no-account relative of Opal's to whom Nat's father had, against her emphatic instructions, loaned three hundred and fifty dollars they could ill afford, while in the lower sash of the casement window behind the stove, a pair of tiny electric fans executed a broad parody of Nat's father (and for that matter, prefiguratively, of Nat himself) going around and around and around, with unimpeachable intentions, to no effect at all. At last with her chicken pieces neatly mounded and her biscuits tumbled into a basket lined with a clean dish towel, Opal would knock on down the back hall in those high heels to the crazed wooden stairway, barrel staves and bent nails, something out of a Popeye cartoon, bolted to the back of their row house, throw open the door, and stand there on the landing, fanning up a hopeful breeze with her manicured brown hands, unimprisoning her soft dark dove-winged hair from its head scarf, saying in that wild negro Yiddish of hers, "That is sure enough a *mechiah.*" Thirty, almost thirty-five years ago that would have been, Nat's professional expertise wanting to sweeten the memory with maybe some fresh-minted Isaac Hayes filtering in from the stereo in the living room, or the first Minnie Riperton album, *Come to My Garden.* Opal had been into poor sweet Minnie in a big way.

Aviva, as in so many other respects, held to Opalish principles when it came to approaching a mess in the kitchen, and she was going to fucking freak when she saw what he had done, *Time machine my* ass, *Nat,* Jesus! She herself had knocked out some kind of semi-elaborate breakfast this morning for the boys, pancakes, bacon, and yet when Nat arose from bed pregnant with his scheme to win the heart of Garnet Singletary, and came into the silent and gleaming kitchen, he found only a corky trace of bacon in the air to betray her. Aviva, first white woman Nat had ever taken a romantic interest in, and the only one of his girlfriends who ever met the standard or received the approval of his stepmother. The latter being expressed, shortly before Opal's death, in a brief speech to Nat that could have been delivered by Aviva herself: "Don't fuck it up."

Forty minutes after the first batch of chicken went into the fat—without his having restored a modicum of order to the kitchen—Nat was

still busy with the tongs and the drumsticks, mindful of Opal's abso-
lute prohibition on crowding the pan. By the time all those hard-ass
little red beans, rushed into their fatback bathwater, had managed to
relax enough to jump on over into a casserole with the rice, it was nearly
10:40. Time to get moving. The King, more often one of his entourage,
could usually be seen passing the windows of Brokeland with a bag of
McDonald's, maybe a fish sandwich from Your Black Muslim bakery,
sometime around noon, twelve-thirty at the latest. Nat needed to get in
there just as the man's hunger was calling to him.

Like a dog in a cartoon, forepaws a turbine blur as he hunted up a
buried bone in a churn of dirt, Nat excavated the cabinets and ransacked
the drawers looking for usable serving containers and suitable platters.
Piling up behind him mountains of mateless lids and lidless bottoms,
rattling cake pans and pie plates. Souvenirs of ancient Tupperware parties, ice cube trays, Thermos cups with no Thermoses, Popsicle molds
with no sticks, roasting racks, bamboo skewers, a kitchen scale! Nat
figured on serving up to five or six Singletary satellites, hangers-on,
maybe even K of B shoppers. He hoped that at least a few of them would
find his arguments rendered sound and his blandishments persuasive
by the invincible rhetoric of Opal Starrett's cuisine. To begin with, he
needed only to reach the King.

And Garnet could be reached. Oakland-born and -raised, his roots
snaked back deep into Texas and Oklahoma. By laying out the meal that
he now carefully packed in tubs, wrapped in foil, stacked into a plastic milk crate (whose freight of unsorted and mostly unsellable vinyl
recordings, among them several offerings by Jim Nabors, Nat freely
added to the disorder of the kitchen), and schlepped downstairs to load
into the back of his aging Saab 900, Nat would be speaking to Singletary
in a deeper language. Like a wizard to a dragon in a novel on his son's
nightstand, speaking in the Old Speech.

"Oh ho ho," said the King of Bling as Nat backed, carrying the milk
crate, through the steel mesh door of the eponymous establishment.
Singletary reigned from his stool behind the glass counter in his cave
of gold, atop his pile of rope and finger rings. Apart from the treasure in
the cases, there was nothing else to look at in the shop: plain white tile

floor, bare walls paneled in Masonite. Singletary himself devoid in his person, as always, of the least gleam or half-ounce of bling, filling out a guayabera shirt, looking sweaty-hot in his Jheri curl, toward which he took a studiously historicist stance. Strapped like Bullitt over the arm with a licensed .44 that, as he never tired of assuring the curious, had more than once, in the service of the King, been called upon to do what its manufacturers had intended. "I had a feeling. Soon as I saw that little flyer you was passing around."

"Did you, now," Nat said, doubting it.

As his trade demanded, Garnet Singletary was a keen assayer of human alloy, though he would say what he needed to say, Nat knew, to induce among the general public, whether buying or pawning, that he was even sharper than that. But it wasn't like Nat was attempting some subtle bit of statecraft, or considered himself inscrutable, a master of neighborhood diplomacy. This was a fairly straight-ahead play.

"Read me like a book," he said.

He winked at Ervis Watson, more often known as Airbus, who quite amply served as muscle for the King of Bling, a six-five, three-hundred-pound first line of defense in a velour tracksuit, weaponless apart from his ordnance arms and his howitzer legs, beyond whose bulk, events rarely penetrated to the point that the services of Singletary's sidearm were required. King of Bling was half the size of Brokeland, dividing with the United Federation of Donuts the former premises of an Italian butcher, and between Singletary, Airbus, and the stock in trade, arranged in two long and two short table showcases on the floor and a tall cabinet that ran the length of the north wall, there was not a lot of room to turn around.

Airbus did not acknowledge the wink or indeed move the slightest feature of his face. Nat understood that the attempt to elicit a superficial comradeship by winking was a standard gambit of the environmentally nervous white man. He was not the least bit nervous, having grown up in the black part of Richmond with a black stepmother, black friends, black enemies, black lovers, black teachers, and culture heroes who, barring a few Jewish exceptions, were almost exclusively black. But he had so profound a horror of black-acting white men, such as Moby, that he drove himself with a near-pathological rigor to avoid any appearance, in manner or speech, of trying to pass. He would let his chicken do the talking.

"I brought you guys some lunch," he said. He set the milk crate on the counter behind which Singletary sat on his stool. "Thought you might be getting a little tired of the Big Macs."

Singletary squinted at the crate, then looked at Nat, running through possible negative scenarios that might arise once Nat opened the containers stacked in the crate: hustles, robbery schemes, some kind of nasty hummus or shit you were supposed to eat off a leaf. Then the smell coming from the food, a breeze off the coast of the past, worked its way into his nostrils, well defended as they were by his Billy Dee Williams mustache, and a wild surmise lit up the chilly precincts of his face. Nat lifted the platter of chicken and paused, milking the moment, fingers ready to peel back the blanket of aluminum foil at any time. All that was required was a sign from the King of Bling.

Singletary stared at Nat with a curious mixture of hopefulness and misgiving. He glanced at Airbus as if uncertain whether to split or double down on a soft eleven. Then he nodded once: *Hit me.* Nat ripped away the sheet of foil.

"Ho, shit," said Airbus.

"I was expecting maybe you might have a few more people around," Nat said as he set out the containers of beans, rice, and greens and tore open the foil packet of biscuits. Forks, knives, paper plates. A small ottoman of foofy Marin County butter. "Maybe feed a couple of your customers, too."

"Aisha was here, but she getting the baby's picture taken up at Hilltop Mall," Singletary said. He smiled. "I might have scared away some of the other people like to waste my time and theirs sitting around here all the damn day. Medication I been taking for my blood pressure have a tendency to make me a little *irritable*, from what I hear."

Airbus looked prepared but declined to comment on this rumor.

"Customers," Singletary continued. "That I don't know. Business been a little slow this morning."

"Fuck the customers," Airbus said. "More for me." He skyhooked a plate piled high with some of everything.

"Hope I brought enough," Nat said.

Singletary contemplated the well-encumbered plate that Nat had made up for him, but held off from tasting the food. He reached around behind him, shuffled through some papers, pulled out one of the flyers printed on blue paper. Nat had typed it up on the store computer, got it copied at Krishna. Singletary lifted to his face the plain black half-rims he wore around his neck on a thin rubber thong—another spurned opportunity to model his wares. He studied, or affected to study, the text Nat had composed last night in a fever of righteous defiance.

" 'COCHISE,' " he said. "That's for Mr. Jones."

"Another little tribute."

"Funeral's Saturday?"

"At the store, two P.M."

" 'Conserve Oakland's Character against Homogenization, Impact, and Stress on the Environment.' "

"I'm open to suggestions."

"That works."

"Glad to hear it."

"Homogenization?"

"In the corporate sense. Chain stores, franchises."

"I see. Yeah, that's real clever."

"Thanks a lot."

Singletary put down the sheet of paper as though it weighed ten pounds, as though, contrary to his stated opinion, its text left him, on the whole, unimpressed. He returned the half-glasses to struggle for purchase, belayed by the rubber thong, atop the Half Dome of his belly. His eyes were the steel pans of a precision scale.

"Let me see if I understand," he said. "In your opinion, the opening of a Dogpile shopping center on the site of the old Golden State market at Forty-first and Telegraph, which has the support of some highly respected figures in the community, such as Chan the Man, coming out of a company that works hard to lift the economic status and neighborhood pride of black people, is actually something that would have a *negative* impact."

"It's called a Thang," Airbus said through a mouthful of beans and rice. "It's really more like a mall."

"Sixty thousand square feet," Nat said. "Two levels of parking. The equivalent of five stories tall. Built right out to the sidewalk all the way around. It's going to dwarf everything around it."

"A lot of things in this neighborhood, I hope you don't mind my saying, could get dwarfed by a midget. Ain't like we got a lot of mansions and terrazzos and whatnot. Historical landmarks."

"True," Nat said. "We also don't have a traffic or a parking problem, but we will if that *Thang* gets built. As far as economic uplift of the community? Gibson Goode is looking out for *himself*. I mean, come on, King. I came in here for two reasons, and one of them is that of all the people up and down this avenue for two miles in either direction, white, black, Asian, or from Tajikistan, you're the only one more willing than I am to come out and say you hate that community-uplift bullshit."

Singletary weighed the intended compliment in those proving steel pans. "The enemy of bullshit," he said at last. "That's you, huh? And this whole thing"—he flicked the sheet of paper—"don't have nothing to do with the fact that a Dogpile *Thang* moving in two blocks from here, it's liable to put you and Archy Stallings out of business so fast you going to have to declare bankruptcy last Christmas to catch up?"

"Of course it does," Nat said. "I should have led off with that. You're right. I guess I just got a little tired of walking around all day saying, 'We're fucked.'" He rubbed at his chin. "I'm going to come all the way out with it, Garnet. I talked to a guy at Councilman Abreu's office." Abreu was the at-large member of the Oakland City Council. He had no particular interest in Brokeland or music generally, as far as Nat knew. Based on his past record, Abreu would have no particular philosophical, environmental, or other beef with a project like Dogpile. But Abreu was rumored to dislike Chan Flowers, and their clashes in session were a matter of record. "He said that Abreu might be willing to show up, talk to COCHISE, hear what we had to say. But not if—"

"Not if at"—checking the flyer—"twelve-thirty or so, you got a store full of sniffy old white people."

"I could use some influential people of color there," Nat said. "For sure. Prominent local merchants."

The King of Bling considered his next words. "Chan and me, we don't see eye to eye on too many subjects," he said. "And he has said things, both to my face and in a way that it got repeated back to me, about my line of business, comparing the sale of gold rope, et cetera, to a cancer, a plague, and so forth. But if this neighborhood have a heart and soul, Chan the Man got to be a candidate for that position. And you ought to know better than anybody, because you a smart, intelligent man with a lot of experience and credibility, that just because it's all right for a cold-eye, skeptic motherfucker like me to go around saying all that community-uplift jive is a bunch of bullshit, don't make it all right for *you*."

"Right again," Nat said. "Point taken."

"What's the second reason?"

"Oh. Well, I know how much you like collard greens."

Singletary nodded and picked up his fork. He got himself a nice mouthful of the collards and chewed, reflectively at first and, it seemed, with a hint of doubt. Abruptly, he closed his eyes and took a deep, slow breath as though surrendering the burden of many long years. When he opened his eyes, they were brimming with emotion in a way that would have astonished the hangers-on recently banished from the premises by his ill temper.

"What time you need me?" he said.

⊙   ⊙   ⊙

Solemn, smiling, mildly puzzled, or with a beneficent swish of Glinda the Good, each Concerned Person put down his or her alphanumerics, then passed along the clipboard and the souvenir pen from Children's Fairyland that was tricked out with pink and purple tinsel as a magic wand: Shoshana Zucker, who used to be the director of Julie's nursery school, a chemotherapy *shmatte* on her head; Claude Rapf the urban planner, who lived on a hill above the Caldecott Tunnel in a house shaped like a flying saucer, where he once threw a party to mark the unwrapping of a pristine original pressing of *In a Silent Way* (Columbia, 1969), which he then catalyzed on a fifty-thousand-dollar analog system; a skinny, lank-haired, Fu Manchued dude later revealed with a flourish to be Professor Presto Digitation, the magician from Julie's fifth birthday party; two of the aging Juddhists who had recently opened a meditation center called Neshama, a block down from the old Golden State, the male Juddhist slurping with a vehement mindfulness from the rubber teat of a water bottle while the female rummaged with melancholy chopsticks through the strips of flesh-gray tofu skin interleaved in her bento box as if ruing the slaughter of innocent soy plants that her appetite had ordained; Moby; that freaky Emmet Kelly–as Gloria Swanson–impersonator lady from the apartment over the Self-Laundry, holding her Skye terrier; Amre White, godson of Jim Jones, now the pastor of a rescue mission adjacent to the Golden State site, his ears, nostrils, and the ridges of his eyebrows cratered with the ghosts of renounced piercings; a city of Berkeley arborist named Marge whom Aviva once shepherded through a grievously late-term abortion; that Stephen Hawking guy who was not Stephen Hawking; the lady who owned the new-wave knitting store, teasing into life from the primal chaos of her yarn bag what appeared to be a doll-sized pair of cock-socked Eldridge Cleaver pants but also might have been a pullover sweater for her pet wyvern; weirdly, the accountant who got caught embezzling minor sums from a number of her clients, among them Brokeland Records, and was obliged (as a result of a bee that flew into a previous bonnet of Nat's) to settle in small claims court; a noted UC Berkeley scholar of Altaic languages who specialized in collecting independent-label seven-inch soul releases of the mid-to-late sixties, carrying on his right shoulder without acknowledgment and for unspoken reasons a ripe banana, onto the nub end of which he (or someone) had drawn in black felt pen a smiling cartoon face; one of the eleven shrinks Nat had seen over the past ten years, a Dr. Milne, who spent the whole time casting a restless diagnostic eye across the framed album covers on the walls, the inoperative iron fuchsia of the fan whose down-rod receded into the time-furred webs and shadows of the high tin ceil-

ing, Julie's painted bead curtain looking more like Sammy than Miles
Davis, the battalion of miniature plastic Shriners in their miniature
tuxes and fezzes massed along the plate rail of the wainscot at the back
of the store, architectural relic of some pre-Spencerian establishment
rumored but not confirmed to have been for a time the Oakland head-
quarters of the Black Hand; Sandy the dog trainer, who had been lobby-
ing the city for nearly a decade to convert the Golden State site to a dog
park and who had taught the Jaffes' beagle-schnauzer mix, Jasper, later
slain by cancer, to play dead; and S. S. Mirchandani, there only because
he was always around that time of day, the wandering star of his mysterious system of motels, nephews, and liquor stores. Last to sign his
name, grunting and shifting and looking like he would have preferred
to consult beforehand with his attorney, the King of Bling on his usual
stool, minimally fulfilling the racial requirement imposed on Nat by
an anonymous aide to Councilman Rod P. Abreu; though Airbus, unre-
corded by wand, was also present, way at the back, to sew a second patch
of verisimilitude onto the motley cloak of diverse community support
behind which Abreu, in his ongoing struggle with Chan the Man for
control of the Oakland City Council, might plausibly clothe his presence and his intentions.

"Let me start by telling you folks," Abreu said, "why, I think, we are
not here."

Rod Abreu was a weary-shouldered, pudding-cheeked lawyer, at one
time the attorney for the electrical workers' union, younger and sharper
than he looked, better educated than he sounded, scented with bay rum
and endowed advantageously with large, moist mournful eyes the color
of watery coffee that were set into his face in a pair of bruised hollows,
prints inked by the malefactor thumbs of life. Yet in spite of his hangdog stoop and sorrowful countenance, his manner leaned aggressively
toward an irrepressible and uniform pep, pep sprayed in snaky jets all
over everything he said like concrete onto rebar.

"We probably should not be here today at this time," he put it to them,
"thinking we're going to try to stop or turn back the clock on the Dogpile proposal. All right?"

Awaiting objection in a way that seemed to promise a swift overruling, courtroom-tested, Abreu held up his chin. No objection was forthcoming, though the lady with the Skye terrier looked disappointed. Nat was disappointed himself but, supposing this might be some kind of Brutus-is-an-honorable-man rhetorical gambit, settled in to hear what came next. The chin was duly lowered.

"To say anything like that, all right, would not only be premature, it would also be unfair. Maybe even a mistake." Talking to a jury, a labor board, people who believed themselves, no matter how scant the supporting evidence, not to be simpletons. "Yes, I have seen the initial proposal, my staff and I have had a chance to look it over, and I would say that the best word for it is 'ambitious.' It is an ambitious proposal, and Mr. Gibson Goode, a terrific athlete, a human highlight reel—I mean, seriously—is an ambitious dude, okay, who has made amazing use of his gifts and his competitive edge, those leadership skills. If you ever saw him play, you know he has the goods. He can do it all. Guy you want in the huddle, third and long, take the ball and run with it, I mean, pick your favorite football cliché, to be honest, I'm more of a baseball fan. Go A's?"

This tentative sentiment was seconded with scattershot but genuine fervor, the Oaklands a game and half out of first that August and seriously contending, and then the hinges of the front door let out a contrarian jeer. Everyone turned to see, hesitating at the threshold, a large man dressed in a stained *Captain EO* sweatshirt, sleeves cropped and curling at the shoulder seams to expose two high-reaching power forward arms. A pair of official Team USA basketball shorts as worn by that summer's inglorious Olympic squad. White-on-white Adidas kicks, scarred as warhorses and wrinkled as elephants. The man looked flummoxed, lost, and, to his business partner, crestfallen, as if a grim fate that he had always feared might befall their establishment—say, a massive influx of strange white people—was now come to pass. He was carrying a square black frame from Blick art supplies, the kind they used to display album covers. He didn't say anything, just stood there sweaty and breathing carefully through his nose.

"My partner, folks, Archy Stallings," Nat announced, aware of a change of pitch, a downshift, in the music he was hearing in his head.

For the first time since he had begun to craft the flyer that summoned COCHISE into being, it occurred to him, maybe a bit late, that he might have wanted to drop some hint of his intentions on his partner, folks, Archy Stallings. If for no other reason—again a bit late, he saw that there might be plenty of other reasons—than to prevent the calamitous breach of personal-style code that his oversight had obliged Archy to commit. Every so often, maybe, if he was running way behind, Archy might stop by the store on his way from the courts at Mosswood Park, before he went home to shower and change. He never did so except with reluctance, discomfort, and apologies to whoever was at the counter to see him looking so raggedy-ass.

"Sorry," he told the room before settling on his partner as the likely source of his underdressed confusion with a frown and a furrowing of eyebrows. "I—uh. Whoa. Nat—"

"Archy, this is Councilman Abreu," Nat said, trying for the sake of appearances to make it sound like he was reminding rather than informing. "He graciously found some time to stop by today and talk to us, give us his views on the Dogpile thing. And," he added, seized by a happy if disingenuous inspiration, "to hear what *we* have to say. Our neighbor and good friend Mr. Singletary—"

Garnet Singletary pressed his fingers against his sternum as though feeling for the bullethole.

"We need to *fight*!" said the lady who lived over the Self-Laundry, goosing her dog on the word "fight" as though encouraging it to second the motion. The dog abstained.

"HELL, YES," intoned the Stephen Hawking guy through his vocoder, rolling his Mars rover out of Archy's way.

"Huh," said Archy quietly. "Is that right? Fight, okay."

Nat noted the passage across his friend's wide, mild features of what appeared to be genuine distress. Eager to ascribe that painful sight to anything other than the fact that, in an access of hypomania, he had convened—without consulting anyone, in the middle of a "transitional" neighborhood in a city that was largely black and poor and hungry for the kind of pride-instilling economic gesture that the construction of a Dogpile Thang represented, however gestural and beneficial only to

Our Beloved Corporate Overlords it might turn out to be—this motley gathering of freaky Caucasians united, to hazard a guess, only by a reflexive willingness if not a compulsion to oppose pretty much anything new that came along, especially if it promised to be big and bright and *bangin*; in the process, creating and abandoning an unholy mess in his own kitchen, a mess that, his rapidly cycling brain chemistry began to whisper to him, was probably a metaphor, a prophecy of how this whole thing was going to turn out; hoping to forestall this realization, Nat sought explanation for Archy's evident dismay in the picture frame. Archy had used it to mount the sleeve of his cherished copy of *Redbonin'*, with its starkly lit, extreme close-up Pete Turner photograph of Cochise Jones looking lean and hale but far more menacing than he ever had in life, cheeks printed with a calamitous history of freckles.

"I just came by to hang this picture up," Archy said.

⊙   ⊙   ⊙

"Aw, man, condolences," said Moby, letting loose some kind of absurd dap congeries which, remarkably, Archy returned slap for slap, flutter for flutter, pound for pound. Then, like sparring bears, they fell into a woozy clinch. "*So* fuckin sorry to hear about that, bro. Mr. Jones was a legend and a hella nice guy."

"True, true," Archy said, wading toward the front counter with everybody goggling silently at him in a way that reminded Nat of Jesus among the moneylenders. Archy took note of the remaining fried chicken, beans and rice, collards, and biscuits laid out on the counter. He pressed his lips together as if in token of a Juddhist detachment from such worldly (not to say unclean) productions. Exchanged with the King of Bling a curl-fingered clasp of Zen simplicity. Went to a shelf on the wall behind the counter, moved aside an old Seth Thomas digital clock, a James Brown bobblehead, and a stack of AT&T bills one or the other of the partners was long since supposed to have gone through with a highlighter pen. He unfolded the cardboard foot at the back of the frame and propped up the album sleeve with its matte-finished border of funereal black. He stepped back to contemplate it and heaved a big old big-man sigh. Then he turned to face the inexplicable room and reached for a chicken leg. He bit and chewed and swallowed without apparent pleasure, by which token Nat saw that his partner was truly angry.

"Arch—"

"I'm here to listen," Archy said to Nat. "You listen, too." Chomp. "Excuse me, Councilman. Please continue."

"Okay," Rod Abreu said. "Well, like I explained, Mr. Stallings, just a minute ago, at this point in the game, I actually *don't* think we should be thinking of fighting anything. I was just saying . . ." He looked sheepish. "What was I saying?"

"Go A's," said Dr. Milne.

"Right. Football. Yes. Folks, there is no question, if you don't know, take it from me, Gibson Goode has done *great* things for the community down in L.A., a community where not a whole lot of great things were happening before. I commend and admire him for that, and I commend the people, some of my colleagues on the city council, who look at what Mr. Goode has done in L.A. and say, hey, wouldn't it be *great* if we could make something like that happen here in Oakland. And hey, he's a hometown boy, right? A homeboy. Wouldn't something like that be awesome? A shot in the arm. Well, yes, maybe it would be awesome. It sounds awesome. It looks awesome on paper. But if there's one thing I've learned, and hey, I'm a homeboy, too? Born in East Oakland, right at Highland Hospital? It's this: I have seen a lot of impressive people come through this city over the years with a lot of awesome ideas that looked good *on paper*. Hey, when you look like I do, *on paper*'s your only hope."

That got a laugh, Shoshana in her chemo scarf nodding, other people nodding. Abreu worked those doleful eyes, those Marrano eyes, *abreu* meaning "Hebrew," as Nat would have liked to inform Archy, in Portuguese, or maybe it was Catalan.

"Whenever you have a proposal as ambitious as this one, and folks, no doubt about it, this is a *very* ambitious proposal, you have to be careful. People tend, when you have a charismatic guy like Gibson Goode, a genuine superstar, hey, somebody like that generates a lot of excitement, people get kind of caught up, right? And when people get excited, they get carried away, then they rush into things. And *that's* why we are here today. Because somebody has to kind of hang back a little, say, okay, let's slow down. Let's take our time with this. That's the message I'm bringing you today."

Slow down, admittedly not quite the message that Nat had envisioned when he first began to lay his fevered plans, but his nose detected subterfuge in Abreu's words, and he did not believe that a mere retarding action was all the councilman had in mind.

"And it's the message that I'd like to take back *from* you and share with my colleagues on the city council."

S. S. Mirchandani leaned in close to Archy. "I have been reliably informed," he said in a portentous and inadequate whisper, nodding toward Abreu, "that he was the one getting Chan the Man's sister fired from the port of Oakland."

Like Archy, making his joyless way through a biscuit that might have brought joy to Eeyore, Nat affected not to have heard Mr. Mirchandani, but he glanced over at the likely source of the information. Singletary arched an eyebrow, then, after taking a look around the room, smiled a dubious but encouraging smile, the way you might smile at someone about to depress the ignition button of a homemade jet pack. He did not look too impressed by the putative founding membership of COCHISE, their ranks drawn largely, as Nat would have been obliged to concede, from the recipients of an e-mail sent in bee-meets-bonnet haste to those addresses in his personal contacts file who shared a zip code with Brokeland, a relatively modest number (Nat at best a fitful electronic correspondent) amassed over a period of several years from a disparate set of social contexts.

"Now, I want to thank our hosts today, you two are really pillars of this neighborhood, for organizing this get-together."

"*Huh*," said Archy.

Abreu turned at the sound and caught Nat in the midst of offering his landlord an elaborate shrug, lips down-twisted asymmetrically into an expression meant to convey 1) that his willingness to concede both the unlikeliness of COCHISE's success and the regrettable preponderance, thus far, of white faces among its membership was accompanied by 2) a respectful suggestion that Singletary reserve judgment, because hey, you never knew what might happen, and a second, still more respectful suggestion that 3) Singletary go fuck himself; such elaborate, densely layered shrugs being a particular specialty of the Jaffes going back to their days of never knowing what might happen along the banks of the Vistula.

"No, really," Abreu said, misinterpreting Nat's shrug as modesty. "Brokeland Records, right, I mean, this place is so much more than a store. It's a neighborhood institution. I know a lot of you folks have spent a lot of your time and money in this place over the years."

"Lot more time than money," Archy said, and Moby, who had dropped thousands over the years, loyally laughed.

"It's the kind of independent, quirky, welcoming place . . ." Abreu went on, voice wavering as though he were picking up on the crackle of politics that troubled the air between the partners. The Spinozan sadness in his eyes seemed to balloon, and the thumbprints beneath them to deepen: ". . . that gives a special character to this part of the city. And it's that special character we're going to have to really consider as we look at the Dogpile plan going forward. There are also possibly some environmental-impact issues to look at. Now, I understand, from talking to, uh, Ms.—"

"Sandy," said the former light in the eye and wag in the tail of poor Jasper. "That's why I was told we couldn't put a dog park there. The back end of the property used to be a factory or something. I heard there was mercury. You can't dig it up without doing some kind of big cleanup."

A number of people nodded and murmured that they had heard reports of some kind of problem with the site, but many more seemed to be hearing the information for the first time, and Nat was gratified by the concern that it appeared to engender, news of the danger forking outward, in his imagination, along a network of gossip and bloggery until it reached a crescendo of outrage that would doom the Dogpile proposal now and for all time, bring it with a creak and a crumble and a great cloud of dust to the ground. He wanted to turn to Archy, standing irritated next to him, turn to Aviva as in his imagination she ran screaming from the devastated kitchen of the home that was, after all, also threatened by the advent of the Thang, turn to the ghost of Opal

Starrett, who always used to say, not without affection, that Nat was incapable of organizing an empty drawer, throw out his arms, and cry, *Da-deeda-la-*dee-*dop!*

Just as Nat was congratulating himself and mentally boasting to the living and the dead for his remarkable aim with the ancestral Davidic sling, he saw Singletary sit up electric-shock straight, then nod cool and wary at someone beyond the frame of the front window, out of Nat's line of sight.

"So the Dogpile folks are probably going to run into some questions right there. And of course, and here's the end of what I have to say, the city council and the planning commission are going to be looking for a lot of input and comment from you—"

And then in walked Chan the Man, in his Sergio Leone hat and funereal suit, steps precise, eye bright and quick as a rooster's. He stopped in the doorway with two of his nephews paired behind him. "Oh my goodness," he said. "I am sorry. I did not realize."

He raised a hand to his mouth and looked embarrassed. Dumbfounded to discover his favorite record store almost if not quite packed with people in the middle of the day. Far more people, perhaps, than had ever been almost but not quite packed into this space at any time in its history, even back when it was Spencer's Barbershop. For a kinescoped instant Nat cut away in his imagination from the scene at Brokeland to an afternoon forty years earlier, men and boys, maybe Chan Flowers and Luther Stallings among them, jostling around a portable black-and-white to watch Cassius Clay take down the Big Bear. Nat wished intensely that this gathering could be that gathering, these people could be those, with all the years of ferment and innovation in the music and the life of black America ahead of them. Hope unfulfilled, not yet betrayed.

The crafty old fucker, acting surprised. It was barely possible that he felt surprised by the decent turnout Nat had managed, but Nat did not buy for a second that the guy was embarrassed, that he just *happened* to walk in on the organizational meeting of COCHISE, oh my *goodness*, so sorry to interrupt, I see I will have to come back later. Flowers made a more rapid but careful survey of the human contents of the room. When he reached the King of Bling, he paused.

"Mr. Singletary," he said with cold affection. "Well, well. An august presence."

Singletary said, "Mm-hmm." Savoring it, all at once content to be there in the room, the King of Bling kicked back on the stool. He smiled slowly. Chan the Man smiled right back.

"So many faces I don't know," he said as if fault for the ignorance were entirely his. "Oh, now, *Elisheva*, isn't it?"

"Yes, hello," said the lady rabbi from Neshama, wagging three fingers Girl Scout–style.

"Making your preparations for the High Holidays?"

"They're getting close," Elisheva said.

"That's right! Rosh Hashanah!" On Flowers's lips, the name of the holiday sounded like something much grander to Nat's ear, *roarsh hashanah!*, a Klingon affair involving ritual combat and lunar howling. "And who else? Oh, excuse me, there, brother."

The Steven Hawking guy joysticked his chair around to make room, causing Abreu to take a step back and thus come into Chan Flowers's line of sight for the first time. He had been concealed by the certificate, mounted on a piece of foam core, advising all comers that in 2003 readers of the *Express* had declared Brokeland records to be the Best Used Record Store in the East Bay, a conclusion they had reached in seven out of the past ten years. Then Chandler Bankwell Flowers III looked, for real, dumbfounded.

"Councilman Abreu," he said. "And very much at large."

"This is terrific," Abreu said with that untouchable chipperness, so like tedium, which must serve him well in his line of work. "I was just about to open it up to questions from these good people here. And you are so much more informed about this project than I am. I'm sure you all know, do you all know? what a big supporter of Dogpile and Mr. Goode the councilman has recently become after a certain period of sharing the reservations that I know many of us in this room also feel. So, Mr. Flowers, I don't know, maybe you'd like to tell us some of the things you learned, or the decisions you came to, that helped you change your mind about this project."

"I'd love to," Flowers said. "Nothing would make me happier. Unfortunately, today I do not have the time. I'm just on my way from one appointment to another. Not even time to stop and browse the new-arrivals bin. Leave a little more of my hard-earned pay in that cash register over there."

This got a bigger laugh than any Abreu had managed to scrape together from this crowd, admittedly, a tough Berkeley/Oakland crowd, its sense of humor reduced, like the sperm count of a man who wore his underwear too tight, by the heat of two dozen outraged brains. It occurred to Nat that Chan the Man appeared to be in fine form and might take it into his head to make a speech. Might even have come today prepared to make one. An address that would reach out to the core of *Nat's* constituency: the soreheads of the neighborhood, the purists, the lovers of minutiae, the inveterate hearers of invisible bees. All gathered together in one room, to be scooped up into the stern but forgiving arms of Flowers. Delivered at one blow like the brave little tailor's flies. Courtesy of Nathaniel Jaffe, let his epitaph be: *It seemed like a good idea at the time.*

"Actually, I was just looking for you, Mr. Stallings," Flowers said. "If you've got a minute?"

It was an artless and genial question, and when the meeting resumed with a question from Dr. Milne about a peculiarity of Oakland zoning ordinances, no one paid it any mind apart from Nat, who happened to be looking at Archy when Archy, wary, unwilling, replied, "Yeah, you bet."

⊙   ⊙   ⊙

In the cool penumbra of Chan Flowers's office, Archy dropped into a wingback chair. It was big and soft as a grandmother, trellised cream chintz overwhelmed with pink roses. A chair for swooning in, for surrendering one's dignity to, safe within the air-conditioned preserve of sympathy where, installed behind his desk, Chan Flowers received death's custom with magisterial detachment, a gamekeeper crouched and watchful in a blind. Sweat cooled in cobwebs on Archy's arms and forehead.

"Thanks for taking a minute, son," Flowers said. "Didn't seem to me you were necessarily involved in that mess over there."

"Not necessarily," Archy allowed. He fought the armchair, resisting its invitation to conform his frame to its armature of grief. Grief was itself a kind of chair, wide and forgiving, that might enfold you softly in its wings and then devour you, keep you like a pocketful of loose change. He found himself slouching in it, off-kilter, legs outflung, bare knees akimbo, covering his mouth with one hand like he was trying to bite back a smart remark.

"I thought maybe if it was convenient," Flowers said, "you and I might have some details to go over for the funeral and all. One or two points that have come up in the fine print, so to speak."

Archy nodded, already feeling some undercurrent in the conversation, this audience with the councilman, that he didn't like. Bankwell and the other nephew, Feyd, stood guard at either side of the office door like a couple of foo dogs, too close to looming for Archy's taste. They were the undertaker's muscle, no doubt or question about that. At a funeral, if things turned unruly, a Flowers nephew might have to step in, keep the peace. If Flowers was burying a murder victim, somebody dropped by the logic of retaliation, if there was some history of blood and bad feeling abroad, a nephew might have to go strapped among the mourners. Bankwell and Feyd, in their copious suits, wore faces you could interpret as reflecting the tranquility of iron harbored at the hip. Archy remembered Bankwell obese and twelve, head too small for the rest of him, a neighborhood scandal after it was discovered that Bank had been getting his addled granny to pay him five dollars per book to solve her Dell Word Searches for her. Helping her to maintain her dignity, he claimed, so she could leave the books around her house with letters neatly circled, words crossed out. Archy wondered why Flowers felt that muscle was a necessary or desirable element for their rendezvous. He craned around to extend the nephews, by means of a bored slow stare, an invitation to go fuck themselves, saluting Feyd by hoisting his chin high. Feyd raised his own with an amiable coldness. He was reputed to be a tight and encyclopedic dancer, up on them all, from the Southside to turfing. Probably knew how to fight, too, did some capoeira, boy had that lean, springy *malandro* look to him. Bankwell, unquestionably, was grown to a very large size.

Archy returned to Chan, ready with a reply. "Do I have a choice?" he said.

"Of course," Flowers said mildly, so mildly that Archy at once regretted his words and wished to retract them. Paranoid, imagining shit, guns and undercurrents. Come at the man sounding flip and disrespectful.

"If this is a bad time," Flowers said, "I'm happy to—"

"Nah, no," Archy said, "just kidding. Let's do it."

"Fine."

"You were saying about Mr. Jones."

"I was. Now, I'm sure Brother Singletary already told you, but Mr. Jones took care of everything, from the financial point of view and also in the matter of choices and selections."

"Everybody knew that." Singletary turning out to be Mr. Jones's executor, fingers in every pie not already fingered up by Chandler Flowers. "I mean, shit, for a while he was carrying around a picture of his coffin folded up into his wallet, used to take it out and smile at it like he was looking at a centerfold or, like, a picture of Tahiti."

"Mr. Jones, rest in peace, the man had his certain type of peculiarity, no doubt."

"Asking to be buried in the Aztec number," Archy said. "I heard."

"Thing is hell of ugly," Feyd said.

"The Aztec number was made by Ron Postal of Beverly Hills," Archy said, grateful for the opportunity, as an alternative to adolescent slouching and mouthing off, to turn professorial and school the roostery motherfucker. "Acknowledged master of the American leisure suit. It's truly one of a kind. Shit ought to be in the Smithsonian."

"People can be very particular about burial attire," Flowers said with all his perfected mildness. "No, the odd thing, what I'm talking about, maybe odd's not the proper term. I was going through his instructions, you know, he has it all typed up single-spaced, six pages." He opened a folder on his desk, forest green with hooks of white metal where you hung it from rails in the file drawer. With the tip of his middle finger, hardly larger than a boy's, he began to tick off items on the first sheet of paper the folder contained. "He wanted the Cadillac hearse."

"Naturally," Archy said.

"Naturally. And we're going to make that happen for him. He wanted it open casket—"

"How's he look?"

"Now? Now he looks peaceful and dignified."

"No sign of, uh, damage?"

"This is our art, Mr. Stallings," Flowers said. "Our profession. Please. Man wanted the Chinese marching band, the Green Street Mortuary Band, from over in the city." He looked up from the folder. "How's that coming?"

"Turns out they're already booked," Archy said. "Morning and afternoon."

"That is going to be a problem, then," Flowers said.

"Please," Archy said. He had been trading messages with Gwen's receptionist, Kai, to see about booking her outfit, Bomp and Circumstance, to play the funeral parade. Mr. Jones had checked them out one time at the Temescal street fair. Bunch of straight-faced, brass-brandishing cute little tattooed lesbianettes playing "What a Friend We Have in Jesus" wasn't ever going to have too much trouble putting a smile on Mr. Jones's face. "This is my art and my profession."

"Fair enough."

"So I'm still waiting for the points that have come up," Archy said. "In the fine print."

"Well," Flowers said, "the gentleman, rest his soul, he had an aversion, you might say, to religion. I'm sure you know."

"He was deep, though."

"Yes, he was. But he made it clear," tapping the third typed sheet of paper in the green folder, "he didn't want a preacher or a minister, didn't want no church. Didn't even want to hold the service here at the funeral home. What with the stained glass and, I guess, the pews in the chapels and so on. We got Bibles, we got hymnals. A general atmosphere of, call it, reverent solemnity. I mean, I try to keep the religious element unobtrusive, respectful. Technically, this is a secular operation. But, well, they are called funeral *chapels*, and Mr. Jones—"

"He was a true-blue atheist," Archy said. "I remember my pops saying how Mr. Jones, at one time he was even a full-on *Communist*."

"How is Luther?" Flowers said, tired, uninterested, milder than ever. Asking it pro forma. But one pop-eye peeper flicked left, checking in on Bankwell, telling the man, *You pay attention, now.*

"I wouldn't know," Archy said.

"You haven't seen him?"

"Not for like two years. What he do this time?"

"Didn't do anything," Chan Flowers said. "I never said he did."

"But you're looking for him," Archy said. "I get the distinct impression."

"I might be."

"If you're looking for him," Archy said, "he must of done something."

A smile opened, thin as a paper cut, at the bottom of Flowers's face. Archy did not know the nature of the ancient beef that Chan Flowers had with Luther Stallings. The history of the matter was banned and obscure. His aunties had made inquiries, put out feelers. For years they continued to probe the gossip pits, turn over the ashes with their sticks. But even those legendary connoisseurs of scandal never found anything to definitively explain the break, apart from whispers of a connection to some mythic murder of the Panther years. As boys, Archy knew, Chan and Luther had been famously thick, chronic co-conspirators. Then, when Archy was maybe four or five years old, around the time Luther started acting in movies, the friendship was abandoned like a house, sealed by law, condemned.

"Whatever he did, I assume it is all his fault," Archy said. "Let me just put that out there to start."

"You may well be right," Flowers said. "Luther may have done something, and whatever he did is probably, I'm sorry to say, his fault. But that's not here nor there. I just need to see the man. I just need to talk to him."

There was a photograph that Archy remembered, hung from the wall of his father's various apartments. It was a glossy black and white, taken by a *Tribune* photographer, at an Oakland Tech dance, Luther Stallings and Chan Flowers and two fly girls of the period. Everybody dolled up and smiling but possessing that precocious dignity of your ancestors when they were young.

"If I knew where he was at, Councilman, I would tell you, straight up," Archy said. "But I don't know. By choice. And I don't plan to find out."

"And you don't know anybody knows where he's living. Not one single soul."

He might have been gently chiding Archy for this ignorance. Implying there could, somewhere, for somebody, still be some use left in Luther Stallings.

"Nope. No, sir, no, I don't."

"Well, let's say that situation changes, or maybe you have some kind of change in the way you're looking at that situation. Say, one day you gaze out at the neighborhood water. See that fin popping up, that old familiar shark come swimming around. Just, you know, let me know. I have something to give him. Something he needs very badly."

"Yeah? What, a sea lion?"

Flowers fixed his sleepy eyes on Archy, laid them on like hands. Slowly, skeptically, the heavy lids lifted. "I am serious, now," he said. "You run across him or one of his known associates and running buddies. Somebody from his old crew that ain't died yet, few in number as they are. Just let me know. Valletta Moore, for example. I heard she's around."

He came at Archy's soul then with the flashlight and the crowbar of his gaze. Archy offered no purchase and gave nothing back. Maybe the man already knew that Archy had seen Valletta; maybe he was only fishing. Archy could not have said why he decided to keep silent.

"If she should happen to show up," Flowers said, "let's say. You just go on and call me on my personal cell. Feyd, give him the number. All right? Will you do that for me?"

Archy said, "I'll think about it."

"You do that," Flowers said. "And maybe, you never know, I might be the one ends up putting in a word for you with Mr. G Bad."

"Is that right?"

"It's not out of the question, by any means."

" 'Community relations,' huh."

"The new Dogpile store, I have been reliably told, is going to have the most extensive, most encyclopedic, jazz section of any store in the country. Also hip-hop. R and B. Blues. Gospel. Soul. Funk. Somebody will have to run that department, Mr. Stallings."

Archy had a choice: Let the significance of these words sink in, or shed it at once without even giving it a try, like a dog encouraged to wear a hat. "Satan," he said, smiling. "Get thee behind me."

Behind him there was only a snort from Feyd, or maybe it was Bankwell.

"Up to you, of course. Baby on the way," Flowers said. "Time you started making some real money. Get yourself that fat package of benefits they're paying."

"He could offer me a ride in the Dogpile blimp," Archy said. "I am not for sale."

"I love the predictions of a man right before his first child is born," Flowers said. "They're like little snowflakes. Right before the sun comes blazing out the clouds and melts those happy dreams away."

"Living in a dreamland," Bankwell suggested.

"Indeed," said Flowers. "But the rent is coming due."

"Hey, yeah, no, I really want to thank you," Archy said, getting to his feet. "You really helped me organize my thinking about Brokeland all of a sudden. I appreciate it."

"Did I?" Flowers's turn to sound leery, doubting the trend of Archy's thinking. "How so?"

"You made me realize, we have to do the funeral at the *store*. Push back all the record bins, how we have them on those wheels, you know? We can fit all *kinds* of people in there. Just like for the dances we used to put on." It was not easy, dressed in skanky b-ball shorts and a *Captain EO* sweatshirt with cutoff sleeves, but Archy dived down deep and hauled up all the dignity he could snap loose from the sea bottom of his soul. "Councilman, you made me realize, thank you, but me and Mr. Jones and Nat Jaffe and our kind of people, we already got a church of our own. You, too, seemed like at one time, up to not too long ago, a member in good standing. And that church is the church of vinyl."

"The church of vinyl," Flowers said, looking half persuaded. But he shook his head and made a snuffling sound of amusement or disgust. "Well, well."

Archy turned and left the office without looking to the Bankwell side or to the Feyd, admiring as he passed between them the echo of his own phraseology as it lingered in his ears.

"You see that fin in the water, now," Flowers called after him. "You just go on and holler out."

⊙   ⊙   ⊙

Wide as the abyss and rumbling like doom, the El Camino rolled into the street of forsaken toys and came to a stop in front of the house. Shudder, cough, soft bang; then the whole afternoon suffused with an embarrassed silence. Late afternoon in late August, the sky limited only by the hills and the imminent wall of night. Palm tree, sycamore trees, soaked in shadow. Slouch-hat bungalows blazing sunshine at their crowns. Archy took it all in with the ardor of a doomed man. Not that he believed himself to be in any danger or was dying in any but the slowest and most conventional of ways. The clarity and sweetness of the evening, the light and the way it made his chest ache, were only the effects of mild panic, panic both moral and practical.

When he got out of the car, the evening laid its cool palm against his weary brow as if feeling for a temperature. He stood on the sidewalk in front of his house. The El Camino's engine sighed and muttered to itself, settling. A toddler archaeologist searched the sandbox with a red shovel. Probably come up with some ancient bit of toy legend, a Steve Austin head, the head of an Oscar Goldman. *Six million ways I use to run it.* He would tell Gwen about Titus. After that there would be other things to say to various other people. A number of crucial decisions remained as yet unmade. At least he would have gotten to square one, if no farther.

"Stay right there," Gwen said, and it turned out that the instruction was meant for young Mr. Titus Joyner, installed on the bottom step of the front porch. Indeed, it might be surmised from his wife's expression, as she came huffing toward him down the front walk of their house freighted with a big green duffel bag, that rather than stay right where he was, the preferred course for Archy would be to turn around and run for those motherfucking hills.

"I took him to Trader Joe's," she said. She dropped the duffel on the ground between them, and it sounded like fifty pounds of property and possessions to Archy's ear. "There's canned black bean chili and frozen taquitos. Eggs and bacon and pancake mix and syrup."

"Okay," he said. "Whatever you— Okay." He bent down and picked up the duffel. Fifty pounds. No way could the things that Archy Stallings required to live free and equal and happy in this world weigh anything less than five, six hundred pounds.

"I bought him new socks and underpants." She shuddered. "And you had better believe that I disposed of the old ones."

Archy looked at Titus, head in hands, studying his Air Jordans. Archy imagined the new white socks on their plastic bopeeps, the fresh Fruit of the Looms in their crinkling package. It was when he looked at his son and pictured the underpants and socks that he first felt truly ashamed. This boy had no one in the world to ensure, to at least check from time to time, that his underwear was clean. And Archy was so low, of so little account as a man and a father, that Gwen, not even a blood relation, had been obliged to step in like Uncle Sam with a rogue state and intervene. Assume control over the situation.

"Hey," he said. "Hey, man. Titus. Is this how you want it?"

The boy thought it over, taking his time. No flicker of the process of thought was perceptible in his eyes. Then he shrugged.

"Okay, then," Archy said. He reshouldered the strap of the duffel and looked at Gwen. "Thank you." He turned away, getting choked up, trying to cover it with a cough, coughing like his El Camino. His broken old car, his broke barbershop full of old broken records, and the broken-down two-tone double town of Brokeland: That was the inventory of his life.

"Excuse me. *Where* are you going?"

He turned back, understanding that he had failed to understand but not yet fully understanding. Gwen came down the walk, snatched the duffel bag from his shoulder, and staggered off with it to her car. The duffel bag rode shotgun as she backed her Beamer out of the driveway. She rolled down the window on the duffel bag's side and waited while Archy, checking the neighbors' windows, finding a face or two, loped over to the car.

"I am going to tell you how to do it," Gwen said, keeping a tight grip, Archy could see. "It is very simple. This is the only advice I'm ever going to give you, because there is nothing else to really say."

"Okay," Archy said. Even though he saw Gwen sitting in her car, getting ready to drive away with her fifty pounds of freedom, he still did not fully understand that she was leaving him. "I'm listening."

"First I want to make sure you understand. You look confused. Are you confused?"

"Yes, I am a little confused."

"I have a patient in labor. Amy. I am going to work her birth. And then I am going to sleep someplace else. I will not be returning. With me so far?"

Archy nodded.

"That child over there is your son. Titus. He just barely fits on an AeroBed in the back room. I have been told that he's capable of speech but haven't seen too much proof of that so far. Taquitos. Bacon." She counted them off on her fingers. "You got it?"

"Got it."

"Okay. Now here is the advice: You have to make them do things they don't want to do, even when you don't really care if they do them or not," she said. "All the rest is, you know."

It took Archy's brain a couple of nanofarts longer, contemplating this Möbius twist of advice and the fine rear end of Gwen's car as it receded, but at last he understood. The packages of underpants, the cans of Trader Joe's black-bean chili. These were not reproaches thrown at him by an angry woman trying to shame him into paying attention to his child by the sacrifice she was bent on making. They were pieces of information that he was going to need.

"I'm hungry," said the boy when Archy turned back to the house.

⊙   ⊙   ⊙

Whenever his mother and her sisters gathered to work hair and pronounce judgments in the kitchens of Archy's childhood, they had two favorite terms of fulmination. The first thunderbolt they liked to throw, reaching back like Zeus to grab it from a bucket in the corner, was *shameless*. You used to hear that one a lot. It had an ambiguous shimmer. Shameless meant you suffered from a case of laziness so profound that you could not be bothered to hide your misbehavior; but it seemed to suggest also that you had nothing to hide, no need to feel any shame.

The second word lofted by the sisters from the heights of their insurmountable outrage was *scandalous*. This term they collapsed, like a switchblade on its hinge, into two syllables, "scanless," so that when he was young, Archy heard it as a grammatical cousin of the first: an absence *of* that was also a freedom *from*. Scanlessness was a magic invisibility, a moral cloaking device wielded by the shameless in order to render them proof against the all-seeing scanners employed by proper-acting people who knew how to conduct themselves, the latter group reckoned by the sisters to be few in number, roughly coextensive with themselves.

Shameless and scanless Archy ducked into Walter Bankwell's car, thus almost by definition up to no good. Back in the day, the vehicle in question would have been a hard-used but well-loved 1981 Datsun B210, the blue of testicular vasocongestion, its rear seat exchanged like the works of Doc Brown's DeLorean for the flux capacitor of a pair of Alpine speakers capable of shaking loose the screws of time and space. Today, twelve-thirty P.M., at the secret bend of Thirty-seventh Street, a rendezvous chosen by Archy according to ancient habits of stealth, the vehicle in question was a sterling 1986 Omni GLH, turbocharged and nasty. Caution-yellow with black Band-Aid strips, its exhaust tuned to a baritone Gerry Mulligan growl. Lest Archy or anyone else currently inhabiting the surface of Sol III miss the homage intended by the paint job to the jumpsuit worn by former Oaklander Bruce Lee in his last, incomplete masterpiece, *The Game of Death*, Walter himself was attired in a vintage Adidas tracksuit, bee-yellow with a wide bee-black stripe up the side, and the requisite pair of bumblebee Onitsuka Tigers.

"Oh my goodness," Archy said, aching with the beauty of the car as he swung his bulk into it, favoring his old running buddy with a long, slow head-to-toe of mock admiration. "Uma Thurman! Love your work."

Walter broke off a piece of a smile and tucked it into his left cheek as if reserving it for future use. Giving off a vibe of irritation, of feeling put upon, as if he had better things to do, wilder geese to chase. He had e-mailed Archy from a Dogpile domain, destination and intentions left unstated and mysterious apart from a terse if not insulting (however accurate) allusion to Archy's inability to decline a free meal.

" 'Uma Thurman.' " He shook his head, sorry for Archy, disappointed in him. "That ain't even a insult."

Archy considered. "You may be right."

"When the mosquito bites her? And my girl Uma comes out that coma . . . ?" Walter laid two fingers against the wheel. "It's, like, a simple two-step process. Step one, regain consciousness. Step two, tear it *up*." He marveled. "When she chews that guy's tongue right out his head . . ."

"Is that even possible?"

"Matter of fact," Walter continued, ignoring the question, "I wish I *was* Uma Thurman. Then I would surely not have to be riding around the tired end of Temescal with no beret-wearing, soul-patch dee-vo-tay of Negritude, Charles Mingus–impersonating motherfucker."

Walter put the GLH in gear, and they loped away from the curb with the engine blowing low notes.

"Ain't like you got the way you are from people changing their minds about feeding you."

There was merit in this reasoning that Archy could not discount. So he removed and folded on his lap the jacket of his linen suit, caramel brown, one-button, knife-narrow 1962 lapel; found the bar that let the seat roll back, all the way back; hooked his feet, shod in sugar-brown size-15 alligator ankle-zip boots, together at the ankles; adjusted the angle of his genuine Basque beret, also the color of brown sugar; and shut the fuck up. He had a feeling this mystery trip might be a sequel to his conversation yesterday with Chan Flowers, but his conscience wouldn't let him take the idea any further than that. As they pulled out, he looked over his shoulder out the rear window to make sure Nat wasn't standing there on the sidewalk.

Old Kung Fu, check him out. All those years scuffling and fucking up down in L.A., offering up his face to any door that cared to shut on it, trying to keep distance between himself and the uncle who loved him too strongly. Now here he was, back in Oakland, working for the fifth richest black man in America, driving this flawlessly restored piece of carflesh, blasting some Zapp or maybe it was solo Troutman on the in-dash factory cassette player, and in general, as he and Archy would have put it during their salad days, *keepin it surreal.*

"So, like, seriously," Archy said. "Where we going?"

But Walter's only reply was to get on the 24 heading west, and before long they were on the 880 with only Hayward, San Jose, and Los Angeles between them and the bleak unrestauranted expanse of Antarctica.

"Someplace by the airport?" Archy guessed. Still one or two old-school dives there, tucked in among the union halls and standardized burger units along the renovated stretch of Hegenburger, dark sub-aquatic holes for labor lawyers to crawl into, bikers, baggage handlers, short-haul stews adding up their croutons in their Weight Watchers booklets. Nothing to look forward to that Archy knew about, except insofar as he lived in constant expectation of discovering or being led, even along the most unlikely and brand-blasted frontage road, to some great unknown plateful of marvels.

"Supposed to surprise you," said Walter. Boy had that raspy voice anyway, but something seemed to catch at the back of his throat, a pill of hesitation. Archy replayed the e-mail in his mind, certain that it had included words that could be paraphrased as *I will buy you lunch.* "Case you too blind, dumb, and stupid to come along under your own recognizance."

"It's a restaurant, though. Right?"

"Keep that a surprise, too," Walter said. "Just for a little bit longer."

Archy's imagination starting to run wild on him, picturing maybe some kind of farm-food bullshit where you had to slaughter your own pig, a deep-fried termite stand, something like that.

"Because, swear to God, if you're trying to punk me—"

"Whoa, ease up, Turtle. I straight-up guarantee, you going be in the hands of a excellent chef. All right?"

Universal and catholic in his appetites, Archy sat back, soothed by this information, allowing the prospect of an enigmatic luncheon—maybe *al pastor* sliced from the rotisserie by some obscure genius in a taco truck—to drive from his mind worrisome thoughts of the boy who was, by some loop in life's tangling, now his responsibility. Stoneface, built and colored so much like Luther Stallings, the sight of the boy like the touch of pincers to Archy's heart, stinging him in the past and the present at the same time, an ache that leaped decades, skipped a generation. Or maybe one of those Korean barbecues where the lady came and dealt out a whole deck of little plates and bowls of kimchi on the table in front of you like she was going to tell your fortune in chili and pickles, let you cook your own short rib sliced thin as lunch meat over your own private grill. For a minute Archy allowed a Korean cookfire in his mind to burn away the bitter consciousness, pressing at him all the time, of the hurt and disappointment he had caused and would no doubt go on causing, through his scanlessness and shamelessness, to the woman he loved. A waffle truck, a gleaming chrome bus that dished up chicken and waffles, where the fate of Brokeland Records, of his long and tricky friendship with Nat Jaffe, could all be drowned in a ribbon of pancake syrup, spreading across the crisp grid of an imagined waffle to impinge, with its sweet hint of smoke, on a crispy drumstick. All those problems, and the loss of Mr. Jones, the calls and arrangements Archy needed to make—so much smoke and vapor to be sucked up into exhaust fans roaring over Hunan woks, bubbling pots of *birria*, grill tops hissing with onions for a patty melt or a Joe's Special.

Then Archy saw, and realized, the surprise. It swung with a slow majesty from its tether at the end of a high steel mast that was in turn mounted on the bed of a tractor-trailer, at the farthest reaches of the Oakland airport, along a bleak, half-wild stretch of marshland.

"The blimp," Archy said. It filled the windshield of the GLH, shiny and black, emblazoned on its flank with a red paw print and bold red slab-serif type. "The Dogpile blimp."

"Ain't a blimp, it's a zeppelin." That raspy Q-Tip voice of Walter's turned soft, choked. Betraying, Archy might have said, possibly the slightest hint of fear. "Got the rigid structure."

"Oh, right."

"Blimp's just a bag."

They rolled up to a checkpoint manned by a pock-faced rent-a-cop where Walter exchanged his driver's license for a long hard fish-eye, which, upon return of his license, he steadily countered. Walter rolled the car right up into the shadow of the airship, and they got out, slammed doors. The zeppelin appeared to be as long as a block of Telegraph Avenue, as tall as Kaiser Hospital.

Standing there, righting his beret, verifying the tuck of his shirt-tails, smoothing the wrinkles from the front of his butterscotch suit, Archy regarded the big black visual pun on centuries of white male anatomical anxiety and felt it trying, like Kubrick's melismatic monolith, to twist the wiring of his brain. The late-August sun goaded him, the way Walter had always goaded him, urging him to give the slip to the thunderbolt-throwing aunties who dwelled in his soul, to emerge from the doomed cavern of Brokeland Records and the gloomy professional prospect of endless Dumpster dives and crate digs, every day dropping like a spindled platter on top of the next, Z out the cash register with its feeble tally, get home at the end of the day humping your box of scratched and moldering treasure to have your wife harangue you in instructive tones with quotes from some self-help book on the moral imperative to strip all that was not essential from one's life. To throw over all ballast and soar. Starting with, say, your record collection, just shed the whole off-gassing pile in a scatter of 180-gram Frisbees and rise up. The high blue curtain of sky overhead, the tender wetlands reek of Alameda on the breeze that took hold of Archy's necktie, seemed to hold a promise to redeem the unredeemed promise that he had always carried around, creased and tattered, in the billfold of his life.

"Lunch, motherfucker," Walter explained.

⊙   ⊙   ⊙

Like a hoard of family diamonds sewn into the hems and hidden pockets of an exile's cloak, Oakland was salted secretly with wonders, even here, at its fetid, half-rotten raggedy-ass end.

The zeppelin's gondola was a streamlined dining car formed from some black polymer glossy as a vinyl record. It hovered just above the ground, a cushion for the reclining god. Through its front viewports, a pair of typecast pilots in captain's hats saluted the arriving passengers, then resumed their preparations for ascent, fiddling with knobs, dialing in shit on their big old zeppelin mixing board. Between the new arrivals and the gondola, a laterally oriented brown man in a toque and white smock stood at a pushcart grill, practicing relentless artistry on two dozen big prawns with a pair of brass tongs and a brush. Wild-style lettering sprayed onto the front of the grill read THE HUNGRY SAMOAN.

"Don't tell me," Archy began, then stopped, for he was not yet prepared to understand or to accept what he knew to be the situation vis-à-vis lunch: that it was to be eaten in the sky. He eyed the smoke as it knit and unknit in dense skeins trailing from the grill top, catching along the flank of the airship.

"Filled with helium," Walter said, following the worried course of Archy's gaze, looking worried himself despite the cool expository tone. Self-reassuring. "Shit's inert. Can't burn. Can't interact with nothing."

Then a hatch in the side of the gondola sighed and swung open, divulging the airship's secret cargo: a basalt monolith, the very thing to set half-apes dreaming of the stars. Black knit polo shirt, skull polished like the knob on an Oscar. Gold-rimmed sunglasses, gold finger rings, black Levi's, Timberland loafers. Pausing at the top of a fold-down stair for a display of freestyle looming, brother looked like a celebrity golfer or as if perhaps he had recently eaten a celebrity golfer. Shoulders thrown back, chest out, he moved with a herky-jerk stop-motion fluidity, a Harryhausen Negro, mythic and huge. Behind him, tall and broad-shouldered yet dwarfed by the dude from *The Golden Voyage of Sinbad*, came a tea-brown handsome man, lithe, slender. He stood considering his guests on the top step, then hopped down and made slowly for Archy and Walter, past the bodyguard, breaking out from behind his blocker, some kind of joint pain or old injury a slight hitch in his gait.

"Archy Stallings," said Gibson Goode, like he was repeating the sly punch line to a joke that had made him laugh recently. "Thanks for coming."

"Yeah, thanks for, uh, having me," Archy said, his voice petering out at the pronoun and the unworthiness it designated. Walter put his fingers to his lips, corking a laugh as Archy fell all over himself trying not to fall all over himself. "Gibson Goode! I mean!" Archy laughing at himself now. "Goddamn."

Print it on the back of the man's Topps card, six-six, 230 pounds, Emperor of the Universe in 1999 when he led the NFC in touchdowns, completions, passer rating, and threw three four-hundred-yard games. Still long and wiry, built more like a center fielder than a QB, mostly leg with that loose equine sense of motion, Gibson Goode, aka G Bad. Head cropped to leave a faint, even scatter of coal dust. Wearing a pair of heavy tortoiseshell sunglasses with dark green lenses that left his eyes to go about the cold business of empire unobserved.

"What can I pour you?" he said.

"I don't drink . . ." Archy said, and stopped. He hated how this sounded whenever he found himself obliged to say it. Lord knew he would not relish the prospective company of some mope-ass motherfucker who flew that grim motto from his flagpole. ". . . alcohol," he added. Only making it worse, the stickler for detail, ready to come out with a complete list of beverages he was willing to consume. Next came the weak effort to redeem himself by offering a suggestion of past indulgence: "Anymore." Finally, the slide into unwanted medical disclosure: "Bad belly."

"Yeah," Goode said looking appropriately sober, "I quit drinking, too. Coke, then? San Pellegrino? Sweet tea?"

"You going to like my sweet tea," said the Hungry Samoan gravely. It appeared to be in the nature of a command.

"Yo, T.," Goode said to the giant in the Timberlands, his bodyguard, majordomo. Wordless and obedient as a golem, the giant returned to the gondola. When Archy stepped up behind Goode into the cabin of the misnomered Dogpile blimp, the giant had a tall tumbler apiece of passionflower tea for Archy and Goode, and a can of Tecate for Walter, with a lime-wedge eyebrow.

The interior of the gondola was cool and snug, the whole thing molded continuously into a glossy surface of black plastic trimmed with brushed aluminum and covered, wherever it was likely to encounter a pair of human buttocks, in spotted pony skin. On the spectrum of secret lairs, it fell somewhere between mad genius bent on world domination and the disco-loving scion of a minor emirate. The decor made references, of which Archy approved, to *Diabolik* and the David Lynch *Dune*.

Goode dropped back to let Archy admire freely. "Welcome aboard the *Minnie Riperton*," he said.

Walter stole a look toward Archy, who rocked back, caught off guard.

"Seriously," Archy said.

"Seriously." Goode was ready for it, had a line. "She's black. She is beautiful. And she goes really high."

The five-octave F-above-high-C singing voice of Minnie Riperton, who died of cancer in 1977 at the age of thirty-one, was an avatar of Archy's mother in his memory; always a vanishing quality to it, an ethereal warmth. The two women, Minnie and Mauve, even looked alike, Cherokee noses, eyes large, deep brown, and pain-haunted. At the unexpected invocation of the name, Archy's heart leaped and he grew confused, assuming for a dreamlike instant that Goode had named the zeppelin in his mother's honor.

"Thank you," he said. "That's so nice of you."

Goode looked at Walter or, at any rate, appeared to be regarding Archy's old friend from behind the blast shield of his D&Gs.

Walter shrugged. "I told you," he said. "You got to feed the man."

"Skip breakfast?" Goode said.

Archy said, "Never."

Goode hung halfway out of the hatch, gripping the frame, and called to the chef to ask him how long it would be until lunch. Chef held up three thick fingers, then commenced plating lunch with DJ aplomb. Two minutes and forty-eight seconds later, Archy found himself sitting at a posse-sized plastic table topped with speckled laminate, called upon to conduct deep research into a plate piled with some kind of Thai-Samoan South-Central barbecued shrimp thing served, with plentiful Sriracha, over coconut rice. Black-eyed peas in a hoisin garlic sauce. A scatter of okra tempura doused in sweet and peppery vinegar.

"Kind of a soul-Asian fusion-type deal," Archy said.

"Hey," Goode said. "That's your thing, right? Soul-jazz. Soul-funk. Walter tells me you like to work the hyphens. Walter— Ah, shit."

Walter had his eyes closed, holding himself like a plateful of water, as, with an eager kick at its traces, the airship bucked gravity and took to the sky. Goode smiled, slowly shaking his head. "Boy spent his life cutting up dead folks, telling a bunch of homicidal rapping gangbangers they got dropped by their label, but he's afraid to go up in a damn *balloon*."

"Uhh," said Walter.

Swiftly, Oakland fell away beneath them. The Bay Area shook out its rumpled coverlet, gray and green and crazy salt pans, rent and slashed and stitched by feats of engineering. Twin Peaks, Tamalpais, then Mount Diablo rising up beyond the hills. Archy had flown in and out of his hometown a dozen times or more but never in such breathless silence, never with such a sense of liberation, of having come unhooked. An airplane used force and fuel and tricks of physics to fight its way aloft, but the *Minnie Riperton* was returning to its rightful home. It belonged in the sky.

When they reached one thousand feet, Walter swallowed and opened his eyes. "Oh, the humanity," he said.

Archy got up to tour the windows, meet the captains, squint through the shipboard telescope at a far-off disturbance in the haze that he was told to call Lassen Peak. He checked out a bunch of snaps and candids pinned to a corkboard beside the jump seat where T., the bodyguard, sat behind his gold-rimmed sunglasses, containing, as a fist might contain a bauble, his unimaginable thoughts. Pictures of G Bad, the man posed against varied nocturnal backgrounds of city lights or flashbulb darkness with famous singers and actors, black and white, holding the Golden Globes they had won for directing or starring in Dogpile films or their Grammys for Dogpile records. Or caught up in the thick of various posses, or maybe it was the same posse, an ontogeny shaped by time and fashion and the whims of Gibson Goode. Brothers in caps and game jerseys, smiling or blank-faced, throwing up gang signs, holding glasses and bottles. Women of the planet dressed in candy colors, necklines taking daring chances, eyelids done up lustrous as one of Sixto Cantor's custom paint jobs. Gibson Goode looking exactly the same in every picture, sunglasses, enigmatic half-smile, Super Bowl ring, might as well be a blown-up life-size picture of himself mounted on a sheet of foam core.

"My peeps," Goode said, taking the pin from one of the photos on the corkboard. "Check out last week."

He passed the picture to Archy. It showed a particularly unruly group of ladies, strewn as if by a passing hurricane along the laps of a number of gentlemen, among them Walter Bankwell, who peered out from behind the wall of horizontal sisters with an expression of evident panic.

"My boy Walter's first flight."

"I never knew him to be afraid of heights," Archy said.

"I hear you and him go way back."

"Heard from him or somebody else?"

"Might have heard it from a number of sources."

You do that. And maybe, you never know, I'm the one ends up putting in a word for you with Mr. G Bad. Undertaking motherfucker worked fast. Wanted to get hold of Luther Stallings with considerable urgency, indeed. Archy telling him, *I'll think about it.*

"So where's the posse?" Archy said, nodding toward the bulletin board. "You leave them at home?"

"Yeah, they okay for a party cruise, but they don't appreciate the, uh, stately pace of the journey up from Long Beach," Goode said. "They just a waste of time anyway. Nobody but Tak around, I can get a lot of work done."

Trying to let Archy know what a serious guy he was, snaps and candids to the contrary, sending himself like his own stand-in to attend such trifling matters while his real self went on tirelessly planning conquests, a hip-hop Master of the World in his Vincent Price airship.

When they reached the featureless blue-gray world beyond the Golden Gate, the pilot brought them back around and they bore down on Oakland again, watching from the port-side window as their hometown gathered its modest splendors.

"Highland Hospital," Goode said, pointing. "I was born there."

"Me, too," Archy said.

"Moved down to L.A. when I was three, but I came back in the summertime, Christmastime. Whenever school got out. Lived with my grandmother in the Longfellow district. Her brother had a record store for a time. Was on Market and Forty-fifth, over by the Laundromat there."

"House of Wax," Archy said. It was almost a question. "Seriously? I used to go in there. Your grandfather, he was, uh, kind of a portly man?"

"My uncle. Great-uncle. Uncle Reggie was pretty much spherical."

"I remember him," Archy said. And then, as if the line that hooked it had been snagged all these years on some deep arm of coral, an afternoon bobbed to the surface of his memory. A boy, the offhand sketch of a boy, reading a comic book or a magazine, long feet hooked through the slats of a metal stool, a pair of brand-new Top Tens. "Maybe I even remember you."

Goode lifted a hand to his cheek and patted it as if checking the closeness of his morning shave or monitoring a toothache.

"You used to read comic books?" Archy said.

"Most definitely."

"You were reading a comic book." Archy took hold of the line with both hands and hauled up the afternoon, streaming years like water. "I'm thinking it was a Marvel book, but—"

"It was *Luke Cage*," Goode said, picking off the memory from Archy like a bobbled pass. Too positive about it, stripping the ball.

"Was it?"

"Yeah, *Luke Cage, Power Man*. And we got into a discussion, a long discussion," turning to Walter, who lifted his head from his hands and stared, the food on his plate sitting there untouched. "Got ourselves way down deep."

With the sunglasses, the smile that twisted Goode's mouth could not be read for levels of irony or nostalgia.

"Well," Archy began.

"This motherfucker was peeling off all these sophisticated interpretations. Inner meanings. In *Luke Cage*. Talking about the American penal system as portrayed in Marvel Comics. Referencing all kinds of heavy reading materials. Eleven, twelve years old, telling me what, like, Frantz Fanon has to say about the possibility of black superheroes in a white superpower structure and whatnot."

"Huh," Walter said, looking doubtful, life returning to him in the form of irritation. This claim was almost certainly 90 to 97 percent false. The shimmer of what Archy remembered from that afternoon at House of Wax was only an awkward mutual series of passwords exchanged, the chance encounter with a random nerd brother in an unexpected location. Right up to this very instant Archy possessed no theory of black superheroics, only a vague idea of who Frantz Fanon was, and apart from the redoubtable Black Panther, particularly during the operatic run of McGregor-Graham on the book, Archy had never taken particular interest in the skin color of the comic book superheroes he loved, most of whom, now that he thought about it, had been white. The world in which those characters lived and operated was plainly not the world in which Archy lived, and on the whole that was the way he preferred it. On that long-distant afternoon at House of Wax, there had been no theory spun, no deep knowledge displayed. Goode was flattering him, either because he was a flatterer or because he wanted to see if Archy was a hound for flattery. Archy had to admit that there was something gratifying about the flicker of envy he saw in Walter's eyes as Goode falsely lionized his critical acumen at eleven.

"You have a better memory than I do," Archy suggested, guarded, leery, unable to shake a feeling not just that he was stepping out on Nat Jaffe, up here dining on shrimp and flattery and all kinds of piquant sauces, but that he was in over his head, that he was going to be edged into doing something or agreeing to something that he did not want to do or agree to, into something at least that he did not understand, some kind of business being transacted by Goode and Flowers that would prove costly to Luther Stallings, maybe other people, too. To judge from things Archy had read about G Bad, as well as from memories of watching him on television as he conducted instantaneous Einstein-deep analyses in the pocket under a heavy rush (not to mention the simple fact that he was visiting the man in the cabin of his personal zeppelin that flew on the gas of burning dollars), Gibson Goode was smarter than Archy on many levels. "But I remember you, and I remember your uncle."

Goode got up and went over to a beautiful Thorens semi-automatic, perched atop a low plastic cabinet that formed part of the plastic wall of the cabin. On a shelf along the bottom of the cabinet, beneath the turntable, a row of LPs lounged like boys at lazy angles. Beside the albums, a steel mesh box held a couple of dozen 45s. Goode flipped through them, chose one, and did what he needed to do to the turntable to switch it over to forty-five revolutions per minute.

"Name that tune," he said.

He lowered the tonearm, and from a pair of speaker grilles, a drum pattern emerged and repeated itself, *b-boom boom CHICK!* in 4/4 time, the kick muffled, mixed very dry and miked with the attention to detail that marked 1970s recording of drums but partaking, through having been sampled so many times by subsequent hip-hop acts, of a timelessness beyond period or style.

"Manzel," Archy said, knowing that he was being tested, thinking it was kind of a bullshit move and yet incapable of resisting the challenge, which was hardly a challenge at all. " 'Midnight Theme.' That was on the, uh, Fraternity label. 1975."

The single played on, adding textures, stacking up layers. A moody wash of piano, a stab of ARP strings. The swirl and growl of a Hammond B-3 played through the whirling orrery of a Leslie cabinet.

Scritch-scratch guitar, coming in on the 2, along with paired lines of space-funk Minimoog that sidled in, late arrivals, to carry the melody and bass line, that Minimoog sound popping the bubble of timelessness and returning the track, comfortably, to its home in the mid-1970s.

"Sounds good," Archy said. "Nice pressing."

"Know where I bought it?" Goode said.

⊙ ⊙ ⊙

"Was on Saturday afternoon," Goode said. "Walter here had told me about you, your store. Thought I should check it out. I had to be up here anyway. So I came in the store, your boy was there. Nat, right? Said you was home, gone for the day, some shit."

"Yeah, I had to meet somebody." Archy kept his thoughts off that last encounter with Mr. Jones, ran back the tape on every conversation he'd had with Nat since Saturday that had contained the words "Gibson Goode," looking for hints of guilty knowledge, a secret suppressed. "Damn. MVP quarterback media mogul comes in our store, cagey motherfucker never says a word to me."

It did not strike Archy as the kind of thing Nat was likely to keep quiet about, let alone forget.

"He didn't know me," Goode said. "I was just a customer. Between you and me, dude didn't seem too keen on making conversation. Up there at the cash register all mumbling to himself, making these fucked-up Keith Jarrett noises, like *hnnh*. Only wasn't any piano around."

"He has days like that," Archy said.

"To be honest," Goode said, "I mean, look here, y'all have a nice store and everything. Really nice. Lot of charm, inventory goes deep, goes wide. But it wasn't just your partner that seemed kinda out of it. Business seemed pretty fucking slow."

"We're doing all right."

"Oh, really? I stayed twenty-two minutes, I was the only one in the place the whole time. That place was *desolate*. On a Saturday afternoon."

"But I mean, Saturday was a beautiful day," remembering the scent of honeysuckle in sunshine, the knock-knock of Mr. Jones's pipe against the sidewalk, "lot of folks were probably—"

"Your partner up by the cash register, all groaning and moaning. Felt like I was in the motherfucking *Omega Man* in there. Last man alive, trapped with a zombie."

For the first time since they came in sight of the *Minnie Riperton*, Walter smiled and burped up something that sounded like a laugh. Archy turned away, watching the approach of Berkeley as they turned to the north. Anger and shame braided themselves like wires through his interior cabinetry, with shame carrying the greater flow. He did not like to stand there while G Bad or anyone tore off woof tickets about Brokeland, which, along with some of the sounds that had issued at times from his Fender Jazz Bass, Archy had always considered the only truly beautiful thing he had ever made. He knew that he and Nat were financially circling the spindle in an ever narrowing gyre. Now here came this man who could afford, even in these times of failing record chains and of infinite free downloadable libraries that fit in your hip pocket, to open a *bangin* used vinyl store, five times as big as Brokeland and tenfold deep and, just for the glory and goodness of it, let it fail, forever, inexhaustibly bankrolled by his media empire, his licensed image, his alchemical touch with ghetto real estate. Breezing into Brokeland on a Saturday afternoon, a king in mufti, come to lay his sandal upon the necks of the conquered.

Archy felt ashamed, too, remembering the longing that had stirred in him, not half an hour before, to throw over, once and for all, the burden of the store. Remembering the first time he had met Nat Jaffe, after that last-minute wedding gig up in the Oakland hills, Archy fresh from the Saudi desert, dragging his honorably discharged ass through the streets of Bush I America, disoriented, lonely, unable to connect to anyone, black or white. How he and Nat had sat on the floor of the Jaffes' living room till five o'clock in the morning, little Julie asleep, Aviva out wrestling some other new human into the world. Nat rolled fat numbers packed with the Afghan butthair, threaded and hoary, that he routinely scored at that time, and stoned and cross-legged, they fell through the circular portals of Nat's record collection, one after another, flat-out tumbled awestruck arm in arm like that team of chrononaut dwarfs in *Time Bandits*, through those magic wormholes in the fabric of reality. Archy was so impressed by the scope and detail but most of all by the passion—relentless, nettlesome, ecstatic, inspiring—of Nat's knowledge when it came to music, "in all its many riches," from Storyville whorehouse rags to South Bronx block-party sound-system battles. It had been a long time since Archy had seen a man so willing to betray himself by exuberance, by enthusiasm for things that could not be killed, fucked, or fed upon. Nat already dreaming of opening his own store, lacking only half the cash, half the records, and half the foolishness necessary for the undertaking.

"My partner is a cantankerous pain in the motherfucking ass," Archy said, recalling the eagerness with which he had leaped at the chance to make up that holy trinity of shortfalls. "Also my best friend."

He gazed down at Golden Gate Fields as it slid under them, the grandstand half full of losers, the horses blowing like confetti along the futile oval. They passed over the giant oil tanks of Richmond, ranked along the slopes like secondhand turntables on a pawnshop shelf. "Midnight" came to an end. The tonearm worked itself loose of the label's edge and sought its well-deserved rest.

"Now," Goode said. "I know you already know what it is we are planning to do in Temescal, and I gather the councilman already made a suggestion of what I might like to obtain from you in that direction."

"You're offering me a job," Archy said.

"You could look at it that way. Or you could look at it, I am offering you a *mission*."

"That's right," Walter said.

"I am building a monastery, if you like," Goode said, warming up, "for the practice of vinyl kung fu. And I am asking you to come be my abbot. And, yeah," with the enigmatic half-smile, "that does make me the Buddha, but don't go too far down that analogy, 'cause, check it out, now I'm a bend it a little. What I am asking you to do, to be— Look here, did you ever read this book, Taku over there turned me on to it, *A Canticle for Leibowitz*?"

"Good book."

"You know it. All right, then, look at it this way. The world of black music has undergone in many ways a kind of apocalypse, you follow me? You look at the landscape of the black idiom in music now, it is *post-apocalyptic*. Jumbled-up mess of broken pieces. Shards and samples. Gangsters running in tribes. That is no disrespect to the music of the past two decades. Taken on its own terms. I love it. I *love* it. Life without Nas, without the first Slum Village album, without, shit, *The Miseducation of Lauryn Hill*? Can't imagine it. Can't even imagine. And I'm not saying, just because we got sampling, we got no innovation happening. Black music *is* innovation. At the same time, we got a continuity to the traditions, even in the latest hip-hop joint. Signifying, playing the dozens. Church music, the blues, if you wanna look hard. But face it, I mean, a lot has been lost. A whole lot. Ellington, Sly Stone, Stevie Wonder, Curtis Mayfield, we got nobody of that caliber even *hinted* at in black music nowadays, I'm talking about genius, *composers*, know what I'm saying? Quincy Jones. Charles Stepney. Weldon *Irvine*. Shit, knowing how to play the fuck out of your *instrument*. Guitar, saxophone, bass, drums, we used to *own* those motherfuckers. Trumpet! We were the landlords, white players had to *rent* that shit from us. Now, black kid halfway to a genius comes along? Like RZA? Can't even play a motherfucking kazoo. Can't do nothing but 'quote.' Like those Indians down in Mexico nowadays, skinny-ass, bean-eating motherfucker sleeping with his goat on top of a rock used to be a temple that could predict what time a solar eclipse was going to happen.

"I'm not going to blame nobody, and I don't know what the reason is, because I haven't studied it, and like with everything misfortunate in life, I bet there's ten, twelve reasons for musical civilization getting wiped out by this here particular firestorm, what's he call it in the book—?"

Goode glanced over at the bodyguard, Taku, who sat immersed in a copy of *Shonen Jump* magazine. " 'The Deluge of Flame,' " Taku said, not looking up.

"Record companies. MTV. Corporate radio. Crack cocaine. Budget cuts to music programs, high school bands. All that, none of that.

Doesn't make no difference. I'm saying we are living in the *aftermath*. All's we got is a lot of broken pieces. And you been picking those pieces up, and dusting them off, and keeping them all nice and clean, and that's commendable. Truly. What I'm offering you is a chance not just to hang them up on the wall of your museum, there, maybe sell one every now and then for some white dentist or tax attorney to take home and hang on his wall. I'm offering you, I'm saying, come on, let's really put them out there where the *kids* are, where the future's spending its money. Teach them. Explain what all those broken-up old pieces mean, why it's all *important*. Then maybe one of those kids, maybe he's going to come along, learn what you have to teach, and start to put things back together. If you feel me."

"Huh," said Archy. "So you want me to be Saint Leibowitz of the Funk."

"More like, T., who was it? In that, what's it? *Foundation*."

"Hari Seldon," Taku said.

"You can be Hari Seldon," Goode said. "Preserving all the science till civilization gets reborn, man had a whole planet—"

"Terminus," said Archy, right before the bodyguard could come out with it. Taku nodded once, solemn.

"Planet of the Negroes," Walter said. "That's what you should call your band. Y'all still play, right? You and your boy Nat?"

"When we can get the gigs."

"What instrument he play, piano?"

"Some guitar. Mostly piano."

"Like Bill Evans."

"A touch."

"Elton John. Barry Manilow."

"Lennie Tristano," Goode suggested.

"Actually," Archy said, "Nat digs Tristano. Tristano sang at his birthday party, bar mitzvah, some kind of shit like that. And we already got a name, Walter, the Wakanda Philharmonic." He looked at Goode, calling him out on the boyhood reminiscences, the secret comics-nerd lore. "I know, given our history, you can dig the reference."

"I like it," Goode said. "And speaking of names. How do you like this: the Cochise Jones Memorial Beats Department?"

"That's nice. That's a nice tribute. You ought to do that."

"Come over, then. I will. I know you don't believe me. But I'm not in it for the money. Record stores, brick and mortar, they're dying. Large and small. Any fool can see that."

"And so alls I have to do in return for this generosity? Is come up with an address for my pops. Is that right? Let Bank and Feyd pay the man a visit so they can give Luther something he wants very badly."

"I don't know too much about that," Goode said. "Don't want to know. Less I have to do with Luther Stallings, the better."

"You know him?"

From behind his *Shonen Jump*, Taku made a kind of rhinoceros noise.

"We met," G Bad said. "Brother came to see me, to be honest, I have to say, he actually did help me out with this Golden State deal. For real. But that was an accident, a side effect. Luther wasn't trying to help nobody but himself."

"You do know him."

"I'll say this: The man already got himself mixed up in it. Nothing you going to do can mix him up worse."

"Mr. Goode," Archy said. "Truly, I thank you for your generous offer, and how you took me up in your zeppelin, and fed me some truly delicious prawns. Oh, man! That hint of mole in the marinade? But even if I, like, followed my general lifelong policy and left the old man out of it? I already *have* a record store. A whole store that's my own, half mine, not just a department in somebody else's chain outlet, with bar codes and inventory software and probably a little badge with my name on it." He tried to look through the lenses of Goode's sunglasses, to send some Nat Jaffe–style gamma rays right on through that polarized plastic. " 'If you feel me.' "

"By this time next year," Goode said, "you won't have a store. You know that. You already dipping one wing in the water. I got three storage units in West Covina, any one of them carries inventory bigger and just as motherfucking deep as what you and your partner have on offer, at an average of three to five dollars less per disc, not to mention all the new music, too. Compilations, box sets, books and video relating to music, I open my doors four blocks away from you with all that, you are through."

"No doubt," Archy said, turning away from Goode to face the wide strip of windows at the front of the car.

"Aw," Goode said. "You're just being *stubborn* now. Stubbornness in the service of a mistaken notion is a vanity and a sin."

"I have proven that many times in my life," Archy agreed.

Gibson Goode joined Archy at the front window. They had turned east of north, and a great barren stretch of empty land forked with silver stretched out below them.

"That's Port Chicago down there," Goode said. "You know about that?"

"Yeah. Munitions ship exploded in World War II. Killed a mess of black sailors. Had to work as longshoremen in the Jim Crow navy. My grandfather was there, he got blinded, burned his lungs. Died like a year later."

"My mom's uncle was left deaf in both ears," G Bad said. "Standing outside having a cigarette on a cargo pier almost a mile away."

"I heard it was really a A-bomb," Walter said. "That's what I heard."

Archy had heard this, too. A test bomb, pre-Hiroshima, that detonated prematurely as it was being loaded on a ship bound for some Pacific atoll. The whole thing covered up without too much trouble, all the victims of the blast being black, with no recourse except to keep on being dead. He did not entirely disbelieve it, thinking of the breast cancer that afterward clustered in Marin County, in the women of his family.

"Fireball was three miles wide," Goode said. "Air was filled with burning Negroes falling out of the sky. Only thing they ever did wrong was try too hard and work too fast to fight somebody else's war."

"It was their war," Archy said.

"Maybe. And Oakland was their town. Our town."

"Giving me a history lesson," Archy observed. "Going to tell me now's my chance to make history as the presidente for life of the Cochise Jones Department of the Oakland Dogpile Thang. And strike a blow for the race by bailing out on my white oppressor, on the Man who was forcing my granddaddy to load so many carpet bombs so fast that he came raining down in pieces."

"I might of been headed in that direction," Goode said, rubbing his chin, little crooked smile. "Be honest, I was pretty much scrambling."

"Got me up here with my old running buddy. Put those classic sounds on through an excellent system, maybe have too much bottom in your EQ settings, but whatever. Start me reminiscing about Luke Cage, House of Wax. Feed me all that good food. Playing on my nostalgia *and* my stomach, that is a highly effective approach."

"So forget about the mission, Turtle," Walter said. "It's a damn job." He had stationed himself on a bench at the precise center of the gondola, equidistant and out of view of all the windows. "Take it or don't. Sooner you say something, sooner we can land this motherfucker."

"It is a job," Goode said. "And from what I understand, congratulations are in order, right? Got a baby on the way? Based on my observations of what you have going on down there at Brokeland Records, you all living up to the name so well, I'd say you might soon be looking for any kind of job. Forget about a sweet opportunity like this one, which, furthermore, as I tried to explain, has a chance to give you something important and meaningful to do with your life. Make your son proud of you."

His son. Goode meant the unborn one, possibly a daughter who would be highly likely not to give anything resembling a fuck about the transition of the James Brown band from the Bernard Odum to the Bootsy Collins era; but Archy thought at once of Titus, face like a false panel, some unknown and possibly hostile intelligence peering out at his father and the world through the Judas holes of his eyes. Archy had only to consult the map of his own feelings toward the father who had abandoned him to know that a feeling of filial pride was the farthest kingdom, unreachable, beyond deserts and ice caps and seas. A job. A baby. Sons, daughters, wives, and lovers. Paychecks and payrolls.

"How far you can go in this thing?" Archy said abruptly, as they sailed beyond the void of dust and brackish silver where seven hundred Negroes had come to grief. Bearing for Mount Lassen, the Yukon, the moon.

"Huh?" Goode said.

"What's the effective range?"

"On a tank of fuel? Five hundred miles. Except for gas and supplies, I mean, she don't ever have to come down."

"That sounds good," Archy said. "That sounds like a plan."

III

A Bird *of* Wide Experience

I f sorrow is the consequence of pattern spoiled, then the bird was
grieving, seeking comfort in the patter and tap of the baby's shoes
against the wooden floor, Rolando whaling away like Billy Cobham
with the heels of his little Air Jordans, working himself around the
room on his back, a human dust mop making a knight's tour of the
emptied-out living room, brown eyes grooving with vacant fixity all
the while on the red tail feather and black eyebead of the parrot, for
whose care, removal, or ultimate disposition no instructions had been
given to Rolando's mother when she was directed to clear out the place
by the executor of the Cochise Jones estate, a modest affair carefully
depleted by sixty-plus years of foolishness, most of what remained of it
tied up in vinyl records, the rest in vintage leisure suits (Aisha had
counted twenty-two), the fatal Hammond, a Yamaha keyboard on a
cross-legged metal stand, furniture fit only for the Ashby BART flea
market, and the Antarctic architecture of Mr. Jones's so-called files,
towers and peaks and drifts of paper everywhere, which Aisha shoveled
into cardboard banker boxes—gas bills, doctor bills, communications
from Musicians Local 6, photos of people who meant nothing to Aisha,
a photo of Mr. Jones at the front counter of his favorite haunt saying
something that was making Archy Stallings smile his big slow smile,
door-hanger menus, bank statements of the mid-nineties, medical and
insurance documents, the yellowing ongoing history of Mr. Jones's battles against record labels and their departments of legal affairs—before
turning at last, with a sinking heart, to the parrot, Fifty-Eight, wordless during the whole time that Aisha had devoted to sorting out the old
man's belongings, the bird expressing itself only by emitting a throaty
musical purr that put her in mind of the old Wurlitzer organ at her
church, singing or playing—or neither or both—an instrumental ver-

sion of a song you would hear on an oldies station, *but it's too late, baby, now, it's too late*, the parrot sounding like a funky church organ and making its musical selection, given the circumstances, with what seemed to be a disturbing sense of the apropos, the endless organ solo after a couple of hours kind of sort of starting to work on Aisha's last nerve, the latter a strand of bodily tissue notorious among her friends and family for its thinness and stretched as well by her ADD-ass little son lying there on the rug kicking his ADD-ass little feet, and also by an eerie dead-old-man vibration troubling the air in the house, a smell of decrepitude and neglected houseplants, water drops hitting the bathtub from a leaky tap like a ticking clock, year after year of debts and depositions, old record albums, the elegiac smell of leisure suit, all of it starting to creep Aisha the fuck out, but at last she got everything tagged and bagged and boxed and, having buckled Rolando back into his car seat for safekeeping, made five trips to the street, arms loaded with exiled shit to put out for curbside pickup, trying, as she climbed and descended the front steps, to reckon once and for all in her mind what was the right thing to do about the parrot, her analysis determining that it could be 1) sold for money, 2) put down, or 3) set at liberty to forge its own fate in the wild, but when she returned for the last time to Cochise Jones's house, having decided to turn the question over to the executor, who was also her father, Garnet Singletary, in spite of the certainty that in consulting him, she would incur the risk of his electing to choose option 4) keeping the gray parrot for himself, a fate that she placed somewhere between 1) and 2) from the parrot's point of view, and worse, from her own, since she had a serious case of birdophobia and, what was more, believed firmly that her father's house already smelled bad enough, thank you very much, she came back into the living room to find her baby just sitting there in his car seat, sucking on his bottle, no longer kicking, studying the bird while the bird, fallen silent, contemplated the baby, and Aisha understood how the part of Rolando that was like a wild animal, all eyes and reflexes, was a part already fading and soon to vanish from the world, understood how fragile was her child and how contingent that world, to her, on Rolando, understood the price in heartache that her child would extract from her in exchange for the ever passing joy of him, and then the parrot aimed a quick eye at her, and there was something about its expression, an air of sympathetic reserve, of pity kept politely to itself, which unnerved her further, so that though it was time to call her father and hand the bird over, time to tell the baby, "Okay, mister, we got to bounce," Aisha looked at the two little animals caught up in some kind of moment, and felt something long-stymied inside her pop loose, and now, at last, the parrot spoke, saying plainly, in the voice of Cochise Jones, "Quarter to three in the *got*damn morning!" and that was when, short story long, Aisha went over to the bedroom window and threw it open to a fine August afternoon, blue sky and green trees and any old thing a parrot might want, some dim memory chiming in her brain of rumored colonies of parrots, or was it parakeets, flying wild over San Francisco and, picturing Fifty-Eight making some local East Bay scene down in Trestle Glen, or up in Tilden Park, and holding fixed in her mind that happy image of sociable birds running loose in the trees, Aisha screwed up her courage and got in close to the bird, scary close, close enough to grab the pole of the perch, to smell the hot-newspaper funk on its feathers, then carried perch and parrot over to the open window, brusquely exhorting the bird to go free, an invitation of which the parrot did not hesitate to avail itself; a rousing of neck feathers, a sidestep, then flap, flap out into the day with no word of valediction, a bird of wide experience and rare talent set free over Telegraph Avenue, catching a scent of eucalyptus in its olfactory organs, banking left and heading north across Forty-third Street, up two blocks, passing over the Bruce Lee Institute of Martial Arts, in whose secret room, at the back of the stairs leading up to the roof, where exiles and religious fugitives and, for nine nights, a Living Buddha from the mountains of Sichuan, had all known bitterness and safety, Luther Stallings and Valletta Moore prepared to flee, neither of them quite clean but both of them dreadfully sober, zipping what all they had into suitcases and gym bags, Luther sending Valletta down to the tiny parking lot out back to load up the car, then at her honk—she was not supposed to honk—coming down himself, careful as a cat, bringing out what he called "the crown jewels," though Valletta was uncertain whether the term referred to himself or to the contents of the bulging

portfolio and plastic storage bin that he carried: the conceptual artwork, promotional designs, notes, treatments, screenplay drafts, and
other creative materials that, in the event he predeceased the start of
production, might someday be packaged and assembled, as it pleased
him to imagine, into a special slipcovered edition entitled, with becoming modesty, *Strutter Kicks It Old-School: The Second Greatest Film
That Never Was*, the number one greatest film that never was being, of
course, Stanley Kubrick's *Napoleon*, curating the bin and portfolio down
the stairs with a tenderness rarely shown, in her opinion, to Valletta,
out onto a back porch of painted two-by-fours which the director of the
Bruce Lee Institute, Irene Jew, was sweeping with a crazy-looking Chinese broom, just a bunch of long twigs witch-knotted together on a
bamboo pole with a piece of straw, a tool for sweeping away demons,
sifu Irene a woman schooled in the art of being haunted, so that two
young black men in ill-fitting suits, trying to appear as if they had
parked randomly outside the Institute earlier that day, in their hearse,
had posed zero challenge to her skills at the kung fu of ghosts, the ap-
parition sending her straight upstairs to tell Luther that his cover was
blown, Mrs. Jew leaving off her sweeping long enough to say "Don't
worry" to Luther as he passed, because, he understood, she was worried, so that all he could reply was "Should have left yesterday," then let
her get back to her sweeping while he loaded the storyboards of his
dream into the trunk of the Toronado, like some kind of deposed tin pot
from Haiti or the Philippines about to get into a Sikorsky and fly to a tax
haven, only without the title, the helicopter, or the income to be taxed, a
king in ruins, still the most brilliant product of the Bruce Lee Institute
and the most talented student Mrs. Jew had ever taught, shoving Valletta's wig box into the trunk alongside his practice *bokken*, nowhere to
really go, no one to help him, Archy never going to drop his permanent
eternal state of beef with Luther, though Luther had tried to make
amends, take responsibility, tried all twelve steps, some of them two or
three times apiece, got the degree in regret and done the postgraduate
work in sorry, but Archy wanted nothing to do with Luther, would not
listen, would not even listen to people, the man's own wife, telling him
to listen, meanwhile Luther living, in spite of sobriety and its promised

advantages, so broke and destitute that he was forced to seek refuge in the bosom of crazy old Irene Jew, God love the little Chinese lady, desperate enough to reach out to Gibson Goode, to undertake the long-contemplated shakedown of Chan Flowers, which he had always been too fucked up before this to attempt, a Hail Mary from the bottom of a deep dogpile indeed, at the far-distant end of whose majestic arc lay enough money—Goode had *promised*—to finance Luther's dream too long deferred, every shot of the film worked out in his mind from the classic slow strut through the streets of Oakland Chinatown on a busy Saturday morning, under the opening credits, Cleon Strutter come out of retirement to pull one last funky heist job, a blast from the past in a three-piece suit and Borsalino, a whup-ass Rip Van Winkle, to the final freeze frame, Luther always having found a strangely fraught pleasure in movies that ended like that, *Butch Cassidy, Fists of Fury*, a shot of Luther and Valletta jumping out of an airplane into an ocean full of sharks with a suitcase full of gold, every detail thought through over the course of long years, from the ad campaign to the casting, so that when the film came out, Luther would star not only on screen but at the center of his own comeback story, saved by no one, unlike Pam Grier or John Travolta, but himself, and by nothing but his own genius, and fuck that little whiteboy Tarantino anyway, passing Luther up for the part of Winston in *Jackie Brown* only because he believed the (perfectly true at the time) rumors about Luther Stallings's uncontrollable drug use, Luther imagining in like detail every shot of his comeback story as well, which would end with himself tossing down, in front of Valletta, a pile of job offers from agents and producers, clearing the way for Luther to take on his dream after next, which was to work with Clint Eastwood, whom he considered, as known at this point by half of West Oakland living and dead, to be the single greatest leading man in Hollywood history, and on whose eloquent taciturnity he had modeled his own reticent style, a style in stark contrast, as much of West Oakland dead and living would also readily attest, to his voluble off-camera self, or hey, maybe at the other end of this Hail Mary pass, he would take all the money he squeezed loose from Gibson Goode, for services rendered in helping change Chan Flowers's mind about the Dogpile Thang, and snort it right on up his nose, an option that, as he helped Valletta load her barbells into the car, struck him as possibly preferable to the comeback story, which was going to be difficult, so much more motherfucking hard than he ever allowed himself to consider; and just before they rolled out of the back alley, Luther saw against the afternoon sky the foreign profile of the fugitive parrot making its escape, taking its bearings generally along the hypotenuse of Telegraph Avenue while parsing light and scent and angles for their information, reckoning a course toward the eucalyptus hills, thrown eastward by a sensation of horror as it skirted the death cloud hovering above the Smokehouse hamburger stand, the sudden detour sending it over the street of forgotten toys, over the tan bungalow lost in flowers, where Fifty-Eight went unobserved by either of the house's present occupants, a man and a boy, side by side on a yellow Swedish sofa from the 1950s that the man had bought because it somehow reminded him of a zoot suit, watching the A's play Baltimore, Rich Harden on the mound working that devious ghost pitch, two pairs of stocking feet, size 11 and size 15, rising from the deck of the coffee table at either end like towers of the Bay Bridge, between the feet the remains in an open pizza box of a bad, cheap, and formerly enormous XL meat lover's special, sausage, pepperoni, bacon, ground beef, and ham, all of it gone but crumbs and parentheses of crusts left by the boy, brackets for the blankness of his conversation and, for all the man knew, of his thoughts, Titus having said nothing to Archy since Gwen's departure apart from monosyllables doled out in response to direct yes-or-nos, *Do you like baseball? you like pizza? eat meat? pork?*, the boy limiting himself whenever possible to a tight little nod, guarding himself at his end of the sofa as if riding on a crowded train with something breakable on his lap, nobody saying anything in the room, the city, or the world except Bill King and Ken Korach calling the plays, the game eventless and yet blessedly slow, player substitutions and deep pitch counts eating up swaths of time during which no one was required to say or to decide anything, to feel what might conceivably be felt, to dread what might be dreaded, the game standing tied at 1 and in theory capable of going on that way forever, or at least until there was not a live arm left in the bullpen, the third-string catcher sent in to pitch the thirty-second inning, batters catnapping slumped against one another on the bench, dead on their feet in the on-deck circle, the stands emptied and echoing, hot dog wrappers rolling like tumbleweeds past the diehards asleep in their seats, inning giving way to inning as the dawn sky glowed blue as the burner on a stove, and busloads of farmhands were brought in under emergency rules to fill out the weary roster, from Sacramento and Stockton and Norfolk, Virginia, entire villages in the Dominican ransacked for the flower of their youth who were loaded into the bellies of C-130s and flown to Oakland to feed the unassuageable appetite of this one game for batsmen and fielders and set-up men, threat after threat giving way to the third out, weak pop flies, called third strikes, inning after inning, week after week, beards growing long, Christmas coming, summer looping back around on itself, wars ending, babies graduating from college, and there's ball four to load the bases for the 3,211th time, followed by a routine can of corn to left, the commissioner calling in varsity teams and the stars of girls' softball squads and Little Leaguers, Archy and Titus sustained all that time in their equally infinite silence, nothing between them at all but three feet of sofa; and the parrot flew on, noting the potent sensory hum of Chimes General Hospital, baffled by the bright blast of humanity the hospital emitted, of which one soft electron pulse was being traced just then by the LCD display and ticker tape of a fetal monitor in one of the nicest LDRs on the fourth floor, an upscale Marriott feel, white curtains, plum walls, Pergo floor, the CTG a thread of lightning, a quickly sketched line of mountain peaks, a drumbeat metered on a mixing board, the dad and the mom holding hands beside the bed watching it, though the word "holding" could not really suffice, for they were engaged in more of a sumo move, a fighting hold on each other, waiting and watching the monitor as, on the other side of the door, not quite audibly, the attending, Dr. Bernstein, told the two midwives with evident regret that he would have to go in there and get the baby out, news that did not come as a great shock to either midwife, since each had seen the printout, and each knew how often hospitals act with precipitate caution, confounding impatience with efficiency, but each stunned nevertheless now that they were obliged to go back into the LDR and gravely disappoint their patient, the mom, whose first child had also come by emergency caesarean and who had been working and visualizing and chanting and Kegeling and meditating and undergoing hypnosis and submitting her perineum every night to be lavishly oiled by the dad with jojoba oil, readying herself for a Vaginal Birth After Caesarean like Beatrix Kiddo readying herself to take revenge on the Deadly Viper Assassination Squad, until her identity, her sense of purpose, seemed to have become subsumed, against the advice but with the sympathy of the two midwives, in the successful passage of her child through her cervix, and who broke down crying when she saw Gwen and Aviva come through the door with tight non-smiles upcurling the corners of their mouths, just flat-out came unglued smack in the middle of a long contraction, the dad fighting to keep his eyes off the fetal monitor as Aviva explained that since the baby, having in its wisdom declined to engage its head with its mother's pelvis, was beginning, after twenty-two hours of labor, to show signs of fatigue, they would all have to abandon their considered and wishful plan and concentrate on what the baby needed right now, an argument that rarely failed to relash a laboring mom to the mast of her purpose and produced its intended effect, the mom nodding as the contraction let go of her, Gwen nodding, too, but saying nothing, avoiding direct eye contact as she had done ever since she first determined, so many hours ago, back in the bedroom of the little bungalow on Ada Street, that the baby was floating, perched too high in the womb, stuck at a fetal station of minus three, running a small risk of cord prolapse that the Berkeley Birth Partners ordinarily would be inclined to take, carrying on with the mom's plans for her home and vagina while they waited for the floater to descend, and even in the cloud of her pain and regret, the mother was not too far gone to notice how squirrelly Gwen was acting, and to wonder if perhaps Gwen felt herself to be somehow responsible for the turn things had taken, if her calm and supportive but somewhat reserved manner betokened some personal failure, or if perhaps Gwen secretly believed a C-section was unnecessary, had not wanted to transfer to the hospital, but for some reason felt like she could not speak up and so had to knuckle under to hospital policy, to her partner, even though the truth might very well be that floating babies were born at home all the time, all around the world, and turned out healthy and fine, but before the mom could ask Gwen what was going on, why she and Aviva did not appear to be on speaking terms except when some exchange of information became necessary, the room filled with strange new doctors whose air of consequence struck the dad as profound and frightening, while a team of nurses got busy with the magic act of converting the birthing bed into an operating table that was rolled through the door, trailing the dad, who had hold of his wife's hand so tightly that Gwen was obliged to separate them, saying, "Okay, honey," saying that it was time to let the mom turn this baby loose, then helping the dad into his scrubs and mask, getting him ready for the brief and relatively honorific series of duties whose execution would devolve upon him: cutting the umbilicus, taking pictures with his digital camera, rooting for good Apgars while his child squirmed under the french-fry lights, he, with Gwen and Aviva—the only three people in the building, the city, or the world, apart from the mom, who cared whether she gave birth through her vagina or through a slit in her belly—reduced to the three least powerful people in the room, an air of dreamy impotence permeating all the proceedings for the dad, who at one point, after the baby was hauled by the armpits from the hole in the mom, a girl at once entitled Rebekah with a K that would encumber her for the rest of her life, made the grave error, just as the doctors were reassembling his wife, of turning his head—he was supposed to be watching his daughter feel light, air, and water for the first time, the first day of creation—and saw things on the other side of the operating room that no husband was meant to see, blood-orange welter of Betadine and placenta and golden fat and chicken-white membrane, but in the end, apart from a disappointment that would linger for years in the mom's heart like a burnt smell in a winter kitchen, everything was fine, a grainy fading vision of the smiling dad with the swaddled floater in his arms the last thing the mom saw before she closed her eyes, exhausted, down a pint, woozy, wheeled into the recovery room beside a tall slit window that gave onto a dazzle of implausibly green and blue afternoon, where the mom conked, and where she remained, still fucking *whacked* by some formidable opiate, when Gwen came in, stood by the bed, clasped the mom's hands in both of her own, Gwen's cool palms destined to linger afterward in some underlayer of the mom's memory and then, minutes or centuries later, when the mom opened her eyes again, just before she turned her head from the afternoon dazzle of the window to greet her daughter and see about rustling her up a little milk, the mom saw a flicker of red in a live oak tree beside the parking lot, a savage red, a bird, a parrot! that stalked along a limb of the live oak, looking as if it were talking or even singing to itself, gathering itself together with a hint of fussiness and then regaining the sky, bearing for the herded hills with their pied coats, fixing a course that carried it over the duplex on Blake Street in whose master bedroom another father and son lay watching something together in lieu of conversation, side by side on the bed, propped up by pillows, faces lit by the screen of a laptop computer that the father balanced on his abdomen angled so that if they lay very close together, they could both get a good view of the movie, one of nine discs that Julie had dug out of the blaxploitation section at Reel Video and brought home by way of research for his Tarantino class at the Senior Center, this one, *Strutter* (1973), starring the current fugitives from the Bruce Lee Institute in the full flame of their youth as a gun-toting, ass-kicking, frequently coupling double shot of funky magnificence, Luther Stallings cast as the ex-marine Vietnam vet trained to the point of artistry in techniques of stealth, infiltration, and hand-to-hand combat, then court-martialed and dishonorably discharged after he intervened to prevent a (white) captain from raping a hamlet girl, set loose with his commando skill set in the world of banks, pirated art collections, shipments of bullion and jewels, who is stalked (the first film in the projected trilogy being an avowed blaxploitation twist on *The Thomas Crown Affair*) by the leggy, implausibly monikered, and scantily clad insurance investigator Candygirl Clark, who must betray him to collect her paycheck, the son delighting in the movie's overall ambiance of insouciant cheapness, his father in its evocation of a time, a year, 1973, marveling at a string of little bits of the past (two-tone red-topped mailboxes, long rows of telephone booths in bus stations, old guys, routinely lounging around in suits and ties) that, without his noticing, had vanished as surely as mushrooms under the passing boot of Super Mario, father and son both impressed, and on a number of levels, by Valletta Moore, for her kung fu skills, for that orange outfit with midriff cutouts and the orange hip boots, for a touch of the doe- or even cross-eyed in her hard-ass glare, most of all impressed by the ineluctable cool of Luther Stallings in his prime, the way he underplayed every scene as if confident that he could meet its needs without resorting to words, the liner notes for the forthcoming DVD boxed edition of the trilogy (packed now in the back of the Toronado) explaining that, on the first day of shooting, Stallings (author of said liner notes) had borrowed a pen from the director (who later went on to direct hundreds of episodes of *Trapper John, M.D.*, *Knight Rider*, and *Walker, Texas Ranger*) and crossed out 63 percent of his lines, violating every code and bylaw of the trade, possessing the gift, rife among failed geniuses (though you would find no such observation in the liner notes), of a strong sense of his own limitations, coupled with the championship kung fu, the snap and the acrobatics of it, its kinship to certain dance moves of James Brown—the Popcorn, for example—its message of bodily liberation from the harsh doom of physics, "so awesome," as the son expressed it, noting several times in an approving way that made the father feel a squeeze of compassion for the son, the amazing resemblance between young Luther and Mr. Titus Joyner, so that when the movie was over, the father, closing the laptop, took an awesome Stallings-worthy leap of his own, plying the son with questions more pointed than usual about his friendship with young Mr. Joyner, and a story emerged, a tale, as the father perceived it, of unrequited love such as teenage boys often undergo in each other's company, with all the emotion on Julie's side, the father aware as the conversation progressed that he was woefully unprepared for this, not the gay part, that was whatever it was, but for the world of hurt and heartache (homo or hetero) into which his son had so rapidly passed, and his heart went all the way out to the boy, giving up that line of inquiry and affording his son an opening to turn the tables with the question "So what happened to him, anyway?," inaugurating a long, close interrogation as to the post-*Strutter* career of Luther Stallings, the exact nature of his relationship to his son, his present whereabouts, if known, Nat lavishing on each question the scant information he possessed, recognizing not without disapproval, and fuck the heartache, that his son was in the early stages of a full-blown obsession, which was why when Aviva came home, giving off an air-conditioner smell of the hospital, and slumped her bag on the bedroom floor, she found them geeking out on the interwebs (as Julie put it) about Archy Stallings's father, watching his collected works in three-minute clips and having a better time than she'd had with either of them in a long time, and for a second she looked hurt and angry, but then that gave way to bittersweetness as Aviva dropped between them on the bed, looking more defeated than either of them had seen her in a long time, and by means of this modest dogpile, they attempted to ensure their mutual comfort as the parrot, tired of flying, came down in a cedar tree in People's Park, where it established a lookout over a small party of feral teenagers who carried on for quite a while, darkness at last rewarding its vigil with half a lemon, the husks and pits of a number of avocados, and an entire tomato, which it consumed with a measured ferocity, then crept for the night into a shallow but adequate knothole, in which it passed the next two days before seeking out fresher fare and settling, after further wanderings, in the untended and paradisiacal backyard of a foreclosed house near Juan's Mexican, where other birds long ago had raided a loquat tree and then dropped or shat out the pits, reared by time and neglect to a fine establishment of loquat trees frequented heavily by the legendary flock of North Berkeley parrots, the Leaf Men of that neighborhood, far from the heartaches and sorrows of Telegraph Avenue.

IV

Return *to* Forever

A change of state. Molecules in transition, liquid to vapor. A Chinatown dollar-store teacup flying a dragon kite of steam.

"No more sleep!" said Irene Jew. With a whoosh, the window shade abandoned its post, and sunshine surged through the breach. "Time to get up. Big day!"

Gwen opened her eyes. Dust motes drew paisleys across the dazzle: molecules in transition. And Gwen just another molecule, a big fat molecule, tumbling random through space.

"Big day," she ironized. "Woo-hoo."

Her world now consisted of four walls and a lone window at the back of the dojo, secreted behind a knobless door that was in turn concealed behind a life-size, full-length still photograph (slick pecs and abs, flying slippered right foot, teeth gritted in a predatory smile) of the eponym and presiding spirit of the Bruce Lee Institute of Martial Arts. Her life was a bedroll and a blue duffel, a meal in a paper bag, every day adding its sorry page to the history of the homelessness.

The thirty-sixth week was fertile ground for self-pity in the gravid female, and Gwen's thoughts upon waking struck her as neatly diagnostic.

Master Jew cupped the teacup with its painted mountain landscape in her tiny hands, trained to mend and heal, as well as to deal blows by Lam Sai Wing, who had studied under the great doctor and righter of wrongs Wong Fei Hung. She squatted beside the sleeping mat in her black cotton pants and shapeless white tunic, waiting out her latest hidden guest and source of irritation until, at last, said individual hoisted herself halfway out of the bedroll. Gwen took the cup into the outsize hands that had cupped the tender skulls of a thousand babies and whose lineage of instruction likewise could be traced directly back to the nineteenth century, to a midwife named Juneteenth Jackson, of Tulsa, Oklahoma, Gwen's twice-great-grandmother.

"Hot *tap* water," Gwen said. She made a face. Her tone damned not only the idea of drinking hot tap water but all the eventualities that had led her to another lonely reveille in this glorified closet, its sole ornament a Chinese dollar-store Ming vase in which stood a plastic red Gerber daisy that was really a ballpoint pen. To this cut-rate futon with its smell like stale waffles. To this moment at which a cup of hot tap water must—she would not have dared to refuse Master Jew—be drunk. "What I need is a cup of coffee."

"Coffee make your baby restless," Master Jew said. "Make him want to run away from home one day."

Along with the cup of hot water, then, Gwen must evidently accept an implicit criticism of her own flight from home and hearth. A ninety-year-old Chinese master of kung fu, even a female one, was not likely to be all that progressive, you had to figure, when it came to the question of proper relations between husband and wife.

Gwen drank and was amazed, as always, by how good hot tap water actually felt and tasted, how well it suited your throat and gullet going down, how drinking it seemed to loosen some inner string or melt an inner coldness you did not even know that you harbored. Master Jew claimed to be able to cure all kinds of ailments with nothing but a mugwort cigar and the regular consumption of moderately hot water. In the darkness of Gwen's belly, the son or daughter of her worthless husband gave a flutter kick of gratitude for the drink.

"How's your back?" said Master Jew.

Gwen reached the fingers of one hand to palpate the muscles at the small of her back. In the past few days, her pregnancy had been finding new, painful uses for the largest knots of muscle on her frame. She woke in the company of charley horses, grandma cramps, stiffness of the joints. She shrugged. "It hurts."

Master Jew knelt and reached behind Gwen to plunge her fingers into the root system of the lumbar like a gardener with a crocus to transplant. Gwen drew in a sharp breath at the pain, yet the abrupt rough contact of the old woman's cool, dry, soft-skinned fingers came as a shock to her exiled heart. Gwen loved Master Jew the way one was supposed to love one's kung fu master: furiously, like a child.

"Better," Master Jew said.

"A little," Gwen admitted.

Here was the reason that Gwen had been drawn into and persevered with her studies at the Bruce Lee Institute for so long, training hard for nearly four years until she had earned her black belt: because qigong, like Master Jew, didn't seem to care if you believed in it or not.

She passed the empty cup back to the old woman, who acknowledged without gesture or word the look of gratitude in Gwen's eyes. Master Jew also noted a thickening of the young woman's pretty features, a blurring of her wide gaze. Overnight Gwen appeared to have moved into the climax of her term. The baby was going to arrive so soon, and here was this woman with her life in disorder. Working too hard. Taking care of other mothers-to-be while neglecting her own health. To make matters worse, she had spent the past three nights sleeping in this tiny room, in a hip pocket world that crackled with male energies. Master Jew hawked up a pill of phlegm and spat it with feline delicacy into a linen handkerchief.

No, it would not do.

When Gwen had shown up for class on Monday night, with a packed duffel bag in the back of her BMW convertible and traces of tears on her cheeks, long-ingrained instincts had caused Master Jew to reach out and catch the falling young woman. But now the teacher saw that she had not handled the matter properly. Irene Jew was a very old woman—she liked to boast, improbably, that she was the oldest Chinese woman west of the Rocky Mountains—and over the long years of wandering and exile, from Guangdong to Hong Kong to Los Angeles to Oakland, she had presented countless students with the black sash that was the mark of longest study and hardest training, pain, devotion, tedium, and work. Some of these students had been capable of magnificence and others of brilliance, and a few had partaken of both qualities. Until now, however, none of them had ever been a pregnant black woman who drove a BMW. Master Jew never quite knew how to behave toward Gwen Shanks.

"This place very bad for you," she said. "Bad smell. Also bad to look at. Ugly."

"Yes." Gwen made a sound, a hoarse intake of breath that might have been the precursor to tears or one of her big sputtering guffaws. She massaged her face, took her hands away, opened her eyes. "I mean, no, it's all right, but. I'm sorry." She reached for the bed jacket in a metallic shade of good brown silk that lay folded by the futon and pulled it around her. She wore silk pajamas that matched the robe, piped with white. "I just need a good night's sleep."

Her duffel lay open, all the clothes and shoes and bottles of lotion encased in Ziploc bags. It was time to get up and get dressed for her big day; at three P.M. she and Aviva were due to go before a board charged with reviewing the status of their privileges. Gwen looked at the clothes she had stuffed into her bag three nights ago, the distended stretch tops and yoga pants, the preposterous bras and geriatric panties. "Just one good night of sleep."

"Need your pillow."

"I do," Gwen said, yearning for the long, cool expanse of the Garnet Hill body pillow that for months, interwoven with her legs, arms, and belly, had been her truest lover. "I do need my pillow, so bad."

"Go home," Master Jew said. "Get it."

"I can't."

Master Jew turned her back to Gwen. Across the scarred and glossy bamboo floor of the studio, four high windows looked out onto the blue glazing of a summer Oakland sky crazed with telephone wires. Behind the concrete hulk of the old Golden State market, a palm tree hiked its green slattern skirts.

"Okay, I know you need me out of here. I'm so grateful you let me stay this long. After today I'll go to a hotel, I'll rent an apartment. One of those little places down in Emeryville by the movie theater. IKEA's right there. Get a crib, some dishes. Whatever I'm going to need. I know I've been kind of lying around here moping and feeling sorry for myself. My back hurts, and I've been maybe in a little bit of shock. There are a lot of things I don't know. If I can take care of a baby on my own.

If I'm going to be able to keep doing the work I have been doing for the past ten years."

Master Jew kept her back to Gwen, who knew that her speech had been disrespectful and poorly judged in both its length and its tone.

"I'm sorry," Gwen concluded. "Seriously. Tomorrow, next day at the latest, I'm out of here."

The teacup—smaller than the first, red and gold with an intricate carpet pattern and a goldfish—was in Gwen's face before she realized that Master Jew had moved, a sudden accident of vision like a blackout or a camera flash, and by the time she realized that the crazy old lady had actually *tossed a teacup at her head*, Gwen's right palm was smarting, and the intercepted cup lay cool against her fingers, where, at the base of her thumb, it gave up one last drop.

"Big day. Get dressed," Mrs. Jew said. "Then go get your pillow."

⊙   ⊙   ⊙

Gwen felt nervous about her footing, her status under her own roof. So she had in mind a kind of marital Grenada, the deployment of massive force in support of a modest, even risible objective. But when she drove past the sleeping house at 6:51 A.M. (an hour with which her husband had never been intimately acquainted), it looked so ordinary, blue-painted cedar shakes peeling, honeysuckle strangling the slat fence, empty tanks from the Arrowhead bubbler ranged along the front porch, that she lost her stomach for a fight. She rolled right past the house and, for an instant, considered driving on.

True enough, as she had told Master Jew, the body pillow did not just preserve her sleep: there were nights when she felt it was the only thing in this world that felt and understood her. True to its name, the body pillow had come to embody the unknown child inside her, mute and shapeless but imbued with some distinct essence or presence of the baby to come. The body pillow was a doll that she nightly cuddled as, in weird pregnancy dreams, the baby was transformed into all manner of beasts and vegetables and stuff a whole lot freakier than a pillow. At the same time, she knew, it was only a forty-five-dollar body pillow she had bought online. It could easily be replaced.

"The hell with that," she said aloud, and parked the car in front of the Lahidjis' house. "I want my damn pillow."

She did not get out of the car. She did some qi breathing. She groped for the shimmery little bead at the center of herself. She tried to harness or at least to tidy up her qi. She had enough conflict to deal with today, she reminded herself, without adding to the toll of stress, measurable in rads, to which she and the baby had been exposed. Still, her sense of outrage over all that Archy had done and failed to do as a husband, a father, and a man remained undiminished by her reluctance to confront him, and that outrage fixated on, swarmed like a cloud of bees around, the sum of forty-five dollars. She was not going to throw that money away. She had left behind many things of value in the house when she left Archy, and if she never got back any of those things, so be it; let the body pillow serve to redeem the remainder of the life and possessions she had abandoned. She got out of the car. Only one course open to her: to come in not like a battalion of marines overwhelming some little isle of coconuts but like Special Forces: surgical. Stealthy. In and out.

Gwen decided to try the back door first. She slipped—without much clearance on either side of her—along the broken snake hide of the brick walk that ran between the house and a hurricane fence, the fence woven with morning glory like some kind of feral basket. She sneaked past the kitchen windows, past the garbage and recycling bins, through that whole shadowy side zone of the house, which she had entered rarely over the years, a dense and leaf-shadowed passage hospitable, or so she always imagined, to rats. That thought hurried her along.

The backyard looked worse than she remembered. Brick barbecue area, angel's trumpet tree hung with yellow wizard hats, chain-link fence obliterated from view in many places by green flows of ivy and jasmine and morning glory. Shaggy stand of pampas grass. The forlorn expanse of concrete that some previous occupant of the house, through an excess of laziness or optimism, had painted lawn-green. It was a mangy, scraggly, jungly mess that must be lowering property values as far away as Claremont Avenue. It was an embarrassment. But Gwen had been gone only a week; this ruin was the work of years. A faithful record of her untended life.

She averted her gaze from the broken latticework around the foundation of the house, the loose weather stripping that peeped like a gang banger's drawers from the seams around the back door. When she and Archy bought the house, it had been a semi-wreck, cheap but ill used. They had prepared a list of the repairs and improvements they were going to make. This list was divided among the required, the optional, and the fantastic. They put in new toilets and sinks, using a book from the library. They redid the floors, rehung the windows, patched the roof. It was the first common project of their marriage, and looking back on that time, Gwen felt a twinge of loss and regret for their happiness. In time they had crossed off all the things that were required, but when they reached the next phase, they opted against the optional. At some point well before they arrived at the fantastic, they had lost track of the list.

Gwen unlocked the back door and pushed, but the door pushed back. The chain was set. It was a formidable chain installed by the previous owner, and to Gwen's knowledge, neither she nor Archy had ever employed it. There was something unnerving about the vigor with which the chain resisted letting Gwen enter the house. It was as though Archy had changed the locks on her. Gwen was insulted. She was about to start pounding, demanding an explanation, but she remembered her maternal resolve to stay calm. It occurred to her that Archy might feel less secure without her in the house, and the thought touched her. She shut the back door with a soft click and crept back around to the front door.

As she let herself in, she realized that a faint rolling hum she had taken, coming up the porch steps, for the vibration through the old fir floor of the refrigerator, or maybe the humidifier in the basement, maybe even some kind of distant cement mixer or the MedEvac helicopter landing on its pad over at Children's Hospital, was in fact the entwined snoring of two boys. Julie Jaffe lay half extruded from Gwen's old sleeping bag, shirtless and shockingly pale, with little pink guineapig nipples. Titus had been neatly interred beneath Archy's *Diff'rent Strokes* sleeping bag, only his weird fingery toes and the upper half of his face visible. A glacier of DVD cases slid across the coffee table, *Strutter*, *Ghetto Hitman*, *Soul Shaker*, all those crazy crap-ass movies that Archy's father had spent the seventies cranking out or being cranked out by. Peeking from under a Styrofoam clamshell from which a couple of french fries poked like the feelers of a large and cautious insect was another disc on whose label she recognized the astonishing Afro of Valletta Moore, along with the barrel and silencer of the .357 she fondled, in that iconic pose from the poster of *Nefertiti*, forty stories of endless brown leg with a pair of highjacked fuck-me pumps for a ground floor, yellow satin hot-pants jumpsuit for a pediment. The room hung heavy with a fug of puberty, microwave popcorn, and something unidentifiable but horrible.

Julie, in his nocturnal wrestling with her sleeping bag, had crawled so far that she nearly stepped on him when she came into the room. The hollow of his hairless chest, the puzzled knot of his brows, the soft straight hair pasted by night sweat across his bony forehead, all stirred deep memories of the nights when she used to watch him for Aviva and Nat, sing him her grandmother's grave lullabies. His innocence then struck her, as she recalled it now, as having also been her own: before Nat and Aviva fixed her up with Archy, before the long, gathering disappointment of her professional life.

She preferred not to look at Titus, snoring away under a goofy and tragic mantle blazoned with an image of Gary Coleman and Todd Bridges in matching sweaters. She felt sorry for him, but she did not want to feel sorry for him, and so she let him piss her off. Meanwhile, the mystery smell, it became clear to her pregnant nose, plain as the pall of carnage, was the smell of old hamburger. She made the mistake of looking more closely at the clamshell package on the table. A pink and beaded gray streak of fat dribbled like candle wax down the outside of it and sent a rocket of hot bile arcing from her belly to her mouth.

She would have been willing to bet forty-five dollars that ninjas and Green Berets did not, generally speaking, incorporate vomiting into their operational procedures. The humiliation of that would be too much to bear; Archy had spent, without complaint, a fair amount of time in the early days of her pregnancy handling her various ejecta.

The molecules of oxidized fat seemed to trail her like malodorous pixies as Gwen crept down the hall to the bedroom and opened the bedroom door. The blinds were drawn, but in the window behind Archy's auntie's old Marie Antoinette–style dresser, the job had been poorly done, so that they hung at an angle to the windowsill. In the daylight seeping under this hypotenuse, Gwen could see Archy heaped up on the bed, flat on his back. It was a round bed that Archy had brought to the marriage—he called it his secret-agent bed—and with his legs and arms spread in four directions, he reminded her of the naked man by Leonardo da Vinci, squaring the circle or whatever it was. Only Archy was not naked; he had on a pair of Cal basketball shorts. Her objective lay right alongside him, bent double, ignored or perhaps trying to wriggle away. All the other, more conventional pillows had been kicked or flung over the side of the bed and lay in dejected attitudes on the floor. Typically, Archy slept flat on the mattress and employed a pillow only to cover his face when a room was too full of light. He was not going to miss the body pillow at all.

The molecules drifting downwind from the burger-joint packaging in the living room seemed at last to abandon their pursuit of Gwen. She could stand to breathe through her nose again, and what she smelled was her bedroom, her husband, her life. The clove-and-citrus redolence of his aftershave, a Christmasy smell. A smell she had fallen in love with early on. Now it struck her as a tonic, bracing and restorative, steeling her to reach for the pillow, careful, moving slow, holding her breath. She grabbed two feather-fill fistfuls of pillow and began to peel it away from the mattress one patient millimeter at a time.

Archy rolled over onto his side and, with a sharp intake of breath, threw his legs around the body pillow. He pressed his hips against it, took it in his arms, drew it close to him. He embraced it, let his breath out shuddering, sighed once, and began to snore. Gwen froze, horrified, thrilled, and pricked by a sense of betrayal, though whether by her husband or the body pillow, she would not have been able to say.

"Don't get up yet," Archy said without opening his eyes. Begging in his sleep. He took another long appreciative sip of unconsciousness, weighing the flavor of it in his mouth, smacking his lips. "Don't leave me."

Gwen considered a number of possible rejoinders to this, among them "Too late, motherfucker," "I'm sorry," "I won't, ever again," and "You are talking to a *pillow*."

She let go of the forty-five-dollar pillow without saying a word. She turned and slipped back out of the bedroom. As she looked up from easing the door shut and releasing the doorknob with practiced soundlessness, she saw Titus standing at the other end of the hall, watching her, not quite smirking, not quite looking confused. Those blue-green Luther Stallings eyes, rimmed with the unreadable force-field shimmer that veiled the light eyes of black folks.

"I just came to get my special pillow," Gwen said in a pathetic whisper.

Titus nodded, then seemed to notice that she was not carrying anything.

"I changed my mind," Gwen said.

She felt a pulse of tightening across her belly that she knew meant dehydration. The boy got out of her way as she moved past him into the kitchen. Standing behind her, he became the only thing that prevented her from backing away in horror at what she discovered there.

"Oh my *God*," she said.

The boy concurred with a mirthless snort.

"What did you *do*?"

"He said you could grind coffee in the blender."

"Who did?"

"Julie."

"Did he also say you could shoot Ragu out of a SuperSoaker? Because that's what it looks like happened in here."

The boy shrugged.

She soldiered in, holding her breath as if walking into a recently vacated portable toilet, and ran herself a glass of water from the sink. "Now I see why you put the chain on the back door." She drained off the whole twelve ounces in one greedy draft. "It was for the protection of others."

"That was Julie, too," Titus said. "He gets scared." Again there was not quite a smirk on his face; his expression held too much curiosity for that.

"I know he does," Gwen said.

Something, some routine tenderness in her tone or aspect of her he had not considered, made him train his curiosity apparatus on her. He measured her circumference and girth. "You got a special pillow for that," he said, pointing at her abdomen.

"A body pillow."

"To hold it up when you're sleeping?"

"I don't really sleep," Gwen said. "But especially not without."

"So, and, that kid in there. That's, like, my brother."

Gwen thought about rinsing the lipstick from the rim of the water glass, but in the unlikely event that anyone noticed it among the marinara Pollocks and the termite mounds of plates and pans, the print of her lipstick could serve as a calling card, a silver bullet, a bent joker.

"Or sister," she said.

"You didn't have no ultrasound?"

"*Any.* We asked them not to tell us."

"You want the surprise."

"Archy does. I don't like surprises." It came out sounding more pointed than she had intended, but not inappropriately so.

"Why don't you just find out and not tell him?"

"I could do that," she said.

"What. Aw, you already did," Titus guessed. "Am I right?"

Gwen took the chain off the back door. "Half brother," she told Titus before she went out into the rest of her day. "And half I don't know what."

⊙   ⊙   ⊙

"Who was that?" man wanted to know.

Nothing but questions ever rising from that quarter, man shaking them up in the cup of his fist like a handful of dice every time he walked into a room that was furnished with his son. *You like Rice Krispies? English muffins? Baseball?* Star Wars? *Peaches? The ladies? Mos Def? Cats? Dogs? Mentos? Monkeys? Nobody ever taught you to brush your teeth when you wake up in the morning? Did that shirt used to be* white? *How you spend so much time playing that damn* game? *What would happen if you read an actual Marvel motherfucking* comic book *one time? You ever hear of washing a dish? Listen to Duke Ellington? Do you know who Billy Strayhorn was? Aw, shit, are you trying to break my heart?* Letting fly the dice. In that regard, the man offered little in the way of novelty; Titus felt himself to be a vortex around which the questions of adults routinely came to circle, like that wheel of plastic he had seen one night on the Discovery Channel, out there past Hawaii someplace, great big endless turning of plastic bags and pop bottles. Every conversation a quiz, a debriefing, an interrogation, a catechism. Every sentence fitted at the end with its whiplash curl, a hook to snare him. And every single one of those questions, at bottom, nothing but rhetorical, admitting of and needing no reply.

"Who was *who*?" Titus said.

Take it in, feed it right on back at them.

"You were talking to somebody, sounded like a woman. Was it Gwen?"

"Who's Gwen?"

"Boy, you know who Gwen is. My *wife*."

Titus produced an elaborate shrug, three-part, multilayered like a Vulcan chessboard. "I guess."

"You guess."

"She was here."

At this news, his father got hollow-eyed, his big old Yogi Bear cheeks going all slack. Standing there by the bedroom door where his *wife* had stood a few minutes ago. Tying and retying an unsuccessful bow in the sash of his playboy bathrobe. Man took in the socks littering the hallway floor, the stink of male habitation in the house. He closed his eyes, working on must be like two, three hours of sleep, eye sockets purple with fatigue. No doubt picturing the devastation in the kitchen, the trash heaps in the living room, the skinny little underpantsed white boy tangled up out there in that crusty old sleeping bag. Reconstructing in his mind the likely path of her visit. Understanding how disgusted she had been by it all. Running through the whole scenario like the flashback at the end of a detective film that shows the murder as it must have gone down, everybody sitting around the parlor or the conservatory or whatever, under the framed butterflies and the stuffed tiger heads, while the detective laid it all out. *She was standing right there; you needed only to wake up and you would have seen her. But you did* not *wake up, did you, Mr. Stallings?* He dragged one hand across his face slowly and with intent, like he was hoping to erase its features. He opened his eyes.

"Fuck me," he said. "*Look* at this shit."

He kicked on down the hallway, trailing that lemon Pledge smell he had, almost but not quite brushing against Titus as he went by. When he came into the living room, what he discovered there seemed not only to confirm but to deepen or dwarf his worst fears.

"What she want to be coming here today," he said, his voice barely loud enough to hear. For once it did not sound like a question.

So Titus didn't answer. Not—this time—because he made it a point of pride to spurn or duck his father's and all the pointless questions of the adult world, but because what was he going to say? Mention had been made of a body pillow, but Titus understood that a body pillow explained nothing, was only what Hitchcock called a MacGuffin. The swell of the woman, the arc of the brother who deformed her, the serious way she had of speaking to Titus, looking at him not boy-you-best-get-yourself-together serious, like Julie's mom, but scientist serious, skeptical, fascinated by what she saw. How was he going to put any of that into words?

His father said, "Jaffe, get up."

Julie sat up at once, pink nipples like a pit bull pup's, not a hair on him anywhere except for, under his left arm, if you knew about it, one coarse wire like an eyebrow whisker, about which it was not unknown for Titus to tease him. Julie blinked, focusing on the man, cross-eyed and hungover on the vapors of his last dream of the night.

"Gwen was here," the man told him.

Julie nodded, then saw that something more was wanted. He shook his head. "I don't know," he tried.

"Not asking you. Titus says Gwen was here. Just now." He turned to Titus. "In this room?" Titus nodded again. "In the kitchen?"

"Had a drink of water from the sink."

"Sweet Jesus," Archy said. He looked back at Julie. "So you didn't see her, then?"

"I was asleep," Julie said.

"Yeah, I was asleep, too. Only one *wasn't* asleep was my boy Titus, here, and as usual, he don't have too much to say on the subject."

Titus got that a criticism was intended by this last remark, although he did not consider it to be so. You could damn yourself with silence but never so effectively as by running your mouth. He hung back as his father approached the disordered and, at best, to be honest (owing to the poor quality of the original film stock, subpar camerawork, third-rate video transfers, routine yet crazy story lines, and wooden dialogue), broken evidence of Luther Stallings's having, at one time, shone forth from the screens of ghetto grindhouses. At first the man seemed not to notice the DVDs, preoccupied instead by the crumpled napkins, the twenty-four-ounce cups, the greasy packages of leftover food. With the hopeless energy of someone trying to save worthless knickknacks from an impending wildfire, he gathered up the cheese-edged clamshell packages, the used forks and straw wrappers, and all the other refuse the boys had left out last night when, at three-thirty A.M., man still not home from a gig in the city, they finally switched off the television and went to sleep. Stacked it all precariously in his arms as if there were a chance that the wife might return any second.

"*Fuck* me," he said again. He stomped into the kitchen, growling once when he comprehended the full disastrousness thereof. Banged around under the sink until he found a garbage bag, tumbled into it all the garbage he was holding. Folding anger up into himself like a hurricane gathering seawater, he swept through the kitchen picking up trash. Came stomping back into the living room, fat ghetto Santa with the soul patch, slinging his Hefty sack.

"I cannot *believe* you little motherfuckers left my damn house looking like this," he said, accurately but without justice, since in so leaving it, they had only been following the principles of housekeeping as laid down after his wife's departure by the man himself. The dire state of the kitchen was as much his fault as anyone's. "Can't believe she came this morning." As if, say, she came yesterday or tomorrow, whole place would have been done up shiny and correct, and today was some freak of the housekeeping schedule. "House looking like a garage full of crackheads. She should of— Wait. Hold up."

Now the cover of *Night Man*, one of the DVDs that Titus and Julie had rented from Videots on College Avenue last night, seemed to catch the man's eye, to register for the first time. He picked up the case, turned it over, read the hype, scholarship, and bullshit written there.

" 'Quentin Tarantino Presents,' " he said. "Huh."

As he made a study of the DVD box, his stance widened, his posture grew straighter. The anger making landfall, moving inland. Feeding on itself, was Titus's impression—and he was schooled in the repertoires of anger. Rifling through the other DVD cases scattered up and down the table. Tarantino was right: *Night Man* was the best thing in the Stallings filmography, a straight bank heist, cops and robbers, light on the cheese, scored by Charles Stepney, shot by Richard Kline, who shot *Soylent Green* and some other cool movies of the day, one of the *Planet of the Apes* movies. Cheap, rough, and uneven, it made plain and proclaimed for all time the truth of Luther Stallings's physical grace in 1975, the beauty of his winged nostrils, the lowdown way he smiled, the fatal architecture of his hands.

Man said, "What is this shit?"

Titus was about to say "It's your father" but, at the last instant, realized it might sound like he was saying that Luther Stallings, his grandfather, *was* shit. When, to the contrary, Luther Stallings at one time had stood in full possession of a definite article, not to mention two capital letters. Was most definitely The Shit.

Before this summer, before last week, the name of Luther Stallings was not a memory to Titus but the memory of someone else's memory, like a minor hit or the vice president of the disco years. A scatter of images caught like butterflies in the grille of his mind. First: an article in an old, a very old, a King Tut–old copy of *Ebony* tucked into a drawer in his grandmother's nightstand. Titus remembered little about the article apart from the name of its subject, the title *Strutter*, and a shot of Luther Stallings sitting in a Los Angeles living room, in tight black pants and white ankle boots, tossing a baseball to a blur of a boy. Second: a scratchy, washed-out clip in a Wu-Tang Clan video, no more than a few seconds long, showing a lean light black man causing grievous harm with his fists and feet to a gang of homicidal Taoists. Third and faintest: the memory, really the acrid residue—and no more—of the low opinion, bottled like smoke in the name Stallings, held by his granny for all the fathers to whom Titus was heir.

None of these echoes prepared Titus for the truth of the greatness of Luther Stallings as revealed in patches by the movies themselves, even the movies that sucked ass. None readied him for the strange warmth that rained down onto his heart as he sat on the couch last night with the best and only friend he'd ever had, watching that balletic assassin in *Night Man*, with those righteous cars and that ridiculous bounty of fine women, a girl with a silver Afro. Luther Stallings, the idea of Luther Stallings, felt to Titus like no one and no place had ever felt: a point of origin. A legendary birthplace, lost in the mists of Shaolin or the far-off technojungles of Wakanda. There in the dark beside Julie, watching his grandfather, Titus got a sense of his own life's foundation in the time of myth and heroes. For the first time since coming to consciousness of himself, small and disregarded as a penny in a corner of the world's bottom drawer, Titus Joyner saw in his own story a shine of value, and in himself the components of glamour.

Man said, "You all having a Luther Stallings film festival?"

"He was good," said Julie.

"No, Julie, he was not."

"Well, at kung fu or whatever."

The man did not look up from the plastic case. He spoke with a soft and furious enunciation. "I don't want this motherfucker in my house," he said. "Not in any form. Not flesh and blood. Not in electrons, pixels. Not even the damn name out your damn mouth. Okay? Got that?"

The man scooped up the rented elements of their Stallings film festival, stacked them haphazardly, and tried to hand them off to Titus. Titus just looked at them. The man shoved them at Julie instead.

"Get them out of my house!" he said.

"Okay, okay," Julie said. "Jeez, Archy, what the *hell*?"

Boy stunned by the abruptness, the violence, of how he found himself in possession of the DVDs. Looking at the man like he was about to cry. "I'm sorry, Archy. I didn't—"

"That's your *daddy*," Titus heard himself say, to his surprise if not horror. "Man was a motherfucking movie star! You should be feeling *proud* of him."

"Huh."

"He *was* good," Titus said. "He could really act. Better than Fred Williamson, and fight better, too. Better fighter than Jim Kelly, who wasn't no kind of actor. Better than all them white guys, Chuck Norris, dude with the eyebrows—"

"John Saxon," Julie said.

"John Saxon. Better than most of them classic Chinese dudes, too. Sonny Chiba, Sammo Hong. You *know* you love that type of shit, got that screen capture from *The Game of Death* for a desktop. Fighting that big dude, looks like some kind of giant emu. It don't even make *sense* for you to not appreciate Luther Stallings. He can play piano. He's like a expert at barbecue and shit." These facts he'd cribbed from a bonus feature on the *Night Man* disc. "But, I mean, even if you don't like him, you got to still *respect* him."

Titus saw that he had afforded the man a fresh surprise on this unusual morning.

"Two weeks you don't say ten words," the man said. "Now you going to make me a whole speech, huh? Telling me what I'm supposed to feel."

"It's your father."

"Uh-huh. So then, by that logic, I guess you must respect me?"

"Nah," Titus said. "Because you just a sperm donor."

It left his bow with a snap of inspiration and hit its target with a thwack you could almost hear. It rocked the man back before he rallied.

"Okay, first of all," he said, "that shit was not 'donated,' okay, it was *bestowed*. Second, that 'emu' is Kareem Abdul motherfucking Jabbar. Third, all right, and listen to me now, I got enough shit to worry about, all right, laying my actual father figure to rest day after tomorrow, providing food and drinks for like a hundred people. Rounding up a marching band. Tracking down a parrot. In my garage, okay, I have the

Hammond organ that killed Cochise Jones just, like, sitting there, need to be patched up so we can give the man a fitting tribute. I got all this personal shit piling up everywhere, baby coming, wife going out of her motherfucking *mind*. Got like three hours sleep. Got this skinny little motherfucker here, wandering around in his underpants, wearing a sleeping bag around one ankle like it's some kind of fucked-up giant *sock*. You two little faggots," yanking out the last couple of Jenga blocks from the tottering pile of his cool, "you come in here, dropping DVDs all over the place, disrespecting me, disrespecting my wishes, messing up my gotdamn house—"

Julie looked up accusingly. Disappointed in the man, wanting him to know it. "Hate speech," he pointed out.

"Think so?" the man said. "Because, brother, that is fucking *mild* compared to what you *about* to hear. You little fuckers can put your clothes on, pack your bags, and get the fuck out, both of you. Leave the premises. And take those piece-of-shit movies with you. I am bouncing your cinephile asses."

"Seriously?" Julie said.

Man seemed right then to want to show Julie that he was in earnest. He picked up the copy of *Strutter* in its box, Luther Stallings's first film, made when he was only eight years older than Titus was today. Threw it on the ground, stomped it four times.

"Get. The. Fuck. Out."

The plastic gave way twice, but on the third blow, the case snapped in half. The last time the disc broke. Three shining pieces of rainbow lying on the rug.

"Asshole," Titus said.

Murderous, hopeful, he took a swing at his father. Twisted stylishly back around on himself, lost his footing, fell. The hand that broke his fall got caught up in the pieces of the shattered case. A piece of broken rainbow cut him, enough to bleed a little, hurt a lot.

"I fucking *hate* you," Titus said, his voice sounding, even to his own ears, dismayingly girlish and shrill. "I hate you so motherfucking much!"

Man stood over him, looking down, hands on his hips, breathing in big wheezy lungfuls of the air they all had soured.

"Now, that," he said, "is what I call hate speech."

⊙   ⊙   ⊙

Two blocks from Brokeland, backing into a space on Apgar Street with a furious swipe of the El Camino's steering wheel, sucking the last charred millimeter of usefulness from a fatty while trying to confirm an order for twenty pounds of *al pastor*, twelve dozen tortillas, and a gallon of pico de gallo from the Sinaloa taco truck down on East Fourteenth, Archy Stallings tripped some inner wire tied to hidden charges of remorse. Remorse for his unmanly and irresponsible outburst with the boys, for the hurt done to Gwen, for Gwen's unveiling of the unanimous squalor into which her leaving had sunk him. Remorse, at last, for his Ethiopian adventure—Archy recalling, with the remorseful acuity of marijuana, the ink of melancholy that flooded the pupils of Elsabet Getachew whenever she looked up at him with his jimmy in her mouth. Regret for his general inability to holster said jimmy, for his last quarrel with Mr. Jones, for his choice of brown wing tips with a suit that had more blue in its glen plaid than he remembered. He cut the engine and sat, a hi-hat of regret, struck hard and resounding.

Just before the taco lady returned from running his deposit to take Archy off hold and inform him, employing a deft and broken phraseology, that the operation was a failure and his Visa card had not survived the procedure, Clifford Brown, Jr., came on KCSM to back-announce a cut he must have played before Archy got in the car, Freddie Hubbard's 1970 cover of "Better Git It in Your Soul," "featuring," as Junior put it, "on the organ, Oakland's late, great Mr. Cochise Jones," and Archy found himself unexpectedly on the verge of tears. That verge was as close to tears as Archy usually allowed himself to come. Regret, hurt, bereavement, loss, to permit the flow of even one tear at the upwelling of such feelings was to imperil ancient root systems and retaining walls. Mudslide and black avalanche would result and drown him.

It was just something in the way Clifford Brown, Jr., said, *Late, great.*

"I knew my card was hurting," Archy conceded to the taco lady, weeping freely. "I did not know it was that sick."

"Is okay," the taco lady said, mistaking the wobble in his voice for simple grief over the loss of Mr. Jones, almost as loyal a customer of Sinaloa as he had been of Brokeland Records, prone to fall into an almost musical rapture at the spectacle of all those rotating slabs of glazed and crispy pork stacked on a spindle like tasty 45s. Or maybe she was making no mistake at all. "You pay me cash when you pick it up, okay? Day after tomorrow, eleven A.M.? Okay?"

Archy said that would be okay. He worked to get a grip on himself. Thinking of Tony Stark, Iron Man, with that shrapnel lodged in his heart's scar tissue, doomed to a life encased in armor, flashing his repulsor rays. That Gwen's departure may have stirred echoes of the death of Archy's mother's—FOOM! Repulsed. That if you went back in time and informed Archy Stallings, at the age of fourteen, one day his own son would be filled with nothing but reproach and contempt for the worthless man who had, Wile E. Coyote–style, left a hole in his life in the precise shape of a fleeing father—FOOM! Repulse the motherfucker.

"Day after tomorrow," Archy said, wiping his cheek with the overly blue sleeve of his suit jacket.

Then Nat Jaffe beeped in on the other line.

"I'm a block away," Archy told Nat.

It was forty-seven minutes past the hour of eleven, only about twelve minutes beyond the usual frontiers of Archy's lateness, and he wished sincerely but without much hope that his partner was not planning on pitching him shit about it. Not this morning.

"You have a visitor," Nat informed him, sounding cool if not frosty.

Dread took hold of Archy, mostly at the scalp, like the lining of a too-small hat. The number of available candidates for the role of Dreadful Visitor was more than sufficient to stock his premonition of doom, but at the core of the feeling sat the memory of a visit paid to his third-grade classroom by the school principal, during current events, on the Tuesday morning of his mother's passing. After that day every visitor was, in prospect, Mr. Ashenbach, all news going to be bad. Enemies, lovers, hitherto unknown children, cops and *federales*, process servers, debtors and creditors, vengeful Ethiopian fathers or brothers or clan elders, any one of the nine thousand and nine fools he had been plagued or influenced by over the years, folks time-traveling forward from any one of a number of doubtful periods of his life. Bankwell, Feyd, Titus, or Gwen. In the end he settled on his father as the likeliest Mr. Ashenbach du jour.

"Man by the name of Goode," Nat said, the temperature of his tone dropping by another ten degrees Kelvin. "Says he's a particular friend of yours. Came with his entourage."

Turned out to be only Walter, skulking around in a five-hundred-dollar tracksuit behind that small moon. *That's no moon, it's Taku*, an earbud in his left ear, another dangling like a locket down his chest. A heavy burden of loot at throat, ear, and wrist, black tee, blue jeans, blue Top-Siders without socks.

"You fucking it up," Walter confided to Archy in a murmur. Archy careful to have on his round tortoiseshell sunglasses, nobody going to catch Diz or Mingus crying over whatever stupid shit they might have done or left undone. "Don't fuck it up."

"I'm not," Archy said.

"Don't let your boy fuck it up, either."

"Nat?"

"Man, what is his problem?"

"He being touchy?"

"Kind of like."

"Dude can be touchy," Archy said.

If upon first arriving at the store this morning, the affable Mr. Gibson "G Bad" Goode had, as might be imagined, attempted to exchange a few pleasantries with Mr. Nat "Royal Pain" Jaffe, by the time Archy walked into Brokeland, the two men no longer appeared to be on speaking terms. They had installed themselves at opposite ends of the store, Nat perched at the cash register, affecting to conduct a careful audit of some check stubs in a scarred black binder, Goode way at the back, fingering a strand of painted beads in the Miles Davis curtain while he flipped through the hip-hop bins. A sweet-sounding copy of *Melt-*

ing Pot by Booker T. & The MG's (Stax, 1971) was playing over the store system, and by the turntablism of chance, the record that Goode was lifting from the bin as Archy came in was a twelve-inch single of Roxanne Shanté's "Live On Stage" (Breakout, 1989), built on the bedrock of sampled Booker T.

Goode spun around when Archy came through the door, but Nat just sat there, hunched on his stool like some high-collared miser out of Charles Dickens, crooked as a finger on a guitar string, humming like a struck length of wire.

"Yo, yo, yo," Archy said. The hat of dread still gripped his brow, but he played things light and innocent, stalling for time as he sampled the atmosphere in the store, checked the thermometer, scanned the length of tape in the seismograph. Needles jigged. Gauges and meters all ran into the red.

"Mr. Stallings," Gibson Goode said.

He stuck Roxanne Shanté under his arm and rolled on the trucks of an invisible skateboard to the front of the store, wearing a thousand dollars' worth of T-shirt and jeans. Archy considered a final burst of evasion, acting as if he had never met Gibson Goode, never flown in his zeppelin, could not imagine what might have brought the man into his little old Telegraph Avenue used-record store on this fine August afternoon. But no, the time had come. Archy needed to man up, take hold of himself. Confess that he had known a moment of weakness. That he was tempted by the offer to run the Beats Department, get a regular paycheck, boss some other folks around.

Then, when he opened his mouth, the usual tangle of lies and evasions came spooling out.

"Oh my goodness," he said. "Look who it is! Nat, you know who this is?"

"I do, in fact."

G Bad and Archy pitched the tent of a handshake over themselves, struck it, folded it up, put it away. Archy glanced over at his partner. Nat wore the look he got when he was listening to something amazing that was new to him. A fleer of analysis, like he was startled to learn that he could have missed this before, given that he knew everything about anything worth knowing.

"Check it out, Nat. Gibson Goode. In our store."

"Totally."

"I know you're excited about that."

"Yep."

"Did you so express it to him?"

"Oh, he did, he did," said Goode.

"You used to get your hair cut here, isn't that right, now?" Archy put the question like an interviewer on 20/20, lobbing him a softball. "Back when it was Spencer's?"

Nat looked up from the three-tier checkbook, betraying the mildest curiosity toward Goode. "Lot of folks got cut here," Nat said amiably.

"Did *you*?" Goode said.

They clocked each other, their gazes two sets of radar guns.

"Before my time," Nat said.

"Get rid of all this vinyl, put a few barber chairs in here, place looks pretty much the same," Goode said. He took out and opened a tin of Flow-brand breath mints, which he had long had a deal to endorse, and offered one to Nat, who shook his head. "Pretty much."

"Stick around," Nat said. "You can come to the second COCHISE meeting, it's at noon."

"Noon? What's the holdup?" Goode said without missing a beat. "Sounds to me like y'all been having meetings every five motherfucking minutes around here."

"I might like to have a meeting right now," Nat said. "Archy? Partners' meeting? Open to the general public. Stick around for that, at least, *G Bad*." He gestured to Walter and Taku outside the window. "They can come, too."

"Nat—"

"You, what, you here to offer Archy a job?"

Goode saw how it was, that Nat knew nothing, had heard nothing from Archy. "That's between he and I." He smiled. "I'm the competition. I don't need to tell you what I plan to do."

"Plan to or already did?"

"He offered me a job, Nat," Archy said. "Manager of the music department."

"The *Beats* Department, I believe it's to be called."

"That is correct," Goode said.

"Manager," Nat said. "Hey, that's great. Congratulations."

"I didn't say yes."

"No?"

"No."

"Well, did you say no?"

Goode taking it all in, scanners lit and feeding information to the option-running brain.

"At one point," Archy said. "Maybe not definitively."

Nat hooked a thumb in Archy's direction. "Get used to that kind of thing," he told Goode.

Archy felt blood in his cheeks, the shame of the ponderer in a world that urged decision. A deliberator nipped at and harried by the hounds of haste. Professing in his heart like some despised creed the central truth of life: The only decision a man will never regret is the one he never made.

"How about that old man of yours," Goode said. "Mr. Strutter. He ever turn up again?"

The question caught Archy off guard, Luther a pot he thought he had slapped a lid onto one time already that morning. He began to understand, though not yet to accept, that sooner or later his father—out there scheming, rolling some kind of Julie Jaffe–style D&D dice—would have to be faced, dealt with.

"Not that I know of," he said, trying to figure where Goode was going with this line of questioning.

"Your *father*?" Nat said. "How is he mixed up in all this?"

"You know our mutual friend Brother Flowers going to find him," Goode said. "With or without your help. Got all his people, got those nephews, out there looking everywhere. Lot of folks owing Brother Flowers something, could find themselves able to wipe out a lot of debt real fast. Come up with a house number. Name of a motel."

"So be it," Archy said. "Whatever. I can't go there, you know?"

"No?

"No, man, I can't think about that now."

"You might want to start soon."

Goode's tone was cool, matter-of-fact, unconcerned with the fate or the whereabouts of Luther Stallings, and Archy saw, catching up at last, that the warning was directed at him. Goode was trying to remind him that the job offer with Dogpile had been, and remained, conditional on his helping Flowers track Luther down.

"I surely will," Archy said. "I will start thinking about it, sure enough. The day after tomorrow."

A beautiful phrase to the ponderer, *the day after tomorrow*. The address of utopia itself.

"Okay, let me try for one second to pretend like I understand," Nat said. "Not only do you, Archy, *not* plan to help me get out in front of this thing, reach out to the neighborhood, start pressing the city, the Planning Commission, on the DEIR, so forth? But you are actively considering going to *work* for this guy at Dogpile. Do I have that right?"

"You might," Archy said. "Or perhaps you might not."

"Archy, what the fuck?"

"Nat," Archy said, "for a good many years, I have been trying as hard as I can, and in good faith, to answer your rhetorical questions. Today, just this one time, I'm afraid this particular rhetorical question is going to have to comport itself in the traditional manner, which I believe is to not need an answer from me or from anyone."

"Arch," Nat said, and for the first time his eyes, his voice, betrayed a certain desperation, a wince of genuine pain. "I need you. You can't just sit this out. We have to actively *oppose* this asshole."

"Seriously?" Goode said, showing pain himself, though it was the broader, more universal pain of reckoning with fools. "You going to do that, Stallings? Cost this neighborhood where you grew up, like, two-fifty, three hundred good-paying jobs? I don't know how much in revenue, tax base? Neighborhood revitalization? Sense of pride?"

"Maybe," Archy said, soothing himself with the feel of the words, two cool sides of a smooth round stone between his fingers. "Maybe not. For the time being, I have a neutral stance."

"Oh, uh-huh," Goode said. "Okay."

"Fuck that," Nat said. At last he abandoned the pretense of book-keeping, closed the cover on the three-level checkbook, slapped his pencil down. Pouring himself off the high stool like Snoopy going from vulture to snake. "No, you don't. I mean it, Archy. Either you are fucking me over here, or you are helping me out. Which is it?"

Archy and his brown shoes made their way around the counter, and he brushed up close against Nat, taking some kind of ugly satisfaction in the way his partner stepped back. Even though he knew that Nat was far from a physical coward, had gotten his hothead self into more fights and public dustups than Archy over the years by a factor of ten. Archy activated all the force fields of coolth, calm, and collectedness built in to the circuitry of his Iron Man armor. Nothing to fight about, no need for alarm. He took down the framed copy of *Redbonin'* that he had hung on the wall the day of the first COCHISE meeting. He propped the frame on its bottom edge along the counter, opened the triangular foot cut into the cardboard backing, angled it so that the photograph of Mr. Jones's freckled face, looking young and fierce, could stare down Gibson Goode. The disc itself stood among the hold items on the shelf behind the register in its paper sleeve. Archy slid it out, held it up to the window, watching the daylight flow like water across the shimmer of the grooves. A Very Fine example of a scarce release, believed to be among the smallest runs of all CTI pressings. He laid the record on the turntable's platter and cued the first track, a cover of "I Don't Know How to Love Him" from *Jesus Christ Superstar*.

Cochise Jones always liked to play against your expectations of a song, to light the gloomy heart of a ballad with a Latin tempo and a sheen of vibrato, root out the hidden mournfulness, the ache of longing, in an up-tempo pop tune. Cochise's six-minute outing on the opening track of *Redbonin'* was a classic exercise in B-3 revisionism, turning a song inside out. It opened with big Gary King playing a fat, choogling bass line, sounding like the funky intro to some ghetto-themed sitcom of the seventies, and then Cochise Jones came in, the first four drawbars pulled all the way out, giving the Lloyd Webber melody a treatment that was not cheery so much as jittery, playing up the anxiety inherent in the song's title, there being so many thousand possible ways to Love Him, so little time to choose among them. Cochise's fingers skipped and darted as if the keys of the organ were the wicks of candles and he was trying to light all of them with a single match. Then, as Idris Muhammad settled into a rolling burlesque-hall bump and grind, and King fell into step beside him, Cochise began his vandalism in earnest, snapping off bright bunches of the melody and scattering it in handfuls, packing it with extra notes in giddy runs. He was ruining the song, rifling it, mocking it with an antic edge of joy. You might have thought, some critics felt, that the meaning or spirit of the original song meant no more to Cochise Jones than a poem means to a shark that is eating the poet. But somewhere around the three-minute mark, Cochise began to build, in ragged layers, out of a few repeated notes on top of a left-hand walking blues, a solo at once dense and rudimentary, hammering at it, the organ taking on a raw, vox humana hoarseness, the tune getting bluer and harder and nastier. Inside the perfectly miked Leslie amplifier, the treble horn whirled, and the drivers fired, and you heard the song as the admission of failure it truly was, a confession of ignorance and helplessness. And then in the last measures of the song, without warning, the patented Creed Taylor strings came in, mannered and restrained but not quite tasteful. A hint of syrup, a throb of the pathetic, in the face of which the drums and bass fell silent, so that in the end it was Cochise Jones and some rented violins, half a dozen mournful studio Jews, and then the strings fell silent, too, and it was just Mr. Jones, fading away, ending the track with the startling revelation that the song was an apology, an expression, such as only the blues could ever tender, of limitless regret.

Archy pressed the button that raised the tonearm of the Marantz 6300 he had restored to its veneer and steel glory after Nat rescued it from a curbside trash heap in Montclair. In the silence that followed, he returned disc to sleeve, sleeve to album.

"Nat," Archy said, "I'm sorry. I know I am the most unhelpful, indecisive, useless partner you could have. And Mr. Goode, I apologize for how rude and how ungrateful I probably seem to you regarding your generous offer. But right now, and for the next forty-eight hours, until I see that man safe and resting peaceful in the ground?" With both hands, like a ring-card girl, he raised the record high, flashing the face of Mr. Jones now at Nat, now at G Bad. "Fuck both of y'all."

He nodded to himself as much as to both his interlocutors and then, tucking the record up under his arm, set out, feeling mysteriously free, for the first time in days, of regret, ready for whatever might come, and bound, as ever, for the day after tomorrow.

⊙   ⊙   ⊙

A last morning flag of summer, blue banded with gold and peach, unfurled slowly over the streets as the two wanderers, denizens of the hidden world known to rogues, gamblers, and swordsmen as "the Water Margin," made their way along the Street of Blake toward the ancestral stronghold of the Jew-Tang Clan, its gables armored in cedar shakes faded to the color of dry August hills. Armed merely with subtle weapons of loneliness, they left behind them, like a trail of dead, the disappointment of their tenure at the School of the Turtle. They were little more than boys, and yet while they differed in race, in temperament, and in their understanding of love, they were united in this: The remnant of their boyhood was a ballast they wished to cut away. And still boyhood operated on their minds, retaining all its former power to confound wishes with plans.

"I ain't staying. Just so you know. Not hanging around."

"Just a couple of days."

"Not even."

"Well, just till we get some money."

"I can get some money today. How much you got?"

"A hundred and seven dollars."

"Huh."

"A hundred and eight. I mean, it's probably enough for the bus, but—"

"Bus will be like maybe a hundred."

Their wish, wearing its mask of planning, was to seek out a legendary master in his hidden sanctuary among the deserts of the south and offer their blades to his service. The journey would be long and fraught with peril and was soberly considered impossible, but one of the boys had mastered the kung fu of desperation and the other the kung fu of love, and armed with these ancient techniques, they passed untouchable, protected from knowledge of the certainty of failure. At any rate, it was the end of summer, a season when the wishes of fourteen-year-old boys are wont to turn heedless of the facts. So they had returned to the house where one of the young men had been raised, in the time before he embraced the bitterness and romance of the Water Margin, hoping to find, by theft or pilferage, provision for their journey to the south.

"I would have had more than a hundred and eight dollars, only, like a fuckhead, I bought that stupid Viking helmet at the Solano Stroll back in April."

"How much that thing cost?"

"Two hundred and twenty-five. Yeah, I know."

"Damn."

"I know. But, I mean, those are real horns. From a real bull."

"Don't even really fit you."

"I have a freakishly big head."

"Anyway, Viking helmets didn't *have* horns."

"I know. I'm sorry. I don't know what I was thinking. I didn't know you back then."

"Whatever. I can get the money. If I have to do some, I don't know, maybe some robbing, or, like, I know the combination of the safe where my auntie keep her money. So, yeah."

"She keeps it in a safe?"

"Big heavy one. She got to, living in that house. She has almost, maybe, three hundred, three-fifty she been saving up to buy a new wig. Like a human-hair wig. Hair comes from India, they got these temples, you shave your head and it's, what's it, a sacrifice. I just get up inside that safe . . ."

"You know the combination?"

"I know everything but the last number. And the dial only goes up to fifty-nine, so."

They approached the Jew-Tang stronghold with the stalking diffidence of cats, employing techniques of Silence and Lightness. In spite of their precautions and the intensity of focus they brought to bear, as they crept around to the back, they felt themselves observed.

"What in God's name?"

"Oh. Hey, Mom."

The matriarch of the clan stood at a kitchen window overlooking the back garden. It was known that she could see through shadows, whether in the corners of the world or of the human heart. At the mere sound of her voice, trained along with her eyes and ears by years of merciless study of the tendency of men and plans to go awry, the grand enterprise they had mutually proposed during the flight from the School of the Turtle fell to improbable pieces in her son's mind. The young men turned to gaze up at her, awful in the slanting light, dressed in sober habiliments as though to go before some tribunal, probing their souls with her picklock gaze. In one hand she held a cup and in the other the strip of transparent little boxes in which she stored her mysterious week of pills, the crushed and bitter formulations from which she derived many of the strange powers for which she was legendary.

"He, uh, we got kicked out," said her son.

"We're fine," said the other.

"Kicked out?"

"No, ma'am."

"Yes," said her son.

All the ancient schools of lying, in their mountain fastnesses, and all the techniques they taught were of no avail against this subtle matriarch with the unbeatable kung fu of her Nine Intensities Steel Gaze. The only hope for escape, her son knew, was to tell a version of the truth, to scoot your lie beneath the fingertips of her attention under a sheepskin of truth and pray for an instant of blindness.

"But, just, only for today," said her son. "Carpet cleaning."

"Archy is having his carpet cleaned."

"Yeah."

"I see. Turn it down?"

"What?"

"Can you please turn it down? What *is* that?"

"Return to Forever."

"Yeesh. Thank you. And what's with the, uh, luggage?"

"The washing machine is broken. We came over to do T's laundry."

The one denoted by that mystic initial nodded, but it was plain to the son that the mother disbelieved every word of the story, as she likely also would have done had he been telling the truth.

"They had a fight," tried her son, hoisting his tattered scrap of sheepskin higher. "Him and Archy."

"He."

"He and Archy had a fight. Archy kicked him out."

"What? What kind of fight?"

"Not, like, violent or anything, but, so, we just came back here to, you know. We're back."

His mother nodded agreeably, a clear indicator of disbelief, and dismissed her son from her consideration. "What do you have to say about it?" she asked the other young man.

For a long couple of seconds during which emperors were poisoned and kingdoms squandered and prophets calamitously disbelieved, there was no reply.

"I'm hungry," said the other young man.

"Are you, now?" said the matriarch. "And, so, why didn't you two come in the front door?"

It took an extended interval of mutual silent interrogation for one of them to devise a plausible reply.

"Because we were hungry? And the kitchen is in the back of the house?" said her son, and saw weariness roll across her eyes like a fog.

"Get in here," she said.

Tired and footsore, they trudged up the steps of a fir-wood terrace that overlooked the raked pebbles and dwarf cypress of the back garden. They unslung their packs and racked their weapons and stepped across the ancient sandstone threshold of the kitchen, haunted by the smoke of a thousand banquets and revels, with its vaulted ceiling and its deep stone walls. By the time they entered, she had already lit fires, rendered fats in mighty kettles, wrung the necks of ducks and chickens.

"I got leftover pancakes in the freezer," she said. "I can microwave them. That's it. I have a meeting, I have a crazy day. I have to go."

"We're fine."

"Honestly, Mom. For real. You can go."

But they sat at the table where, over the years, noted rogues and gentleman killers had gathered to praise the hospitality of the house and empty its cellars of rice wine, its larders of ducks hung from hooks like pleats of a long curtain. And the matriarch of Jew-Tang lay before them a feast of noodles leafed with fat, roasted organs, pickled trotters, eggs that had lain treasured for three winters in the ground.

"Take some syrup," she said, arms folded across the front of the short gray silk jacket she wore. "So you want to move back in?"

"He— Oops."

"Oh, for God's sake, Julie. Here's a napkin. Mop it up."

"You know I don't," said the other. "And you don't want me to. You don't like me."

"If I didn't like you," said the matriarch of Jew-Tang, in the epigrammatic style she favored, "I would never give you the satisfaction of telling you that I didn't."

"I ain't staying."

"Okay. So what's the plan, then."

The boys consulted each other by not consulting, spoke without speaking, sought each other's gaze by keeping their eyes resolutely on their plates.

"I *will* break you down, Julius."

Her son laid down his eating implements, carved from the tooth of a sea unicorn, and sighed. "It's all stupid," he said. "Come on, Titus, you know that it is. Like Quentin Tarantino is ever going to let you, just, 'Oh, hi, I'm fourteen and I look twelve, so, like, which way to my trailer, motherfucker?'"

And his companion hid his face behind his hands and wept.

"You had a fight with your dad," the matriarch said after a decent interval had passed, handing him a cloth to wipe his eyes.

"Whatever."

"You can stay here," the mother said. "You can stay here as long as you want to or need to, Titus."

"I ain't staying."

"Look, I'm sure you are a genius of cinema in the budding. No, I'm serious, I read your screenplay, and what do I know, but I thought it seemed very good. But Quentin Tarantino needs you to be at least eighteen years old before he can take you under his wing. If nothing else, I'm sure they have union rules to govern that kind of thing. Now, look, I have to go. I'm already late. Can you tell me in twenty-five seconds or less what is making you sad?"

The knight of secret grief seemed to ponder this question for a period whose duration impressed his stout companion.

"She didn't get her pillow," he said at last.

"What? Who didn't?"

Quickly, her son narrated, as well as he could, the failed early-morning raid by the Empress on the School of the Turtle.

"She can't sleep without it," Titus said. "It's, like, stressing her out. It's probably stressing my brother out, too."

"I'm sure your brother is fine," said the matriarch. "But I tell you what."

She left and returned a minute later carrying a cushion crafted, in barbarian lands of the north, from the innermost down of the snow goose.

With an awful solemnity, bowing her head, she entrusted them with the Long Cushion of Untroubled Slumber.

"What you boys need," said the matriarch, "is, clearly, something to do."

⊙   ⊙   ⊙

Gwen crept up the narrow stairs, let herself in with the spare key. Slipped off her espadrilles to cross the polished wood floor of the dojo, with its faint Parmesan dusting of the smell of feet and, by the weapon racks, its dark, aqueous mirror wall. She was stalked as she passed by the hiss of her soles sticking to, peeling away from, the cold bamboo floor. The mirror wall seemed to harbor as much shadow as it banished, as if it bottled the reflections of past students, forty years of West Oakland youth trying to kick, punch, and style their way out of their lives.

Though it spooked her to be alone with that shade-haunted mirror, Gwen was glad to find the place deserted. She did not care to face her teacher again so soon. She planned to retrieve her scant belongings and be gone before Irene Jew returned from her Thursday-morning appointment with the traditional Chinese doctor who rectified her qi.

Master Jew had sent her out that morning, her resolve cinched with the knotted black belt of the old lady's counsel, to accomplish a clear, simple, even rudimentary objective: Retrieve one pillow, used, not especially valuable. But, like everything she did nowadays—as she had realized aloud while talking to the state senator from Illinois—the rescue mission turned out to be wasted time.

It seemed probable that she had been wasting her time from her arrival in California in 1994. She looked back with embarrassment now on that Gwen Shanks, showing up in Berkeley with her nursing degree from Hopkins, a letter of recommendation to Aviva Roth-Jaffe, and grandiose plans to restore, to her obstetrically diplomate family and to the black community at large, its rich ancestral heritage of midwifery. For a long time Gwen's gifted hands, steady nerve, and the way patients tended to fall for her skeptical good humor about their hippy-trippy whoop-de-doo had served to mask the cavernous echo, when you tuned your ear for the sound of black voices, of the waiting room. Now that silence was all she could hear. As for her marriage, she had fallen in love with Archy Stallings having no illusions about his sexual past or his strength of character. But the outbreak of forgiveness that followed each new transgression of her husband's, as typhus followed a flood, called into question the difference, if any, between illusion and its willful brother, delusion, with its crackpot theories and its tinfoil hat.

It was not supposed to have gone like that for Gwendolyn Ward Shanks. From Mrs. Hampt's kindergarten at Georgetown Day School, which she had entered already knowing how to read *Little Women*, through Jack and Jill, to Howard University, where she had graduated first in her class and been elected president of the Alpha chapter, Gwen had been trained, equipped—her father would have said that she had been bred—to succeed. To fulfill the ambitions of her ancestors and justify the care they had taken to marry well, aim high, climb hard, and pull together. Gwen recalled a lecture of Julie's, delivered one night when he was ten or eleven, on the difference between terraforming and pantropy. When you changed a planet's atmosphere and environment to suit the needs of human physiology, that was terraforming; pantropy meant the alteration of the human form and mind to allow survival, even prosperity, on a harsh, unforgiving world. In the struggle to thrive and flourish on the planet of America, some black people had opted for the epic tragedy, grand and bitter, of terraforming; others, like Gwen's parents and their parents and grandparents before them, had engaged in a long and selective program of pantropy. Black pantropy had produced, in Gwen and her brothers, a clutch of viable and effortless success-breathers, able to soar and bank on thermals of opportunity and defy the killing gravity of the colony world.

It had turned out that Gwen was unprepared for life on the surface of the planet Brokeland. Over the past week, at last, she had begun to succumb to the weird air and crushing gravity of it all. Little by little she had surrendered every gift and hard-won attribute of dignity and ambition until, finally, following the incident at Queen of Sheba and the bloody mess of Baby Frankenthaler's birth, she had lost the one remaining advantage she possessed, the most precious, the hardest-won: her cool. As Julie Jaffe would no doubt put it: *Fail!*

Now there was the board that had been called into session for this afternoon, empowered, duty-bound to drag Gwen through the whole botched delivery all over again. She couldn't face that, and she couldn't face Aviva. She no longer wanted to be a midwife, any more than she wanted to be married to Archy or stepmother to his child. She loathed kung fu, herself, and Oakland. She had never liked the Bay Area, with its irresolute and timid weather, the tendency of its skies in any season to bleed gray, the way it had arranged its hills and vistas like a diva setting up chairs around her to ensure the admiration of visitors. The people around here were fetishists and cultists, prone to schism and mania, liable to invest all their hope of heaven in the taste of an egg laid in the backyard by a heritage-breed chicken. She had to get her shit out of the little upstairs room before Irene Jew got back from the qi fixer, pile it into the back of the car, and light out for someplace. Some town without fixations, one that had sent its vinyl records to the dump and would eat any kind of an egg you set before it. She had hoisted every sail to catch the rising wind of her panic; there was no telling what bleak tropic she might yet strike.

As she crossed the floor to the poster of Lee rampant, another door swung open, nearly smacking Gwen in the face. It was the door behind which lay a half bath with a PVC stall shower, one that boomed like a drum whenever Gwen rotated herself inside it.

"Oh, I'm—Oh, *hi!*"

It was Valletta Moore. Though she was ravaged by time, smoke, and a ponderous hand with the makeup brush, there was no mistaking her. A pinup photo of the woman in her heyday, clipped from an old *Ebony*, hung on the wall of Gwen's father's basement workshop back in Mitch-ellville, where, taking pride of place among the tools on their hooks and the screws in their baby-food jars, it had troubled Gwen's adolescence with all the ways in which Valletta Moore—tall, light-skinned, with planetary breasts—differed from Gwen, while evidently constituting her father's ideal of black womanhood.

Even without the stiletto heels that, in the picture on her father's wall, had launched Valletta like Saturn V rockets into the stratosphere of her Afro, the woman was tall, a couple of inches under six feet. Had to be at least fifty but showing, with the help of a skirt that seemed to have been made by taking a few passes with a black ACE bandage around her hips and upper thighs, enough leg to string with telephone wire, carry startling messages to the world. Hair pulled back tight and glossy against her head, lips shining with purple paint. Her madly green eyes, in the instant before they vanished behind a pair of big Dolce & Gab-banas, betrayed an unmistakable half-canine look of guilty surprise. Caught, Gwen thought, in the act.

Valletta Moore put her head down, shouldered a large red plastic handbag, and with a cool nod, slid past Gwen. In a blasphemous pair of heeled pumps, she went clicking across the sacrosanct floor of the dojo.

The officious swagger in her gait might have been some flavor of self-possession or the cool skedaddle of a shoplifter making for the door. In either case, the streamer of toilet paper that trailed from the waistband of her tiny skirt like the banner of an advertising airplane pretty much spoiled the effect.

"Oh! Um. Miss—Ms. Moore."

The woman stopped, and in the instant of her hesitation, the clatter of her exit echoed in the empty studio. She started to turn back to Gwen, then reconsidered. She shouldered the bag again, walked away with no reply.

"Go on, then, Valletta. Fly that flag," Gwen said. "Always good to have some extra toilet paper on you. You never know."

A taut-fleshed, claw-fingered, but elegant hand emerged from Valletta's front of haughtiness like a stagehand sent backstage to retrieve a leading lady's tumbled wig. The hand felt around behind with a frantic helplessness that touched Gwen enough to impel her forward to help. Valletta whipped around and jumped back when she saw what Gwen was up to.

"Hi," Gwen said, dangling the strip of toilet paper between three fingers from about the height of her right shoulder, as if she expected a yo-yo to materialize on the other end of it.

"Look at that," said Valletta Moore with a hint of accusation and reproach.

Like boxers or circling cocks, they appraised each other. Their respective cryonic targeting arrays were brought online and deployed. Where their gazes met, great snowbanks heaved up between them. The air chimed with the crack of ice.

"Any other way I can help you?" Gwen said. "Does Mrs. Jew know you're here?"

Valletta Moore took in the spectacle of Gwen's belly, squinting one eye as though staring along the edge of a plank to gauge its trueness. "Who you supposed to be?"

"Who'm I *supposed* to be? Like I'm trick-or-treating?"

Gwen caught a whiff of the other woman's perfume, something dense and somehow reminiscent of the smell of Froot Loops, maybe Poison.

She recalled having detected a whiff of it, like the pressure of an incipient migraine behind the eyeballs, her first night in the secret room. If Valletta Moore was not herself a former pupil of Mrs. Jew, then Gwen reasoned that maybe Archy's father had returned to the Bruce Lee Institute, seeking refuge and shelter in the hands of his old teacher, departing just before Gwen showed up.

Great. It had been shameful enough fleeing to the dingy spider hole, behind the hidden door, when she could at least imagine herself to be following, as Master Jew had given her to understand, in the footsteps of fugitive lamas and persecuted practitioners of Falun Gong. But maybe all this time she had been filing herself alongside a squirrelly old no-account basehead and his washed-up ex-ex-girlfriend in a drawer marked, everlastingly, *Fail!*

"How'd you get in here?" Gwen said.

"I have a key."

"I heard there was only one extra key."

When Valletta snapped open her handbag to fish out and brandish her own key to the door of the institute, Gwen glimpsed against the red satin lining a hole in the universe that was exactly the shape of a large handgun, just sitting there absorbing all light on the visible spectrum.

"How'd you get a key?" Gwen said steadily, though her heart swam in her chest, kicking like the boy who inhabited her. "You take lessons here?"

She glanced across the studio to the glass cabinet where Mrs. Jew had amassed a gold-brass conurbation of trophies ranked in dusty skylines. Generations of insect citizens had abandoned their husks and limbs in its necropolitan streets. Propped along the back of the topmost shelf, a half-dozen framed black-and-white photographs depicted Mrs. Jew with some of her most successful colleagues and students, among them the future Kato, looking grave as a mycologist in a white gi, and a handsome brother in a tall natural, bent down to get his smiling face alongside that of his tiny *sifu*, a man whom Gwen had long since identified as Archy's father, Luther Stallings. She first learned of the Bruce Lee Institute from Archy, who recommended it solely on the basis of the sheepish nostalgia that informed many of his recommendations, back in the fall of 2000, after somebody told her that martial arts might help with the lingering stiffness that getting rear-ended by a Grand Wagoneer had left in her knees and lower back.

"You used to be a student here, too?"

The "too" hung there, unglossed, a pin to hold the map threads strung by Gwen as she worked her way from the woman standing in front of her; to the photograph of Luther Stallings in the trophy case; to his estranged son, a memory of him crying in the bathroom at their wedding, relieved and crushed because his daddy, conforming perfectly to Archy's expectations but not, alas, to his hopes, had failed to show; to stories she had heard from Archy about crack houses and court appearances and, long ago, a naked woman shaving her legs in the bathroom of a Danish modern bachelor pad in El Cerrito.

"I know you?" Valletta Moore said, clearly doubting it.

"We've never met," Gwen said. "My name is Gwen Shanks. I know who you are." Knowing it was probably a mistake yet unable to let the woman, pathetic as she might be, have the satisfaction of thinking that Gwen had recognized her famous face from the movies or from, say, a glossy pinup stuck to the wall of a garage workshop twenty years ago, Gwen added, "I'm married to Archy Stallings."

"What? Get the fuck out." Valletta Moore pushed up her sunglasses and dazzled Gwen with green. "You *are*? You and Archy having a *baby*?"

"No, I'm just incredibly fat."

"Not really?"

"No," Gwen confessed. "I'm just feeling sorry for myself."

"Oh, honey."

"I mean, wow. Valletta Moore. How are you?"

"How am I?" She seemed to teeter on some edge. "I am doing what I have to do, you know what I'm saying?"

"I ought to by now."

"And I am *trying* to stay fly."

"Oh, you are. Most definitely."

"Thank you, honey. What are you . . . You living here now?"

"I was just— No. Right now I'm moving."

"You and Archy aren't together?"

"No, ma'am. Not right now. I guess we—"

"You don't need to say nothing. If that boy has, like, only ten, fifteen percent of what his daddy came equipped with, then you got my full sympathy, and you don't need to say nothing else."

"Is he all right? Luther? Is he . . . in trouble?"

Valletta seemed to try to decide how best to answer. "I'm sorry," she said. "It's nice to meet you, Gwen, but I really have to leave." She took a step toward Gwen. Leaned in. Swept Gwen up for three seconds in a riot of perfume and hair oil and piña colada–flavored gum. "All right, now. You take care." Again she adjusted the heavy burden on her right shoulder and started to turn away.

"Are *you* in trouble?" Gwen said. "Is there anything I can do to help?"

"Stay fly," said Valletta Moore, hurriedly reversing the terms of her equation. "And do what you got to do."

Then she was gone. Gwen weighed her parting words, wondering at how a certain warmth kindled in her chest at the sound of them, almost like the flame of nostalgia. They rang a bell; a snatch of lyric, a parting line tossed to the crowd at the end of a live album. A catchphrase. Ah. It must be something that her character said in one of those dreadful movies she was in. Taking the yoke of a plummeting cargo plane, just before leaping from a fire escape to the roof of a passing uptown bus, strapping on for a showdown with a gang of heroin dealers. Or with a hospital review board.

Gwen went into the secret room, and instead of packing up her things and lighting out, as she had planned, she submitted her clothing to harsh inspection, trying to find something that would do for the board. Nothing: She would have to go shopping; there was just enough time for that and a trip to Glama. All the while the words echoed and re-echoed, and finally, in mid-carom, she caught them: *Do what you got to do, and stay fly.* They were the parting words of Candygirl Clark, the character played by Valletta Moore in the *Strutter* movies. As she undressed, Gwen wondered whether the phrase was something cooked up by the screenwriter, some Jewish dude trying to think like an ass-kicking soul sister, or if they had started out as an ad lib, something that Valletta used to say for real. She went into the bathroom, wrapped in a towel that strained to girdle her, her hair tucked under a shower cap, and noticed that the lid of the toilet tank had been knocked off-kilter. She looked inside and saw a plastic bag taped to the inside of the tank, slit open, empty. The lid of the tank tolled like a bell as she restored it.

There were all kinds of things wrong with her life, and as they swarmed her, she did an admirable job of identifying and taxonomizing them. As a meteorologist of failure, she had proven her mettle in the teeth of an informational storm. That was how troubles arrived, mourners rushing the bar at a wake. Though they came in funereal flocks, they could be dismissed only one at a time, and that was how she would have to proceed. She ran the water in the shower, letting it get hot, watching her face in the steel mirror until it vanished like San Francisco into a summer fog. She took the water onto the load-bearing points of her body as hot as she could stand, hoping to undo some of the kinks from another night without the body pillow. When she emerged from the bathroom, feeling luminous, giving off steam, she found that the most recent of her troubles had taken it upon itself to find its own way, literally, to the door. To *a* door, at any rate. Against the bottom of the black-and-white photographic poster of Bruce Lee, propped against the sheet of Lucite that covered it, bent at the center as though to duck and allow Bruce, feet and fists flying, to hurdle it in a single, unending, eternally incomplete bound, lay a large, plump pin-striped body pillow. On the floor beside it lay a square of yellow sales slip on the back of which Julie Jaffe had written, in his antic all-caps hand, DO WHAT YOU GOT TO DO AND STAY FLY.

⊙   ⊙   ⊙

In the seat by the center door of the 1, a young Latina mother with her hair pulled up into a palm tree atop her head sat yoked by the string of a pair of earbuds to a little boy on her lap, a bud apiece in each left ear. The little boy was holding by its remaining arm what appeared to be a Goliath action figure from the old animated *Gargoyles* program. Long ago, it had been Goliath's orotund voice, stony musculature, and leonine coiffure that stirred in little-kid Julie, as he watched *Gargoyles* on the Disney Channel, what he recalled with poignance as his first conscious erection. The show had since gone off the air, and the little boy probably did not even known who Goliath was, how much tragedy there was in his gargoyle past, in the lives of all the gargoyle race. To him the toy was only an imperfect enigma, at once cool and ruined. His mother probably bought him broken old secondhand toys off of eBay, to save money, or shopped for him amid the desolation of the children's bins at Goodwill. Or maybe she worked cleaning houses for women who gave away to their servants their children's old, broken things. The little boy probably thought of Goliath as simply a toy monster. Such bias and ignorance were, after all, the usual portion of monsters. Julie felt a stab of sympathy toward monsters and toward himself, but most of all, he felt sorry for the little boy with his armless plaything and his one earbud. Julie always found ample cause for sorrow in his fellow passengers on the bus.

"Ain't *my* grandma," Titus was saying.

"I know, but still."

"You saying you would not want to get up in that."

It was hard to imagine wanting to, but Julie felt no need to say so. Nor did he point out that, for example, a swordswoman wearing a steel brassiere and chain mail, occasionally subject to fits of magical bloodlust, was theoretically awesome in more or less the same way that Valletta Moore was awesome, but if, say, Red Sonja were to turn up on the Number 1 bus, headed for downtown Oakland, the question of whether or not to, quote, get up in that, unquote, would not necessarily feature in Julie's first series of internal discussions on the matter. And that was leaving aside the whole question of her possibly being somebody's grandmother.

"Sure," Julie said presently. "Totally."

"Faggot."

"Hate speech."

As if in reply—a reply uttered in the silent and intricate language they used to transact the secret business that underwrote their friendship—Titus took hold of Julie's hand and pressed it against the fly of his jeans. They were at the back of a spiffy new Van Hool, segmented and capacious, and there was no one in the seats behind or around them, but the bus was far from empty, and you would not have said that Titus's move was quite covert. Julie pressed his palm against that straining arc of denim, rocked it back and forth, fingers spread. Titus kept his eyes on Valletta, imagining, Julie understood, that he was *up in that*. In the rape scene that opened *Mayflower Black*, Valletta Moore bared breasts that had the graceful architecture of eggplants, paler than the rest of her, nipples fleshy, aureoles far-flung. When she stabbed her white rapist in the throat, improvising a shiv with a shard of broken vinyl LP, rolling off him, you could see, in freeze-frame, *there!* and *there!* the tangled shadow of her bush. No doubt Titus was making use of some of that material now. He was not, Julie knew, picturing Julie naked. He was probably not even thinking that it was Julie reaching to unbutton his fly.

Julie's fingers staged a brief bit of comedy with the buttons and the waistband of Titus's boxer briefs, in which Titus's dick played the role of clown bursting from a pint-sized car, snake liberated from the fake can of nuts. Smooth and cool against the hand as gargoyle stone. As he played with Titus, Julie tried to look at Valletta Moore the way he imagined that Titus was looking at her, but all he could manage was the idea that his lips were Valletta's, a vivid O painted red around Titus's penis. That his head was bobbing up and down and mechanically in Titus's lap the way Valletta's had done during her love scene with Luther Stallings in *Strutter at Large*. The idea that Julie could ever resemble Valletta Moore, in this or any way, struck him as only slightly more likely than his being able to get up in her, and he smiled at his poor little gargoyle self. Things went as far as they could between Titus and Julie's fingers without causing cleanup issues. Titus brushed Julie's hand aside and, still looking at Valletta, buttoned himself up. He gave Julie's fingers a gentle squeeze.

Julie said, "Seriously, dude, you shouldn't say 'faggot.' "

"Yeah, whatever."

"I'm serious. It's—"

Titus said, "You go right ahead, call me 'n—' "

"Oh, yeah, right."

"I really don't care."

"Yes, you do."

Titus frowned, half-closed his eyes, rehearsing the scene in his mind. Slouched low next to Julie, legs sprawled out into the handicap area, Nikes slanted like a couple of Easter Island heads. Taking up about a third of Julie's seat, too. "Probably true," he conceded.

"Anyway, I never *would* call you something like that."

"Yeah, whatever, Wavy Gravy. Peace and love."

"Want some tempeh?"

Titus's eyes behind his Run-DMCs bore in on the back of Valletta's head as she stared at the bus window opposite or, less likely, at whatever there was to see on the far side of the glass. As though to offer evidence of the terminal crunchiness, the megadoses of rainbow radiation, to which Titus felt Julie had been overexposed in his sheltered Berkeley youth, they rolled past the ruin of the Bit o' Honey bar. The Bit o' Honey, owned by some Black Panthers, was mentioned twice in a book on Panther history that Peter van Eder had loaned them. The Minister of Defense, Huey Newton, had been jumped and beaten in the parking lot, and a few nights later, perhaps in retaliation, someone named Everett "Popcorn" Hughes had been shot inside the bar. Now, affixed to one of the Baghdad-quality blast shutters that blinded the Bit o' Honey's face, a bold if oddly worded sign announced, in lean sans-serif letters, that the site would soon be home to the MindBridge Center for the Study of Human Consumption.

"I think I know where tempeh comes from," Julie said.

"Okay," Titus said to the back of Valletta Moore's head. "Where we going?"

"The Number One goes to East Oakland. Out, um, International, kinda like, Fruitvale, I think."

Julie knew that Titus had not been asking about the bus route and where it might lead them. The gist of his question had been: Where is *she* going? They had literally bumped into her, emerging with a dreamlike matter-of-factness from the front door of the Bruce Lee Institute. The body pillow serving to absorb, like an air bag, Julie's impact with the woman. At that point, enveloped in the deep, cool cushion of her fragrance, Julie had sort of recognized her, thinking, *That woman looks like her and smells how I would imagine her smelling how funny since I have just seen all six of the nine films in which she appeared between 1974 and 1978 and which are available on DVD or VHS I wonder how old she is if she was born in like 1954*, and then when they came back outside, having left the pillow and note for Gwen, and saw the woman waiting by the bus shelter across Telegraph, he had known her for certain: Valletta Moore, in the flesh. High, fine, feline, with that Candygirl Clark aloofness, but looking, to the eye of a rainbow-irradiated East Bay boy, maybe a touch on the tranny side.

Titus got very quiet when he recognized her, the way only Titus could get quiet, shutting down nonessential systems, patching all available impulse power to the sensors. There was Valletta Moore, waiting for AC Transit, tapping her cell phone against her hip, face unreadable behind her foreign-dictator shades but standing folded into herself, with impatience or the need to pee. Her head fixing like a radar dish on every car that passed her. Going somewhere. Looking out for someone.

The possibility that she was on her way to a rendezvous with Luther Stallings occurred to both boys simultaneously, since in the interval between the doorway collision and now, they had not only deposited the body pillow by the door behind which (a thought as fearsome to Julie as that of having sexual intercourse with Valletta Moore or Red Sonja) the naked expanse of Gwen Stallings was evidently being lathered and rinsed. They had also seen a framed photograph in the dusty trophy case: the picture of Luther Stallings in his prime, posed beside the crazy little Chinese *sifu* lady when she was only one hundred, and not one hundred and thirty-five, years old.

"Okay, check this out," Titus had said, watching her in the bus shelter. Power restored to all systems. He'd patted at the side of his tidy natural with his dazzling palm. Then he had crossed the street in disregard of a don't-walk signal and converging vehicles, with Julie bringing up the rear like an old worried grandpa. When the lady's bus came, the boys got on it. They drew a line from the photograph, lost in the dust of kung fu oblivion, to Valletta Moore, and now they were riding the bus along that line as she took up the pencil and marked the course they might follow to find the magical man.

It would not be accurate to claim that Julie had no illusions as to whether Luther Stallings would turn out to be worthy of the admiration, regard, and even—in a way that was, at this point, almost pure fanboyishness—the love that Titus and, loving Titus, Julie felt toward the man. True, Julie Jaffe was one of those rare beings capable of adopting an optimistic view toward the past, and furthermore, he had experienced while watching the available filmography of Luther Stallings the kind of sexual arousal that must afflict Titus as he stared at Valletta Moore. Not because Stallings was beautiful—though he was, his litheness in fight scenes and action sequences like a base stealer's, head down and ready to get some dirt on his pants. What got to Julie was the way Luther Stallings off-gassed something invisible that Julie wanted to call *equipoise*: unruffled, confident, prepared to improvise. Something so rare and fragile could not be entirely faked. Archy had the same quality, softened up, and so, in his turn, did Titus: There had to be some kind of genuine basis in the famous original.

A number of Julie's illusions remained intact, therefore, at the end of the ride as he followed Titus, who was following Valletta Moore, east to Franklin Street, where she opened her phone, made a brief call, then went into a takeout whose sign argued, with a certain apathy that must have been the fruit of language heedlessly applied, that it was properly known as EGG ROLL LOVING DONUT. But even without having heard the disparaging words and tone his father and Archy had used about Luther Stallings, Julie had read enough books and seen enough movies to suspect that if Titus ever did meet his grandfather, he was in for a disappointment, perhaps a grave one. Julie was so conscious of this possibility that as great a part of him hoped Valletta Moore was only stopping for a donut on the way to pay her electric bill, say, and had not seen Luther Stallings in twenty years, as hoped that they were seriously on the man's trail. Titus showed nothing but scorn for Archy and had never said anything remotely to the effect that he had a hole in his heart in the shape of a father, but like an astronomer with an exoplanet, Julie could infer that hole's presence from distortions in the field around Titus. It was there in the ambition and the scorn. It was there in the daring that led Titus to cut past Valletta Moore, duck ahead of her into

Loving Donut with its brushed steel and white tile like a police morgue, and get in line before she did. Julie recalled having read in a spy novel that the best way to tail somebody was to walk ahead, but there was an élan to Titus's move that went beyond spycraft.

Titus put in an order for six egg rolls and two glazed raised donuts; Julie paid the bill. Valletta Moore, taking no notice of either boy, ordered a chicken chow mein and a dozen egg rolls to go.

She paid for her food using coins of small denomination, slowly, seeming to get angrier with each one that she snapped down on the counter, as though the Asian lady at the cash register were rushing her or fouling up her math. The Asian lady said nothing at all, and her face gave away little, but in her very silence and patience, there was something that might have passed for contempt. Settling the tab took every nickel that Valletta Moore could raise in the clatter of her handbag. When the Asian lady offered to make up the four cents' change, Valletta stared at the proffered pennies with distaste, as though they were something the Asian lady ought to take care of with a Handi Wipe. Then she carried her white paper bag out to the sidewalk, where the boys, cleverly, were already hot in advance on her trail. Their cover: two boys patronizing Loving Donut. Easy to remember, diabolic in its simplicity.

Julie declined to touch the paper bag that Titus held out to him, let alone its contents, whose reek of cabbage and burnt sugar caused his stomach, already twisted by the dread and bus-borne hand job and the thrill of pursuit, to seethe. "Did you see the oil they had those things cooking in?" he said.

"Biodiesel," Titus said. "Run a Jetta."

If you recorded Titus eating the six egg rolls and two donuts on film, Julie thought, and then ran the film in reverse, it would look as though he were firing them out of his mouth, pop, pop, like cannonballs from the mouth of a cannon. Thirty seconds after commencing his meal, he went inside to wash it down with a half pint of milk, also on Julie.

When Titus came back out of Loving Donut, he was just in time to witness the arrival of a very unfortunate Toronado. It juddered, and heaved, and disputed with unseen antagonists like some kind of Telegraph Avenue hobo. Rust had left bloody tooth marks along its underbelly and wheel beds. It might once have been gray or green, but since that remote era, the most irresolute painter in the history of automotives appeared to have tested out every known make and formulation of primer on all of its surfaces. Its driver slowed without stopping and leaned over to unhook a loop of yellow nylon that connected the right-side grab handle to the lock button of the passenger door. The door groaned open. Valletta effected a kind of flying hurdle into the passenger seat. She slammed the door shut and relooped the nylon cord over the lock button. Without missing a beat, she and the driver seemed immediately to resume some earlier argument, the report of which contended, as the car pulled away from the curb, with the hawking and rattling of the car's emphysema, arthritis, TB.

At the wheel, indisputably, unmistakably: Luther Stallings.

"Damn," said Titus, not without an air of truest wonder.

The hunt would have ended there, with the boys left to find their way back from Franklin Street, if Julie had not happened to spot a man in a turban coming out of the one-story office building next door to Loving Donut. He was holding a package of Rolaids and a small spray bottle of Febreze.

"This is going to be incredibly racist," Julie warned Titus, or himself, or the censorious gods of his hometown.

The pathetic Toronado hit a red light at the corner of Twelfth and Broadway. Julie approached the gentleman in the turban and asked if he was, by any chance, a taxi driver, and if so, did he happen to have his taxicab handy?

Julie was to be spared having the racist underpinnings of the structure of his consciousness exposed to the world, at least for now, because it turned out that the door from which the man in the turban had emerged belonged to the dispatch center and main office of Berkeley-Oakland Yellow Cab of Oakland, Inc. Thus Julie's rude and bigoted inquiry was transformed by chance proximity into a reasonable if not logical inference.

The man in the turban looked them up and down, holding the bottle of deodorant spray with a hint of admonishment, as though to suggest that he might be obliged, if they were planning to fuck with him, to Febreze them. "Who is wanting to know?" he said.

They found Mr. Singh's Crown Victoria parked around the corner, bearing across the bottom of its doors, under the stenciled logo of Berkeley-Oakland Yellow Cab of Oakland, Inc., in slanted capital letters, the surprisingly furious legend GOD DAMN INDIA IMPERIALIST DESTROYER OF PURISTAN! The boys got into the back. Julie had twenty-one dollars left in his wallet. He hoped it would be enough to get them wherever they were going.

"Follow that car," Titus said. There were a lot of ways to play the line; Titus chose to go with a touch of BBC, John Steed from *The Avengers*. That left Julie to fill out the role, at least in his mind, either of Mrs. Peel or of Tara King. It was not an easy decision to reach; each had its appeal.

"No, no. No games," said Mr. Singh. "No, no, no. When you are getting onto an airplane, you do not tell the pilot, 'Follow that Boeing.' "

"Maybe I might," Titus said. "You don't know."

"I know this, 'Follow that car,' that is the way a taxi driver gets shot. No, no. No 'Follow that car.' Leave that car *alone*."

"No, that lady left her wallet on the bus," Julie said, brandishing his yellow plastic 21 *Jump Street* number. "We just want to give it back to her."

"This is clearly a lie."

"Seriously, yo," Titus said, assuming a ghetto accent as freely and sincerely as he had the voice of Patrick Macnee. "Tha's my moms in that car, *aight*? She been drinkin and dopin all day, and she don't really, like, *know* that guy she with? And he be all *dangerous* and shit? Come on, man. We just trying to keep an eye out for my *moms*."

A quaver came into his voice as he made the speech, authentic enough to spook Julie. The scenario came to Titus's lips with a freedom, a note of faithfulness to lived experience, that made Julie ache as surely as the little boy with his one-armed gargoyle on the bus.

"That is sounding to me like a police matter," Mr. Singh said.

"Nah. They just gon say it a waste of they valuable time. Know'm sayin?"

Mr. Singh considered Titus's reflection in the rearview. Mr. Singh's eyes in the mirror, in Julie's opinion, were of a doleful beauty.

"I will try to catch up with them," Mr. Singh said, putting the car in gear. "But I will not exceed the speed limit."

"Yeah, okay," Titus said. "Not too close, though."

Mr. Singh looked disgusted. "Playing games," he said.

Ghost Town, Dogtown, Jingletown, there were large swaths of Oakland all but unknown to Julie, among them that ragged old ill-used selvage between the bay and the tangles of the 880 and 980: abandoned army bases and naval stations, depopulated blocks where everything seemed to have been flattened by some economic meteor impact, tattered wetlands ribboned with egret. And, of course, the string of loading cranes massed along the westernmost edge of town, the 1st Oakland Cavalry readying a charge on San Francisco, shipping containers stacked around their feet, like bales of hay by giant quartermasters, to fuel the final assault. The container boxes of the port of Oakland, as seen from the Bay Bridge, were a lifelong source of fascination to Julie, monster piles of colored brick like stabs at some ambitious Lego project left unfinished, interchangeable as casino chips and yet each filled potentially with something new and surprising, soccer balls, polyurethane replicas of sushi, blue lasers, Santa hats, twenty-pound bags of *chicharrones*. In theory they were in constant motion, imports, exports, transshipments caught, swung, and dangled over the beds of trains and eighteen-wheelers and over the decks of the dull ships that brought and carried them away. Julie could never seem to catch the cranes in motion, and the loose but tidy piles of containers never seemed to move, as if the business of the port were a magical one like that of the toys in *Toy Story*, a secret work that would be spoiled if he observed it.

"You see those?" said Mr. Singh as they followed the Toronado down a broad avenue that cut across the former site, according to a historical marker at the old entry gate (tagged with an orc-ish graffiti rune), of the Oakland Naval Depot. Immense railway buildings of concrete and gray stucco awaited damnation on the east side of the avenue. Along the harbor side, a fence of steel unscrolled in woven sheets, topped with razor wire, beyond which the steel cavalry readied its attack. "The big metal things, some people say they are looking like horses?"

"George Lucas," Julie predicted under his breath. "AT-ATs."

"You know in *Star Wars*?" Mr. Singh said. "Those big walking things. Big walking robots."

"AT-ATs," Julie said. "In the snow." He knew that his father, were he present, would feel compelled to point out that this was an urban myth of the East Bay, like the claim that the name itself had been bestowed upon the region by a pioneering coven of Satanists who spoke pig latin. It was very difficult for Julie, committed as he was to being like his father in no respect or particular, to resist the temptation to correct Mr. Singh.

Titus didn't say anything. He just kept watching the back of the Toronado, the same way he watched the back of Valletta Moore's head on the bus.

"Exactly! And there! Look at them! You see? George Lucas used very often to drive, you know, back and forth across the Bay Bridge, from what I have been told, he came originally from Stockton or Fresno."

"Modesto," Julie said.

"Modesto, still worse. Driving up to San Francisco as a young man to drink espresso coffee and experience French cinema, then returning in the small hours of the night to Modesto, which is a real armpit, I am attesting personally to that. And this, you see, was the inspiration for the AT-AT walking machines of the *Star Wars* films."

"Cool," Titus said, taking his eyes off the Toronado long enough to relive those giant legs astride the ice of Hoth, those darting starfighters trailing cable from their spinnerets. "Hold, hold up."

They had come to a stretch of old rail yard where the buildings had been maintained and even renewed. In the trackless void of concrete, a number of metal sheds and depots huddled together around one immense train barn, like a feudal stronghold. A totem pole of signs advertised the services of welders, makers of specialty furniture, tool cutters, fiberglass fabricators and, at the foot of the pole, Motor City Auto Body and Custom Jobs. As the Toronado rolled, popping gravel, into the commons and slowed, its fits and spasms increased. It executed a kind of drunken rumba toward one of three open bay doors in the front of Motor City Auto Body, heaved itself halfway into the bay, and then, with one final shake of its castanets, died. The Toronado's driver got out, and the shadow of Valletta Moore slid across the front bench to take the wheel.

He wore a Raiders jersey, number 78 with the name SHELL across the shoulders. Kung fu pants, some kind of sandals or leather flip-flops. He was carrying a long billy club, a kung fu *bo*—no, it was a walking stick—twirling it like an old-school beat cop.

"Okay. I am now leaving," Mr. Singh announced as Stallings emerged from the car swinging his truncheon thing. "And I am taking you with me, no charge."

Stallings did not look in their direction or appear to notice the taxicab at all. He came around the back of the spavined Toronado and studied its trunk for an instant. Then he raised the walking stick, reared back on his long scarecrow shanks, and gently thrust the stick against the circular keyhole in the lid of the trunk. He bent one knee, gave his wrist a twist, and either by means of qi or pure panache—should there prove any difference—gave the Toronado a baby push. It rocked back, then surged forward and rolled the rest of the way into the body shop. With Blofeldian alacrity, a steel door rolled down behind it. Luther Stallings stood studying the sealed steel door as though it allegorized something. Then he whipped around and pointed the end of his cane at the Crown Victoria.

"Ho, shit," Titus said.

Mr. Singh and Julie came to rapid agreement on the advisability of their turning around now and driving as far as Mr. Singh felt twenty-one dollars would go.

Before Mr. Singh could put the car in drive, Titus got out. He took from his shirt pocket a small number of bills folded tight with origami precision. It might have been a packet containing some kind of sterilized pad. He unpleated a twenty and handed it, halfway to a peace crane, to Mr. Singh. "I got this," he said.

Julie climbed out of the taxi. Titus had never paid for anything before.

"Here is my card," Mr. Singh said, passing an oblong imprinted with his name, his contact information, and the surprising avocation of PUNJABI CHEF.

"Okay," Julie said, too awed or afraid or embarrassed to mention that while he traveled with a portable eight-track player, he did not own a cell phone. "Thanks."

He reached into his Johnny Depp wallet and pulled out one of his business cards at random and had already handed it to Mr. Singh before he noticed it was the one that read:

JULIUS L. JAFFE
libertine

This was a word he had encountered in the pornographic Victorian novels kept by his mother in a shoebox in her closet, among the ordinary shoeboxes. It was less pragmatic though no less hopeful a declaration of calling than Mr. Singh's. The Punjabi chef eyed the card, then glanced over at Luther Stallings. Leaning on the cane, Stallings had begun slowly to walk in the general direction, without any set goal, of Titus. Mr. Singh's mustache did a slow hula over his pursed lips as he contemplated Julie's card. Then, with a number of backward looks, Mr. Singh turned his taxicab around and drove away.

The libertine without portfolio came up alongside his friend, who had fallen, perhaps helplessly, into an arrant imitation of his grandfather's trademark gait, intensified by whatever injury or infirmity required the use of a cane, so accurate it verged on mockery. Stallings angled his head to one side, sizing Titus up; Titus hitched his to the same inquisitive angle. Neither of them appeared to notice that Titus was running a Harpo Marx on Stallings.

"Huh," Stallings said, and Titus duly said, "Huh."

Stallings's hair was densely threaded with ashy gray. There was a good deal less flesh on him than in his heyday. His teeth had not done well; some were lost. Otherwise he seemed okay, not obviously fucked up or sick, and if he was not looking quite so fine as his former costar, he was in far better shape than his Oldsmobile; a state fairly close, all in all, to the original, right down to the chill twinkle in the conman eye. The shoes on his sockless feet were not sandals, Julie saw, or flip-flops, but Chinese cloth slippers, the kind sold out of tubs in Chinatown for five dollars a pair. The kung fu pants had the sheen of doll pajamas or a cheap Halloween costume. Without taking his eyes off Titus, he raised the outstretched walking stick. Leveled it, in a broad sweep, at Julie, the tip of it unwavering, locked as though dowsing at Julie's soul, a move right out of *Witchfinder General*. Julie found himself blushing deeply, as if his pockets held henbane and mandragora.

"Who's the white boy?" Stallings asked Titus.

Julie did not catch the reply, it was tendered so softly.

"It's *who*?" Stallings said. Not angry, not impatient, not unwilling yet to suffer fools or boys who muttered, but ready to go in any of these directions if need be.

"My *friend*," Titus said loudly, ashamed.

Stallings lowered the cane and checked Julie out, once vertically, once horizontally, the process leaving him unconvinced if not outright skeptical. "Your 'friend,' " he said, as if Titus had claimed that Julie was his invisible potato or his talking blue ankylosaurus.

"What they want?"

Valletta Moore stood in the second garage bay. She had her hand tucked inside her red handbag.

"Archy's my father," Titus said.

"Archy Stallings?"

"Yes, sir."

"For real? You my grandson?"

Titus nodded.

"Boy got kids all *over* town," Valletta said.

Luther came in a hurry, with a destination. Titus went stiffly into his grandfather's arms. Holding back. But he went. Luther Stallings—at one time, many, many years earlier, a viable pretender to the fiercely disputed title of Toughest Black Man in the World—brushed away a few ill-suited tears.

"Well, goddamn."

He let go of Titus, stepped away, and cleared his throat. He took hold of the silver-tipped head of his cane with both hands and planted it square on the ground in front of him. Looked down the avenue across the barren expanse of the old depot, then up the other way where there was not much to see, at first glance, but razor wire and morning glory in wild contention. And sky. Lots of sky, torn into scraps of silver and blue. Eighteen-wheelers like beads on an endless strand, creeping along the flyovers toward the docks. And containers stacked everywhere you looked, painted with names that sounded to Julie like the names of opponents in *Street Fighter*: "K" Line, Yang Ming, Maersk, Star. Beyond that the gray planes and facets of San Francisco.

"Best get inside," Luther said.

Titus started toward the garage. Stallings turned to Julie, who hesitated, paralyzed by a ridiculous fear that Valletta Moore might be keeping a gun in her handbag. Afraid, too, of the man with the cane, of this nether zone of Oakland, of certain shadows in the garage that he saw gathering into the shape of man, large and portly, with fearsome mustaches somewhere between biker king and generalissimo.

"What?" Luther Stallings said to Julie. "You want a hug, too?"

"Okay," said Julie. Then he realized that Luther Stallings had only been joking, and even before the man turned and loped, without looking back, into the garage bay of Motor City Auto Body and Custom Jobs, he felt sharply bereft.

⊙   ⊙   ⊙

"Oh, look at that cute little boy," Aviva said bitterly. Frog Park, lunchtime, babies and herders of babies pastured in the sunshine. The boy was as strawberry blond as Julie had been once. He lounged against his mother with his toddler overalls unsnapped and flapping, feeding her a garbanzo bean. "Could you die?"

The boy looked nothing like Julie had looked, apart from the hair. It was the angle of his slouch, the way he carelessly depended on his mother to hold him up, that killed her. Or maybe it was simply the avalanche of years. She looked away. She almost regretted having proposed to Nat that instead of eating at the store, they find someplace nice to sit and have an early lunch together. A bag of sandwiches from Genova Deli, some fried artichokes, a pair of Aranciatas. Her last meal, she had styled it, aiming for wry, hitting brittle. Taken aback when Nat only assented to her terminology, hunched over the counter of Brokeland, chin in hand, flying black sails from every mast like the ship in Greek mythology. Sailing as ever toward her, from yet another labyrinth, aboard the *Moody Dude*. No sign of Archy. Explanation of that absence, of what was wrong around or between the partners, awaited only a formal request from Aviva; but she had withheld it. For once, let Nat do the listening. Let him look for something to grab on to, someplace to hunker down and watch as she unstoppered a genie of panic and did whatever it was that you called the opposite of wishing.

"If I go to prison," she said.

"Ho, boy," Nat said, fishing Möbius strips of onion out of his sandwich with a feline prissiness, piling them on the white sandwich wrapper spread between them on the bench. "Here we go."

"You're going to have to make Julie come visit me."

"Aviva."

"He won't want to come," Aviva said. "He'll be too angry."

"You aren't going to prison."

"Oh, no?"

The boy reclined against his mother the way a god might recline in an Italian fresco, against a favorite cloud, in the heaven of his mother and her bare brown shoulder. Maybe around his eyes, too, there was a touch of Julie, a histamine puffiness in the cheeks.

"Aviva, it's a hearing in a hospital. Not a courtroom trial. And it's about something that *Gwen* did. You're just along for the ride."

"Gwen didn't do anything, Nat."

"No, of course, I'm just saying—"

"That's the *point*. Gwen's real mistake wasn't mouthing off to a doc. I mean, it was a mistake. But she was tired. She was drained. It was a really long day. And the guy totally, *totally* provoked her."

"Had to be," Nat said. "Gwen Shanks losing her cool is kind of hard to imagine."

"It was unreal. Impressive." Delicious, sickening, like eating an entire birthday cake between them. Aviva had found herself reveling in Gwen's outburst with all the horror of fifteen years spent putting up with the highhandedness and disdain of doctors, dusting it like dander from her shoulders. Fifteen years of valorous discretion, unspoken retorts, and *trepverter*. "But a mistake."

"It's always a mistake to lose control like that," Nat said without apparent self-irony.

"Huh," Aviva said.

"Shut up."

"Anyway. This fucked-up hearing we have to endure today? It's not happening because Gwen lost her shit in the ER. And Gwen's blowup won't be the reason when I have to go to prison."

"Good to know."

"Gwen thinks Lazar disrespected her because she's black. And look, I mean you're aware of my policy when it comes to that type of situation."

"Your policy is 'What do I know about being black?' "

"What do I know about being black? I'm sure that when she went after him, calling him names, pointing her finger at him? To Lazar, it was just another stereotype from the ER deck of cards, you know, the Angry Black Woman. But being a black woman wasn't Gwen's big mistake, either. Her big mistake was being a *midwife*. A nurse-midwife who does home births *and* hospital births."

"They hate that."

"They hate all midwives, but they especially hate the ones who do home births. They want to make us go away. They want to say to us, 'Pick. You can do births here in the hospital, or you can do them at home with your patchouli, and your placenta-eating, and your mandala tramp stamps. But if you choose to keep doing those home births, ladies? Then you lose your privileges.' "

She became aware that some of the women around them, moms,

babysitters, were looking to see who was ranting on this fine August afternoon at some poor old slumped guy in a pool-hall suit, picking at a sandwich. At least one of the moms was a patient of the Birth Partners, Dina or Deanna, looking half embarrassed and half entranced, the way you looked at your rabbi when you saw him mowing his lawn in a pair of Bermuda shorts.

"I mean," Aviva said, lowering her voice, "we know this. This is a proven, established fact. Every other hospital in the East Bay has already done it. Chimes is the last one that still lets midwives do both home and hospital births. They're just looking for an excuse to go the same direction. And, of course, they have all the power, right?"

"Right."

"Meanwhile, if *they* have a birth that goes like Lydia's? It's 'Oh, hey, shit happens. Mom's fine, baby's fine, let's move on.' I don't know, maybe if Gwen didn't lose her temper, maybe we would have been able to skate past. But Gwen did lose her temper, and when it came time to say she was sorry for losing her temper, God bless her, she didn't want to do that. So now? Today, at this hearing?"

"What happens?"

"I figure we'll get our privileges suspended. A month, two months. Six months. Just to give us something to think about. And then two or six months from now, they'll make it a condition of our reinstatement that we stop doing home births. Then once they've got me, they'll make all the other midwives stop, too. And here's the thing, Nat."

She put down her sandwich, wiped her fingers, took a long acrid swallow of orange soda. The little boy had wandered away from his mother, tacking across the grass toward the play structure. His mother watched him go, proud, tickled, unaware that every time they toddled away from you, they came back a little different, ten seconds older and nearer to the day when they left you for good. Pearl divers in training, staying under a few seconds longer every time.

"I'm not *going* to stop," Aviva said. "I will tell them I'm stopping, and then I will continue to do home births in secret. I'll do them in yurts and tree forts, in Section Eight housing, on top of Grizzly Peak in some million-dollar glass palace, you can see the Dumbarton Bridge. And then one day, sooner or later, something will go wrong. I'll have to transfer to the hospital. And the secret will get out. My privileges will be terminated. I'll be investigated, and brought up for review, and after dragging the process out until our family is broke and in debt for all kinds of legal fees, the state medical board will take away my license."

She knew a strange sense of exhilaration and saw it reflected in her husband's face, a question forming in his eyes, probably something along the lines of *Is this what* I'm *like?*

"And after they take away my license, Nat, I promise you: I will *still* do home births. I will do them for people who live off the grid. Marginals. Illegals. People, I don't know, moms on the run from the law. Moms in cults, moms living in communes. Whatever insane, highly inadvisable scenario you want to imagine where somebody would hire a rogue midwife. Because babies should be born at home, and midwives should catch them. That is the sum total of my system of belief, all right? It may seem trivial or quaint or crazy to you—"

"When did I ever—"

"—but I want you, okay, to take a minute—or, honestly, given the fact that we have been married for seventeen years, take two *seconds* and ask yourself if I would be willing to go to prison for that simple belief."

"No need to ask," Nat said. "I'm going to start stocking up on files for the cakes."

She smiled and punched him on the shoulder, hard, not without affection.

"Ow."

"Asshole."

The genie had drained, a dark smoky funnel, back down into the mouth of its flask. She tamped the stopper and dropped the bottle into some deep irretrievable abyss where it belonged.

"I'm sorry," she said. "I had to vent."

"I get it."

"I had to say it to somebody."

"That's what I'm here for," he said.

"That's your job."

"Great," he said. "Pretty soon I'll be able to go full-time."

For the first time she caught the note of sorrow in his voice, something catching at the back of his throat.

"Hey," she said. "Honey, what's wrong?"

"Nothing," he said. "It's just a fucking record store."

⊙   ⊙   ⊙

"This is sacred ground," the old man was saying, or words to that effect. Titus, to be honest, was only half listening, or put it this way: He was listening as hard as he could but to a different story. A bigger story, *The Titus Joyner Story* as it culminated, for now at least, here. Here in the fluorescent chill of this funky old lost-Atlantis grotto of a body shop, Motor City Auto Body and Custom Jobs having turned out to be a cabinet of wonders, the final resting place of Inca submarines and Nazi saucers and the death-ray cannons of ancient Egypt. Here where, from steel hooks along two of the cinder-block walls, there hung the bones, hides, and organs of legendary whips—grilles, slabs, chrome intricacies looted or preserved from dozens of monstrous automobiles. Here where, beside the long wall opposite the rolling steel doors, a Smithsonian of parts and hardware stood racked and labeled in bins, baskets, and pin drawers. Here. Now. Hiding out in the shadow of the AT-ATs on the ice world of Hoth. Co-conspiring in the secret lair of Cleon Strutter and Candygirl Clark to hit the vaults of his impregnable self and rob them of the treasure that he had been guarding for so long. With the whole of that guarded and time-locked heart, then, Titus was listening. Not to the science that Luther Stallings was dropping but to the mysterious story of his own life from this moment forward, a tangled tale of which the old man's rambling lecture formed a mere strand in the overall weave. "Holy ground. Oakland, California. End of the dream. End of the motherfucking line."

"But not the end of the lecture," said Valletta Moore, and under her breath, almost but not quite below the human hearing frequency, "Apparently."

She perched on a bar stool, hunched like a jeweler over an upturned steel drum that was covered in a cut sheet of glitter-flecked upholstery vinyl, in the "office" that had been carved out of the back corner of the echoey cinder-block barn by means of two grease-furred sofas, a wooden rolltop desk, and a filing cabinet, under a poster of a mad orange hot-rod pickup truck advertising something called the House of Kolor. Valletta had a white earbud tucked into the ear that was farthest from Luther, and the near one dangled as she leaned to study the little tools and bottles spread across the glittery tablecloth: Everything she needed to execute custom work on her fingernails. From time to time she lowered a pair of half-glasses from her forehead to the bridge of her nose but refused to keep them there for longer than a few seconds at a time. A veddy-dry British man droned from the speaker of the neglected earbud, narrating all about *The Autobiography of Miss Jane Marple* or some such shit. The submarine cave of Valletta Moore's cleavage, glimpsed through the open collar of her shirt, a further, smaller Atlantis lost in freckles and rumors of cranberry lace, formed another vivid tangle in the tale of Titus Joyner.

"Man has a audience," said the old roly-poly Mexican or Spaniard or whatever he was. Owner of the place, Sixto Cantor. Mustached face made out of orange rocks seamed together like the Thing in the Fantastic Four, slung wide as the cars by which he got his living, thick white hair streamlined back into a swan, the fin on some heap of the Fonzie years. Across the name patch of his blue coverall, it said EDDIE in red script. Behind the prescription lenses of black safety glasses with cheese-grater sides, Eddie's eyes patrolled like fighting fish in a tank. At least one of those eyes, at any given moment, was on the crew of six over in the first bay, three Latinos, two black guys, and a little punk-rock body-art dude, who were busy gutting some gray eighties box, maybe a Citation. Just feeding on the thing like a swarm of piranhas. "We gonna be here all night."

"Yeah, well, I'm talking about the nighttime," the old man said. "So that's okay. 'History is made at night,' Henry Ford said that. That is what they mean when they talk about the American *Dream*."

While he professed, Luther Stallings lay on the floor on his back, stripped to his white kung fu pajama pants, balanced at the tailbone on a foam rubber mat, snapping off stomach crunches by the hundred.

Bicycle crunches, twisting crunches, rope climbs, the steady scis-
soring pulse of it marking the progress of a lecture interrupted only
by an occasional wince as his hip bone cracked or by the odd snort of
impatience from Valletta Moore. Every time Titus glanced over at Julie,
boy was watching the ripple and swell of the old man's abdominals, the
play underneath that leather stitched tight as the rolls in a bucket seat.
Julie looking half queasy, half hypnotized, as if watching a sneaker go
around inside a clothes dryer. "Everything got started for us, minute
the white man wanted to get some sleep on a train."

The discourse had been riding this particular local for most of the
past fifteen, twenty minutes, *The Secret History of the Black Man in California According to Luther Stallings*, the old man backing up his claims
with cites and quotes drawn from irrefutable authorities whose names
always seemed to be on the verge of being divulged or else, when spoken
aloud, meant nothing to Titus. Claim Number One, front and center,
being something along the lines of how, when you tunneled deep, the
way the old man had done during the long years of his exile, going way
on down into the mines of knowledge, Oakland was literally the Land of
Dreams. After that, well, between the growling and barking of the air
compressor, the ceaselessness of the trash being talked by the Motor
City crew, the sight of what appeared to be the right (i.e., Robin-side)
door of the Batmobile from the old-school TV show hanging hooked
like a side of beef in the far corner of the garage, and the undersea world
whose gates parted every time Valletta Moore bent over to French the
tip of another fingernail, frankly, Titus did not follow it too closely,
though he understood and even felt prepared to endorse the view that
the Secret History of the Black Man in California truly was all tied up
with the sleep and sleeplessness, the insomnia and dreams of the white
man. Because, because, hmm, something about how white folks back
in the day, needing to catch their beauty sleep as they traveled west sub-
jugating and conquering, turned to a man named Pullman. And this
one white dude, Joe, no, George Pullman, turned right around and,
not out of any kind of wanting to do the right thing but only because he
was cheap and needed an instant pool of skilled but low-pay servants,

started hiring up free black men of the time and setting them to work tending to the slumber of white people. Punctuated by grunts that at times seemed to elide or bleep out the parts of what he was saying that would help it make some kind of sense, the old man evoked the nightly scene, vigilant black men studying the sonorous nocturnal rumblings of wealthy sleepers in the sleeper cars, dreamers rocking through the great western darkness toward the land of sunset, the far shore of the American Dream, which for reasons no doubt made clear during a particularly loud grunt, was all because the word "America" was actually a broken-down version of "Amenthe-Ra," the Land of the West in Ancient Egypt, where you went when you died, though not in a train, of course, but in a boat, a westbound boat like those that had freighted the sorrows of the Pullman porters' African ancestors, even though to the ancient Egyptians, the death journey to Amenthe-Ra was only a kind of sleep, in fact a dream—not Dream as in "I Have a Dream" but, rather, the strange journey taken every night by the sleeping human brain, although, as an aside, the connections were interesting, you had to wonder why Dr. King, whose father was a Prince Hall Mason, had chosen to couch his message using a term so central to the Secret History of Black Men in California, the language of the Pullman porter, raised up and set to rights and liberated while the white man was literally asleep.

"The freest black men that ever lived," Luther Stallings told the boys, "but it was like a kind of secret freedom."

He described the Pullman porters in terms that conjured up giant sleek-haired warriors of the night, armored in smiles, how they went from place to place, all these little backwoods, boondocks towns, seeing the world, carrying like undercover spies, hidden about their persons, all the news of the clandestine world of black America, the latest records, gossip, magazines, hairstyles, spreading the lore and the styles across the country, to every place where black people lived, and most of all singing the song of California, to be specific the city of Oakland, where Pullman porters got off the trains to rest on their sunset couches in the houses they bought with the money they wrestled loose from Mr. George Pullman, houses in which they built up families that sent children and grandchildren to college and trade school and eventually to the United States Congress, then getting back onto the trains in the morning to ride south and east, spreading the news of their own prosperity, so that by the time World War II blew up, Oakland was the Hollywood of middle-class black aspiration, except that unlike in Hollywood, once you got to Oakland, you actually stood a chance of making good.

"Hollywood," Titus said, feeling like he was expected to say something. "Well, all right."

The Secret History came off kind of boring in its particulars, truthfully, built on events and details and historical phenomena whose obscurity to Titus only deepened as his grandfather strung them together: strikes and black labor unions, bourgeoisie and Seventh Street nightclubs, shipyards, the Klan marching down Broadway in broad daylight as white Oakland lined the streets cheering, and yet the arc of the narrative, the sense of sweep across time and territory, stirred, in Titus's mind, a sense of revelation.

"That was the real underground railroad, a railroad underneath, inside another railroad. And this here was the terminus. This building you in, it was a train barn. You see that line there in the cement, crack like a big circle going all the way around? That's where the turntable is. Big old concrete turntable, spinning the music of dreams."

The old man seemed to have concluded his remarks. He sat up, winded, shining from his hairline to his shins.

"Only it don't turn no more," Eddie said.

Luther Stallings looked from Titus to Julie and back, wanting to know what they thought, how they were handling it, what they were going to do with their little minds now that they had been blown.

Julie glanced at Eddie. "Is that from the real Batmobile?" he said.

Valletta Moore said, "Huh." She shook her head. "Luther, they are *not* listening to you." She was tucking little foam spacers between the fingers of her left hand. "Nobody is listening to you."

"Man should have got a Oscar," Eddie said. "Always playing the silent type."

He and Valletta Moore fell out laughing.

"*I'm* listening," Titus said, trying not to sound contradictory, since contradicting Valletta Moore was painful to him and, in the movies of hers that he had seen, occasionally dangerous.

"All right," Luther said, firing off a scowl at his old lady, then giving Eddie the other barrel, mopping his face with a ragged but clean square of polishing cloth. "There you go. Now," he told Titus, "boy, what you got to do, if you want to absorb knowledge, you have to ask questions. So go on. Go ahead."

Titus understood that he was meant to build off the lecture just completed, but that understanding was unable to outrun the natural impulse of his true curiosity. He knew he should ask a question about Egyptian funeral traditions and Prince Hall Freemasons, but to his dismay, he heard himself saying, "Why you have to live in a garage?"

Another laugh arose irresistibly from the neighborhood of Eddie Cantor, a repressed, apologetic series of semi-coughs. This time Valletta Moore contented herself with studying her own reflection in the clear-coat shimmer of her left index fingernail and muttering a few words to herself in a parody of a stage whisper, hard to make out, something along the lines of *Oh, now, I want to hear this.*

The old man sat, long arms hugging knees to chest. He pursed his lips and gave his head a slight shake, leading with his jaw. Closed his eyes, opened them again. For what felt like a long time, he said nothing. Titus began to regret the question, particularly when he saw a brief upwelling in the old man's eyes, though it passed without a tear having been permitted to fall. Titus was on the verge of withdrawing the question and shifting about for a replacement when his grandfather said, "I did some stupid shit in my life. That is the truth."

Titus glanced at Julie, whose face grew solemn and knowing, a touch pious. "Drugs," Julie said.

"Even stupider shit than drugs," the old man said. "And that's saying a lot, y'all can take my word. But I'm clean and sober, thirteen months, one week, and two days. I have my shit together. I officially have a movie in the active stages of preproduction—"

Valletta Moore pronounced another observation whose syllables hovered just that side of audible. She was like the magic harp from that Disney movie *The Black Cauldron*, popping a string every time the harp-playing dude, the bard, came up with some new exaggeration of his exploits or abilities.

"*Strutter 3?*" Titus said.

"You guessed it. But uh, something of that nature, independent type of venture, operating on the kind of small nonstudio level that Stallings Productions operating at, you have to, look here, sometimes you need to get a little creative in your financing. That's why, to try to answer your question, wasn't exactly the question I was expecting, but uh, I came up with a way to, uh, make one of those stupid things I did a *long* time ago, way to turn it around a little bit. Hook up to a major player in the industry."

"Or so you thought," said Valletta Moore.

"Goddammit, Valletta—"

"Thinking you could shake down that—"

The old man was up and on his feet like an umbrella opening. In the passage of another half second, he had organized his arms and legs according to a logic more direct than whatever had guided his verbal teaching. There was an impression of wind and gyration contained within a modest ambit, like the procedures of the Tasmanian Devil in cartoons, and then, as with the push given to the back of the Toronado by the tip of his walking stick, it all came down to the point of his left foot, one square inch of contact. The steel drum pitched over, resounding against the cement floor with a Chinese-gong finality. All of Valletta's little bottles and implements went flying. Over in the bay, the hydraulic pump cut off with a gasp.

"Uh?" Julie said to Valletta Moore. "You okay?"

They were the first words he had directed toward her since the minute they walked into the garage.

"Oh, I'm fine, honey," Valletta said, all cheerful. She crept around on her hands and knees, trying to put things right, checking bottles for cracks and spills. "Thank you."

"Well, I better go check on those yo-yos," Eddie said.

The fighting fish flitted back and forth behind the panes of their aquarium as Eddie surveyed the mess he had permitted in his otherwise spotless body shop, looking like his reasons for having permitted it were no longer apparent to him. Figure his eyes must be trained by now to gauge possibilities for recovery, salvation, hidden in the ruin of a once fine machine. Titus tried to read those eyes for signs of hope, but Eddie was looking at him; Julie; him.

"You boys need a ride anywheres?"

"Uh, well—"

Julie got to his feet, hugging himself, used to hanging with the kind of people who talked it out, shared their feelings, everybody circling up like Care Bears for a big hug when it was through, nobody kicking shit over, spattering the walls and floor with bloody nail polish.

Luther Stallings reached for his walking stick and leaned on it with both hands, watching his grandson but not giving any indication of what he wanted Titus to do or to say.

"We're fine," Titus said.

Eddie nodded and, yelling in a contemptuous dialect of Spanglish, went over to critique the efforts of his crew. Luther's stick banged against the concrete floor as he padded in his Bruce Lee slippers across the stained seas and continents that mapped it, toward the Toronado in the nearest bay. He reached in through the driver's window to take the keys from the ignition, then went around to the back and popped the trunk. He took a plastic bin with two lids that interfolded out of the trunk, huffed it over to one of the workbenches. He looked at Titus.

"Thought your ass wanted to see my movie," he said.

⊙   ⊙   ⊙

She would do what she had to do; staying fly, alas, might not be an option. It implied the sustainment of a metaphysical state from which Gwen, a house on a rain-swollen hillside, had long since slid. But she gave it her best shot, determined to quit sneaking around, put an end to the hiding, all the craven marital and professional ninjutsu. To come on as straight and strong and brazen as Candygirl Clark, unreachable as that aspiration might remain to a woman in her thirty-seventh week who had spent the past three days with a suitcase for a wardrobe and a foam pad for a bed.

With three hours to go before the showdown at Chimes, Gwen drove through the tunnel to the Land of the White People. Her BMW faded incrementally into the local autosphere as the freeway stretched and flexed for its run toward the Sierra foothills. Shadows sharpened, and the afternoon took on a desert shimmer. Sprinklers chittered. Titleists traced white rainbows against the blue Contra Costa sky. Along the forearms of hard-shopping women in tennis skirts, sunshine lit the golden down.

At A Pea in the Pod, Gwen consigned her cubiformity to a simple A-line dress of stretchy gray jersey with a matching gray blazer. The jacket came with shoulder pads that lent her an uncomfortable resemblance to the flight deck of an aircraft carrier. Because it rode up so high on her belly, the dress appeared to hang down at the back a good three or four inches in a kind of impromptu train. She would spend the rest of the day tugging her dress down at the front like a half-bold teenage girl in a micromini.

Up at the cash register, she asked for a pair of scissors to cut out the shoulder pads, which, given the shock on the face of the downy golden salesgirl as Gwen vandalized a dress on which she had dropped $175, felt like kind of a kick-ass thing to do. Then it was on to the Easy Spirit store, where, employing a pair of vanadium tongs and a portable blast shield, she consigned her depleted espadrilles to a trained hazmat team and walked out in a stolid gray pair of modified Mary Janes. They had the charm of cement and the elegance of cinderblocks, but they held her feet without pain or structural failure, and it seemed to her that the librarian-nun vibe they exuded was also not incompatible with the kicking of ass.

Thus equipped, she returned through the Caldecott Transdimensional Portal to Oakland, to submit her hair to the subtle if not silent artistry of Tyneece Fuqua at Glama. To meet Gwen's hair emergency, Tyneece had been obliged—she explained in irritable detail—to reschedule a telephone consultation with a psychic in Makawao, Hawaii, a woman who, during their prior phone session, had come close to locating the two bars of looted Reich gold that Tyneece's great-grandfather had brought home from the war and buried, it was said, in one of three backyards belonging to three different Oakland women who were the mothers of his nineteen children. While she lectured Gwen on the intricacies of Nazi gold registration numbers and of her abundant and goldless cousinage, Tyneece serviced Gwen's worn-out locks, picking out slackers, stragglers, and lost souls, then twisting them tight, as if winding the very mainsprings of Gwen's resolve. She massaged Gwen's scalp, neck, and shoulders and put the new girl on Gwen's sore feet. Finally, having done what she could, she called in Mr. Robert, whom she had sent for as soon as she learned what Gwen was up against today.

Mr. Robert came in wheeling a scuffed pink plastic art box on an airline-stewardess luggage trolley. He was a dapper little gentleman in green plaid pants, a short-sleeve lime turtleneck, and zip-up white ankle boots, with Sammy Davis hair. Nowadays he mostly worked weddings, proms, and the odd quinceañera, but at one time he had been the go-to Hollywood black makeup man, relied upon by an entire vanished generation of television actresses, from Diahann Carroll to Roxie Roker, to combat the visual and technical biases of white cameramen and lighting directors. After a few seconds of intense scrutiny, Mr. Robert shrugged and looked confused.

"I heard this was supposed to be an emergency," he said. "But honey, you're so hot, I'm afraid you going to set fire to my cotton balls."

"Now, don't lie to me, Mr. Robert."

"I'm serious! You're radiant! I need a Geiger counter! I need to get me one of those lead suits like Homer Simpson wears."

Mr. Robert was a scabrous if outdated gossip with a brusque, pointillist touch and a habit of asking questions without waiting for answers. When he had finished, he took hold of her chin in his slim, dry fingers and turned her head this way, that. One eyebrow lifted in a skeptical arch. Then he let Gwen get a gander at herself in the mirrored wall of the salon.

"I almost look beautiful," she told his reflection.

"Almost?" his reflection said, looking hurt. "Honey, fuck that, Mr. Robert doesn't leave no one looking *almost*."

"No, you're right, thank you, Mr. Robert," she said quickly, as he began with an angry clatter to return his brushes and bottles to the pink tackle box. "I look *fly*."

He didn't say anything, but she caught the shrug of the left wing of his mustache, a half-satisfied half-smile. He packed up his gear, slow and deliberate, from time to time rubbing the ache of age out of his fine brown long-fingered hands. Tyneece had already collected Gwen's money for this emergency session, but when Mr. Robert looked up from his kit, Gwen was holding out a twenty-dollar tip. Mr. Robert shook his head and pushed away her proffering hand.

"Hit me next time," he said.

"No, Mr. Robert—"

"I was born in my momma's kitchen," he said. "In Rosedale, Mississippi. Was a midwife like you brought me into this wonderful world."

"Yeah, well," Gwen said, touched, embarrassed, regretting, in spite of the progress it seemed to imply, the loss of the world of black midwives catching black children, grappling the future into the light one slick pair of little shoulders at a time. "After today I might not *be* a midwife too much longer."

As appeared to be his habit—maybe Mr. Robert was a bit deaf—he ignored her. "Before she called my daddy in to see me for the first time," he continued, "this lady, the midwife, she took a lipstick out her purse? And made up my momma's mouth. She combed my momma's hair. Fixed her up, you know? Got her ready. That was how my momma always told it, anyway. Sometimes I wonder, you know, hmm, was that, did that give *me* the idea," hand on a hip, pointing with the other hand, the genie of himself addressing himself in far-off Rosedale long ago, " 'Mr. Robert, when you grow up, you going to be a makeup artist!' "

He hoisted his tackle box onto the wheeled trolley and bound it carelessly with loops of green bungee cord. "Do you think something like that," he said, "something that happened in the room when you were born, you could notice it, and it would stay with you the rest of your life?"

"I wouldn't put anything past a baby," Gwen said.

At 2:55, her Chimes General parking ticket tucked carefully into a zip pocket inside her handbag, Gwen trundled through the high, wide sliding doors she had come through so many times before, having so much more at stake, those other late nights, long afternoons, and early mornings, than her own small, personal fate. The feeders and freshets of East Bay humanity flowed through the filter of the hospital lobby, all the wild variety of life in the local pond. A gang banger rolling toward the elevator with a bouquet of lilies and Gerber daisies stuffed under his arm, a sunburned old buzzard with a physicist shock of white hair and camp shorts, a one-legged, three-fingered bearded biker dude she figured for a lax diabetic being eaten by neuropathy, two new moms—one Asian, one veiled and tented in the laws of Islam— waiting in festive wheelchairs with their babies for their husbands to bring the cars around. Scrubs, coveralls, nightgowns, baller jerseys, and patterned hippie-chick skirts, a pair of Buddhist monks flying the saffron, probably Thais from over at the Russell Street Temple. At the sight of them, Gwen was rapt by a need for the little coconut- and-chive pancakes they served there Sunday mornings, but it was a Thursday, and anyway, Candygirl Clark never would have permitted a craving, even for Thai temple pancakes, to divert her from a mission.

"Wow," Aviva said, taking in the fruit of Gwen's resolve. Shoes, dress, jacket, the exuberant coils of her restored coiffure. "Don't you clean up nice."

Gwen gave a tug on the front hem of the dress.

Aviva was at her gravest, slim and efficacious in a taupe suit with a skirt that fell to just above her knees. Her hair, regularly—you might even have said *carefully*—threaded with gray, was pulled into a wide bar- rette of chased Mexican silver. No makeup at all apart from a touch of color on her lips, a shade or two more vivid than her own natural rose- pink. Rested and collected and projecting, Gwen thought, the slightest touch of resignation to her fate. Having given Gwen's appearance a good going-over, she lingered on Gwen's eyes, as if trying to discern in them some clue to her partner's thinking or state of mind.

"You ready for this?" Aviva said.

"I am *so* ready for this," Gwen said.

"Yeah?" Alerted, curious. "Know something I don't?"

"Not so far," Gwen said, sweet as pie. "But it's only been ten years."

"Huh," Aviva said, bullshit sniffer set as ever to a brutally low ppm.

Gwen tried to go wide-eyed and innocent, feeling, of all things, strong and positive and—but for the lack of six little coconut milk pancakes, steaming and flecked with green onion, nestled in their paper cradle—surprisingly ready.

"I'm just going to try to, you know, maintain my dignity in this matter," she said. "I don't intend to embarrass myself ever again."

"Sounds like a plan," Aviva said. " 'Kay, then. I guess we should probably head on up."

Gwen checked her watch. "Let's give him a minute."

"Give who a minute?"

"Moby," Gwen said, and then she saw the big man stutter-stepping leftward to avoid collision with an elderly black couple helping each other out the front door, a human lean-to, temporary shelter against the day.

She had called Moby right after the fateful shower, her last ever at the Bruce Lee Institute, during the course of which, caught in the brainstorm breeze of all those negatively charged ions, Gwen had found herself imbued with the spirit of Candygirl Clark.

"All your little self-deprecating pregnant-lady fat jokes to the side," Moby had told her over the phone, "I really only represent whales."

"Yeah, *I* know that," Gwen had said. "But Chimes General doesn't."

"Did they suggest y'all bring a lawyer along?"

"No, on the contrary, technically, it's just an informational thing. But that's what makes it such a good idea. Look, Moby, you don't even have to *say* anything. Just sit there with, like, your necktie, your briefcase, all big and intimidating like you are."

"No shit. You think I look intimidating?"

"You definitely have the potential."

"To be badass?"

"Like, a form of badass."

"The intimidation fac-tah!"

"Sure."

Admittedly, she felt a doubt then, hearing the eagerness kindle in Moby's voice along with that horrible *Electric Boogaloo* accent, but today was not about doubt, second-guessing, hesitation. Today was about doing what one had to do while approximating, to the best of one's own and Mr. Robert's abilities, the condition of flyness.

And here the man showed up wearing brown Birkenstock sandals with his baggiest navy suit over black socks.

"Good Lord," Aviva said.

"Whoa."

"What's he doing here?"

"I was trying for a certain intimidation factor," Gwen said. "Frankly, I had not counted on the Birkenstocks."

"Gwen!"

"It's fine."

"It's *fine*?"

"He just needs to sit there. To be there, physically, taking up that much lawyer space in the room."

"Okay," Aviva said, meaning it was not okay. "I'm confused. When Garth Newgrange threatens us with a multimillion-dollar lawsuit that not only could put us out of business but also could leave us both totally fucking bankrupt, you won't even *talk* to a lawyer."

"Garth has no grounds for a suit. His baby was fine, Lydia was fine."

"Then for this thing," deaf as Mr. Robert when she needed to be, "you bring in a guy, the venue of his last trial was *SeaWorld*."

"Ladies," said Moby with the most terrible suavity imaginable. Gwen felt another tremor of uncertainty. On the way up in the elevator, however, Moby assumed a surprisingly professional demeanor, speaking low and fast, buoyant and aswim in his own expertise.

"I spoke to the general counsel," he told the partners. "She said that even though a formal complaint has been brought, it's not like it's, you know, can't be expunged. Written in stone. The board has discretion, and they have authority to toss the thing out as long as we can satisfy Lazar and give them a reason to let it drop. Maybe they keep you, Gwen, on probation for six months, a year. Then everything goes back to normal."

" 'Give them a reason,' " Gwen said. "What kind of reason did legal affairs have in mind? How'm I supposed to 'satisfy' Lazar?"

"Oh, for God's sake, Gwen, you know what you have to do," Aviva said.

"What?"

Aviva didn't say anything, didn't feel she needed to say anything, smug as ever in the telepathic power of her self-evident correctness. Gwen refused this time, knowing the secret word was "apologize," but staring right back at Aviva as the elevator opened at the fourth floor for a ghost, closed, carried on.

"Apologize," Aviva said at last, giving it a slight hint of the imperative.

" 'Apologize?' " Gwen feigned a degree of shock at the revelation. "To Lazar? For what?"

"For nothing. It's a meaningless, empty formula: 'I'm sorry.' Literally? It means you are in pain, you are sore. But nobody knows that, and nobody means to say that. They're just words, Gwen. It's a token, a little box on somebody else's checklist, you take your pencil and you go . . ." She ticked off a little checkmark in midair. "You just mouth the words, take your medicine, and we can all—"

"Take my medicine," Gwen said, breaking out another package of ironizing quote marks, her supply maybe starting to run low. "Okay, sure, hey, they're doctors, right? As long as they don't try to administer it rectally—"

The doors opened on the sixth floor, and Gwen shut up. They briefly became quite lost, looking for the conference room, wandering through an intricacy of corridors and sub-lobbies until they ran into Lazar himself, wiping his mouth on the back of his sleeve, turning from a drinking fountain halfway along a blue-carpeted branch corridor behind Personnel. He was in a light blue button-down shirt with a square-tip knit necktie and a pair of blue twill trousers so tight that his bicyclist thighs hoisted the cuffs to floodwater levels.

"I'm sorry it got this far," Aviva told him.

"I'm sure you are," he said, pointedly avoiding eye contact with Gwen. He opened the door to the conference room and stood aside to let them pass.

As they made the introductions, Gwen saw that she had lucked out: the midwifery review board as currently constituted was three OBs, all of them men. She knew and had worked with all three over the years, and her relations with them, like Aviva's, were in each case at least cordial and, in the case of Dr. Bernstein, who was chairing the proceedings, warm. Bernstein had referred dozens of patients to Birth Partners, and Gwen at various times had formed the distinct impression that old Aryeh Bernstein was macking, in that pass-the-time doctorly way, on Aviva. But none of that formed the basis of Gwen's luck.

3 WHITE MALE OBS, Aviva wrote on the topmost sheet of one of the legal pads that the hospital stenographer had distributed to the partners when they sat down. VS. 1 BLACK MIDWIFE = TOTALLY FAIR.

"Totally," Gwen said aloud, though she wasn't entirely sure where to place Dr. Soleymanzadeh on the whiteness scale.

The stenographer, a formidable older Filipina who was also tape-recording the proceedings, frowned, then typed seven letters into the transcript. Bernstein started, caught off guard by the tap of the keys, obviously fearing maybe that things were starting without him.

"Okay, then," he said, with a nod to Soleymanzadeh and Leery on his left and right. "Ms. Jaffe, Ms. Shanks. Gwen, Aviva. As you know, we're here today to follow up on a complaint filed by Dr. Lazar, here, Paul Lazar, following from an incident that occurred in the ER back on the twentieth. At this point, the hearing is purely for the purpose of gathering information, trying to fill out a more complete picture of what transpired, which Doctors Soleymanzadeh, Leery, and I will use to come to some kind of recommendation about the status of your privileges here at Chimes General. Now, this is a serious complaint, and there's no question it's an important matter. Also, I should probably mention that whatever our recommendation should be, that is likely to become the action taken by the hospital. But—"

"Or not taken," Moby said as if helpfully.

"*But*," Bernstein resumed, "I'd like to begin by reminding you, Gwen, Aviva, that this hearing falls strictly within the purview of hospital and departmental policy regarding the conduct and status of nurse-midwives with privileges at Chimes. It is emphatically *not* a legal proceeding. You do not need a lawyer."

"Dr. . . . Bernstein. Here's the thing, a lawyer is sort of like an umbrella," Moby said, looking more relaxed and in his element than Gwen had ever seen him, not a trace of Boogaloo Shrimp in his manner or his voice. "You don't bring it, it rains."

"I understand, Doctor," Gwen said. "I'm just being careful. I hope you'll be careful, too."

She saw how it landed, the way Joe Leery's eyebrows shot skyward before parachuting back down to the ridge of his brow.

"Okay," Bernstein said, "and, well, you are certainly free to do so. Mr. Oberstein."

"Doctor."

"Before we get into the serious charges and issues that have been brought up in this case, I think we should all take a moment to remind ourselves of the most important thing, which is that the mother and the baby are both fine. That isn't the issue here."

Seven different variations on the pious nod, everybody safely in agreement on that score.

"Now, Dr. Lazar," Bernstein said, "we've all got your complaint, and I think it's pretty clear you feel that Ms. Shanks's conduct not only lacked professionalism but diminished the quality of care—"

"Look," Lazar said, the man everlastingly an asshole, through and through, a common enough trait among doctors statistically and one not necessarily falling, therefore, under the heading of Gwen's good luck. "I'm not going to get into a pissing match, okay? I'm not interested in who screwed up, or how they screwed up, or whether or not it makes sense for people to have babies in their bathtubs. To me, this all boils down to the fact that Ms. Shanks, here, when I confronted her, as I was well within my rights to do, was belligerent, threatening, and aggressive. Okay? And if that isn't considered inappropriate conduct toward staff by somebody with privileges at this hospital, then, I mean, what the fuck is?"

He glanced at the stenographer as if considering whether he ought to ask her to strike or let him rephrase his rhetorical question.

"Belligerent, aggressive, maybe," said Dr. Soleymanzadeh, a handsome, hawk-faced man with preposterously beautiful brown eyes. He flipped through Lazar's statement on the table before him, two double-spaced pages more or less free of specific detail or, for that matter, readerly interest. All of it heavily distorted but, in essence, Gwen supposed, true. "Threatening, I'm having a hard time, Paul."

"That's the heart of the matter, isn't it?" said Dr. Leery, an old guy, the sweetest and least competent of the doctors in the room. "Aggressivity, belligerence, it's hard to know whether—"

"You say Ms. Shanks threatened you," Bernstein said, "but in your account, Paul, I can't really say I—"

"Not physically, okay."

"But she did threaten you."

"I guess it was more like she *menaced* me."

Gwen could feel Aviva and Moby watching her, waiting for her to interrupt, to deny, to argue. But she had not come here to argue with these motherfuckers. She waited, looking for her chance.

"Okay," Bernstein said. "That's sounding pretty much like a semantic shading to me. Could you, could we get you to possibly be more specific?"

It was weird; Lazar seemed abruptly to lose all interest in the proceedings that he had instigated. He sat under the humming CFL lights, looking wearier and more dead-eyed than ever. He shrugged, utterly bored by himself and all of them. "She got in my face," he said, as if definitively, and though they waited for him to continue—even Gwen found herself perversely hoping for more—he seemed to have arrived at his conclusion.

Bernstein turned to Gwen. "Ms. Shanks, would you like to respond?"

Gwen made a show of checking with her attorney, who sat up

straighter in his chair, mildly panicked. Patting his mental pockets as if he had left his wallet on some bus. His eyes reminding her, *Silent and badass.* Then, slowly, seeing she expected it, he nodded. Gwen rose as if obediently to her feet, knowing what she had to do and, worse, knowing how to do it, telling herself that it needed to be done.

"Thank you, Dr. Bernstein," Gwen said. "Yes, I would like to respond. Dr. Leery, Dr. Soleymanzadeh, I'm not going to lie. I was very angry at the time. I'm sure that I was standing pretty close to the man, maybe even 'in his face.' But look at me."

She stood up and completed one languid rotation on her own axis, reveling in her bulk. "First of all, I'd like to point out, I could plant my feet as appropriately far away from Dr. Lazar as he might want me to get. Large tracts of me would *still* be 'in his face.'" A string of laughter cinched up the doctors; even the grim stenographer parted instantaneously with a smile. "Second," Gwen went on, "do I look dangerous to you? *Menacing?*" No need, at this juncture, to go into her black belt, how, if she wanted to, even giving up a foot of height to Lazar and with all the litheness of a sandbag, she could snap any bone in the OB's body. She glanced at Moby, the big man loving it, nodding, jowls shaking, as proud as if he had coached her every step of the way. "All that aside, fine, let's give it to him. Let me concede his point." Moby stopped nodding. "Aggressive. Belligerent. *Menacing.*" Old Moby wishing he had stuck to orcas. "Like I said, I was angry. Doctors, I had a *right* to be angry. I had just been subjected to the kind of vile, ugly treatment by that man, Paul Lazar, that I know, I would like to hope, would have made you angry, too." She kept her gaze steady on the faces of the three inquisitors, fearing that if she glanced at Aviva, she might lose her nerve. "This man, Paul Lazar—I know you don't want to hear this. And I didn't want to tell you. I didn't want to tell anyone, not even my lawyer, because I knew that if I did, he would advise me to file a complaint with the EEOC. But I can't just stand by in the end and let the man get away with it. Not when he is guilty of the worst kind of racist—"

"Ho," Lazar said. "Whoa, hold on—"

"The worst kind of derogatory racial remarks."

"Oh, come *on*, lady."

"He made a crack about my hair. About black people's hair, about processed hair."

"I . . ."

The memory, then; a pinprick, the air whistling out of him, while understanding, troubled and shifty-eyed, flowed into the faces of Leery, Bernstein, and Soleymanzadeh. Seeped like the stain from a teabag darkening a cup of hot water. Gwen turned to Aviva, daring her partner to back her up or back away. The doctors—Lazar, too—turned to see what she would say, Aviva Roth-Jaffe, the Alice Waters of midwives, the rock upon which modern East Bay midwifery had been founded.

Aviva looked shocked; as shocked as Aviva ever looked. She hesitated for a long second, her full lips flatlined with unhappiness. Finally, she nodded. "That is true," she said.

"He called me a witch doctor."

"I never said that!"

"He accused me of practicing voodoo."

"Ary, that's not true," Lazar said to Bernstein. Awake now, alive, working as much truthfulness into his voice as he could, more than was compatible with telling the truth. "I didn't mean—"

"There was a waiting room full of witnesses," Gwen said. "They all heard what you said. These people checked in with the intake clerk, I'm sure they can be tracked down. They'll all verify it. You said, 'Five more minutes of burning that incense, or whatever voodoo you were up to, and that mom doesn't make it.' "

Lazar opened his mouth as if to protest, then closed it again.

Bernstein turned to Aviva, who shot a look at Gwen, hoping and doubting and most of all, Gwen thought, fearing that her partner knew what she was doing.

"I do remember that," Aviva said. "I'm not sure those were the exact words, but Dr. Lazar did say something about us practicing voodoo."

Bernstein looked at Lazar. "Paul?"

"How is voodoo racist?" Lazar said. "I just meant, like, you know, all that bullshit new age aromatherapy crap."

"If you meant 'aromatherapy,' " said Moby, going with it, ready to help Gwen press the advantage, "why did you say 'voodoo'?"

"Why, indeed?" Gwen said.

"Maybe we ought to get general counsel in here," Moby said.

"I really don't think—" Bernstein began.

"I wish I had done a better job of controlling my temper," Gwen said. "I truly do. I have devoted my entire professional life, my entire life *period*, to maintaining a consistently calm demeanor. I have always fought successfully to rise above. But when people start getting into that kind of rhetoric, that kind of hate speech, I'm sorry—in my view, I have an obligation to stand up to it."

"We all do," Moby said.

"Of course," Bernstein said. "Gwen, nobody expects you to put up with that kind of talk. Paul, I have to say, I'm very surprised by this."

"I'm sure," said Leery, "that it was all a big misunderstanding of some kind. A misjudgment."

"It was the end of his shift," Soleymanzadeh said. "Clearly, the man was tired."

Gwen saw that Aviva was chewing on a fingernail, a habit she reviled in herself and had struggled for years to defeat. She looked like she was feeling ill, about to get up and walk out of the room.

"Okay, here's what I'd like to propose," Bernstein said. "I'm going to say we review this, in light of what we've just heard. Take the matter under advisement for the time being, and—"

"I'm sorry," said Lazar from behind his hands. "All right?" He lowered his hands, and the imprint they left in the sallow flesh of his cheeks glowed red for an instant like the residue of rage, then faded. "I was tired, just fried, and pissed off. I mean, you tell me I'm an asshole, okay, that's not going to be news to me, right? Not to anybody in this room, maybe. But I'm an equal-opportunity asshole. I'm an asshole to everyone, black, white, blue, green." Somehow, imperfectly, as if calling on rumor and hearsay and long-forgotten lore, he worked his features into something that meant to resemble a smile. "Ary, help me out here."

"You have an edge," Bernstein suggested.

"That's what I'm saying. I totally have an edge. And that's why, look, Ms. Shanks. Gwen. I'm sorry for what I said. Okay?"

Everyone turned to look at Gwen, ready for her to accept Lazar's bullshit apology—that weary old dodge, *I'm not a racist, I hate everybody equally!*—and more important, ready for her to go on, break down, give in, and apologize right back. Just bat Aviva's meaningless tennis ball of language over the net. Check the little box on Paul Lazar's list.

"Nice try," Gwen said. She picked up the legal pad on which she had jotted not a single note. "Aryeh, Dr. Soleymanzadeh. Dr. Leery. I appreciate your time."

"Ms. Shanks," Leery said, sounding woeful.

"Gwen, for God's sake," Aviva said, and then, to the doctors, with remarkable sincerity and warmth of tone, "she's sorry, too. We both are. Our good relationship with Chimes is important to us. Personally and professionally." As she came out with the second adverb, she underscored it on her own pad with four scratched words: COST OF DOING BUSINESS!

"No, Aviva," Gwen said. "I don't know what's wrong with me, but I'm not sorry. Must be a black thing, huh, Paul?"

"I wouldn't know."

"Doctors, I look forward to hearing not only what you but also the EEOC have to say about all this. Now," Gwen said with a wave to Moby, on a roll, talking mostly to herself, "if you'll excuse me."

Thus, feeling something very close to fly, and doing what she had to do, Gwen went to see about taking back her house.

⊙   ⊙   ⊙

"Mr. Stallings," wrote A. O. Scott in his *New York Times* review of *Strutter Kicks It Old-School*, "has not only redeemed himself, he has also redeemed the genre of American cinema known so crudely as blaxploitation, and let us hope that this marvelous new film lays in its grave that ignoble moniker for all time."

That was only one of the clippings. There were positive reviews from

Time, *Ebony*, and *Entertainment Weekly*. Cover stories in *People* and *Esquire*. Quotations from these articles and reviews had been excerpted to run in print ads and on the packaging of the DVD, useful exclamations like BOLD! and TERRIFIC! and A NONSTOP ACTION-PACKED THRILL RIDE! Across the film's poster, above a full-length image of Candygirl Clark and Cleon Strutter leaning together, each of them three quarters turned to the camera, her left shoulder against his right shoulder, giant letters proclaimed TWO THUMBS UP!!! EBERT & ROEPER.

"It looks so real," Titus said.

That was not true at all, but he sounded like he meant it. Everything had been collaged using text, drawings, graphics cut from the pages of real newspapers and magazines, and computer-printed text that attempted with moderate success to match the fonts of the original publications. Leafing through this homemade archive, Julie felt an ache in his chest, though he wasn't sure whether it was for the crude sincerity of the archive's fakeness or for the faked and heartfelt sincerity of Titus, saying it all looked real.

"Totally," Julie agreed.

The bin also contained seven drafts, six of them handwritten in slanting longhand on prison stationery, of the film's script; a thin sheaf of old head shots of Luther Stallings when he was Luther Stallings, poker face but with that Strutter twinkle in the eye, beautiful and young. Synopses and diagrams done mostly by hand. A red folder tabbed BUDGET that held official-looking spreadsheets, and a blue one tabbed LOCATIONS that bulged with dozens of four-by-six photographs of Chinatown, East Oakland, the museum, and the interior of a restaurant that Julie recognized as the Merritt bakery.

A leather-grained pasteboard portfolio divulged a stack of storyboards for the film, strips of cartooned panels, executed in a style perhaps half a step above stick figure, that had been Scotch-taped to panels cut from pizza boxes. The greatest treasure and the pitiable heart of the whole archive was undoubtedly the poster, so large that it had to be folded in half to fit into the portfolio. It had been executed in colored pencil, no doubt over a long period of time, the colors laid down faint but smooth and even, as if rubbed with a tissue, giving everything the appropriate mistiness of a dream. The posed figures of Strutter and Candygirl were awkward, leggy even for Valletta Moore, and you could tell by the dead eyes and smiles that the faces had been copied, pretty accurately, from photos.

"Jailhouse artist," said Archy's dad, sounding apologetic and regarding the poster with a critical expression. He smiled; there was the twinkle from the ancient head shot. It reminded Julie of Archy, and then he thought of Titus, standing on the sidewalk outside the Bruce Lee Institute, scheming this whole adventure. "But I got to say, I think it looks pretty good."

"Where you going to get the money to make it?" Titus said. "To make it for real, I mean."

"Here and there." Luther tried to come off as playful, having a secret, then seemed to worry that he might sound like he was full of shit. "You heard of Gibson Goode?"

Naturally, they had, Titus talking about rushing records, Grammy Awards, Julie basically grasping that the ex-quarterback had bent his wealth, legend, and magic on the destruction of Nat Jaffe and Brokeland Records.

"Some of it's derivating from him, payment for services rendered. Some of it, I'm going to be relying on cash flow from another source of funds, a local businessman. A, uh, a former associate, you know, an old homey of mine, always been reliable. Between what he's willing to part with and what Goode already committed to, all told . . ." Luther tapped the red folder with a finger. "I figure I can make this movie for, like, call it a hundred K. And that's about what I'm hoping to raise."

Luther's fingers, his hands, amazed Julie. The backs of them were red-brown, fading to gold at the meridians where they met the palms. The fingers were slender, long and fluid, but you did not question their storied lethality. They looked like they had been shaped with fine tools from a regal pair of antlers.

"You have an old friend," Titus said, "man has that kind of money, but you sleeping in a garage."

Valletta laughed a low, unhappy laugh and got up from the table where she had progressed from her fingernails to painting her toes. "Boy has sense," she said. She tucked her feet into a pair of blue Dr. Scholl's sandals and then went tocking across the cement floor to the bathroom door, on which some airbrush master had rendered a photoreal image of a Conan the Barbarian–type character in the style of Frank Frazetta, sitting on a toilet with his ax and his sword on the floor in front of him, squeezing out a shit with a look on his face of barbaric joy. "Must come from his momma's side of things." She slammed the bathroom door behind her.

"Boy, we are comfortable as hell here," his grandfather said. "Truly. Not that I don't hope to improve our situation. But I would prefer if you didn't keep harping on it like that."

The compressor clanged the entire building like a single great fire alarm reverberating in the rebar, the air itself ringing as though struck. The noise of it was starting to get on Julie's nerves. Somebody had started to brew up a batch of a noxious substance needed for bodywork, and it smelled to Julie like burning bananas.

"I'm sorry," Titus said. It was the first time Julie had ever heard him employ those words in that configuration.

"Man ain't exactly a friend, is the answer to your question. Let's just say, he and I, we have some history. *Long* time ago, back in the Jurassic Age." He gestured toward the ruin of the Toronado. "Motherfucking dinosaurs roamed the earth." He interrupted himself to chuckle at his self-mockery, then seemed to lose the thread, maybe recollecting those dinosaurian days. "Dude and me, we had our misunderstandings, know what I'm saying? Water has for sure flowed under the motherfucking bridge. But he'll come through. Basically, he wants to keep up the prosperity as a local businessman, he *has* to come through, is the type of situation we're talking about."

It sounded sketchy to Julie, and he guessed, given what he knew about recent decades in the history of Luther Stallings, that it might have something to do with drugs. Maybe the reason that Luther had "taken a rap" and "done a bid" was so the mysterious old friend from the Jurassic Age could stay free, and now, by prior arrangement, it was time for him to repay Luther for "carrying the weight." Or maybe, Julie thought, wildly quoting from his cinematic syllabus over the past week and forgetting that Luther was not a master thief and had only played a master thief in one semi-bad and one wretched movie, maybe it was like in *The Getaway* and the mystery "running buddy" had *arranged* to get Luther released from prison because he needed him for a job. The shadowy benefactor in Julie's imagination took on a distinct resemblance to the actor Ben Johnson, so he was bewildered to hear Titus's grandfather say, "Your pops knows him. Chan, Chandler Flowers, the undertaker."

"*I* know him!" Julie said, startling himself along with Luther Stallings, who seemed inclined to forget that Julie was there. "He's on the Oakland City Council. He's a customer at Brokeland. He likes King Curtis."

"King Curtis, Earl Bostic, Illinois Jacquet," Luther Stallings agreed. "He loves all them honkers."

"Chan the Man," Julie said.

"So-called, so-called," Luther said. "Old Chan, I tell you what, old Chan never was the flexible type. A stubborn, stiff-necked man. Eventually, I feel confident, he is going to come around."

"You best hope he *don't*, you old fool."

Luther Stallings was caught as helplessly off guard as Julie and Titus. If it had been some hood or, like, Ben Johnson standing there with a .45, Luther would have been toast. So much for instincts honed by years of arcane martial arts training or by the harsh realities of prison life. Presently, Luther remembered to brandish his walking stick, but it was too late, and he knew it. Phantom slugs starred his head and torso with phantom squibs. He lowered the stick, looking disgusted. "Goddammit, Eddie!" he said. "What the hell kind of hidden refuge you running here?"

Eddie called back to him, offhand, bored, "Oh, yeah. You have a visitor."

"Yo, what up, Ed?"

"Hey, Archy. How's the whip?"

"Running well, looking good."

"Baby?"

"No, nuh-uh, not yet. Julie, Titus. Go get in the motherfucking car."

Julie had known Archy Stallings since he was four years old. He tried to remember if he had ever, in all that time, seen him angry twice in one day. Luther was smiling, or showing his teeth, anyway, a weird smile, as if he had lost money betting against some outcome that would be worse than losing. "Look at this," he said. "Big shorty."

A little white mint appeared for an instant in Archy's mouth, surfing the curl of his tongue. "Boys," he said. "Car."

"Man, *fuck* you," Titus said.

For the past little while, the hour, hour and a half they had spent at Motor City, rattled by the air compressor like bones in a blender, watching Eddie Cantor's blowtorch pirates butcher the Citation so it could be rebuilt, that magic slaughter like something out of *Norse Gods and Giants*, hot rod dwarves intent on replacing its headlights with diamonds and its tires with wild boars and its engine with the heart of a dragon, Valletta Moore moving on from fingernails to toes, crooking one long leg against the steel drum, craning forward so the boys were granted a fitful vision of the shadowland between her legs, which forever afterward would remain confused in Julie's retroimagination with the vision of his homeland articulated by Luther Stallings as he snapped off stomach crunches by the abs-rippling dozen, that whole ancient Egyptian take on Oakland being a land of rebirth for the Black Man because of Pullman porters—all that while, sitting there on that skanky old sofa, Titus had seemed for the first time to relax. His angles softened, and his cords went slack. The things he said sounded sincere, unbracketed with an ironic formulation, a celebrity impression, or a parody of a gang-banging TV hood rat. His string had been jerked taut again, and Julie could not tell if it was Titus or some imaginary street Negro who said, "Man, *fuck* you."

"We having ourselves a visit," Luther said. "My grandson and me. And my man Julius. Ain't that right, boys?"

"Yes, sir."

My man. Julie reveled in the designation. "Yes, *sir*," he said.

"Something wrong with that?" Luther wanted to know. "You got an objection?"

"Oh, huh, suddenly he's your grandson."

"Not sudden. Been, what, how old are you, boy?"

"Fourteen."

"Been fourteen years."

"Fourteen years of you not knowing or giving a shit."

"You should talk."

"Ho, snap," Titus said, as if he had enjoyed the retort, even though Julie could not imagine what there was to enjoy in the idea that for the fourteen years of your life, your father had cared as little about you as your grandfather. But Julie had observed that, like other black kids he knew, Titus seemed able to find humor in things that only would have made Julie feel sad.

"How'd you find us?" Julie asked Archy.

"A customer, owns the cab company. Mr. Mirchandani. You gave the driver your card?"

"Oh yeah."

"Mr. M. recognized your name, he called my cell."

"Mr. M. is nice," Julie said.

"Yeah, yeah," Archy said. "Okay, come on, you been rescued, now we got to go."

Julie started to walk toward Archy, more than ready to go home, but when he turned to look back at Titus, he saw that they were going to be standing around having generational difficulties for a while longer.

"Come on! I got to go to Costco, meet up with my marching band. You boys get your asses in the damn car."

"Go on," Titus said. Then, softening it, "Yo, Julie, you go on home."

"You are planning to stay here," Julie said. "In, like, a garage."

"Hello, Archy."

"Hey, Valletta. What's up?"

"Oh, you know. Just another motherfucking day in the ancient Egyptian Land of Rebirth."

"Say again?"

Valletta only shook her head in an infinitesimal arc, almost a tremor, as if saying it again would cost her too much dignity.

"So, you up for the stepmom gig this time? Step-*grand*mom. Seems like you're about to have another mouth to feed."

"I had not heard that."

"That the deal, Luther? Titus gonna stay here with you?" Archy took a slow, theatrical, but keen look around the premises of Motor City Auto Body. "Doesn't look too comfortable. You and Valletta really sleeping here?"

Julie had been wondering that, too. He dreaded to consider the possibility that the two gray sofas, their original coloration lost to time, might be converted into places where human beings passed the night.

"It's all right," Luther said.

"Glad to hear it. Y'all got room for one more?"

Luther didn't answer, just stood there with his arms folded and an offended expression, moving his lips as if trying to formulate an argument for why Archy ought to show more respect. At last he shrugged and turned to Titus. "Go on, now," he said.

Titus crumpled. Everything bright, all the fierceness, drained out of his face. He didn't move, didn't say a word. It hurt Julie to see it, not because his friend was disappointed so much as because he ever could have thought Luther was going to let him stay.

"Go on!" Luther repeated. "I know Eddie Cantor don't plan to start running no group home anytime soon."

Over in the service bay, Eddie nodded, slow and firm, looking like he might be considering whether to point out to Luther that he was not running a hotel, either, or a halfway house, or a B&B.

Titus made a wild experiment. "Grampa," he tried. The word sounded exotic on his lips, unlikely, as though it referred to something mythical or long extinct.

"One step at a time," Luther said.

"If that," said Archy, and Valletta said, "That's right."

"Go on," Luther said. "We'll see you again."

In one final, loose-limbed access of emotion, Titus went slack as a child and groaned. Then he stood up straight and rolled, walking like

Strutter, past Archy and toward the open doorway of the middle bay. "Man, how can you let your father live that way?" he said.

Julie, feeling unexpectedly that Archy, historically his favorite person in the world, was being a total douche toward Luther, who had straightened himself out and was really sorry about everything and simply needed a little help, could not bring himself to say so, but he went over to the bin on the workbench and pointed. "Do you think I could maybe have one of those head shots?" he said. "I really like your movies."

"What?" Luther said, watching his grandson strut angrily out into the giant blank where at one time the trains and ships of a mighty nation had come to exchange cargoes, and Oakland had fattened on war and on the flesh of San Francisco. Walking out into the ghost footsteps of his great-grandfather, who worked the docks here and got blown up one day during World War II when Vallejo, or maybe it was Martinez, exploded. "Sure, go ahead. Help yourself."

Julie went over to the plastic bin. He was about to pick up the photo when he noticed, lying in a corner of the bin, the faded and wrinkled husk, like a vacated chrysalis, purply blue, of what could only be a Batman glove. It was stained dark along the fingers and fraying at the seams. It had the little old-school fins, and Julie guessed it was the same vintage as the door that hung from Sixto Cantor's wall, with its red bat logo. In his imagination—patrolling the streets of Genosha or Wakanda or the corridors of Blue Area of the Moon in MTO—Dezire wore long purple gloves. It had never occurred to Julie that they ought to have fins. He snatched up the stray glove and shoved it down into the pocket of his cutoffs.

"Do you have a pen?" Julie asked Archy when he had chosen the picture he wanted and turned away from the bin.

Archy put a warning in his voice. "Julie."

"I want to get an autograph. Come on. Don't be a dick."

" 'Don't be a dick.' That's how you're going to talk to me."

"I want. An *autograph*."

Archy fished a pen out of his pocket and click-clicked it. Then he handed it to Julie.

"You tell him it's just a matter of time," Luther said in a low voice as he scratched the pen across the bottom right corner of the photo. "Soon as my associates come through. After that, him and me can talk it over, see what's possible."

That was when Julie knew the *Strutter 3* venture was doomed, if not imaginary. He determined on the spot to see that it came true, that it happened, that Strutter was resurrected one last time to kick it old-school, for the sake of Titus, for the sake of Luther, and for the sake of the world of cinema, too.

DON'T LOSE THAT DREAM, Luther wrote. BEST WISHES, LUTHER STALLINGS .

⊙   ⊙   ⊙

The late Randall "Cochise" Jones, his mortal remains. Washed, powdered, painted. Conduits and chambers flooded with aldehydes. Broken ribs set. Eyelids sealed, jawbone wired shut, fingernails trimmed close as in life, fingers woven into a trellis on the belly. Vestigial smile of forgiveness. Hallucinogenic Ron Postal leisure suit that cost three hundred dollars in 1975. Stacy Adams Spectators, two-tone blue and white. Thick ginger-gray flag of hair flown stubbornly to the left, as in life. Stashed like some fine tool or instrument in the velour darkness of a casket prepaid since 1997. The velour a specified shade of purple called zinfandel. Satin pillow propping up the ten-pound head. Exterior of the casket done up in a rich oak finish like the cabinet of a Leslie speaker, then trimmed out like the lost ark with finials and gargoyles of gold plate. Loaded onto a mortuary cot, ready to ride up the freight elevator to the garage at the back of Flowers & Sons Funeral Home, where a pristine 1969 Oldsmobile 98 Cotner Bevington, borrowed for the occasion from a funeral home up in Richmond, waited to ferry it over to Brokeland Records. Here the body would be laid out for a combination wake and funeral scheduled to begin at eleven A.M. and to last until three P.M. or the refreshments ran out. When the living had concluded their business of farewell, the casket would be rolled back to the capacious rear section of the hearse. Half an hour later, at Mountain View

Cemetery, it would be put into the ground alongside what remained of the dead man's second wife, Fernanda. And that would be the end of that. Mr. Jones's funeral plan had called for the use of Flowers and Sons' vintage 1958 Cadillac, but the Caddy had come down with a pain in the alternator. Even if Mr. Jones had known of the substitution, he hardly could have faulted the magnificent Olds 98, batlike and swooping, ready to haul ass through even the shadowiest valley.

⊙   ⊙   ⊙

"You need a permit, anything like that, lay a body out in a record store?"

"I don't know. If you do, I guess Chan Flowers took care of it. Man took care of everything."

"No doubt," Singletary said. "No doubt. Now, seriously, watch out, ain't no light, the upstairs switch is broken."

You might have tunneled, given time enough and shovels, from the basement of Flowers & Sons, where the body of Cochise Jones lay in zinfandel darkness, to the basement of his house on Forty-second Street, but you probably would have run into problems trying to get in. It was a basement of the 1890s, resolute and dry. The house had been built by a retired riverboat captain from Sacramento who married a Portuguese girl of whom there were still living memories among a few of the very oldest neighbors, like Mrs. Wiggins. The smell of thousands of record albums submitting themselves to the depredations of bacteria and mold could not entirely erase the lingering smell of the cardoon cheeses that the old woman had manufactured for decades, along with hams and pickled tomatoes, in her basement.

"I hope he ain't mad about the Cadillac," Singletary said.

"If it's the same Olds they had at Ardis Robinson's funeral," Nat said, citing the funeral two years back of a mainstay of the Bay Area funk circuit during the seventies and eighties, "it'll work."

Nat and Archy groped after Singletary down the basement stairs of Cochise's house. The wall of the stairwell was smooth, cold Oakland sandstone.

"And you got the Chinese, right? I like that Green Street band. All military and proper. Ain't one of those motherfuckers really Chinese, though."

"No, they were booked. I had to go in a different direction. Hired this outfit, Bomp and Circumstance, you know them?"

"The lesbians?"

"They got the set list together, they know how the Chinese do it, the hymns and whatnot. Kai, Kai Fierro, works for Gwen? Plays the sax. She promised me they would send Mr. Jones home right."

"But still," Singletary observed, "lesbians ain't quite what he asked for, either."

"True, true."

"That must nag at you."

"At times it does."

The downstairs light switch snapped. Ceiling fixtures gapped by dead tubes flirted with darkness. Then, with a click, they shone steady. Something on the order of, at Archy's eyeball guesstimate, seven, eight thousand records, lovingly and helplessly amassed.

"I had no idea," Nat said. His suit was an Italian number from the sixties, narrow lapels, no trouser cuffs, textured black silk flecked with gray. Skinny tie. Pointy little black loafers. He looked like Peter Sellers trying to recover from a very long night in 1964 and needing a haircut. "I mean, I knew, but I didn't comprehend."

"Man's habit was out of control," Archy said admiringly. His own suit was his least interesting, just a plain old Armani bought on sale at Men's Wearhouse, two-button jacket, center vent. He wore it only to funerals and once, a long time ago, when he and Nat had gone to a Halloween party as the Men in Black. "God love him."

"Fuck God," Nat said. "Bastard killed our best customer."

"You have fifteen minutes. Ten if you keep on blaspheming." Singletary took out his phone and frowned at its display. "You ain't interested, I'm calling Amoeba."

The only son of the captain from Sacramento and the Portuguese lady had a son who died in Korea and a daughter, Fernanda, who passed the house on to Cochise Jones when she left him a widower. The Joneses never had any children, and Mr. Jones's heir, his late sister's daughter, lived somewhere down toward San Diego and wanted everything sold. So Garnet Singletary had gotten the house cleaned, painted, and patched and, in his capacity as executor, had hired himself to sell it. Archy got the strong impression that Garnet Singletary was also arranging to have one of his many shiftless relatives and hangers-on, whom he kept in a state of cash dependency on him for such eventualities, front a company that would buy the house from the estate, Garnet Singletary preferring, if possible, as a rule, to negotiate with himself. It seemed like a pretty good system to Archy. The King of Bling knew how to get over.

"We aren't here to conduct business?" Archy looked at Nat. "Not today, right?"

Garnet and Nat said nothing, though neither appeared to see any cause for alarm in the prospect of dealing for the old man's vinyl on the day of his interment.

"I thought we had just came to, like, admire," Archy said.

"You go right ahead and admire," Garnet said. "It's your fifteen minutes, you spend it however you want to. Then I'm calling Amoeba records."

The albums were in poly sleeves, for the most part, and for the most part had been kept edge-on in crates, but here and there in tottering piles, discs lay ruined by the horizontal, and some of cheaper stuff was not in plastic or was missing its paper inner sleeve. The crates were stacked into alleys and bends that lacked only a Minotaur.

After a ten-minute walkabout, Archy was prepared to pronounce the collection first-rate. He guessed that not quite half of the records had flowed through Brokeland on their way to this subterranean catchment. Another 20 percent, call it, bore price tags indicating provenance in the bins of other used-record dealers here in the Bay Area and all around the country. Ten percent was flotsam and jetsam, the random shit—fifties gospel, old Slappy White and Moms Mabley records, a surprising amount of Conway Twitty, George Jones, Merle Haggard. The rest—about 25 percent—was in the nature of Mr. Jones's personal collection, as it were: recordings of sessions and dates he had played, the work of friends, colleagues, and rivals, maybe a hundred rare stride and boogie-woogie 78s, and a couple of complete sets of ten-inch LPs from the forties of classical works for organ, Bach, Buxtehude, Widor. These had belonged to Mr. Jones's father, for many years house organist of Flowers Funeral Home as well as a number of local churches. There was no way to be sure after such a cursory sniff, but Archy figured the collection be low five figures, at least. Likely more.

"What do you think?" Nat said, turning out to be the Minotaur trapping Archy at the heart of the labyrinth. "Call it, what, fifteen? Offer twelve-five?"

He spoke in a low voice, not quite a whisper, but Singletary was busy grilling somebody on the phone, possibly Airbus.

"Who did?" Singletary was saying. "Well, where'd they see it? Uh-huh. Did it say anything? What did it say? Goddammit, Airbus, what did it say?"

"Twelve-five," Archy said. "Nat, look here. Maybe this isn't the right time to be . . . You are talking about putting more money into the business."

"That's right."

Archy studied Nat's face, trying to see if his partner was fucking with him. Nat believed that he owned a top-notch poker face, but in this belief he was sadly mistaken. His eyebrows in particular were unruly and signifying. The man thought he could conceal the contempt he felt toward his benighted fellow creatures, but the best he could arrange was to immobilize every part of his face, apart from the eyebrows, into a leaden mask through whose eye slits leaked an incandescent scorn. Right now, though, all that Archy could see on Nat's face was enthusiasm, a certain smug pursiness to his lips that Nat got whenever he believed himself (again mistakenly, most of the time) to be about to get the upper hand in a negotiation. Nat had descended like Orpheus to this basement full of forgotten music, dressed in a funeral suit, hoping to bring Brokeland Records back to the upper world, the land of the living, with a vibrant infusion of collectible stock, stock that they would catch the scent of as far away as Japan.

"But, uh, I don't—I'm not sure, even if I had that kind of cash—"

"I have it. Or I can get it. If you—Oh." The truth that Archy was not ready, not today, to confess, had begun to seep in through those eye slits. The mask gave way, Nat's jaw softening. "Archy, there is some shit here, in Japan, France, we could sell it for easily—"

"Did it know German?" Singletary called out to them from the stairs. "Mr. Jones's parrot, could it speak German?"

Archy looked at Nat, who shrugged impatiently.

"Not to our knowledge," Archy said.

"That ain't him," Singletary said to Airbus. "I never heard that bird do anything but sound like a Hammond B-3."

"Can't rule it out, though," Archy called. "Bird knew all kinds of unlikely shit."

"Maybe I should have gone into business with *him*," Nat said.

"Oh, okay, now you're all mad at me."

Nat didn't answer. He ran a furry finger along the printed spines of the records in a nearby crate. Archy saw that it was all Mr. Jones's labelmates from his time on CTI. Hank Crawford, Grover Washington, Jr., Johnny Hammond. A number of them would be records that Mr. Jones had played on. Archy had probably owned most of the Creed Taylor catalog at one time or another, but it made an impression, seeing the records all together in that crate and those immediately above and below it, all those discs produced by Taylor or Don Sebesky back when Archy was a youngster, recorded by Rudy Van Gelder, pressed at some plant in New Jersey, then shipped by the scattered millions to the vanished mom-and-pop record shops of America, to the local chain stores of the seventies that had long since folded or been absorbed into national chains that had in turn folded, all those tasty beats and (mostly) tasteful string arrangements marbled together in a final attempt to reclaim jazz as popular music to be danced to and not just an art form to be curated, all those beautiful records with their stark jacket photography and their casually integrated personnel, reunited through the efforts of Mr. Jones. Archy had been breaking up estates for years and selling them off in pieces, but until now he had never felt the vandalism inherent in that act, his barbarity amid the crates of so many ruined empires.

"Nice," Archy admitted, running his own finger along the spines of the records.

"Beautiful," Nat said, giving the word the full benefit of his residual Tidewater accent.

"Nat," Archy said, "nothing would make me happier than to let you take twelve thousand five hundred dollars you don't have and buy these records for us, then you and me sit on top of them for two, three years like a couple of dad penguins. Listening to Idris Muhammad all day long, all that crazy old Willie 'the Lion' Smith he had, that Versatile side he did with Grant motherfucking Green that never got released, I mean—"

"I know, you saw that?" Nat hung on, fanning the little spark of it.

"But I have been fucking off, fucking up, and fucking around for too long. I need to get real, else I'm going to end up living in an auto body shop. I need insurance, a paycheck, all that straight-life bullshit. Gwen goes out on maternity, she doesn't work, I'm going to need to take care of her, the baby. I got to settle some shit with Titus, Nat, that boy—"

"You guys back together?"

"Huh?"

"You and Gwen. She moved back in?"

"Last night."

"Hey, all right."

"Uh-huh, she moved in, then she threw my ass out. Said it was her house, too, and so on. She came home, I don't— Something got into her. Had the gain on the flamethrower turned *all* the way up."

"Yeah, I heard she was in fine form yesterday. I heard she did the full mau-mau routine on those assholes at Chimes."

"Is that the term Aviva used to describe it, 'mau-mau'?"

"That was just my interpretation."

"Black midwife standing up for herself to a bunch of white doctors, that makes it a mau-mau?"

"I don't have a problem with mau-mauing," Nat said. "It's a valid technique."

"I'm glad to hear that," Archy said. "Black folks been holding off on the mau-mauing lately, till we got a ruling from you."

"Where are we?" Garnet Singletary said, sounding prepared to be disappointed by the answer. He filled the space at the end of the narrow alley in which Archy and Nat seemed to have lodged.

"Where we are is, Archy is 'getting real,' " Nat said.

"That doesn't sound like an offer," Singletary said.

"Nat, man, please. We can get into all of this tomorrow. We don't need to get into it now. Mr. S., respect, I know you're in a hurry, but today I am about trying to do this one thing of sending off Cochise Jones how he expected and how he deserved. I can't be about anything else."

"Are you going with Gibson Goode?" Nat laughed, a single incredulous bark. "Ho! Wait! Is that what you're doing right *now*? You already took the job! Jesus Christ, Arch, is that why you're here? Did he, did your friend Kung Fu give you his checkbook, tell you, go ahead, get in there, start stocking your *Beats Department*?"

"Hold up, Nat. Now you're getting toward paranoid."

"A short journey," Garnet Singletary observed.

"I seriously doubt if the offer is even out there anymore," Archy said. "Maybe I put the man off too long."

"I can't *believe* I told you what my number would be."

"Why don't you tell *me* your number?" Singletary suggested. "I'm the one selling the damn records. No, I tell you what. Do it this way, I give *you* a number. Seventeen thousand dollars."

"I am supposed to give you seventeen grand to buy back a bunch of records I already bought and sold once before," Nat said. "Some of these records are like children to me, you're going to make me pay for them twice."

"Give me a offer, then," Singletary said, declining to acknowledge that Nat was starting to get bothered. "Then you get to sell them twice, too."

"Fuck it," Nat said. "We're already having one funeral. Let's bury everything. Right here and now. Have done with it." He brushed past Singletary, in his pointy little loafers went banging back upstairs.

"Seem like maybe you been putting a *lot* of people off a little too long," said Singletary.

"I know it," Archy said. "I wish I knew what was wrong with me."

"I got a theory."

"Which is?"

"Maybe you are sick to death of mold-smelling, dust-covered, scratched-up, skipping, wobbly old vinyl records."

"You said 'no blaspheming.' "

"Maybe you sick of Nat Jaffe. Man started to get on my nerves five minutes before I met him."

Archy experienced a certain temptation to assent to this theory, but it felt disloyal, so he only said without enthusiasm, "Huh? Nah, man, Nat's my nigger."

Singletary seemed to weigh this claim. "Was just a question of knowing how to fry a chicken leg," he said, "I might almost be prepared to agree to that description."

"So, yeah. I guess you better call Amoeba or whoever. Call Rick Ballard down at Groove Yard."

"Now, wait a minute," Singletary said. "Okay, now, hold on. Let me just ask you. What was his number going to be?"

"He said something about eleven. Fifty-five apiece, but I don't have it, and as far as I know, neither does he."

"And if he did, if he came up with the money, and you all acquired Mr. Jones's collection here for something south of fifteen but north of eleven, would you be able to make money on that?"

"Hard to say."

"Oh, no doubt."

"A little, maybe. Maybe a little more than a little. Nat was saying about France and Japan, but that's no sure thing. It would improve our inventory, I mean, damn, there is some tough stuff here. Maybe if we expanded our website, did more of the shows. Put a little more push into the business side of the business, spent a little less time shooting the shit around that counter."

"Aw, no, don't say that," Singletary said. "I might back off from the fool offer I am about to propose. Because you know, truth is, I don't give a shit about some scratched-up vinyl Rahsaan Kirk, Ornette Coleman sound-like-a-goose-trying-to-fuck-a-bicycle bootleg pressing from the rare Paris concert of 1967. I spend five minutes listening to that, I'm like to want to slap somebody. I don't really like *any* jazz, to be honest. The kind of style Mr. Jones played, mostly have a steady groove to it, that was all right, but when I get home at the end of a working day, Miller time, put some music on, you know what I like? I like Peabo Bryson."

"Peabo had his due share of jams."

"Here's my concern in this matter. I know you think I am messing around in all that protest shit your partner's stirring up to annoy Chan Flowers. Just because I maintain historically cool relations with the councilman. And true, that is part of the reason. But the real reason is something that's not that. The reason, I remember when that record store used to be Eddie Spencer's. And before that, when I first got out of the army, right after the war, it was called Angelo's Barbershop, and those old Sicilian dudes used to go in, get their mustaches looked to or whatnot. I have known Sicilians, and so I feel confident saying, your store been full of time-wasting, senseless, lying, boastful male conversation for going on sixty years, at least. What that Abreu said the other day at that meeting, he was right. It's an institution. You all go out of business, I don't know. I might have to let in some kind of new age ladies, sell yoga mats. Everybody having 'silence days,' walking around with little signs hanging from their neck saying 'I Am Silent Today.' I would take that as a loss."

"Garnet Singletary," Archy letting amazement show on his face. "One-man historical preservation society. Turning soft on me."

"Lot of bad things happen once you start to get old."

"So, what? You going to just *give* us the records?"

"Now, how can I do that? These are Mr. Jones's records. They are not mine to give. You know that. But maybe the estate could advance them to you all on consignment. And you all could pay the estate back at some later date. Once you done selling them in France and Japan."

"Huh," Archy said. "Well, thank you, Garnet."

"It must be the funeral has me feeling sentimental."

"You're a good man."

"You put that around, I will have to deny it."

"Same with what I said about Nat being what I said, to me. Do not tell anybody. Least of all Nat. It'd go right to his head."

"Maybe after he earn a few more merit badges, we let him in the club."

"All right."

"Meantime, you need to figure out what you want to do about your-self, Archy Stallings. You need to make up your mind."

"Common refrain," Archy said.

When they went back upstairs, they passed Mr. Jones's living room, which had a denuded air but with that fussy feel, crewel and fake fruit, as if it had been decorated by ladies of a former age, maybe by the Portu-guese lady herself. In the center of the room, two steel suit racks waited side by side, hung thick with the dead man's leisure suits. The collective palette ran to bold, even heedless, in the seventies manner, or to muted potting-clay tones, something a touch Soviet or even Maoist in the olive tans and rose grays. The plaids had left Scotland far behind and struck out for new worlds of gaudiness, including one in red, white, black, and sky blue that always reminded Archy of a place mat at IHOP.

"Look at that," Archy said. "Look at those things. And I've seen him wear them all."

"Believe it or not there is actually a lively market," Singletary said. "I looked into it."

"Maybe I need to get into a new line," Archy said.

"Here go Airbus."

The big man met them at the top step, wearing a beautiful midnight-blue tracksuit, his hair razored down to a glaze on his scalp. Singletary's car, a late-model Toyota Avalon, stood double-parked in the street, flashers going. Kai Fierro, Gwen's receptionist, got out of the passen-ger side. She wore her hair greased back à la Fabian Forte and carried her sax in a soft gig case. She had on a blue brass-button high school marching-band jacket like they all wore in Bomp and Circumstance, corny yacht-captain hat complete with scrambled eggs on the visor.

"This suppose to be the, uh, leader of that Chinese marching band," Airbus said as though humoring the ranting of a nutjob, so as to keep her calm. "Was outside your store with another white chick named, uh, Jerry something, and two older ladies, trumpet and a sax. She say they made a appointment with Stallings. Want to know what the deal is, what the route is."

"Hey, Arch," Kai said. She shook hands with Garnet Singletary, all square and manly, telling him, "I'm Kai."

Something kind of a turn-on for Archy, funny, in the way she shook Singletary's hand. "Thanks for coming," he said.

"It's an honor," Kai said. "Cochise Jones, that's a name that, well, a lot of us in the band, it means something to us."

"You know he was born in New Orleans," Archy said. "That's why he loved the whole funeral-band thing. Always said Chinese people was the only ones around here really knew how to do a proper funeral."

"Tell you what, though, those guys over in the city, it's not like New Orleans. They don't really *swing*," Kai said. "Stuff we rehearsed for today, Archy, I mean, it's all that straight-ahead military funeral stuff. Is that okay? A lot of hymns, 'Onward, Christian Soldiers' and that type of deal."

"Okay," said Airbus, big man looking positively offended, " 'Onward Christian Soldiers,' now, how is that Chinese?"

"But we practiced a lot, you know. And plus, I have to say we put together a pretty swinging arrangement of 'Redbonin' ' that we'd like to do."

"That sounds just fine," Archy said, but he was frowning as he took in Kai's tacky little tenth-grade band jacket. "Now, let me ask you this. What size you wear?"

Softly, under the sound of traffic from Telegraph and the idling of Singletary's car, almost beneath the threshold of audibility, a bass note sounded and then went up a step. To the south, down over West Oakland, a black zeppelin sniffed at the sky with its pointed snout.

"A's playing Tampa today," Archy said. "Everybody's going to look up, see that, get all excited. Talking about, 'There go the Dogpile blimp!' "

"I was in the Dogpile down in L.A.," Kai said. "It was awesome."

"You're killing me," Archy said.

⊙   ⊙   ⊙

God said, "What the fuck is this shit?"

In the cabin of the *Minnie Riperton*, Walter Bankwell did not bother to try to look at ease. He did not enjoy the experience of flying in the dirigible, too nervous to have a drink, get loose. And he did not like it when everybody else got loose on board the *Riperton*, either, though the primary, express purpose of the airship (apart from its function as an irresistible eye magnet) turned out to be corporate entertainment of high-rolling clients, actors and singers and rappers, media folk, athletic shoe barons, that bunch of inner-city librarians won some kind of contest or something, got up there in the sky with G Bad and his posse and went *completely* out of control.

Walter was not afraid of heights per se; it was the gasbag that worried him. He understood perfectly that there was a difference between helium and hydrogen, but inert and gigantic as it might be, there was something fragile, insufficient, about the *Riperton*; its name, with its hint of tearing fabric, didn't help matters. Zeppelins had had their chance, and they had failed. The world had moved on, like with eight-track tapes. Though an eight-track, sure, it might gum up, eat its own innards, one of the little plastic wheels might crumble away to dust. But it was never going to blow your ass up.

Walter felt ill at ease; and surely the truth was that he was not *meant* to feel at ease, even if he had been willing to drink and get loose. That, and not public or client relations, was the true point of owning a zeppelin; it affirmed the godhood of Gibson Goode, living in his heavenly mansion. Today Walter had been summoned to the throne in the sky to learn of His displeasure.

God picked up the *Oakland Tribune* that lay on the little plastic hump of a coffee table. "You saw this?" he said.

Headlines, thought Walter bitterly. " 'VINTAGE RECORD STORE OWNER TURNS IT UP TO 78 IN BATTLE AGAINST NATIONAL CHAIN,' " he read. "Yeah, I saw it. Man comes off sounding like a dick. Turn it up to seventy-eight all the time, you end up sounding like Donald Duck."

"That is a valid comparison," Gibson Goode said. "In those kind of environments, I don't know why, sports cards, rare magazines, autographs, the dicks tend to, like, attract a following. But that ain't even what I'm worried about," Goode said. "Man, I could give a fuck about that little squirrel-nut-zipper white boy trying to rile up twenty-seven lactose-intolerant white people."

"All right. Then what are you worried about?"

"I'm worried about *you*."

A large white envelope, a mailer with green hash marks around the edge, had been exposed when Goode lifted up the newspaper. The man had at hand all the materials he needed for his presentation, including the bodyguard, Taku, sitting in the dining nook, seriously compromising the vehicle's vertical lift. Carrying a gun on board an airship, accidental discharge might happen anytime.

"This came to my office in Fox Hills," Goode said. "Looking like it was sent by a nutball."

It was a color photograph printed on plain paper, the colors at once sickly and vivid, a starfish thing, purple-blue twisted against a moiré of pale blue-green. A scan, on second thought: a 3-D object laid on the glass and photocopied, dark against the infinite, blank, pale blue-green dazzle of whatever you were taking a picture of when you left the cover open on a Xerox machine. The unscannable world.

"Looks like a glove," Walter said.

"Letter that came with it says it's a glove."

"Letter from who?"

"Luther Stallings. Saying how it ties your uncle to the killing of Popcorn Hughes, has blood on it, DNA, kind of thing they can test even after all these years."

"Huh."

"Chan Flowers having some history he'd like to keep hidden? That was fine back when him and me were on two different sides of the question. Know what I'm saying? Now that we're on the same side, I am not comfortable having all this, uh, memorabilia, floating around out there. Getting photocopied and shit."

"A purple glove?" Walter said.

Goode threw the photograph at Walter's head. "How the fuck do I know?" he said. He got up and went to the window and looked down at the bowl of the stadium. "You know I was drafted by the A's," he said. "As a pitcher."

"I saw you," Walter said. "USC against Cal, like '85, I was after this girl Nyreesa, used to work food service over at Evans Field. Everybody was talking about how there was scouts there from the A's and Giants both."

"I threw a two-hitter. Had no run support. One guy gets a cheap little inside-out hit, then I left a mistake hanging over the inside corner to the next guy. RBI double. That was all they needed."

"I got shut out, too," Walter said. "Only by Nyreesa."

"Okay." Goode whirled from the window, catching Walter off guard. Walter jumped back, lost his footing, and fell on his ass. Goode came to stand over him, staring down at him, his eyes not entirely devoid of contempt. "After he puts in an appearance at the funeral, Councilman Abreu is going to join me at the game at his own suggestion. I thought he might enjoy sitting in a corporate box, but he said he likes to sit in the stands. I got us seats right behind the A's dugout."

"Abreu."

"For some reason, he got the idea that it might be worth looking into the tax structure and other elements of the deal I'm making with the city, thanks to the hard work of your uncle, to develop the old Golden State market site. How the EIR was conducted, what kind of ties I have to the planning commission, et cetera."

"He's shaking you down, too."

"What is it about Oakland? Dumb-ass city always has to do the last-minute Gilligan, fuck it up for itself somehow or other. Okay, not this time. This time Skipper's going to do what's *necessary*. And if I decide your uncle Chan's carrying too much liability? Up here, I have to, you know, you got to consider the excess weight."

Kung Fu thought in that case, maybe they should have left Taku back at the airport, but he kept the thought to himself.

"You show your uncle the picture, show him this letter that came with it, all about the night of Popcorn Hughes. Show him the whole mess. See what he wants to do about it. Tell him I would like it smoothed over. Tell him I require reassurance. Else maybe I can get that reassurance from Councilman Abreu, know what I'm saying?"

"Most definitely," Walter said. "Now, when do we land?"

⊙   ⊙   ⊙

After the fathers left to meet Singletary in the dead man's basement, the boys worked. Rolling the big bins out of the way, carrying stock into the back room, elbow-deep in the smell, the leaden gravity of records. The revealed floor of Brokeland, a palimpsest of red and white linoleum worn here and there to an underlayer of green and cream, proved to be skankier than Archy had suggested. Titus grabbed the broom and assigned Julie to the dusting. They were being paid for their time, and this had the interesting effect of making Titus happy. He had located a sister of his mother's somewhere down in Los Angeles. She would not send him any money, but she had told him that if he could make his way to her, she would take him in. He had a purpose in life; that purpose was to break poor Julie Jaffe's heart.

There was an old-fashioned feather duster, comical blue plumes plucked from an old lady's hat or the ass of an ostrich in a Warner Bros. cartoon. Julie went after the dust with it, feeling like Bugs Bunny, keeping an eye all the while on Titus. Titus took his broom work seriously, gridding the floor with grit and bug legs, neatly collapsing everything into tidy mounds, crouching to whisk it into the pan. His undershirt white against the skin of his shoulders, no belt, the plaid of his boxer shorts visible where the waistband of his jeans gapped. Julie, flicking here and there with his feather duster, felt that confusion of desire, remembering how, when he was little, he used to get turned on by Bugs Bunny, something in the hips, the pert cottontail, the way Bugs Bunny's ears lay back when he was pretending to be a girl, lipsticked, kittenish.

"Who's that suppose to be again?" Titus was resting on the broom, looking at the beaded curtain Julie had painted the summer before last, literally all summer, from the end of fifth grade to the beginning of sixth, one infuriating bead at a time.

"It's supposed to be Miles, but—"

"Miles Davis? Trumpet? See, I'm learning it." Titus turned and caught Julie studying the long, lean Bugs Bunny arc of his waist and hips. Julie pulled a feather out of the duster without quite meaning to. "We all done for now?"

Julie pretended to take a look around the store. They had brought nice shirts and clean pants for the funeral, neatly folded by Aviva, in a Berkeley Bowl tote bag in the back room.

"They'll be back in a few minutes," Julie said. "We could get dressed, or—"

They went into the back room. Julie pulled his pants down and opened himself up, and Titus spit into his hand and put his dick into Julie for a minute. It hurt, but in a way that Julie found interesting. The pain, he felt, bore further examination; he would have liked to study it for a while. There was something that happened every time Titus drew back for the outstroke that was closer to relief than to pain. But Titus pulled out after a minute or two. "I thought I heard the door," he said.

He went into the washroom and got up over the little sink, straddling the basin. Julie took off his dusty jeans. The foaming soap, Titus's fingers, the astonishment of his penis.

"I am not gay," Titus said when he came out of the bathroom. "If I was gay, I would tell you. I would not tell anybody else, but I would tell you."

"Okay."

"It's like, I don't want to kiss you or nothing. Like, be your boyfriend." He shook his head firmly. "I'll fuck you, though."

"Okay."

"But you are. Gay."

"Uh."

"You know that, right?"

"I guess."

They put on the clean jeans, two short-sleeved shirts with button fronts, new from Target for the occasion. They might, Julie thought, have been brothers. In Berkeley it was far from impossible.

Titus reached his right hand to Julie, slow, fingers spread, arcing toward him. They hooked hands at the thumbs and bumped chests. Titus wrapped an arm around Julie. Julie felt protected in the lingering embrace, though he knew that when Titus let go of him, he was going to feel nothing but abandoned.

⊙   ⊙   ⊙

Nat left the basement of Cochise Jones's house prepared to impose on his erstwhile partner a life sentence of silence. At the peak of his game, he could maintain a state of angry monosyllable for days on end.

For the first hour or so, he proved able with no trouble to sustain a nice meaty silence as he, Archy, and the boys moved aside the record bins and humped piles of rare vinyl into the back room, set up tables for the food and the booze, and hung the place with photographs of Cochise Jones. On Mr. Jones's customary stool, they set a large-format photo of him dressed in chaps, vest, and Stetson, riding a piebald horse in the Black Cowboy Day parade. Julie appeared to mistake his father's reticence for due funereal solemnity. Titus seemed not to notice or to give a shit or both. As for Archy, he was used to weathering Nat's silences. It was going to take longer than an hour for Nat to begin to see any effect in that quarter.

But then the Olds 98 showed up at the store to deliver the guest of honor. Two of the Flowers nephews wheeled in the remains of Cochise Jones, inside a coffin that looked like Chitty Chitty Bang Bang, everything but the candy-stripe wings and Dick Van Dyke. Archy directed Flowers's crew to install it behind the glass counter. When they had everything squared away, the nephews palmed the lid, preparing to lift it off the coffin, and that was when Nat found himself obliged to ruin a perfect start on one thousand years of silence and converse with his betrayer.

"We really are doing the open casket?" he said.

"You have a problem with that?" said one of the nephews.

"Just, I've bought records in a lot of sketchy joints," Nat said. "None of them ever had a dead body you could look at."

Archy seemed to weigh this as if searching for a counterexample, a used-vinyl store on the South Side of Hades or Philadelphia. Then he turned to the nephews. "Well," he said. "How's he looking in there?"

After a few seconds of mutual consultation, the larger of them nodded slowly, once.

"Real nice," the other one said.

Archy said, "Go on, pop the top on that thing, we can take a look."

The Flowerses lifted the lid, and Julie and Titus pressed in close to see what would be revealed. Julie's first dead body: Nat felt a sudden panic at the thought. He had prepared no words, no commentary, no sidebar or protective formula to contextualize or cushion the moment for Julie or, for that matter, for himself. In his lifetime, Nat had seen maybe half a dozen people laid out dead, and each time the sight seemed to brown the page of life, to tarnish the world's silver and dull its gold. For no good reason but the paralysis of masculine panic, he suppressed the urge to put his arm around Julie, turn him away from the sight.

"Damn," said Titus with unfeigned admiration.

"Come on, Nat," Archy said. "How you going bury that, not even take a look?"

The leisure suit that Cochise Jones had prescribed for his interment was nothing so common as loud, ugly, or intensely plaid. The gem of his collection, it was profound and magical in its excess. White, piped with burnt orange, it had a rhinestone-cowboy feel to it, except at the yoke and at the cuffs of its sleeves and trousers, where it flamed into wild pseudo-Aztec embroidery, abstract patterns suggesting pink flowers, green succulents, bloodred hearts. Cochise had worn this suit, which he always called "my Aztec number," three times before: once backing Bill James at the Eden Roc on the night when Hurricane Eloise hit; once at the Sahara in Las Vegas, where it attracted favorable comment from Sammy Davis, Jr.; and once, with improbable consequences, before a hometown crowd at Eli's Mile High. After that storied night in the annals of Oakland rumpus, Cochise had retired the Aztec number, sensing that it was a leisure suit of destiny. A suit not to be squandered on an ordinary day in a man's life, even if that man, on an ordinary day, rocked the B-3.

Nat looked at Julie. The boy was hugging himself. It took another few seconds for Nat to shame himself into providing this service for his son, and put his arm around the boy. Julie wore a too-tight short-sleeved button-down shirt patterned in black-and-white microcheck. His shoulder bone found a familiar notch in Nat's inner elbow. His broomstick arm still had an infantile give. As soon as Nat touched him, the boy relaxed.

"He looks awesome," Julie said.

"Yeah?"

"Totally."

"Okay," Nat said to Archy. "We do it open."

⊙   ⊙   ⊙

Aviva showed up at a quarter to eleven, snaking a spot as it opened up for her, in front of the hearse parked outside of Brokeland Records.

Nat was hanging around on the sidewalk, trying to look like he was not waiting for her. But she knew how he looked, standing at a bus stop when it was raining and the bus was late. He was waiting.

When she pulled into the spot, he got into the car and closed the door. Kind of a bank-robber move, Aviva thought. A man in a hurry to get away.

"Doris Day spot," he said.

"Totally. Anybody here yet?"

"Just the home team. And, of course, the corpse. The cadaver."

An off note in his voice, a hollow thud of irony. Looking rumpled and disenchanted in his Belmondo suit. Not even a glance at her to see what she had chosen to wear to Mr. Jones's wake or whatever this thing today was supposed to be. For the record, she had on a black Donna Karan pantsuit, bought at Crossroads, over a pearl-gray shell and a staid pair of walking sandals. All business for the business at hand, except for the scarf, which she had tied into a headband. A birthday gift one year from Mr. Jones, it had belonged to the late Fernanda. It was patterned with peaches and peach-tree leaves, and it was a fiery thing for a funeral. Nat really ought to have remarked on it.

"I went to Smart and Final. It's all in the trunk."

"Thank you."

"What's wrong?"

"Nothing," he said. Then he hid his face in his hands. That was as close to a breakdown as Nat ever got, the heroic attempt to confine his weeping to the region encompassed by his palms. It always slew her.

"Oh, baby, what is it?" she said. "Come here."

She held him, ready to ride it out while he massaged his sadness, pushed it all back up into his face. During the first part of their marriage, Aviva would have encouraged him to go ahead and let himself cry. But Nat, she had finally learned, would not, possibly could not, let himself cry, and maybe it was not fair to try to make him all the time. Maybe it was better to leave the poor man alone.

So now Nat really shocked her as his hands fell away, like youthful illusions, to reveal a man in the grip of a full-fledged jag. Soft, damp, and almost grandmotherly in his sorrow, mooing dolefully. Shoulders shaking. And all for old Mr. Jones. Imagine that. After so many years of wishing and resignation, Aviva saw her husband dissolved in tears, and found that the sight, this soft crumbling of his castle, kind of irritated her. It was not Nat: a dweller at the poles, prone to transports of anger and tantrums of joy.

"I know how much you liked him," Aviva said, taking some Kleenex from her purse. "I liked him, too."

Nat blew his nose, took a deep breath, let it out. "I did," he said. "I really did like him. But that isn't—that's not why—"

"Then what's wrong? Nat, what happened?"

"I had a fight with Archy. We're breaking up."

"What?"

"He's divorcing me. Because? He's sick of all my fucking bullshit." He gave another snort into the Kleenex, equal parts mucus and derision. "What the hell kind of reason is that?"

"He's taking the Dogpile job?"

"I hope he is. I sure as fuck don't want him around anymore."

"Nat." It was not that Archy wanted a divorce; Nat, she understood from his petulant tone, felt like he was being dumped. "Archy and Gwen are clearly going through some kind of a thing right now."

"Yeah. It's called real life."

"You're saying that until now Gwen Shanks and Archy Stallings have been living in a fantasy world."

"I bet Gwen feels like she's been living in a fantasy world. Black midwife and a million white mommies. Black people live their whole lives in a fantasy world, it's just not *their* fantasy."

"Uh-huh," Aviva said, sensing with a migraine throb a session in Jaffean theoretics coming on. "So, okay, let's talk about what you're going to do."

"What I'm going to do. Okay. Let's. One thing? I don't want to sell fucking used vinyl records anymore."

"Nat."

"I actually, you know, I actually hate records. No. Let me restate that: I hate *music*. All music. Yeah, I repudiate it. Fuck you, music! Music is Satan. We serve its hidden agenda. It's like a virus from space, the Andromeda strain, propagating itself. We're just vectors for the contagion. Music is the secret puppet master."

"Nat."

"Think about it, Aviva. Music actually has us to the point, we're walking around with fucking pods, with buds in our ears. Nah, I'm out. I think I'm going to get into, like, I don't know, cheesemongering. I'm going to monger cheese. You can help me. Forget birthing babies. Christ, we already have enough babies in the world. What we need more of is really good cheese. I mean, tell me, why should we have to go all the way up to North Berkeley, there, to go to the Cheese Board for the top-quality cheese product? Why shouldn't Oakland have a cheese collective, too, you know, South Berkeley/Oakland? Wait, no, fuck cheese. Cheese is all about spores and, and, molds and all that shit. Maybe cheese is trying to colonize our brains, too. Cheese and music duking it out for control of the human nervous system."

"Nat—"

Rap of a hand. They both jumped. Nat rolled down his window, and Julie was there, looking cute in his little-boy grown-up shirt, with Titus beside him just looking grown up. Two boys, chomping two big hunks of gum.

"Hey, Ms. Jaffe," Titus said.

"What are you guys doing?" said Julie, making a quick study of the dishevelment of Nat's face, hair, and suit. "What's wrong with Dad?"

"What's wrong? It's a funeral, Julie," Aviva said. "I want you and Titus to unload all that crap out of the back of the car. The ice, the sodas. Carry it in."

Chomp, chomp.

"Okay," Julie said eventually. "Come on, T."

The boys went around to the Volvo's hatch and threw it open. Aviva watched in the rearview mirror as Titus encircled four bags of ice with his long arms and hoisted them, his face showing only a faint tautness from the strain. Duly, Julie tied the ribbon of his arms around four bags and lurched, pitched forward like a man with a stomach cramp, away from the car.

" 'Come on, T,' " Nat said. "Fucking little poseur."

She laughed, happy to see him irritable again. She let go of every part of him except for his hand, which she squeezed between both of hers until their wedding rings clinked like flint and steel or a pair of champagne flutes. "You'll be all right?"

"Yeah," he said.

"You know it's all going to work out in the end?"

"No," he said. "But I guess I can probably fake it."

They got out. He grabbed two cases of Coke pony cans, and she grabbed a case of orange Jarritos, and they followed the boys into the store.

"Whoa," Aviva said when she saw the body laid out in a casket pimped with brass like something from Jules Verne. On a flood tide of burgundy velour, the face of Mr. Jones bobbed like a hunk of driftwood worn smooth. The leisure suit gave way at its extremities to the devouring work of fire and vines. "Is that the famous Aztec number?"

"Its farewell appearance."

"Hey, Aviva."

She turned to Archy, standing by the food table, stuffed with partial success into an undertaker suit. She searched his face, legible as a baby's, and saw only a mournful squint appropriate to the occasion. No sign of guilt or remorse over whatever had passed between him and Nat this morning. No hangdog skulk to his shoulders. She knew enough of his history with Gwen—in fact, she knew well more than enough—to know that regret might be days in making its appearance.

"You are looking fine, Aviva," he said. "Wore Fernanda's scarf, I see."

"Thank you, Archy," Aviva said.

Nat put a hand on her shoulder. She felt the weight of him transfer like a message. Without turning around, she knew that he was scowling at Archy, who bunched up his lips and rolled his eyes in an impatient way that confirmed her intuition.

"Sure you got enough fried chicken?" Aviva said.

Along the food table ran a sawtooth of fried-chicken mountains. Wreathed in clouds. Air tanks and Sherpas were required to reach its peaks.

"You're kidding, right?" Nat said. "Wait, seriously, should I go get some more?"

They had brought the food in from Taco Sinaloa and from the Merritt bakery, Mr. Jones's favorite places to eat. Endless llanos of green enchiladas and tamales, a Popocatépetl of *al pastor*. From Merritt, that high sierra of fried chicken. Aviva knew it pained Nat not to serve his own fried chicken at this of all parties, but Aviva had made him promise, like God postdiluvian, never to destroy the kitchen again.

"I'm kidding," she said. "But I will mention, when black folks and Jews feed a crowd, you know many chickens will die."

"I told Aviva how we're closing down the store," Nat said. "For good. Per your wishes."

"You're—closing—the store?" Julie said, the words emerging between grunts as he staggered past on his way to the drinks table with two cases of Martinelli's.

"Never you mind," Aviva said. "Archy, is it true? Did you take the job at Dogpile?"

"No," Archy said. "I didn't do anything, which I intend to keep on doing for as long as I can, at least until tomorrow. Nat's just bugging out."

Aviva grabbed hold of Nat by the elbow and turned him, boxing in his gaze with her own until he gave up and met it. "Nat, are you bugging out? If so, I need you to stop. For like the next four hours. No bugging, no tripping, no rapid cycling. You need Archy. And Archy needs you. Right, Archy?"

"From time to time," Archy said.

"You have, what, fifty people about to show up, plus a dead guy."

"More like a hundred," Archy said.

"So man up," she told her husband. "Maybe you won't be partners after today, maybe you will. But today you definitely very much still are. And as partners, you have an obligation to stand up, to represent, for Mr. Jones."

"That all sounds great, Aviva, and you're such a grown-up, my hat is off to you," Nat said. "But there's a level underlying this thing between Archy and me that you can never hope, for all your wisdom and maturity, to understand. And that level is the one that's all about vinyl."

Aviva considered a number of possible replies, pointed, dismissive, sardonic. She held her tongue, because if it was about vinyl—and men like Archy and Nat would wage wars, found empires, lose their dignity and their fortunes for the sake of vinyl—then Nat was right. She would never understand.

"But I take your point," Nat said. "And so I'm going to think of this as our last day, and live it accordingly, and do my best to honor the memory of Cochise Jones. All right? Just don't expect me to speak to Archy."

"He give you the silent treatment?" Aviva asked Archy.

"Might have. I didn't notice."

"He did," Titus said. "Most definitely."

Everyone turned to look at him. For Titus Joyner, in the presence of adults, it was a pretty long speech.

☉   ☉   ☉

Gwen showed up almost twenty minutes late, working on fifteen hours of sleep in her very own bed, feeling like she had taken a powerful cortico-stimulant. Feeling dauntless, even when it turned out she could barely get in the front door. All kinds of people had come to represent for Mr. Jones. Neighborhood folks, hipsters, beefy and bearded record collectors. Kai and her bandmates, eighteen women all resplendent in leisure suits from Mr. Jones's collection. The regulars, Moby, Mr. Mirchandani, Singletary. By the casket, Chan Flowers, arms folded, that James Brown shine on his big old hair, eyed the face of the dead man with a critical squint. Everybody standing, except for a few lucky folks right toward the front counter who had been granted the use of folding chairs.

Gwen's gaze found Archy's. He stood way at the back by the beaded curtain, towering mournfully over the buffet. Gwen did not linger on his sweet, sad, pouchy eyes. They had brought in some kind of platform and shone a light on the killer B-3. Nat stood beside it, arms folded, as though to restrain it from further acts of violence. He arched an eyebrow in greeting and then returned his attention to an unknown old white man standing on the far side of the organ, in front of the Leslie. In an indefinite European accent, the old man was speaking earnestly to the crowd, talking about Mr. Jones's political beliefs, of which Gwen (like most people in the room) had been ignorant until now. Red, as it turned out, as Cochise himself.

Aviva's jungly head scarf caught Gwen's eye, in the row by the front counter. Aviva was one of the people in chairs. She raised a hand to Gwen: There was an empty seat beside her. Gwen would have to take it. She knew that Aviva was angry, and knowing that was enough to make Gwen angry, too. But she was too pregnant to stand.

As Gwen worked her way into the crowd like an icebreaker shouldering the floes, Aviva picked up her purse, which she had been using to save the seat for Gwen.

"Who is this guy?" Gwen whispered into Aviva's ear when she sat down. Aviva's hair had a bay leaf smell.

"He's from, I guess a Marxist library down the street."

Gwen had been unaware, as well, that Telegraph Avenue featured a Marxist library. She tried to imagine it as a place that would feel congenial to a man who not only dressed the way Mr. Jones dressed but also understood, according to the fluty-voiced old Marxist librarian, the interactions of base and superstructure, the way ultimately, class struggle underpinned all the racism in America.

"That the Aztec number?" Gwen whispered, grasping for the first time the splendor of the corpse.

Aviva nodded.

"Shh," said the woman on the other side of Gwen. She was a freaky-looking old Cruella with a brindle shih tzu perched on her lap.

"Sorry," Gwen said to the scary old lady.

"Me, too," Aviva said to Gwen immediately, as if she had been holding that for Gwen's arrival as well.

Gwen considered correcting Aviva's misapprehension that she had apologized for what Aviva had called her "performance" in the hearing at Chimes. But some impulse restrained her. It was not a qualm—far from it. Maybe it was the soft, snowy mantle of sleep under which she had passed the previous night, but she felt more justified than ever in taking on those tools of the insurance companies, more justified at having thrown Archy out of the house so that she could at last get some rest. It was not the possibility that she might have been wrong, excessive, manipulative, over the top yesterday afternoon, which led Gwen to let stand the misapprehended apology. It was pure calculation, albeit buried deep: Let Aviva think she had been apologized to; it would make things easier later.

After the man from the Marxist library, there was a gap-toothed drummer who looked older than he probably was, a hundred and ten in dope years, and then Moby got up and told a story about how the first time he came into Brokeland Records, Mr. Jones had been sitting at the counter in his usual spot, rewarding his parrot, Fifty-Eight, with sunflower seeds from his jacket pocket, trying to teach him, with a deck of playing cards, to recognize the difference between the red and black suits. " 'This bird smarter than anybody you know,' " said Moby, quoting Mr. Jones too faithfully, maybe, laying on as usual with the Ebonics. " 'He don't learn how to play poker, just mean I didn't give him a adequate schooling.' "

Most of the room broke up into laughter. Gwen looked over at the organ to see how Nat was taking the lawyer's routine. She knew how much he detested the way Moby slipped into his wannabe shtick. And he was really ill equipped for it, there was no denying that. If he were not so sweet and fat with that preposterous swoop-back haircut, Gwen might have taken a measure of offense at the way Moby talked, the style cobbled (with unquestionably sincere intentions of tribute) from the discarded materials of rap records, Grady Tate on *Sanford and Son*, a touch of Martin Lawrence, and then at the core, something really questionable, maybe Morgan Freeman as Easy Reader on *The Electric Company*. It sure bothered the hell out of Nat, though, look at him up there, turned around on the organ bench, working the pedals of his irritation, shooting his cuffs. If you were trying to pass as white, the thing was always to keep your distance from your darker relatives, but if you were a white guy living along the edge of blackness all your life, the worst thing was somebody around you trying to do the same.

Having concluded his remarks, Moby worked his way back to his seat, free throws made, pounding and dapping folks right and left.

"Thank you, Moby," Nat said from the back. Everybody craned around to look at him. "You would not be so fond of that bird if you owed him as much money as I do."

He meant it as a joke, and Aviva laughed, but it came out sounding angry, and if Gwen were a detective investigating the bird's disappearance, she definitely would have brought Nat in for questioning.

"I'm going to play a little now," Nat announced, as if it were a procedure and he a periodontist. Making it sound like it was not going to be any fun for anyone. "And then Mr. Stallings is going to offer the eulogy."

Gwen tried to remember the last time she had heard Nat call Archy "Mr. Stallings." She turned to Aviva to see if she might have picked up on something amiss between their men, but Aviva had eyes only for Nat. She was sitting up and watching him as carefully as Flowers was watching the body in the casket: wanting him to be perfect.

Nat turned to the Leslie amplifier and honored it with a bow, snapped it on. It rose throbbing to life. A wind flowed through its mysterious antique machinery. Nat sat down at the Hammond that had taken, in every sense, Mr. Jones's life. It was not Nat's instrument, but he had a gift, could pick up pretty much any instrument and quickly figure it out well enough to fake it. He played piano, and Gwen assumed that his organ playing would resemble that: modernistic, angular, Monk-style stuff, hard to listen to.

Nat loosened his tie. He mediated a dispute among his shirttails, his waistband, his belt, and his ass. He fiddled with the drawbars and switches of the Hammond, more for the sake of ritual than precision. With a count and a duck of his head on four, he began to play. She recognized the song as the old Carole King number "It's Too Late." The organ had a reedy, bluesy sound, smoke in its throat. Nat did not fool around with angles and flatted notes. His feet stoked the pedals. She did not remember any of the lyrics apart from those of the chorus, though those were enough to convey the melancholy of the song. She wanted to look for Archy, but she was afraid that if their eyes met while this song was being played, he would think she intended to send the message that Carole King had been sending to the man in her song.

Part of her, call it most of her, knew that to some extent she had been playacting, licensed by her hormones to express through the theater of her departure and her return all the humiliation that Archy had forced her to endure. As Nat played, she avoided meeting Archy's gaze and wondered if the sadness she had seen on his face was for her and him. Archy had decided to leave right after the funeral, she decided, his duffel bag and ten crates of records loaded into the back of his El Camino. She had thrown him out in pique, but now he would be leaving in earnest, just as she had always known and feared he would do. The certainty of his imminent departure came over her so strongly that she was confused by it and wondered if Nat had selected the music on purpose as a comment on her relationship with Archy.

Aviva leaned over and whispered into Gwen's ear without taking her eyes off her husband. "This was Mr. Jones's theme song," she said. "According to Nat."

Gwen understood then that whatever its ostensible subject or situation, "It's Too Late" was about Cochise Jones. Lying useless in his casket. Sitting at the bedside of his wife when she had lain dying. The song was about the people gathered here who might never have had the chance to meet Mr. Jones, and those who might have spoken differently, said more, the last time they saw him, had they known. It was about Titus growing up with no father, and Aviva trying to hold on to her one and only baby, and the dream of Brokeland Records. It was about some large percentage of the aggregate wishes, plans, and ambitions espoused by the people gathered here today. Nat had not needed to choose "It's Too Late" in order to comment directly on her situation with Archy. It was Mr. Jones's theme song, and its sentiment was always appropriate.

"Perfect," Gwen said.

⊙   ⊙   ⊙

"My name is Archy Stallings. All right, now. Thank you. Yes. Thank you. Those of you, some of you who don't know me, I am one of the co-proprietors of these premises, Brokeland Records, thank you, a neighborhood institution since, count it one way, twelve years, but really, you have to count back a lot further than that. For real. Back, like, before they had vinyl records, back before they even had Mr. Jones, and Mr. Jones was here a good long time. And I mean he was right *here*. Seriously. Right there, on that stool, where his picture's looking at you, in prime form if I may say, got to love that Borsalino. Mr. Jones spent a lot of time and money at this address over the years, first when it used to be a barbershop. Spencer's Barbershop, that's right. I got my hair cut here quite a few times, I was a youngster. And then Mr. Jones spent even more of his money here, the past twelve years, buying records! A whole lot of records, from me and my partner, Nat Jaffe, who just now tore it up, am I right? Yes, I am. Tore it up on Mr. Jones's signature tune, 'It's Too Late,' thank you, Nat, for that.

"Now, if you talked to Mr. Jones for any length of time, and it took a long time to get anything out of Mr. Jones, man preferred to listen, witness, I bet most of you had no idea until this very afternoon, all due respect to Dr. Hanselius from the library, oh my goodness, Cochise Jones, look at you, dressing like that all the time, riding around town in your big old van with your gold toothpick, and all the time you secretly a *Communist*! Mr. Jones was like, almost like a father to me, used to pass me a little cash every now and then, kept an eye on me. Talked to me, and like I'm saying, that was, you know, it took an effort for him.

"Anyway, if you could drag it out of him, you found out sooner or later that Mr. Jones came here to Oakland from somewhere down in Louisiana, outside of New Orleans, was it Slidell? Yes, when he was fourteen, fifteen. His dad got a job working at the cannery, the one where the DMV is now? The Lusk Cannery, yes. That is all long before my time. But Mr. Jones used to tell me things, you know, every so often the parrot would lay off talking, Nat there just about finished up with the daily rant, ha, ha, something used to bubble up out of Mr. Jones. About the neighborhood. Things he remembered. Coming up a little boy in Louisiana, hearing things from the old folks, some of those people went *way* on back, back up almost to slavery times.

"I don't know how many black folks came up to Oakland from Louisiana, Alabama, Texas, you know, back at the time when Mr. Jones and his family came here. Many, many thousands, tens of thousands. Yeah, so, they left most of what little they had down south, but they brought the music they liked, going back to like Congo Square or whatever. Jazz and boogie, church music. And then getting off the train in Oakland, everything's booming. That's when, if you came inside here, you most likely would be hearing that rocking postwar blues, that jump music, coming out of the radio Eddie Spencer used to keep on this shelf behind me.

"You listen to that music now, like Joe Houston, it's rock and roll, right? Same music. Joe Turner. And that's the kind of music Mr. Jones started out playing in public. That and church music, and church music, that's like, that's the original rock and roll. I can tell, looking at his face, my partner has certain bones to pick with my theorizing on this subject, but hey, we did that roshambo and I drew the eulogy, so hang with me, all right? I think you are going to like where this is going.

"Yeah, so, when he was in high school, Mr. Jones had a band, they were all black kids, played rhythm and blues, Drifters covers. But he also used to play sometimes with a bunch of white boys, I think they were called the Pearl Tones, was that it? Based out of Skyline High. Even when he first got known, in like '64, '65, playing straight-ahead jazz, kind of following on the organ a little bit what Ahmad Jamal was doing on the piano, even then he never totally lost that rocking touch. I know it always used to, not bother him, but make him a little sad the way people sat around *listening* to jazz. To those Eric Dolphy joints he played on, people nodding a little bit, tapping their feet, but not, you know, not up jumping around, getting wild, the way black folks generally, historically speaking, have tended to do.

"Meanwhile, on the radio, Mr. Jones is hearing Jimi Hendrix, hearing Sly Stone. Not just white boys playing black music, like always, or even black dudes playing in a white style, but really, like, this moment, this one moment, lasted four, five years, when the styles and the players were mixing it all up. The Temptations, some of that late stuff is *heavy* in the true rock-and-roll vernacular. And Mr. Jones, he knew Sly Stone, they was even related by marriage somehow, he started working some of that same idea into the jazz that he started to play.

"And even though he never lost that smooth approach, that soft touch on the right hand, his left hand, '67, '68, it started to get *extremely* funky. But Mr. Jones didn't call his style 'funky,' I don't believe I ever heard him use that term at all. Church music, jump music, rock and roll, hard bop, soul-jazz, none of that. We get into a lot of, like, genre arguments around here, like, is Donald Byrd's *Street Lady* soul-jazz, or is it more to the side of jazz-funk? Is 'hard bop' redundant? Mr. Jones never took part in those discussions. But one time, I do remember, he called what he played 'Brokeland Creole.'

"Creole, that's, to me, it sums it up. That means you stop drawing those lines. It means Africa and Europe cooked up in the same skillet. Chopin, hymns, Irish music, polyrhythms, talking drums. And people. Cochise Jones, his mother was mostly, uh, Choctaw, I think it was. Me, my father's half Mexican, which is already half something else. Brokeland Creole. Around here used to be Mexico, before that, Spain, before that, Ohlone. And then white people, Chinese, Japanese, black folks bringing that bayou, that Seminole, that Houston vibe. Filipinos. Toss 'em on the grill, go 'head. Brokeland Creole. And some more Mexicans, Guatemalans. Thai, Vietnamese. Hmong. Uh, Persian. Punjab, Mr. Mirchandani. Mr. Mirchandani, here's an example right here. All them good samosas back there, piled up next to the fried chicken? I— Yeah. I know I had a point I was going to make. Ha, seriously. Yeah, no, okay.

"Only that Cochise Jones— Oh. Excuse me. Whoa. No, I'm good. Mr. Jones was like a father to me, which I seriously needed. That's one point. And the other point is, since I'm here doing this eulogy, I have a responsibility to have us, you know, take a look at the life the man led and, like, extract some kind of wisdom out of it. Right? So here goes.

"Seems like, I don't know. When people start looking at other people, people not like them, one thing they often end up liking about those people is their music.

"There's sort of a, what, an *ideal* that I know Nat and me always had in mind for this store. Not, like, anything we ever planned out or talked about. But it's something like this: on the old Silk Road, you know, between Europe and China. It's all tribes and deserts, and then you've got this long, hard journey, take you a couple of years to get there if you go quick. It's a hard road, it has bandits, sandstorms. You carrying the light of all the civilizations back and forth, but all around you, the tribes just want to keep up their warring, and killing, and keeping track of what makes them better than everybody else. Like you know how every tribe's name, when you translate it, turns out to mean 'the people,' like nobody else but them is really *human*? But you keep on because you are trying to earn a little cheese, right, and you spreading the collective wisdom back and forth. Forging that Creole style. And every so often, every few hundred miles, maybe, you got these oases, right, these caravansaries, where they all get together and chill, hang out, listen to good music, swap wild tales of exaggeration. Nat, man, you know what I'm saying, right? That was kind of our dream. The Brokeland Creole dream.

"Mr. Jones was a mainstay of this caravansary. He was, like, our idol in the corner, the household god. Now he is gone, and we, me and Nat— Whoa. Okay, yes, could I get that tissue, Aviva? Thank you."

⊙   ⊙   ⊙

"You can ride with us," a voice was saying, sounded like the undertaker. "Funeral can't start without the deceased."

In reply, only a silence, partial, intensified by the sounds of departure from the front of the store, chairs scraping, people offering rides, vouching for their own or somebody else's sobriety. Burial-suit thugs from the funeral home handing out maps to the grave: *Miss, a map?*

Titus zipped his pants. The way to play it, saunter out of the bathroom into the workroom, alone. Kid coming out of the toilet zipping up his Levi's, so what? He communicated his intentions to Julie by means of Special Ops hand signs: *I, turn out light. You, stay. I, go, create diversion. You, count thirty, exit bathroom, slip out the back.* Julie nodded: *Understood.* That turned out not to be the case, because the minute Titus switched off the light, Julie just went and opened the bathroom door. Eased it open, at least a show of stealth, half an inch, an inch.

Then the answer: "I'll give you five minutes."

His father. Archy. Tightness in his voice. Fronting. Bored with the undertaker, bored with using boredom as a front. Angry, tired.

Titus and Julie exchanged a look in the darkness: change of plan. The lonely science of eavesdropping, another mad love they shared. Two of Julie's fingers keeping the door open that one little inch.

"All I need is five *seconds*," the undertaker said. "To say you are the stupidest, most self-defeating negro I have ever seen. And my experience in that category is long and bitter."

Archy said, "Let me save you the five seconds, then, 'cause I already know that."

"How about this, then? You have played yourself now."

"No surprise there, either."

Archy was leaning against one of the rolling bin tables they had humped into the workroom that morning, his wide ass in those ugly black suit pants pinned against a corner of the Disco section. On the tab of the white section divider behind him were written, intriguingly, the words YELLOW MAGIC ORCHESTRA. Titus briefly imagined the warm, candy-flavored music that might go by that name.

"I hope you were not counting on going to work for Gibson Goode anytime soon. Because as far you are concerned, Gibson Goode has moved on."

Archy Stallings looked uncomfortable and unhappy, arms crossed, scowling, sharp corner of the record bin poking him in the ass. Maybe he was using the pain to focus himself, keep himself on his guard. Titus was not sure how loaded or sober the man was.

He had made his funeral speech, flowing all over the place, Indians, Vietnam, gumbo, Sly Stallone. At the end of his disquisition on what an undifferentiated mess life was to him, the man had choked up. In that instant, Titus had played a scene in his mind: The pregnant lady got up, put her arms around her baby's daddy, he put his hand on the giant-size belly, and they decided that in the end, as long as life was going to be an undifferentiated mess, they might as well not fight it anymore. Make a place in the mess for a baby, a baby who would have a mother and a father, one small victory for the good kind of doubt and confusion over the bad. But in reality, when the movie in Titus's mind came to an end, it turned out to be Julie's father, Nat, giving Archy the hug of consolation. The box of tissues got passed around.

Then there was some drinking, for sure. Beer, wine, Cokes. People drank it all. They ate up the food, bum-rushed the buffet like freed prisoners, bees on a melting Popsicle. An hour later, it was all gone. A lone can of tonic water floated in a cooler, untouched among the ice cubes for quite some time, and eventually found its way into the company of a bottle of gin that never made a public appearance. The last Saturday afternoon of the summer went about its business, and it got to be time to ride on over to the cemetery, if you were going.

When the food was gone, the undertaker gave out instructions to his nephews and organized the procession to the cemetery, suggesting to some people that they let others do the driving, speaking in a kindly whisper far from the warlock voice he was using on Archy Stallings. Then the lid got lowered for the last time on Cochise Jones, and Titus played a scene in which he persuaded a few trusted confederates to join him in a heist operation to steal the clothes off the dead man before they were lost forever to rot and darkness and oblivion. Trap the hearse between a couple of tractor-trailers at an intersection, pull up in another hearse, switch caskets. Never let that beautiful thing, the Aztec number, go wasted in the ground. By the end of the scene he was cutting in his head, Titus found himself deep into creeping himself out, picturing a piebald cadaver rotting in the stainless leisure suit. Thing was made of space-age materials, no worm was ever going to touch it. Eternal as a Twinkie.

"So, you and he," the undertaker was saying, "you are calling it quits. Is that what I am to understand?"

"I know you would be happy about that."

"I would only be partway happy," the undertaker said. "Which is the same as not happy at all."

"We close the store, Nat's bound to drop this whole protest thing. You won't have to worry about that anymore."

"Your friend already did his damage to me," the undertaker said. "Now Rod Abreu has come sniffing around this whole deal, acting to the world like he is trying to eighty-six it. Letting Gibson Goode think he's an enemy and needs to be kept close, as the saying goes. Needs to be *won over*. Right now, today, Rod Abreu is sitting at the Coliseum, letting G Bad pick up the tab for the nachos."

Titus could not see the undertaker's face, only the steely curl of the pompadour thing at the back of his head. But from the sound of his voice, he must be looking disgusted, contemptuous. It was an easy enough expression to imagine on the undertaker's face.

"Tell me this," he said, "if you close your store, curl up in a ball like a little pill bug, what are you going to do for a job to support your child?"

Only a second before, Archy had seemed fucked up, puzzled. He had this pudding look to his cheeks. Now it was all concrete and stone.

"I am going to see Mr. Jones on home," he said. "And we ain't finished doing that yet. I don't need to ride with you. I have my own car."

"Do you have a map to the gravesite? You're going to need a map."

"I'll be fine."

"Mountain View, two hundred and twenty acres. Hundred and fifty thousand people buried there. Five, six funerals a day. You got the Jews in one place, Chinese over there. Black folks sprinkled all through it. Talk about Brokeland Creole. Mountain View Cemetery, that's the only place you ever actually going to find it. But you need a map. You need *guidance*."

"Oh, okay. You're going all Jedi on me now."

"Hear me out."

"Going Morpheus."

"You don't deserve it, boy. But I am still willing to help you. We can get this mess straightened out. Luther has something I want. Nothing crazy, illegal, not drugs, guns, stolen goods, none of that. All right? Or yes, the thing was stolen, but it was stolen *from me*! It's mine! I mean, seriously." His voice broke, raspy almost to the point of a wheeze. "It's mine, he has it, and I want it back. I have money, Luther's broke. I figure maybe you've heard one or two things about me over the years that might have planted a seed in your imagination. When you are an undertaker and you come from a whole family of undertakers, people are going to hold all kinds of wild beliefs about the way you go about your business. So I want to reassure you. I don't want to hurt Luther, do not want to mess with him, the Lord knows, Archy, I want nothing to *do* with that man any more than you do. That old boy wore me out a long time before he got around to wearing you out. I am a respectable businessman, I sit on the city council. I am not a gangster, and I know what people say about me, but it's lies and rumors and folks letting their imaginations run away with them. One time when I was a young man, I made a mistake. A long time ago, right out of the navy. I made a mistake, but I was lucky, and one way and another, with some help from your father, credit where credit is due, I was able to put it behind me. Stopped running wild and acting a fool all the time. Got serious about life and settled down and did good for myself. Things did not go so well for your father. The whole time I was rising, he was sinking down. For the past ten, twelve years, he's been coming around here, sometimes sober, most of the time so high or so drug-sick, he could not even really talk. But most of the time he managed to get his palm out, and I always crossed it with some cash for him."

"He was blackmailing you."

The undertaker didn't respond to that. "Everything gets put where it belongs," he said. "You can still find yourself standing behind the information desk in the Beats Department at the Dogpile store on Telegraph Avenue, dropping science on the youngsters when they stop in to pick up the new Lil' Bow Wow, getting that employee discount to bring home one of those *Baby Mozart* DVDs, teach your new child to play the cello while he's sleeping."

"And I have to do what?"

"Son, I know you know where he is."

"I honestly don't."

Crouched down in the bathroom with Julie leaning in over him, Titus heard the man lying. At the body shop, it had made him furious to see the contempt his father showed toward his own pops. Now Titus felt sorry for the dude, so twisted up with hate that he could not even let his poor, old kung fu ex-junkie daddy get paid back money he was free and clear owed.

"Have it your way, then," the undertaker said.

For the first time, you could tell, Archy was thinking. Going back over it all. Making up his mind to do what he was going to do.

"I have no reason to want to enable that man," he said. "And I have known you all my life, Brother Flowers. But I can't help feeling like I'm seeing a side of you I never really believed was true."

"Just conducting business."

"Nah. You're an undertaker. A mortician. Burying a dead man, supposed to be more than just business."

"Well—"

"You never once told me, 'I'm sorry for your loss. Mr. Jones was a fine man and a sharp dresser,' or anything of that type."

"Well, I *am* sorry," the undertaker said.

But by that time, man was already on his way out the workroom door, headed for the cemetery and whistling "It's Too Late."

⊙   ⊙   ⊙

Look at this. Here the boys come out of the bathroom, Alfalfa and Stymie. The only thing missing, the little eye-patch pit bull. Both of them with their eyes wide, boy detectives, the black one saying nothing, the Jaffe kid all, *We know where he is.*

"You were eavesdropping," said Chan Flowers. "That is wrong, morally and ethically. Every civilized people from the dawn of time has recognized that fact."

"We didn't mean to." Julie, his name was, a girl's name for a girlish boy. "We're sorry."

Flowers said the one thing there was to say to an eavesdropper. "What do you think you heard?"

Julie said they had not really heard anything, just that Flowers was trying to find Luther Stallings to pay him back the money he owed Luther. Also that, while they had been sworn to secrecy, they would be willing to act as messengers.

"Messengers? What do you mean, messengers? Why do I need a messenger? Can't you just tell me where he is?"

The boys exchanged looks. Flowers was busy managing his impatience, a skill he had acquired without ever quite internalizing, but despite his irritation, he did not fail to detect a spark of genuine friendship between them. It astonished him.

"We heard there was maybe, some kind of"—the boy turned bright red—"uh, beef."

Flowers asked Titus, didn't he know how to say anything? "You two remind me of the old man and that parrot," he said. "Frick and Frack."

He glanced through the door, across the deserted store to the front door. Feyd and Walter, Bankwell waiting in the hearse. Time to start the parade.

"Fine," Flowers said. "I tell you what." He reached into his breast pocket for his checkbook. Then and there, leaning on a stack of records, he wrote out a check in the amount of $25,000.00, payable to Luther Stallings. Signed it with a flourish that he hoped implied magnanimity. "There is no beef," he said. "That was all a long time ago and far, far away. You can tell him I said that. Bygones be bygones."

"Forgiveness is an attribute of the brave," Titus said.

Julie almost smiled, looking pleased and dubious. But Flowers recognized it as one of forty-nine Proverbs, Meditations, and Words of Comfort printed in the last two pages of every funeral program that Flowers & Sons handed out.

"I'm going to have to be careful around you," he said, handing the check over to Titus. "I can see that. Here. You take that to him. Put it in your wallet. You carry a wallet, don't you?"

No, of course he did not, just a dense wad of small bills. So Alfalfa put the check into a toy plastic wallet he carried around. Flowers waited until this business had been seen to, concerned about the fate of that check, which he had postdated and would cancel first thing Monday morning.

"That's no strings attached, right? He doesn't have to forgive me. It's his money, he can do what he wants with it. Got that? We good? All right. Now, I know you boys want to ride with the body."

⊙   ⊙   ⊙

Having laid aside their frogged jackets this once in favor of the drab and Day-Glo splendors of the Jones Memorial Leisure Suit Library, Bomp and Circumstance cut loose. They played "Nearer My God to Thee." They played "The Old Rugged Cross." Their order was good as they led the caravan along Piedmont Avenue to the cemetery gates. Perhaps the brass sounded a touch pallid, like the headlights of the cars in the cortege. Maybe the drumbeat got lost in the heat and hum of the afternoon. But once the casket had been fed by the belts into the ground, they turned from the graveside, the bass trombone taking up the opening groove of "Redbonin,' " which had gone to number thirty-two on the R&B charts in July 1972, and began, as promised, to swing.

Brokeland

T hey were like the kids in that newspaper comic, white nerd, black nerd, pretending at the bus stop on this fine Sunday morning that they were Jedi knights, samurais. Lost so deep in the dream, they didn't have the sense to be embarrassed. *FoxTrot*: Bankwell read it sometimes, though the light had pretty much gone out of the funny papers for Bank Flowers back when the *Chronicle* got rid of the strip with the English basset hound.

Shorties rode the bus downtown, got off by Fourteenth Street, walked down to Franklin Street, where there was a donut place, egg roll place, the decor Chinese but the calendar by the telephone printed in some alphabet of snakes. Bank had long since incorporated the house bear claw into his ongoing survey of donut shops from Fremont to Richmond; this one was a notch above the run of the mill. If you were downtown and couldn't hold out for the Federation or, farther north, the mighty Dream Fluff, Loving Donut would do.

White nerd, black nerd got off the bus and, for once with no swordplay, waited on the empty sidewalk in front of the donut shop as if something real was about to happen. Playing some kind of classic rock, had a flute in it, out of that old green-and-orange shoulder-strap eight-track the white nerd carried everyplace he went. Waiting for another bus to come along, tornado drop a house on them. After a minute or two with no tornado, the black nerd, Titus, said something out of the side of his mouth. Then they waited awhile longer. Titus was built lean, harder than the glasses and that retard bounce in his step led you to expect. Still growing, bound to work out to be tall like his father, maybe not as chesty. In response to whatever Titus said, the other one took out a plastic wallet, yellow and blue. Nestled it close to his chest as if it held magic ducklings, tiny orphan bunnies he was nursing back to health.

He tweezed out a bill and passed it to Titus, who went in and returned a minute later holding what appeared to be a dead puppy.

"I see you a bear claw man," Bankwell said to Titus through the windshield of the hearse, not the brokedown Cadillac or the borrowed Olds 98 but the Flowers & Sons workhorse, a 1984 Crown Vic. No fear or hope of Titus hearing him, kitty-corner away and through the safety glass. "Interesting."

"You mean 'nasty,' " said cousin Walter. Prince Walter, the favorite nephew, more like a son to a man who never had any sons of his own. In trouble, now, though. "What you always get."

"It's a longitudinal study," Bank said. "Bear claw is my, what you call, control."

"Uh," Walter said, hand to his belly. "Like eating a deep-fried sock."

"That is why bear claw have to be the control," Bank explained patiently. "You want to see how much love and affection the chef put into the bear claw. If the bear claw's good, the standardize donuts be even better."

"You already had your donut for today," said Feyd.

"Feyd, shut up."

"You his conscience now?" little Walter said. "Fucking little Jiminy Cricket motherfucker."

Walter in a pissy mood, squeezed into the front seat between Bankwell and Feyd. For many of the more reluctant passengers obliged in the past to occupy that spot, the back of the vehicle had come to seem preferable. But Prince Walter only saw his position, no doubt, for the indignity it was. Walter had graduated from the hearses years ago, from handling the dead, washing their horrible feet. Ushering crazy old ladies, keeping an eye on the gang-bang element, enduring the gusts of drama that caught people up, women especially, whenever funerals came along. Then from time to time, like today, paying a visit on behalf of Chan Flowers to somebody who did not want to be found, was not necessarily in the mood for visitors. Walter had left it all behind years ago, moved down to L.A. to work in the record business, come back from time to time showing off pictures of himself with Tupac, Jada Pinkett and Will Smith, Johnny Depp, Snoop Dogg. Finding his way into Gibson

Goode's circle of love. Now here he was, back riding a hearse, not even driving it. Stuck between two cousins he used to know only as likely vessels for the downflow of family beatdowns.

"Feyd keeping track," Bank said. "Everything I put in my mouth. Sometimes I see him writing that shit down. Boy is spying on my food."

"Uncle Chan said put him on a diet, one donut a day," Feyd said. "He said, uh, 'Big bank,' you do realize that's just a figure of speech, right?'"

Walter laughed his scratchy laugh, Ernie from *Sesame Street*, working something loose at the back of his throat. Feyd took out his pocket vaporizer. He and Walter were well and fully vaped, deep into a fresh, veiny hank of Vineland County kush bought with Feyd's auntie's glaucoma prescription. Bank did not imbibe. Didn't drink or eat swine, either. Seventy-five percent of the way to a five-percenter and thus enjoined to respect his elders, try not to violate Uncle Chan's rules, which definitely included No Partying in the Funeral Vehicles. Also, No Profane Music, and here they were with Ghostface Killah playing on the CD, softly but the music so soaked in the world's profanity that it bled like a saturated bandage.

"Shit," Bank said. "You just a damn food spy."

They watched white nerd watching black nerd ingest the bear claw, an alien feeding in a horror movie, even its teeth had teeth. White nerd looking duly horrified. Then it was his turn to go into the shop, but when he came out, he was holding a pink box tied up with white string.

"Bringing somebody a present," Bank observed.

"Oh, shit," said Walter happily. "No. Oh, no. It's her, here she come."

Here came Candyfox Brown, whatever her name was in the movies, that highjacked, big-titty mature, muscling past the boys on her Preakness haunches. Walking right past them without a glance.

"Valletta Moore," Walter said, praying it. Sounding like he was feeling sorry for her or for himself. "Damn."

White nerd black nerd swung their heads to watch the tick-tock of her bodily clockwork as she made her way past them. The motion of the two heads, whup-whup, so uniform, so abject, like those dogs they used to feature at the station breaks on Channel 20, whipping around with their tongues hanging out whenever somebody off-screen waved a pork chop.

"Why she didn't stop?" Walter said. "Seem like she don't know them."

"She know them," Bankwell said. He put the car into drive and turned right at the intersection, away from the boys and the donut shop. "She being careful. She going to come back around in a second, long as she doesn't see us sitting here."

"Where are you going?"

"Around the block."

Somebody had speculated that Valletta Moore and the man, Luther, were most likely geeked up on crack, that it was just a matter of finding whatever hole they crawled into. But they had eluded Uncle Chan for some time, and obviously, she, at least, was capable of taking basic precautions. Maybe she was not as far gone as rumor had it, or maybe chronically paranoid. In any case, a hearse was by no means the ideal surveillance vehicle. Usually, by the time Uncle Chan sent Bankwell and Feyd around in the Crown Vic, the point was not about concealment. If Batman wanted to observe the thug life of Gotham City, he would not dress up in black rubber and drive around in a Batmobile; he would send Alfred in some poot-butt Daihatsu. The Crown Victoria was intended to make a Batmobile statement, a message of intent. But Uncle Chan, up against it, woke this morning willing to take his chances.

"There she is," Walter said when they had circled around Fifteenth Street and Broadway. Two blocks down the street, Valletta Moore was opening the passenger door of an old, tired muscle car, looked like a Toronado, mottled gray and beige, streaked with green, like a slice of Oscar Mayer bologna after two months in the refrigerator. Titus and the other one fell into the backseat, then Cleopatra Clark or whoever got in and eased the door shut.

"Go," Walter said, watching them pull away from the curb.

"You see I still got a red," Bankwell said. "You want me to get a ticket? Police pull me over, how we going to follow them then?"

Bankwell was not afraid of Prince Walter.

When the light turned green, the Toronado was far enough ahead to be tailed with ease and discretion. Bank had himself ready, to tell the truth was hoping, to see the Oldsmobile put some evasive maneuvers

into play, a Jim Rockford fishtail, something, but the driver of the Toronado, likely the very man they were supposed to be locating, made no
efforts in that line. Right turn on Telegraph, up to MacArthur, then into
the parking lot of a motel, the Selwyn, one of a number of fine establish-
ments along the boulevard, looked like it catered to a select clientele of
crankheads, day-raters, and the insects who loved them. The office was
an A-frame, the motel a two-decker box, with a covered drive-through
between them that the Toronado just managed to thread.

"Parking lot must be in the back," Walter said. He settled between
his cousins as if they were a couple of pillows and it was nap time for the
little baby prince. "Go on, then."

"What about you?" Bank said. "You coming, too, right?"

"Huh? I'm supposed to stay here."

"What?"

"Monitor the situation."

Bank stood there with the door open, patient. A man with time
to burn. Presently, shaking his head at the low state to which he had
fallen, Prince Walter got out of the car. "You strapped?" he said as they
crossed the boulevard. Bank did not bother to dignify the question with
a response.

In the front parking lot, there were three cars, a Band-Aid-tan VW
square-back, a Jeep, an ancient B210. A housekeeping cart had the upper walkway all to itself. There was nobody in the office A-frame they
could see. Two security cameras on light poles, but whatever. They were
here only to pay a visit.

As Prince Walter had guessed, the covered area led to a smaller parking area behind the motel, gravel, subservient to a row of Dumpsters.
The Toronado was tucked into a spot between the trash bins and the high
stucco wall that kept the motel quarantined from the house behind it.
The backside of the motel was blank stucco and frosted windows, a face
that was minding its own business. On the ground floor beside the gas
meters, a fire door warned that it must be kept unlocked at all times.

"I'm a wait here," Walter said. "Case they see you coming, try to run
out the back."

It sounded cowardly, but it made sense, and some allowance needed to be made for Prince Walter's likely uselessness in the event of trouble. Bank hiked up the left leg of his suit pants to take his little Beretta Bobcat out of the holster that was Velcroed to his ankle.

"Here you go," he said, handing it over to Walter, who took it without bothering to hide his reluctance. "Remember to shoot at the horses' legs."

Prince Walter nodded solemnly before he caught what Bank had said. Scowled. As they went through the fire door, Bankwell was obliged to tell Feyd to shut up, man, quit laughing. They found themselves in a harsh-lit room, lollipop smell of laundry, a couple of coin-op washers and dryers. Something like a pair of sneakers was turning one of the dryers into a tom-tom. Purple tumbleweeds of lint rolled scattering as they passed through another door into a dim hallway, past an ice machine, and outside, under the second-floor walkway, right next to room 112. Aimless little flies hovered in the cool of the stairwell like the dots on a lacy funeral veil.

"You check out down here, I'll go up," Bank said. He had a feeling they would be on two.

It was not that he looked forward to trouble or violence. But he felt that it was better to rush up on it than to let it rush up on you. He rang his way up the steel stairs and was about to step onto the landing when somebody stuck out a leg. He fell hard. A lightbulb broke on his head. The stairway was a gong, resounding. While Bank was falling, though, he reached out to take instinctive hold of someone who turned out to be Titus. Shortie fell down beside him.

There was blood in Bankwell's mouth, possibly a loose tooth.

"Motherfucker!" he said. Scrape against the concrete of the soles of his loafers as he reared up on his legs, flapping his necktie, flapping the tails of his jacket. Without intending to, he stepped on Titus's stomach, and ho, shit, here came the bear claw, acrid brown slush in a jet. Bank jumped back, lost his footing, and then was attacked by a swordsman.

"Ya!" said the boy with the bunnies in his wallet. "Hiya!"

The first blow glanced off Bank's right arm, just above the elbow, but the second caught him square on the back of the head. It was a practice

katana, see them racked in a dojo, solid wood. Coming after Bank's interaction with the concrete landing, the blow to his head did no favors
to the clarity of his thought process. Luckily, he was armed with a fully
licensed Sig Sauer .38 that he was more than qualified to use. Thinking
was not required.

He stuck the gun in the face of little, what was it, Julie. Julie Jaffe.
Five feet five inches of redhead Mr. Peabody samurai fury. Bank could
not help smiling. "Check this out," he said to Feyd when his cousin
came running up the steps. "Check out little white-boy Zatoichi."

Mr. Peabody lowered the sword, possibly because he now had two
guns pointing at him and a sword made out of wood. But it looked more
to Bank like amazement than surrender. More like Bank had guessed
his secret identity. Bank twisted the sword free of the boy's grip.

"Zatoichi!" Feyd said. "That's good, I could use me a massage."

Feyd looked down at Titus, saw what had become of the bear claw,
wrinkled up his face.

"Look at you, bitch," he said to Titus, who rose dripping to his feet,
boy full of hateful thoughts he sent out his eyeballs toward Bankwell
Flowers III. "What the fuck you do to yourself?"

"It's okay. Okay, come on. Leave them alone."

Bankwell turned to see Walter bringing up the rear of a short procession, the apex of a loose triangle whose remaining points were Valletta Moore and Luther Stallings with their hands up. Walter held the
Beretta high and crooked, one-handed, in that movie style Uncle Chan
abhorred.

"You found me," Luther Stallings said, the old-school kung fu movie
star, wiry and fit in a kimono, parachute shorts, pair of black cloth
Bruce Lee slippers. Gray in his hair and chest fur, more lines on his
face than Uncle Chan. "Put up the thumpers. Let me get my clothes on.
Go on home, boys. I'll be fine."

Bank had seen, not recently, a movie or two with Luther Stallings
in the lead. This was pretty much what he remembered: to the point,
monosyllables, the lazy smile. So either this was acting, too, or there
was no acting involved.

"Go ahead, Julie, Titus," said Valletta Moore. "Boys, go on. You can go."

"Fuck they can," Bank said.

"It's all right," Walter said. "We got no room for them, anyway."

While Bank was distracted by how stupid Prince Walter could be sometimes, Titus woke up. He grabbed hold of Julie's shirt and dragged him down the stairs, four feet in sneakers chiming on down to the parking lot, sneakers against the blacktop.

"Dammit, Walter!" Bank said.

Now that he was thinking again instead of just doing, he made a futile show of going to the railing, weighing whether it made sense to take a shot at the runners. But it was only a show, and everyone knew it.

"It's a hearse, you dumb-ass!" Bank said. "We could of fit Nell Carter in that thing, in a extra-large box."

"Whatever," Walter said.

"Kung *Fu*?" Luther Stallings said. He turned to take a closer look at his captor. Valletta Moore turned to look at him, too. "Kung Fu Bank-well!"

"Yo, what up, Mr. Stallings. How you been?"

Sheepish, Prince Walter underwent a headlock at the mercy of the old movie star. Valletta, though; the lady was not prepared to join in the warm and heartfelt reunion just yet.

"Walter Bankwell, Lord have mercy," she said. "How did it ever come to this?" She lifted up her sunglasses to beam her most full-strength shaming rays at Walter. "Mixed up in this kind of fool behavior."

"What I been saying to myself all day," Prince Walter said. "Word for motherfucking word."

⊙   ⊙   ⊙

In Archy's last dream of the night, he was a youngster and yet also his present-day self, talking to his mother in an apartment of the 1970s. Mauve was healthy, no shadow hanging over her, and although he was dreaming, a part of Archy's mind marveled at how much clearer and more present she seemed in this dream then she ever did when he tried, in waking life, to picture her. It was that type of dream—self-conscious, fathomable as you were dreaming it. All the pain and longing that had to do with his mother's death, the untouchable spot lodged inside him like the black meteorite in the Kaaba, was palpable as he sat with her, making absurd conversation. As he dreamed, he understood that the conversation didn't make any sense, that the dream was a form of grieving, with the passing of Mr. Jones acting as a trigger, an undercurrent. In the dream, it felt good to grieve. The record playing in the background of the dream apartment was a classic collaboration between Maceo Parker and Curtis Mayfield, the soundtrack from a well-known blaxploitation movie called *Top Hat and Elbows*. He listened to the beautiful music, fat beats, sunshine horns and shadow bass, and talked nonsense to his mom as she would always be. *Thank goodness*, thought his present-day self, *I am having this wonderful dream*.

Then the song playing in the background of the dream apartment, with its silver wallpaper, rolled slowly over into "Trespasser" by Bad Medicine. Archy woke up on the floor of the dead man's house, stacked into a pile of moving-van blankets. He saw Julie's number lighting up his phone and knew that his mother was dead, and that *Top Hat and Elbows* would be a horrible title for a movie regardless of genre, and worst of all, that except in a vanished dream, there was no soundtrack album, no visionary collaboration between Maceo and Mayfield.

"Your phone," said Kai. Supposed to be a lesbian, with that Bowser haircut and how she filled out the shoulders of her borrowed leisure suit, but at five in the morning—after they sneaked in through a basement window in the backyard of Mr. Jones's house to let Kai, who turned out to collect gospel and Southern church music, hold a private listening party with Mr. Jones's small but interesting selection of rare Savoy and Checker sides—the picture had turned out to be more complicated than that. "Yo, your *phone*."

"What's wrong?" Archy said into the phone.

"This is Julie."

"Yeah, I get that. What's wrong?"

"Okay, first of all, I know we totally messed up."

"That's first of all?"

Archy hauled himself with a wobble to his feet, hangover gumming up his inner gyroscope, and went to the dormer in the parlor. The sun fell in bars through the iron on the windows, and he slotted his eyes into a line of cool shadow and looked out at Forty-second Street. A peanut-butter-colored cat skulked, hunting, along a bed of nasturtium and blown newspaper. It was Sunday morning, August 29, 2004. The funeral was past. Today was the day he was sworn to get serious about his life.

"This has to do with Luther," he said.

"How did you know?"

"Man, I thought I told you two, keep away from him."

"Archy, they got him. They went into his room and they carried out his, you know, all his file boxes. And they took him. And then Valletta started to, like, she was kicking them and stuff. Not like some kind of Wing Chun roundhouse kick or something, just straight-up knee in their crotch, biting them and shit. So they had to take her, too."

"Who?"

"Oh, and I hit this one guy with a *sword*."

Titus came on, talking on top of Julie in a put-on voice like some old white chemistry teacher from Iowa. "That is a true story," he said. "I can vouch for that."

"Julie? Hit *who* with a sword?"

"Those guys from the funeral home. I think the big one is named Bank."

Archy felt the sense of relief, or at least reassurance, that came with certain kinds of failure. Yesterday Chan Flowers had asked him to choose between his future—responsible dad working for an admirable employer with a good job doing what he loved—and protecting his no-account, pipehead, washed-up, full-of-shit, lying, smiling poor excuse of an absent father. Archy had walked out of the situation, which was a weak-ass way of choosing Plan B, for no good reason at all except some pathetic residual loyalty to the man who had done nothing but squirt some key proteins into his mother's belly. And because, why not finally admit it, a man like Archy was never likely to go for a plan like Plan A. Come on. He was no better than Luther Stallings, and the theoretical loyalty to his father on display yesterday consisted of nothing more than that. Like so many kinds of masculine loyalty, it was really only a manifestation of cowardice. Now Luther was beyond protection, Archy's lack of resolve having outlasted both Plans A and B, a proven technique otherwise known as Plan C.

"Where'd they take him?" he said.

"We don't know. They had the hearse, so . . . yeah."

"Okay. Where are you and Titus?"

They were at an Eritrean restaurant, way down Telegraph by MacArthur. They had cash and a phone. They knew how to get the bus back to the Jaffes' place. Julie said they would definitely be okay, but Titus did get a bloody nose, plus he had vomited on himself, his nose wasn't bleeding anymore, but it looked gross, and he smelled bad, and also he had a headache.

Archy had known Julie since he was not even two, from a little old man wringing his hands in a bouncy chair hanging in a doorway. Bouncing never did much good, but you could settle the kid right down by putting on the most Out shit you had on tap, the deepest kind of Sun Ra jazz-as-cosmic-background-radiation. Long as it was playing, little Julius would stop looking like he was about to be audited by the IRS and just sit there, watching the music like a cat watching ghosts. It was not hard for Archy to hear in his voice that the boy was freaked out.

"Are you going to call the police?" Julie said. "Or should we?"

Archy perched in his underpants on the windowsill. He looked at Kai in the bed, born a girl but not feeling it, maybe 50 percent of the way toward becoming a man. Still carrying all her reproductive organs of origin but unwilling to let Archy make use of them, asking him to please fuck her in the ass, nothing to ease the passage but a handful of spit. Kai was following a recipe, a series of steps: hormones, paperwork, surgery. And then one day she would wake up and be a dude, and in all likelihood, credit where it was due, a fairly dope one at that. Archy wondered if all the mental and emotional side of being a man flowed in with the hormones, like when you were digging in the sand and broke through to water. Maybe if you actively chose to be a man and followed all the prescribed steps and procedures, you would end up with some kind of clear convictions and never find yourself, say, walking out as a weak-ass way of implementing some dumbshit Plan B that you hoped would simply expire before you had to go through with it.

"Stay where you are," he told Julie. "I'll see to Luther and Valletta, have your dad come get you."

"No."

"No?"

"Okay. Just, yo, don't tell my mom?"

"Promise you'll never say 'yo' again."

"I swear."

Archy sorted out and put on his sour shirt and funeral suit, cupped water at the bathroom sink, tried to ignore the lunar ruin of his hair. Patted the hip pocket of his jacket.

"I took your keys," Kai said. "Your car is parked by the store."

"Thank you," Archy said. Something else from one of the short night's vivid dreams bobbed at the surface of his memory. "Right." He rummaged through Kai's leisure suit and came up with his keys. She had pulled the moving-van blankets up to her chin. Her small brown eyes were watching him. "I have to go."

"Sounds like it," she said.

"Are you okay?"

"Um, *ow*?" She sat up, uncovering her wide mouth, those smart-ass lips. "Good luck in Belize."

"Yeah—what?"

The bobbing memory surfaced. Driving by the house on the Street of Lost Toys in the indefinite time after the lights came on at the Lakeside Lounge. Gwen standing on the front porch in her robe, silent as an idol to be robbed of its forehead ruby. Archy telling her to get *out* the way, grabbing a suitcase from the hall closet. Shoving all kinds of miscellaneous belongings in there, cans of tuna, probably a bra. Belize!

"Yeah, uh, thanks for getting me out of there in one piece."

"Oh my God, I'm *so* fired. Gwen was *pissed*."

"Yeah, I'm, uh, I'm sorry." He glanced around the room one last time, then nodded goodbye, wishing he had a hat to cover the abomination of his hair, all shoved up to the front of his head. "As of now, okay, like two, three hours from now, I'm out of the picture."

"In Belize."

"I got all the maps."

The eyes, the snarky mouth. Disappointed in him. Thinking he was better than that. "Have fun," she said after a pause.

"Huh," Archy said. "Not what I thought you were going to say."

"What did you think I was going to say?"

" 'Man up.' "

"Fuck you."

He took her yacht-captain hat out of the grocery bag she was using to carry around her discarded band uniform. "Yo, can I borrow this?"

"Keep it," she said. "It looks stupidly good on you."

Archy walked down to Telegraph in the L. Ron Hubbard hat, flipping open his phone, thinking about Julie's question. First thing Aviva was going to say: Call the police. Tell somebody, don't keep it a secret. Silence equals death. Take back the night. Aviva had been trained by bitter experience, like a lot of women doing the kind of work she did, to go by the book. Same with Gwen, her family packed with cops and lawyers; she would almost always throw in on the blue side of a question. Neither of them understanding that Chan Flowers would be only too happy to have the police in the mix. He was a city councilman, chair of the Public Safety Committee, tight with a lot of OPD captains and brass. When they died, patrolmen, firefighters, Chan Flowers buried them gratis, with somber pomp universally commended. The police would always be there to protect Chan Flowers. Once the man got back whatever Luther had taken from him, it would be full-on *Patch me through to McGarrett, motherfucker*. After that, you could tell the story of what happened when OPD met the sad old ex–kung fu champ blackmailer, and at the end of that story, in the way of the aptly named criminal justice system, it would probably be the woman, poor lost-tooth Valletta, who might have tried to be a mother to Archy if Luther had been willing to let her, who ended up doing the time.

That was something Aviva could surely understand, but Archy had no time to explain. He was reasonably certain that Chan Flowers would not endanger his position and reputation by doing anything to hurt Luther, have a couple Flowers boys curb-stomp him out behind the mortuary, but then again, within the shroud of power and funereal dignity, something internal to Chan Flowers was still on fire. Maybe the odd exemplary curb-stomp was the exact means men of position and reputation employed to stay that way.

"He around?"

"He is," Aviva said, a warning in it. "How are you, Archy?"

"Gwen's there?"

"Right here in my kitchen."

That was good, in a way; Gwen could sit there saying, *Fuck it, I can have a damn cup of* coffee *if I want to*, calling down curses on Archy's head, finding the strength at long last in the cheerful kitchen of her best friend to do what she ought to have done so long ago, see Archy for the feckless showboat he was. Brewing up the Peet's in that fancy French cyclotron coffee drip of Nat's while they handicapped divorce lawyers, Aviva naturally pushing the do-it-yourself model, talking about how you can go on down to that Nolo Press on Parker Street in Berkeley, they have all the forms and books you need. Frigid weather had obtained between the women lately, and something like this was all they needed to thaw things out. Meanwhile, Nat could slip out the door without attracting too much attention, too many questions.

"You hearing all the dumbshit things I got up to last night?"

"Probably not all," Aviva said. "Enough."

"So can I get with Nat?"

"What?" Nat said when he came on the line, the sulk laid on thick so one might think it was for show, but Archy knew that sulking was a gift Nat could not control, the lonely gift of Achilles in his tent.

"You have to drive to that Eritrean restaurant on Telegraph, the one down by MacArthur, pick up the boys, they're waiting for you there. Okay?"

"You can't be serious." Deep in that dive helmet of his, down in the Yap Trench with his lead-soled boots. "I'm in my underpants."

"I know Gwen's loving that."

"Eat me."

"I got to run, Nat. You know the place, we went there that time."

In a few blocks, Archy came upon his car. Last night's madman suitcase was still in the truck bed, half hidden under the furniture blanket. Furniture blankets, motif of the day. Symbolizing nomadism, impermanence, the need to coat yourself against the damage of transit. He pulled back the blanket and looked at the old blue plastic Samsonite, blinking away a few more jump-cut memories from last night, at the house, him doing all the yelling, Gwen not saying a word, eyes measuring him, seeing him for what he was, loud and drunk and fixing to leave. Three thousand seven hundred and fourteen dollars in the Brokeland Records account at Wells Fargo. Draw it out. Get in the car, start driving, 680 to the 5 to I-10, turn south at Tucson into Mexico. Chihuahua, Zacatecas, Veracruz. Hit Belize in three, four days. Find a hammock and a breeze, eat tacos made with the meat of some large jungle rodent. There was nothing a man couldn't do with three thousand dollars and a suitcase full of canned tuna fish and pregnancy brassieres. The car was called an El Camino for a reason.

He threw the blanket over the suitcase and walked up the street to Flowers & Sons, stopping in at the Fed to pick up a sack of holes. There was bound to be a funeral today, but as of nine A.M. the august pile sat dozing under its eaves and ivy. Nothing moving, doors shut tight. Archy walked around to the back of the building. Two hearses, the old LTD Crown Victoria and a newer Town Car, waited calmly in their stalls. The hood of the Crown Vic ticking like a pot on the boil. Archy went up to the service door and knocked twice, polite but with intent.

"What's up, Bank?" he said when the door opened up to him. "Here to pick up my pops." He tried to make it sound prearranged, part of everyone's schedule for the day.

Something above and to the left of Archy's head, possibly something microscopic or invisible, interested Bankwell more than Archy did. "Can't help you," he said.

For the first time, somewhat belatedly, Archy gave serious consideration to the danger of this, huh, undertaking. "Bank, look here," he said. "Check it out." He held out the sack, a plain white paper bag free of logos or labels, but there was no mistaking it. Chance and their connoisseurial natures had brought Archy and Bankwell together at the counter of the United Federation of Donuts at least twice in the past few years. The man would know that promising bulge, the neat pleat across the top when Mrs. Pang filled your sack.

"Raised glazed," Archy said. "Six, have them all."

Bankwell could not help glancing at the bag, but in the end not even half a dozen raised and glazed could compete with the invisible or microscopic thing behind Archy's head.

"Geeked old fucker told me everything," Archy tried. "Blabbing, all rambling. Talking about that killing him and Chan did back in the day, the gangster in the Panther club, killed him with a shotgun, nobody ever got charged?" It was a wild guess, a string of them, charms of rumor and gossip hung from a chain of audacity. Half-remembered talk in the kitchens of his earliest childhood, mingled with the acrid hiss of a hot comb and the chink of ice in glasses of Flavor Aid. A strange look of recollection on his father's face once, halfway through a broken anecdote about Huey Newton. For all he knew, it might be his father and not Chan Flowers who had pulled the trigger. "So, Bank, you not letting me come in there off the street, I don't know. I can easily hear your uncle characterizing it in the future as stupid."

For the first time, for a second or two, Bankwell's eyes lingered on Archy, and they were not cold or hostile. Only weary, worn out, like he was just so fucking tired of trying to avoid doing any and all of the ten thousand things that Chan Flowers might one day, reviewing them, come to characterize as stupid. Then—resembling Gwen last night to a degree, when she had swung aside to let Archy come ranting into the house, looking to equip his journey to Belize—Bankwell stepped back. A stone gate rolling away to let the doomed archaeologist into the snake-riddled temple.

"Do come in," Bankwell said.

⊙   ⊙   ⊙

Along with the backyard coops of heirloom laying hens, the collectively owned pizzerias, the venerable Volvos that had rolled off the line at Torslanda before ABBA first went gold, the racks of Dynaco tube amplifiers, the BPA-free glass baby bottles, and the ramshackle wonderland known as the Adventure Playground, one minor component in the patchwork of levees erected by the citizens of Berkeley, California, in their ongoing battle to defend their polder against the capitalist flood tides of consumerist uniformity, was a telephone hanging on the wall of the Jaffe family's kitchen, a model 554 with a rotary dial, smiley-face yellow, its handset connected to its plastic shell by a snaking twenty-five-foot helix of yellow cord, kinked by old and unsolvable knots. In conspiring with Archy to retrieve the boys, Nat was obliged to tax this cord to its limit, stretching it across the living room with its gray-green shag carpeting (another little dike against the flood), right to the point where the carpet trim met the inlaid oak border of the front hall floor. Then, little by little, Nat wound himself up, looping himself in coils of yellow cord like a fork involving itself in a plate of spaghetti, Cleopatra sending herself to Caesar in a carpet. By the time his conversation with Archy was over and he went to hang up the phone, Nat had coiled himself all the way back to the kitchen and was as thoroughly tangled as Charlie Brown in kite string.

"Why do you do that?" Aviva said from somewhere behind the haycock of balled-up tissues that Gwen had been heaping on the kitchen table over the past hour or so, bringing in the harvest of her marital woes. "I worry it's a bondage thing."

"What did he say?" Gwen said, blowing her nose, tossing the Kleenex onto the pile.

"What did he *say*?" Nat repeated. A shameless bit of cheap stalling. He wondered—it was a new variation on the question that had been preoccupying him all morning—how much to share with the women in the kitchen. Before he could resolve the question, the phone rang again. A woman at the other end of the line identified herself as Officer Lester of the Oakland Police Department.

"Are you the owner," she wanted to know, "of a black Saab sedan, a 1990, California license plate 3AUH722?"

"Uh, yes," Nat said, feeling a lurch in his chest, "yes, I am, why?"

Gwen and Aviva looked over, alert to the crease in his voice as Nat backed out of the kitchen. Tangled up from ankle to waist in the phone cord, moving too fast. Hungover, if not still slightly drunk, from last night. Losing his balance, struggling to stay on his feet, he put out a hand to grab hold of the back of the Morris chair. The cord ripped loose from the telephone and, at this sudden release of tension, began to unwrap itself from Nat's legs, arcing outward with a kind of majestic sweep, accelerating as it spun faster and faster until, as the last loop arced free, the severed tip of the cord lashed up and stung Nat on the cheek, painfully.

"Ow," Nat said, feeling his cheek for blood. "I have to go."

"Go where? Who was that?" Aviva said, and then her cell phone rang, and once again Nat was saved from having to come clean. Aviva studied her phone, snapped it open. "This is Aviva. Yes? Oh, hi. Are we on our way? Okay, now. Listen to me."

Hours, inches; water broken, the bloody show; contractions coming with some urgently measured regularity. Even at times when he was not wanted by the Oakland police, Nat had long since stopped attending to the variably unvarying particulars that accrued by telephone as his wife went about her work bringing new hotheads, failures, and fools into the world. But standing at the kitchen sink, printing roses onto a paper towel with his cut cheek, Nat noticed an uneasiness creep into Gwen's face as she listened to Aviva patiently instructing the latest father to drive the latest mother to Chimes General, where every day new fools were minted by the dozen. The mournfulness, the air of resignation that been there from the time Gwen came in the front door, seemed to give way to something colder, something closer to resolve.

"Audrey and Rain are headed to the hospital," Aviva told Gwen, closing the phone.

"Uh-huh," Gwen said, as though Audrey and Rain were the stuff of rumor, friends of friends. "Well, good for them."

Aviva pushed back from the table, scooping up blooms of tissue and herding them into the kitchen trash. "You okay?"

"Kind of wrung out, but."

"Let's test-drive those privileges."

"Ah . . ."

"I know you're— I mean, honey, I know you're hurting. That's why you need to work. Work is good."

Moving around the kitchen, Aviva a series of dissolves, seven things at once, stacking rinsed tea things in the dish rack, zipping a fresh package of Chux into her bag, tying back her hair with a scrunchie, fishing a Band-Aid out of the hell drawer, taping it to Nat's cheek. Only thing she was not doing: seeing what Nat saw as it gathered in Gwen's face. Across the background noise of panic and impatience, he began to detect a steady signal of regret.

"I mean, Gwen, I love you," she said. Whiff of chocolate on her breath as she leaned close to tend Nat's wound, sour, burnt, almost smoky. "And Archy's acting like a complete ass. But in the end, how far is sitting around crying going to get you."

"I agree."

"I mean, if you aren't *feeling* well, or—"

"I feel like shit, actually, but otherwise I'm fine."

Now Aviva picked up on it. Turned, shouldering her go bag, to see the face that matched up with Gwen's tone. "What?" she said.

"I've been trying to tell you, wanting to. But I just—"

Aviva sat down heavily and lowered her bag to the floor. It was an authentic replica of the kit bags carried by the crew of the *Nostromo* in the movie *Alien*, something Julie had picked up at WonderCon a couple of years back. Nat was not sure how ironically Aviva intended her patients, as they contemplated the fearsome creatures who were about to burst from their abdomens, to take it.

"Let's hear it," Aviva said.

"This whole thing with Archy," Gwen continued. "It's just, seriously, it's not the main thing. I mean, it *could* be, but I'm not going to *let* it be the main thing. This baby, whoever he turns out to be? *He* can be the main thing. Him and my work."

"Well, that's what I'm—"

"My real work."

"Your real work. What's your real work?"

"The other night, somebody told me how Archy is lucky to have found something that he can really put his heart into. However wrong or crazy it might look to some people."

"Yes?" Aviva said, sounding wary. "Well, that's true, isn't it?"

"I'm sure it is," Gwen said. "You have that, Aviva. Nat, too. But I . . ." She hesitated and seemed to change her mind about what she was going to say. "And then at the review board, with those doctors. Those smug, cocky, self-satisfied—"

"Gwen, it's fine. You stood up to them, and they caved. Now you're good. I— Nat? What are you looking at?"

There was a patch of sky fringed with Indian paintbrush, visible through the kitchen window, devoid of anything but blue. Nat could not keep his eyes off it. "Hummingbird," he said.

"Gwen," Aviva said, "you don't need to worry about those assholes anymore."

"I'm not worried," Gwen said. "It's just . . . I'm sick of having no power in this game, Aviva, and them having it all. Of always fighting against feeling useless. Of how sad it makes me feel that sisters won't go to a midwife. Also, frankly, I'm sick of overprivileged, neurotic, crazy-ass . . ." She stopped talking. She tucked her crossed arms between her breasts and belly like a pencil behind an ear.

"You were going to say white ladies."

"Yes!" Gwen said. "With their white-lady latex allergies, and their white-lady OCD birth plans, and that bullshit white-lady machismo competition thing they all get into," putting on a whiny white-girl voice, " 'I went twenty-seven hours without an epidural! Oh, I know just how you feel, I went forty-four!' I'll take out loans. I talked to my mom and dad, they're willing to help me. My mother's overjoyed, in fact."

"Overjoyed, help you *what*?"

"I figure I start studying now. As soon as I have this baby, I mean. For the MCATs. By next September, I get my application together, this guy's going to be a year old."

"You're going to *medical* school?"

"I told you. I don't want to be fighting them anymore. So I'm just going to, I figure, I'm just going to go ahead and *be* one. Then when I reach out to a black woman while she's having a baby, maybe then she's going to reach back."

"Okay," Aviva said. "Great. Thanks for sharing." She got up from the table and picked up her *Nostromo* bag, her eyes two small dark Ripleyesque coals. "I'm going to go be useless. Audrey is so overprivileged, she's paying for this birth with her unemployment."

Nat started toward her, but she was out the door before he could reach her. Down the stairs of the deck to the backyard. A few seconds later, they heard Hecate's agitated rattle, the inveterate scrape as she backed down the curb.

"Whoa," Nat said.

"I know." Gwen looked dazed. "Crazy, right?"

"So you aren't going to the birth."

"No. No, I'm not."

"Can I ask you a question, then?"

"Sure."

"Can I get a ride?"

"Huh? I mean, yes, yeah, but where's your car?"

Nat returned to the kitchen window and found again only a trackless, shadowless, and above all, zeppelin-free patch of sky. This benign expanse of blue offered, alas, little in the way of reassurance.

"Let's go," he said. "I'll explain on the way."

$$\odot \quad \odot \quad \odot$$

Flowers had stashed them in a visitation room, under a gable of the sweeping bungalow roof. It was a minor room, cramped and out of the way, with latticed wallpaper that invited tedium. Window curtains the color of scorched ironing, a disturbance of pigeons outside. A room reserved for dead folks who were forgotten or unmourned, with the strange angles of a theater carved from the balcony of a chopped-up movie palace. In his spaghetti-western black suit, Flowers straddled a backward chair facing Luther and Valletta, who sat installed on an armless sofa side by side, like mourning parents. A closed coffin on a velvet bier held someone unknown.

"Look here," said Flowers as Bank showed Archy into the room. "We got Thurston Howell III."

"Luther," Valletta said, and gave his knee a shove.

In Archy's dream, it had felt like such a revelation to encounter again, to recall with such force, as if he had forgotten them completely, the crook of his mother's fine Cherokee nose, the down on her forearms, the lingering hint of her childhood lisp. The dream had returned all that, the way a day at Stinson—the sourdough bite of a Negro Modelo, the rattle of a kite on the wind—could be restored to you by an old calendar page in a bottom drawer. At Motor City the other day, Archy had come in so pissed off at Titus and Julie, so unwilling to be there, wedged so deep in the pocket of his fury, that he hadn't been able to see the real Luther, only the Luther required by his anger. Only whatever you saw when you pictured a dead mother and a father you had long since cut out of your life, for your own protection. Photographs and phantoms on the retina.

Now he remembered: The man sat low and scatter-limbed, but he could bounce up out of a chair, on his feet and ready to go, faster than anybody Archy knew, as if someone had dropped a coffee in his lap. That was still true. The cleft in his chin, how it seemed to have been incised by a pottery tool, deft and deliberate. The way he would scowl at you just long enough for it to make you uncomfortable, long enough for you to wonder whether he was kidding around or if you'd actually committed some sin, some forgotten transgression, before he finally pulled the rip cord on the Cleon Strutter smile.

But he was so wintry now, snow in his hair, frost on his eyebrows! Though the height and the breadth of him remained impressive, he had lost mass, gravity. He scowled at Archy from under the icy ledge of his eyebrows. Clear-eyed, possibly sober, but Archy had seen Luther sober before. That was no big thing. With Luther, a period of sobriety was a kind of Groundhog Day, a shadow needing sunshine to foretell interminable gray. Archy hung back by the door and waited. At last, like a fading custom, the Stallings smile revived.

"I hope you don't mind, Chan," Luther said, still looking at Archy, "if I asked my mediator to join us."

Here it came: Time for Luther to put on a show. Archy's heart sank, and he was about to say *Hold up* when it occurred to him that he had come for no other purpose than this.

"I parked my zeppelin in the clergy spot," Archy said. He settled the yacht cap more firmly on his head, thinking it best to own the hat, to live up to it. "Hope that's all right."

He let his father take hold of him for the first time in a decade, maybe longer. Laundromat, motel air freshener, no shower, Valletta's perfume. The bones of his shoulders. Luther making a sound, deep down, sounding like Cochise Jones at the foot pedals of his B-3.

"Hey, Valletta," Archy said, getting free of Luther.

"Hello, Archy. I'm sorry you got mixed up in this."

"You okay?"

"I'm just fine, thank you, honey."

She looked like she had been fighting. No doubt, she had directed some energy toward putting herself together that morning, sleeveless white blouse, clementine-red skirt short enough to arrest the breath in your lungs. But she had since come apart here and there. One shirt-tail was untucked. Springs and coils broke the long rolling sweep of her hair. Luther had his bathrobe on, blue happi coat patterned with white cranes, gray kung fu shorts, Yip Man slippers. Bank and Feyd must have rolled him out of bed.

The nephews had taken up their accustomed foo-dog posts on either side of the door. Feyd looked correct, even daring, for a nephew, in a brown suit with an orange shirt and a dark purple tie, but the *malandro* swagger was out of the boy, standing with his head hung and his toes together, freshly scolded by Uncle Chan, Archy would have bet, for the spectacle they must have made beefing with a couple of *bokken*-wielding, vomiting fourteen-year-olds in the stairwell of a MacArthur Avenue motel. Bank looked *abused*, his right cheek chewed up, his tie askew, radiating an air of outraged humility, as if he had been assaulted, say, by a skinny little gay kid armed with a hickory sword.

"Who's in the box, Kung Fu?" Archy said.

Walter stayed behind his glasses, saying nothing. He picked at the zipper of his midnight-blue tracksuit, stitched with the name Ali in huge red script, slumped in a bentwood-back chair reserved around here for the worker, often one of the younger nephews, who was supposed to sit up with the body, keep it company when there was nobody around. A job that, in former days, often fell to little Walter Bankwell. Boy and a *Sports Illustrated* could feign wakefulness for hours on end.

"That is Mr. Padgett," Flowers said. He uncrossed his legs and, reaching out a hand, got up to give Archy a straight up-and-down funeral-director special. "He was a teacher. Called home last Tuesday. He's our two o'clock."

"*Terrell* Padgett? From Oakland Tech? I had him for algebra."

"Least he survived that," Luther said.

"He was a pussy," Walter said from behind his hand, into which the entire lower portion of his face was sunk glumly.

Flowers uncurled an index finger and jabbed it three times at Walter as if shaking out an umbrella full of rain. "Not. Another. Word."

Walter lost himself in the false-color planet charted across the surface of his late-model kicks.

"Councilman," Archy said. "Chan. What is all this? What are you doing?"

"I—I apologize, Archy, for how this went down. I think, if you hear me out, you're going to acknowledge that I did not have a choice but to do it in this manner. Please, sit down."

Flowers looked at Bankwell, Feyd. "Go on, clear out, now. Ms. Moore, my apologies. You want to go, you are free to go. Feyd, help Ms. Moore to the door." He turned to Walter, narrowed his eyes to lizard slits. "You, too, fool."

Valletta warned away Feyd when he came to clear her out, and set about doing what was necessary to remove herself from the room, sweeping herself up off the mourners' couch, a cyclone gathering its skirts for a run at a trailer park. For a second or two she hung above Luther, looking down at his bald spot like she was willing it to widen, to engulf him in a hairless shine of ruin. Or maybe the poor girl loved him in some way that was even more incomprehensible to Archy than his own love for Luther, under its bell jar of years, flickering impossibly on. Maybe as she stood there, she was wishing that bald spot away, ungraying the hair, unlining the face, unburning the days. As far as Archy knew, Valletta had been in love with his father, on and off, high or straight, treasure to trash, since the Monday morning in 1973 when he first walked onto the set of *Strutter*. You had to figure thirty years of on-and-off love was some kind of heroic feat. Not even God could hold onto the love of Israel in the desert without the jewelry getting melted down, now and then, to make a calf.

"Give it to him," she said to the bald spot.

Luther didn't move or otherwise acknowledge her words, smiling at Flowers as if he had come of his own free will to sell him a magazine subscription or the formula for eternal salvation.

"Motherfucker," she said, "you don't give it to him, I'm gone. I'm serious. You won't be able to find me with a satellite and a X-ray machine."

Luther and Valletta had been costars in their mutual disaster for too long not to milk the beat, Valletta darting her eyes back and forth to read Luther's the way that only actresses in close up ever did, reading his gaze like the screen of a teleprompter.

"Go, then, bitch," Luther said, not without tenderness. "I ain't folding on two pair."

Valletta rocked back. Wavering in her resolve. Knowing she should make good on her threat and go, but trained by the Pavlovian bell of love to confuse contempt with affection and indifference with reserve. Then she shrugged, kissed the air between her and Archy, flashed her palm like a badge. "Bye," she said.

Archy watched her and that swinging ass of hers as they headed for the door, pendulum going tick, tock. Waiting to see if she would look back at Luther, but she was true to her promise and gone. The three nephews trudged after her, and it turned out to be old Kung Fu who cast a backward glance—at Archy—as he stalked out, head down, hands shoved into the muff pockets of his track jacket. Backward and sidewise, filled with reproach, as if all this were Archy's fault. Maybe resenting the fact, on a more basic and juvenile level, that Archy got to stay in the room and he did not. Embroidered across the back of the jacket in big red letters were the words I AM THE GREATEST. *Greatest bitch*, Archy thought, as Walter slammed the door behind him.

⊙   ⊙   ⊙

It was Archy's fucking plan in the first place: Meet back at Brokeland after the burial, smoke a bowl, put a dent in the mess from the old man's funeral. Spin a few records, restore some order. Say what there was to say, see where things stood: Dogpile, COCHISE, their lives. As friends, partners, bandmates, fathers. Decide to go down fighting on the burning deck of the *Brokeland*, or scuttle her and try to jump clear of all the flaming flotsam.

"He say anything about Belize?" Gwen wanted to know.

They were in her BMW on their way to pick up the boys, KMEL playing some 120-bpm thumper, girl singer, the usual combination of finger-crooking and sass homiletics. Gwen had fitted herself improbably into the space between seat and wheel like some novelty marvel, a ship in a bottle, a psalm on a grain of basmati. Still a great-looking woman, even this close to the event horizon, maximum gravidity. Hair wrapped up in a Ghanaian head scarf, sunset reds and oranges. Pistachio ice cream—colored cat's-eye sunglasses. Those hands of hers gripping the wheel, beautiful freaks, almost as big as her husband's but long and supple, fingernails clipped man-short but glossy as meringue.

"He didn't say *anything*, is my point," Nat said. "Dude never showed up. At the cemetery, he got into his car, he waved, that was the last time I saw him."

"I wish I could say the same," Gwen said. "I'm *still* not sure how Kai fits into it all. If I wasn't already messing things up for Aviva, I'd say she was fired."

"I mean, at least you know Archy didn't fuck her."

Gwen said, at least that.

"So, wait, you really are quitting?" Nat said, the news seeping in along with the first fizzy milligrams of panic and dismay. For years his life had balanced like the world of legend on the backs of great elephants, which stood on the back of a giant turtle; the elephants were his partnership with Archy, and Aviva's with Gwen, and the turtle was his belief that real and ordinary friendship between black people and white people was possible, at least here, on the streets of the minor kingdom of Brokeland, California. Here along the water margin, along the borderlands, along the vague and crooked frontier of Telegraph Avenue. Now that foundational pileup of bonds and beliefs was tottering, toppling like the tower of circus elephants in *Dumbo*. Not because anybody was a racist. There was no tragic misunderstanding, rooted in centuries of slavery and injustice. No one was lobbing vile epithets, reverting to atavistic tribalisms. The differences in class and education among the four of them canceled out without regard for stereotype or cultural expectation: Aviva and Archy both had been raised by blue-collar aunts who worked hard to send them to lower-tier colleges. The white guy was the high school dropout, the black woman upper-middle-class and expensively educated. It just turned out that a tower of elephants and turtles was no way to try to hold up a world.

"You think I was playing with the poor woman, saying I was quitting when I'm not?"

"No."

"Nat, do you seriously think I was *taunting* her?"

"No, ma'am."

Sounding annoyed, she said: "So, okay, you went back to the store."

He told her how he had found himself alone in the horror that was the aftermath of Mr. Jones's wake. Bones and scattered beans, puddled sauces inter-oozing on discarded plates in Mandelbrot sets of grease and tomato. A stack of uneaten tortillas swollen and curling like the pages of a book that had fallen into the bathtub. And Cochise Jones officially and forever dead. Over everything, over life itself, that sense of encroaching shadow Nat was always left with when someone he loved had died. A dimming, the world's bulb browned out. He remembered taking Julie to the Gardner Museum on a trip to Boston a few years earlier, seeing a rectangle of paler wallpaper against the time-aged wall where a stolen Rembrandt once hung, a portrait of the very thing that perched atop the stool where Mr. Jones used to sit: emptiness itself. Empty cans, empty bottles, empty store, empty night, Nat's empty life lived fruitlessly and in vain.

"A Nat Jaffe alone," Gwen summarized, "is a dangerous thing."

"Bitch," Nat said, trying to jaunt himself out of it. "I'm always alone."

"Hello, and welcome to another exciting episode of *Existential Drama Queen*."

"Born alone, die alone."

Nat keeping up his end by saying what was in his heart, leaving out only the secret central event of his proposed human time line, namely *Do a bunch of stupid shit alone, repeatedly, because you can't control your dumb-ass self*.

"Okay, now," Gwen said, "ease up, big guy."

On the dilapidated sign of Steele's Scuba, a ghostly diver confronted the lost submarine mysteries of Telegraph Avenue. Gwen slowed as the bus in front of them knelt like a cow before the newborn Jesus to take on, was it, yes, the Stephen Hawking guy. Nat watched the poor bastard increment himself and his chair, patient and stubborn, onto the bus's power lift. Talk about alone. But look at him, dude was unstoppable, ubiquitous. Basically, a head on a meat stalk, strapped into a go-kart, motherfucker would take a bus to Triton if AC Transit ever put it on a route. Nat might have felt ashamed of the self-pity in which he currently wallowed, if self-pity knew any shame. He looked away, left, right, and then, tasting his hangover at the back of his mouth like a flavor of dread, up at the sky. Afraid he might see above him, at any moment, the evidence of last night's stupid shit, looming and vengeful as Spiny Norman in the old Monty Python sketch.

"Whatever," Nat said. "I'm going to tell this or not?"

"Let me guess. You started drinking."

"I found a six-pack of warm Corona. Some miracle it didn't get drunk."

Nat had opened the first beer, found a slice of lemon, poked it through the mouth of the beer can. Knocked the photograph of Mr. Jones from its ceremonious stool with a satisfying sense of desecration. Got up into the old man's chosen spot, maybe trying to dispel the emptiness that had gathered there. Figuring he would wait for Archy, who lived in his own personal CP time zone, his own little Guam of lateness. In the meantime have a beer, try to think his existential drama-queen way out of—or anyway, around—the situation. Then, for sure, do a little cleaning up.

By the fourth Corona, Archy had not showed or called, the store was no nearer to being clean, and Nat no longer bothered with the lemon. The goal was still to think his way out of or around the situation, but by this point, admittedly, his grasp of the complexity of the situation was pretty diminished. The improvidence, carelessness, and lack of acumen that he and Archy had shown in operating their business; their tendency to view the taking on of responsibility for every task, errand, or chore that Brokeland Records required—to conduct their lives, mutual and individual—as a prolonged if not infinite game of chicken, each waiting for the other to blink, to give in; the rise of electronic file sharing of digital music; the low revenue generated by the bargain-hunting and transient crew of dormitory DJs and homeboy mix-tapers who made up the greater share of their customer base, far outnumbering the high-roller collectors; the collapse of the Japanese and overseas markets generally; not to mention Archy's evident dissatisfaction with the nature of their partnership and the algae bloom of financial panic, of provider anxiety, in the normally tranquil pond water of Archy's soul: All these proximate and precipitating causes of the imminent failure of Brokeland Records seemed by the fourth Corona to have been rinsed from Nat's mind, leaving only a mildew-black residue of rage against Gibson Goode. Alcohol as helpful to the making of scapegoats as mud to the shaping of golems.

When the beer was gone, Nat poked around amid the dead soldiers stacked on and under the folding tables until he came up with a bottle of Hungarian slivovitz, God knew who had brought it. It was a quarter full. Nat sloshed a little into a red hot-and-cold cup, then quickly knocked back two or possibly three shots. Slivovitz was the cordial of grief, the mourner's brandy. Nat could remember his newly widowed father, the first Julius, lost in a helpless scrum of uncles in somebody's kitchen after his first wife's funeral, gasping at the fire in his chest as the slivovitz went down.

Nat climbed back onto Mr. Jones's stool with his glass of burning wine, put on *A Love Supreme*. Reliably, it destroyed him. Yes, it had passages of lyric majesty, passages that embodied the modernist union of difficulty and primitivism, and some kind of groove beyond groove, funk beyond funk; and yes, it had been intended as a kaddish of sorts, an expression of praise in the face of all sorrow for the Creator of John Coltrane, with thanks from His magnificent creation; but to Nat, it had always come off as music that was—like Nat himself— secretly powered by currents of rage. Probably that was a projection of Nat's own feelings toward his own fucked-up Creator, some lesser cousin twice removed of the Perfect Being that had made John William Coltrane. But as he listened to the A-side, with its furious repetitions, the saxophone bashing itself over and over against some invisible barrier, a bee at a windowpane seeking ingress or escape, Nat felt his low-frequency rage with motherfucking Gibson Goode and his motherfucking Dogpile Thang begin to spike. The stylus dragged itself to the locked groove, and he needed to take a piss, and it was at this point, as far as he could remember, that he decided it would be a good idea to forgo the routine pleasure of pissing in his own toilet, in the bathroom behind the curtain with its bug-eyed portrait of Miles Davis. He decided that he would walk down to the future site of the Dogpile Thang and piss on that instead.

"They put that sign up," he said to Gwen. "You've seen it? Big black and red sign. With the paw print, future home of."

"You peed on the sign."

"I thought it might feel good."

"Did it?"

"Well, I mean, it always feels pretty good. But, like, in terms of my *morale* . . . ?"

"And what, somebody saw you peeing on it?"

"Oh," Nat said, grabbing at this possibility, "do you think it's that?"

"Do I think what's that?"

"What the police want to talk to me about."

"Why, did you do something *else*?"

"The whole," deciding to adopt Gwen's word, which sounded so much more innocent and harmless than "pissing," "peeing thing, I don't know. I was kind of drunk. But I wasn't drunk enough to kid myself that it wasn't kind of a lame thing to do."

" 'Kind of.' "

"It pretty much made me feel *more* useless. So that's when I decided to head out to the airport."

"You drove drunk."

"If you want to get technical."

"What's with everyone making travel plans all of a sudden?" Gwen wanted to know. "Where did you think you were going? Belize?"

" 'Travel plans'? How well do you know me?"

"No, of course, right."

"I just wanted to get a look at that motherfucking zeppelin."

"Why? So you could pee on it?"

"Pissing on a zeppelin," Nat said, regretting bitterly the loss of this opportunity. "Why didn't I think of that?"

$$\odot \quad \odot \quad \odot$$

He kept the radio off, making the argument to himself that if music divided his impaired attention, then logically, silence would augment it. It was a timeless, placeless transit through a strobe-lit hyperspace of beer and slivovitz, scored only by the quarter-note rumble of I-880 under his tires. Vaguely, he remembered someone reporting a sighting of the airship early that morning, moored somewhere off Hegenberger Road. If it had not already returned to its home base in Southern California, he might find it there, shiny and gigantesque as the ego of Gibson Goode. Let it be huge, shiny, and awesome, then. Nat was prepared—maybe even hoping—to be awed. At least let a failure of his, just this once, partake to some measure, however indirect, of grandeur.

He traced and retraced the barren cipher written in the darkness by airport roads whose names commemorated heroes of aviation. The silence in the Saab was replaced by humming as Nat's original curiosity about the zeppelin, half larkish, half irritated, mounted in the darkness, until it became a full-blown longing and, as with Ahab's fish, the airship came to bear the blame, in Nat's imagination, for all the ways in which the world was broken. And then, right around the time Nat began to understand that he was drunk and lost and would never find the motherfucker, and furthermore had probably already attracted the notice of Homeland Security's flying robot thermal cameras—around the time he realized that for some reason he was humming the chord changes to "Loving You"—it startled him: a zeppelin-shaped hole cut into the orangey skyline of San Francisco.

What happened then: He must have swerved. Someone threw a big luminous net at the car. After that—all within the span of the three or four seconds it took him to crash through the chain-link fence—came a lot of really interesting sounds. A ringing of bells. A raking of tines. A boing, a thump, a scrape, a crunch. Finally, a gunshot bang, as the same clown who had thrown the giant steel net at the car decided it would be funny to give Nat a face full of airbag.

After that there was a gap in the archive. The next things Nat remembered were a taste of salt in his nostrils, the blacktop sending the day's heat up through the soles of his socks, the dwindling hiss of the Saab's radiator, and the consciousness—alas, not yet sober—of having benefited from a miracle. He was fine, whole. And the God of Ahab at last had delivered him from his lonely quest. He stood a hundred feet from his beast in its nighttime pasture. He was not sure what had happened to his shoes.

As he started across the sweep of pavement toward the zeppelin, he tripped some kind of sensor. Stanchions studded with floods lit up all around the airship, snapping it on like a neon sign. Nat fell back into shadow and waited to see what happened. Expecting to find himself confronted by a Bronco full of security guards, an android sentry equipped with lasers, a lonely old night watchman named Pete or Whitey who would leap up from his chair, already halfway to cardiac arrest, as the latest *Field & Stream* tumbled from his lap.

Nothing. Most of the light from the stanchions was squandered on the gasbag, or whatever it would be called on a zeppelin—the word "envelope" slid in through a slot in his memory—but Nat thought he could make out a few small buildings over on the far side of the asphalt field. Maybe Gibson Goode and his entourage were asleep inside that glossy plastic gondola. It was not hard to imagine somebody in that crew feeling obliged to bust out with a gun and take a few shots at the intruder. Nat wondered if he ought to be afraid. But no light came on in the windows of the gondola.

The zeppelin floated three or four feet off the ground, lashed at the nose to a steel mast that rose in turn from the wide bed of a parked truck that looked small next to the airship but must in fact be massive. The airship lay perfectly still, as if listening for Nat. The breeze off the bay did not appear to trouble it. Yet at the same time it thrummed, verging on some kind of outburst of motion. It reminded Nat less of a whale now than a Great Dane or a thoroughbred horse. An animal strung with nerve and muscle but, for all that, lovable.

"Poor thing," he said to the zeppelin.

He came out of shadow and went over to the truck, across whose grille in chrome letters ran the weighty inscription M · A · N. The mooring mast was a business of telescoping poles, like the arm of a cherry picker without the elbow. As Nat drew closer, the mast chimed deep inside itself, and the breeze sang along the length of guy wire that held the zeppelin fast. The truck was meant, from the ground up, to be climbed. At the back, three steel steps led up the bed, and then you scooted around the base of the mast to the bottommost of a column of metal spikes or cleats, like the steps on the side of a telephone pole, which led up the lower segment of the mast to a narrow steel ladder, which in turn carried Nat all the way to the top.

Here his lingering intoxication, and maybe a touch of loopiness from the collision, contended against his desire to set the noble zeppelin free. He spent awhile clinging to a cold rung at the top of the mast. He reached a hand, palm outward, fingers spread, like a man feeling for the kick of a child in a woman's belly. In the instant before contact, he recalled having heard that a static discharge had ignited the *Hindenburg*. But there was no spark, only the cool taut bellying of the airship against his palm. He wished wildly for an ax, a pair of shears, a torch to cut the cable. Then he noticed a heavy lever on the shaft of the mast, alongside the spinneret from which the cable emerged, helpfully labeled EMERGENCY RELEASE. He opened the clasp that held it in place, snaked his shoeless feet around the poles of the ladder, and dragged down on the release, wrestling its rubber grip with both hands. The lever shunted out and down, and with a whistle of steel against steel, the guy wire whiplashed loose of the mast and swung from the big carabiner that clipped it to the airship's nose.

"Go ahead, Arch," he said, perhaps uncovering the source of the sudden flood of tenderness he felt toward the zeppelin. "Fly and be free."

The zeppelin disdained his gesture of liberation. It continued to hang, drifting minutely, almost invisibly, three or four feet off the ground.

"Ballast," Nat inferred. "Right."

He climbed down the mooring mast, dropped to the ground, and took a slow walk around the gondola, looking for something to release, a system of weights, bags of sand like in *The Wizard of Oz.* There was nothing. He sat down on the ground, abruptly tired, and looked up at the gondola's underside. There were two round hydrants, sealed with caps. Modest red capital letters identified them as ballast tanks. Nat reached up, went on the tips of his toes, and got hold of one of the caps. He got just enough purchase on tiptoe to pop it loose. The cap tore loose of his fingers. He felt himself hammered by something cold and implacable that turned out to be a hundred gallons of water. The shock of the water sobered him at once, enough to drench him in an equal or greater quantity of cool, clear regret for what he had done, as the zeppelin, with appalling grace and lightness, took to the luminous night sky.

⊙   ⊙   ⊙

"How did you get home?"

"Walked. Found a cab."

"You just left the car there?"

"I now realize the folly of that."

"That's how the cops found you. From your registration."

"No doubt."

"Oh, Nat."

"I know, I know."

"You *stole* the damn Dogpile blimp."

"Liberated," he suggested, but he knew that in all its long history, the word had never sounded more lame.

"Where is it now?"

It occurred to him that a grave and narcissistic fallacy lay at the heart of the fear that he was going to look out the window of his house or Gwen's car and catch sight of the zeppelin. The zeppelin would not be stalking him. It was mindless, trafficking only with gravity and wind.

"Up in the sky?" he suggested.

"You *hope*! Let me ask you a question. When the police called? Can I ask why you did not immediately confess?"

"Panic? Shame?"

"Nat, the thing could crash into the Transamerica Pyramid, the Bay Bridge."

Privately, Nat wondered if a celebrated giant landmark was more attractive to catastrophe than, say, an egg farm or a Best Buy. "Maybe," he said, wishful, "it'll just keep going up. Right on into space."

They were a few blocks north of MacArthur, and here came Merkata on the left. It was clad in fake half-timbering and stucco with a concrete thatched roof, leftovers from the day, three or four cuisines ago, when it had been a fish-and-chips joint.

"If you want to pull over," he said, happy to change the subject, "I can go get them."

"Here they come."

"Uh-oh. What's wrong?"

The boys came shuffling out of Merkata like prisoners chained at the ankle. Curtis & Poitier, brothers in woe. Something weighing on them, the burden of captivity, their secret escape plan. Julie clutching that portable eight-track to his chest with a weird, splay-fingered fierceness. Nat got out of the car, remarking the boys' sheepish and hangdog expressions, wondering if maybe he needed to prepare his angry-dad routine. If he had it in him right now to do that; not to mention, given the events of last night, a moral leg to stand on.

"Julius Lawrence Jaffe, what did you do?"

He was shocked by the influx of his son into his arms. The bony shoulders, the soft lank hair against his cheek. Shocked by the tears that wetted the front of his shirt.

"Pop, I broke my tape player," Julie said.

Disconsolate. Going slack against Nat like one of those little wooden puppets when you pushed the button in the base.

"It's okay, buddy," Nat said. For all the loneliness and anger, for all the stupidity and shame, for all the pain that losing Archy, the store, the vision that Brokeland had always—exactly like Archy said in his eulogy—represented to Nat, with a warrant out for his arrest on a charge of zeppelin rustling, and the possible destruction of the Bay Bridge or, who knew, the Sphinx, the Leaning Tower of Pisa, on his conscience; right then, with his little boy restored sobbing to his embrace, it honestly did feel okay. This was something useful, maybe the sole useful thing, that he still knew how to do. "Let's go home."

Julius nodded, then looked up into Nat's face. "Titus, too?"

"Sure, of course. Titus, you okay? Oh, Jesus, look at you, what happened?"

There was blood on Titus's face, his shirt collar, and something else staining his shirt. His eyes were wide and shining, about to well over, and his expression was yearning as he watched Julius crumple into Nat's arms. Standing there, blood on him, no one to hold or be held by. Looking at him, Nat felt ashamed. He opened his arms to make room in the embrace for Titus.

Titus shook his head once, disgusted, cool returned. Then he turned and ran away.

"Titus!" Julie called after him. "Pop, come on! Titus!"

He started to drag himself loose, but Nat held fast, and after a brief struggle, Julie gave up and turned to Gwen in the car, watching them.

"We have to go get him," Julie said. "Gwen, let's go."

"I really don't think he wants to be around us," Gwen said. "And I need to go in and talk to these folks about something."

⊙   ⊙   ⊙

There was no *suff* on the menu, but an understanding was reached, and after a brief wait and some blender activity, Gwen was able to allay this unlikely pain at last. She took the tall clear plastic tumbler filled with what Nat understood to be the thin beige milk of roasted sunflower seeds and tipped it to her lips. The joy and sweetness of it on her face, the orgasmic flutter of her eyelids, was stark, arousing.

"Oh, baby," she said.

But then the weird-looking infusion seemed to go down badly.

"Excuse me," she said. She put her long and beautiful fingers to her lips, opened her eyes wide, closed them again, and ran to the front door of the restaurant. Out on the sidewalk, she bent double and spasmed, making a sound that Nat would never afterward be able to unhear, a kind of robotic braying, over and over. Nat, an atheist, prayed for it to stop. It sounded like her stomach was tearing itself in two. When she returned, her cheeks and forehead were lustrous with sweat.

"Wow," she said. She breathed, and swallowed, and breathed again. When she opened her eyes, Julie passed her a napkin, and she dabbed her lips with an improbable daintiness. "Thank you, baby."

She stood still, scowling, as if listening for something, probing a tooth with her tongue, trying to remember whether she had left a burner lit on the stove at home. And then Nat smelled something that reminded him abruptly of Cochise Jones's basement. That cheese-cellar whiff, faint as a whisper, of rot. A darker shade of black seeped across the front of Gwen's stretchy black leggings.

"I'll be right back," she said with a chilling show of cheeriness. Her progress toward the bathroom was slow, her waddle exaggerated by the need to keep her legs apart. Behind her, splashes of water marked her passage. When she came out, she had pulled off her leggings and apparently disposed of them. The sight of her bare legs, emerging from the tails of one of Archy's shirts, came as a shock to Nat. She looked vulnerable, and he understood that she was about to set out for a place, come what may, where she would be completely alone, so much more alone than an existential drama queen like Nat could possibly imagine.

"You need to get me to the hospital," she said.

⊙   ⊙   ⊙

With Valletta gone—beyond the reach of X-rays, uplinks, and his unquenchable thirst for an audience—old Luther had lost his defiant aspect. He sat shifting in his chair as if it were greased or electrified, not meeting Archy's eyes. Eyebrows arching, lips moving, telling Flowers to go fuck himself, saying nothing out loud. A whole great big argument going on there, inside his mind. A knife fight, a televised debate, a sumo match.

"Your father," Flowers began. He paused, ordering his next words, putting them through their paces before he set them loose in the room. "Your *dad* has been trying to blackmail me," he went on, keeping his tone light, amused by the idea. "Over something that happened a long time ago, that no one even cared about at the time, to somebody no one remembers. Been skulking around from rathole to rathole. Leaving scurrilous messages. Spreading scandal and lies."

"Scandal, maybe," Luther said. Shake of the head, going jowly, trying to match his old friend's affectation of amusement with a show of moral severity every bit as unconvincing. "Not lies."

"Naturally, I have a problem with this behavior," Flowers went on, ignoring Luther, making his case directly to the appointed mediator, who was already five minutes past regretting having gotten mixed up in this shit in the first place, even though he knew that the choice not to get himself involved would, in the end, have proved just as big a pain in the ass. "But given the nature of the accusation, I haven't felt—yet—that it would necessarily help clarify the situation to call in my good friends at OPD."

"I hope you do," Luther said. "I would love to tell them all about you." He looked around, seeing if somebody might give him a high five, pound his fist. But it must have been looking right then like a pretty tough room.

"Let him say his piece," Flowers suggested to Archy, speaking through the interpreter, "after I say mine."

"Shut the fuck up," Archy told Luther.

Luther shrugged, clapped one of his big paws to his mouth, Black Bolt holding back a fatal syllable. Scattered his limbs farther and looser in his chair.

"Even though I have been tied up with a number of other important matters," Flower said, "I've also been trying to dig this man up out of whatever hole he was hiding in so I could bring him here, sit him down in front of me, and make him at *least* look me in the eye while he was trying to shake me down."

"Here I am," Luther said, knitting himself together, sticking out his jaw, as if being here were all his idea, a man of integrity walking the lonely path of truth and honor. When really he had been turned over like a worm on the blade of a trowel. "And I ain't threatening you with nothing, Chan. What did I ever say, what note or message did I ever leave, besides, basically, the gist was, if you don't want to help out your oldest friend, a man who been working so hard to clean himself up and get himself back on his feet, what's that say about you? Which," turning to Archy, "is more or less the message I been trying to convey to you, too."

"Yeah, whatever," Archy said. "Convey all you want, I'll stamp it 'Return to Sender' every motherfucking time." He turned to Flowers. "This is about that dude that got shot back in the seventies? Do I have that right? At the Panther bar, what was it, the Bit o' Honey."

"His name was Popcorn Hughes," Flowers said. "He was a gangster, a cheap, ignorant, worthless East Oakland pimp. Wound up right where he was supposed to, a year, maybe two, ahead of schedule."

"And you're the one who hurried him along."

"I had no reason to want to hurt the man," Flowers said carefully.

"He was trying to make his mark," Luther said. " 'Establish the legend.' Impress Huey Newton. See, Huey, when he wants somebody gone, he knows all he has to do is wish it out, loud and clear. Like Peter O'Toole, what's that movie?" Arranging his features into a kingly scowl, busting out a fairly respectable O'Toole. " 'Will nobody rid me of this troublesome priest?' Chan the Man's standing right there to make old Huey's wish come true."

It was not easy to read the face of Chandler Flowers. He had long since, years ago, composed its features with the same care that he had brought to interweaving the dead fingers of Cochise Jones. If you were telling him a joke or a sad story, he would smile as need be or incline his head in sympathy. Mild amusement, ready understanding. Archy had never seen anything in that unreadable fist of a face like he was seeing now. It might have been pain or regret. Maybe it was only wistfulness. His eyes were a pair of shadowy tunnels boring deep into the mountain of the past.

" 'Establish the legend,' " he said almost fondly. "That does sound like me at the time. I will give you that."

"Ready, willing, and able to do whatever you needed to do, not to have to end up right where you are now. Whatever was the opposite of this." Luther opened the compass rose of his right hand to direct their attention to the zones of irony all around them. "The opposite of what Chandler the Second wanted you to do. Shining on going to college. Dating white girls. Enlisting in the navy as a common seaman. Joining the Black Panther Party."

Flowers crinkled his eyes with pleasure, enjoying the memory of the industry he had shown in scandalizing his father. He started to laugh, a scattering of droplets on a hot skillet, sounding like his nephew Walter. "That is the truth," he said. "You got that right."

"Trying to give your old man a epileptic seizure," Luther said, keeping a straight face around the edges of which laughter leaked like light around a door. "Infarction of the heart."

"I did my best," said Flowers.

" 'You're a stain on the name!' " Dusting off, like an old side of vinyl, the tight-assed, stuffy-nosed voice of some long-dead black man, putting it on. " 'Chandler Bankwell Flowers, you are a stain on the name!' "

"A stain on the name, good God, I totally forgot he used to—"

"Surprised you never tried turning faggot," Luther said. "That would of done it real quick."

The silence that followed this declaration, while nanometric, was abrupt and revelatory.

"Uh," Archy said, feeling his cheeks flush, but Flowers's face had resumed its folded-hands composure. "So, what, were you both in the Party, or . . . ?"

"Nah, that was his bullshit," Luther said. "I didn't want no part of that business. I just went along for the ride."

"Oh, yeah, okay. Because you are so opposed to *bullshit*," Archy said. "You and bullshit, strangers to each other."

"It was all a long time ago," Flowers said, and in his voice there was a nasal, seddity echo of Luther's impersonation of Chandler the Second that had, Archy realized, been there all along. "Water under the bridge."

"Yeah?" Luther said, playing with the man, enjoying the company, Archy would have said, of his old running buddy. "Why you still so worried, then?"

Placid, leaning back, hands folded over the convexity of his abdomen in a weird echo of the way he posed his dead men, Flowers said, "I'm not worried, Luther."

"Then why'd you change your mind about Dogpile? All of a sudden. The minute I go around, pay a visit to Gibson Goode, suggest that he ask you what happened to Popcorn. How come you threw in with Dogpile, then?"

"I'd like to hear the answer to that one," Archy said.

Flowers just smiled that unreadable smile, forged in the fire of a hundred sessions of the Planning Commission, people popping up all around Hearing Room number 1 to ask the unanswerable, demand the undeliverable, give vent to the unassuageable.

"I told you my reasons, Archy, the other day when we spoke. I realized that however much personal love and loyalty I might feel toward that beautiful store of yours, not to mention all the history it contains—black history, Oakland history, neighborhood history, *my* history—it was selfish of me to oppose Mr. Goode. A Dogpile Thang is an opportunity for the community as a whole. Now. Today. In the present moment. Not to mention, and now I'll be honest, an opportunity for some people near and dear to me, too, such as my sister Candida's youngest son, my nephew Walter, in all his rack and ruin. An opportunity for people such as yourself, if I'm not mistaken."

"Now, that is *truly* some bullshit," Luther told Archy. "Chan, you knew this thing with Popcorn was going to come back on you someday. From the day you settled your ass down, followed in the footsteps, started pumping that formaldehyde, you been living in dread it would come out." He turned to Archy. "I got evidence, son. DNA." It was his turn to lean back in his chair, hands clasped behind his head, flapping the rooster wings of his elbows. "Shit lasts a million years. Put it under a microscope, clone yourself a damn triceratops. One day, check it out, some *Jurassic Park* motherfucker's going to come along, clone Chan Flowers for a prehistoric Oakland ride, Chan be standing there when Laura Dern goes by in her Jeep. Shit, Chan, I bet I can even lead them to the gun! That Mossberg's probably still there in the woods, tangled up in some weeds and shit."

"You're in the weeds right now," Flowers said. "Way out in the weeds, Luther."

"What *do* you have?" Archy said.

"A glove," Luther said. "Chan was wearing it when he did Popcorn Hughes, has Popcorn's blood DNA all over it."

"A glove," said Flowers.

"You remember, it was your brother's, Marcel's. Little purple glove from the costume he was wearing—"

"A glove!" Flowers enjoyed or pretended to enjoy the idea that an accessory, a minor item of haberdashery, could ever inspire the kind of anxiety that Luther had described. "A glove, been in some crackhead's back pocket thirty-one years? Even if it turned out to be real," wanting Archy to come in with him on scorning this one, "I mean, even if the blood on this *glove* turned out to be mine, or Popcorn Hughes', or Jimmy Hoffa's, what does that prove?"

Here it came, bright and true as a streaming banner: the smile of Cleon Strutter, showing his hand.

"Just give me a hundred thousand dollars," Luther said, "we never need to answer that question."

"Luther, for real?" Archy said. "Blackmail?"

Tossing the word across to his father like a grappling hook, feeling one small barb catch hold. Luther looked down at his feet in their slippers, then up at Archy. Nodding. Good with it. "If you want to call it that," he said.

"It's true, you really clean and sober?"

"Thirteen months, one week, and five days," Luther said.

"For, like, honestly, the first time in, since, what, the late eighties?"

Luther allowed that was probably accurate.

"So this is the *real* you, then. That right? Luther Stallings, clean and sober: a scumbag blackmailer."

The flag of Luther's smile failed, then caught a fresh breeze and streamed freely.

"I'm just trying to make a movie, son. Revive my fortunes. Maybe that seems like an impracticable plan to all y'all cynical motherfuckers, don't have dreams of your own. I guess I'm sentimental. Foolish. I just thought maybe my oldest, longest friend might want to help me out."

"Help you *again*," Flowers corrected him. "Archy, he's been trying to blackmail me on this alleged murder for *years*. It is not a recent phenomenon linked to sobriety."

Archy picked up that bit about *alleged* murder and worked it like a smooth stone in the palm. He went back over the conversation so far, trying to remember if Flowers had admitted to or acknowledged any wrongdoing at all. He didn't think so.

"Help me *again*," Luther conceded. "On a grander scale. Basically," he told Archy, "what happened, see, I had kept the glove the night of the killing. I don't know why. Just held on to it like a souvenir of, you know, wild times. A few years down the road, when I got deep into the deepest badness of my life, and I'm not proud of that, I know I let you down, everyone down, but, uh . . ." Losing the thread, picking it up again. "I went looking for the glove. Thinking it might be, like they say, fungible. But it seemed like I had lost it somewheres, moving around all the time, in and out of jail and whatnot. Then I hooked up with Valletta again. Right after I got out of rehab. Turned out she had the thing all along."

"So, Mr. Councilman," Archy said. "Do you want this glove Luther has?"

Chan Flowers spoke slowly, through his teeth, as if it killed him to have to admit it. "I might," he said.

"And let's say, for whatever reason, Luther doesn't give it to you, what are you going to do?"

The answer to this question was even slower in arriving, but when it did arrive, it appeared to cause him little pain. "I have more to lose than Luther does," Flowers said.

"Oh, I see," Archy said. "Going with cryptic but scary. And what about me, now that I know about the glove, too? Do you have more to lose than I do?"

"You aren't ever going to blackmail me, Archy. I know that. It's not in your nature. You must have got your mom's strength of character."

"Let's don't bring her into this, all right? I'm glad she never lived to see this sorry day." He dared his father to challenge this asser- tion, and Luther quietly let it go by. "So, then, what?" Archy said. "If I promise not to say anything, then you just going to kill Luther over this but not me?"

"I deal in dead people every day of the year," Flowers said. "Remem- ber that. And I am looking to find a little security in these uncertain times. Whatever form that security might take."

Archy wondered where the glove was right now. Luther must have it salted away someplace, stashed with some lowlife, some ex-cellie of his. Taped inside a toilet tank, inside a Ziploc bag. The thing to do, he thought, just get hold of it somehow. Take it to the police, let them de- cide the outcome. It might lead nowhere, point to nothing, incriminate no one. Or it might be the end of Councilman Flowers and, quite pos- sibly, the Dogpile plan.

"If I walk out of here right now," Archy said to Flowers, "leave this asshole to your ministrations—and I think we are all familiar with the quality of the work y'all do here—you say, you are going to trust me on this."

"I do trust you, Archy. I respect you, and I know you would never disrespect me. You walk out of here, I will personally guarantee to make sure you and that little family you got on the way are well taken care of as long as I'm around. You just go with an easy mind. Let me and Luther settle this thing out."

"So, for instance," Archy said, "how about, would you back me up at Brokeland? Because, I mean, once our friend G Bad doesn't have anything to hold over your head anymore . . . assuming you, uh, obtain this famous glove. In return for me keeping quiet." As he said this, a rotor began to whirl in the Leslie cabinet of his chest. "Maybe you could, say, withdraw your support for the Dogpile Thang. Come back over onto the side of Nat and me? Because, you know, in our own small and modest way, we're good for the community, too."

"I will do better than that," Flowers said. "I will *truly* back you. As a silent partner. Pay down your debt for you. Get your creditors to step off, whatever it takes."

"I have to say, that sounds very attractive."

"Archy," Luther said. "Son, come on."

"And all I got to do, let me get this straight, is walk out of here. Leave you and him to, uh, was it, 'settle this out'?"

"That's all," Flowers said. "Of course, you have to remember, if it ever turns out to be the case the police *do* take an interest in this old unsolved crime? You might wind up being charged as an accessory after the fact."

Archy stood up, nodding, as if all this struck him as a reasonable, even enviable, proposal. Then he reached down and smacked his father hard on the back of the head, as if swatting a particularly vicious and slow-moving horsefly that had settled there. "Give him the motherfucking glove, Luther," he said. "And then get the fuck out of here. I can't stand the sight or smell of either of you blackmailing, lying, murdering old motherfuckers. Give Mr. Flowers the glove before I *take* it off you and give it to the police myself."

"I can't do that," Luther said.

"Why not? Because you're going to take all that money he ain't never going to give you, use it to make a movie you ain't never going to make?"

Archy might have counted on one hand the number of times in his life when he had left his father with nothing to say. He figured it was the slap on the head, or maybe there was something persuasive in the nakedness of his contempt for Luther's project. Luther fell back to muttering, shaking his head. Reminding Archy of that wino on his crate the other day outside Neldam's, clinging to his little sack of rolls.

"Give him the glove," Archy said, fighting—for his own sake, not for Luther's—to keep any tone of compassion out of his voice. "And I will pay for your movie."

Steak through the bars of a shark cage. Luther looked up, wary and hungering. "How?"

"Sell the store. Whatever I get from my half, I give it to you."

"Now, why would you do that?"

"I don't know," Archy said. "It can't be because I give a fuck what happens to your worthless black ass."

"Boy," Luther said, drawing himself up out of the chair, still with a good two inches on Archy though giving up at least twenty-five pounds, "I am grateful for the generous offer, but I am tired of your disrespect. I am going to issue a warning. You speak to me again in that fashion, you going to find yourself in possession of one genuine, old-school beatdown like you haven't had in thirty years."

"Man," Archy said in an unconscious echo of his own son's words to him the other morning, "*fuck* you."

"Gentlemen," Flowers said. It was too late.

Archy's historic decision, taken sometime around 1983, no longer to give a shit about his father, coincided almost precisely with the last time he had attempted to kick Luther's ass. Like the five or six preceding it, that attempt also failed. Even big and strong and flooded with the manhood that he was then well on his way to attaining, and even with Luther geeked and anorexic, Archy's bulk and raw anger were no use against his father's deep-grained skill.

But this was a sneak attack, and Archy exploited the advantage. He hurled himself onto Luther, toppling him over onto the little couch, which in turn tumbled over backward, and the two men fell on the floor. Before Luther could begin to recover, Archy scrambled across him, straddling him, and flipped him over so that Luther's face was pressed against the low-pile gray carpet. He sat on his father's ass and pinned his wrists together with one hand while, with the other, he grabbed hold of his hair. Digging in his fingers, he jerked his father's head back. "Give it to him."

"Fuck you."

Archy dug deeper, jerked harder. "Give him the glove, Luther."

"I can't. Get off me."

"Why not?"

"Because I lost it."

"Lost it? You mean you never did find it? Valletta didn't have it?"

"She had it. But in the last move we did, I don't know, it got lost. I can't find it. I swear. Get the fuck off me."

"*What?*"

"I had it," Luther said, writing his own epitaph without trying. "But I lost it."

"I would really like to believe that," Flowers said. "I'm going to need some kind of guarantee. What happens when it turns up again?"

"How about a sworn statement," Archy said. "An affidavit he writes in his own words that he's been blackmailing you for years, that he made up the whole story about the glove and the murder, how you didn't have nothing to do with it." He gave his father's head another jerk, for emphasis, really. "You do that, confess that you've been blackmailing, Luther? I'll give you whatever I manage to get from selling the store. Then you get to keep on living this admirable life of yours."

"That would be acceptable to me," Flowers said. "But huh, we're going to need a lawyer for an affidavit like that. I can't imagine what kind of lawyer. I know mine wouldn't want to even *hear* about this. "

Archy said he thought that Mike Oberstein might be prevailed upon, but first of all, what did Luther have to say about it?

"Had three things on my wish list," said Luther, "coming out of the program last year. And one of them was not 'Please let my son slap me upside my head, pull my hair, and sit on top of me, motherfucker must weigh two hundred and forty, two-forty-five.' "

"Yeah," Archy said. "Oh. Sorry about that." He unstraddled his father, lurched to his feet. Luther rolled over onto his back and lay there, staring at the cottage-cheese ceiling, at the box that held Terrell Padgett. His eyes brimmed over, but he blinked the tears away, and they were gone.

Archy reached down and held out a hand to Luther. Luther took it. He let Archy pull his weightless wiry armature off the floor. When Archy tried to get his fingers loose, Luther held on to them. His grip was the inveterate iron thing that had punished cinder blocks, pine planks, Chuck Norris. Archy gave up and let his father shake his hand.

"That was number two on the list," Luther said.

⊙   ⊙   ⊙

The mom was a kid, two months shy of twenty-one, her baby's father out of the picture. She worked the line at Chez Panisse and from time to time sold cupcakes out of a taco truck. When Aviva had first met her, she was a strawberry-blond third-grader named Rainbow, the daughter of the facilitator of a women's-business network Aviva had belonged to at the time. A wordless slip of a girl, moving sideways at the edges of rooms. Now she was dyed to a shade of blackberry brunette, had dropped the second syllable of her name, tattooed maybe 60 percent of her body with a gaudy loteria of half-allegorical objects (a bee, an umbrella, an egg in an eggcup), and, for today at least, taken center stage in her world. In *the* world; Aviva still felt that way after all these years, after having caught a thousand babies and been afforded every opportunity by routine, patient-borne neurosis, or the health care industry to grow disenchanted, jaded, or bored with the work. A person tended to see herself as a streetlamp on a misty night, at the center of a sphere of radiance, but that was a trick of the light, an illusion of centrality in a general fog. A laboring woman, though, while she endured her labor, lay at the center of something truly radiant in four dimensions; every birth everywhere, all the vectors of human evolution and migration originating and terminating at the parting of her legs.

"I feel like I'm going to shit," Rain said. She had gotten all the way to eight centimeters within two hours of her first contraction, but the journey to the hospital seemed to have slowed her down. "What if I shit in the bed?"

"I dare you," said Aviva.

Click of the door latch, inrush of hospital hum. Aviva had her back to the door of the pretty new LDR that Rain had lucked into, blond wood and chrome trim, a suggestion of slim Danish moms giving birth to strapping young socialists. Audrey, Rain's mother, leaped up from the armchair to drag the curtain around the bed with a rattle of BBs.

"Ms. Jaffe?" It was one of the nurses, a Filipina named Sally, a good nurse, with the same well-trained way Gwen had of being sugar-sweet and kick-ass at the same time. "Your darling husband is here."

It was Aviva's turn to leap to her feet. She could not recall Nat ever having shown up at the hospital, unbidden. Maybe to bring her a more comfortable pair of shoes, something to eat. For him to turn up out of the blue had to mean bad news, disaster. As she followed Sally down to the nurses' station to meet him, she fished her phone from her back pocket, looking for the voice mail she must have missed. No calls from Nat or Julie. No calls from anyone at all.

He was drawing an invisible mandala across the glossy tile with his high-top Chuck Taylors, head down, hands in the back pockets of the jeans she liked best on him, humming the soundtrack to his impatience. When she saw her, the panic in his face gave way so suddenly to relief that she thought he would cry.

"What's wrong?" she said.

"Gwen's in labor."

"Is Archy there?"

"No. She's not home, Aviva. She's here."

"Oh, no."

"Yeah. Her water broke, there was meconium?"

"A lot?"

"Not a lot, but some. The doc said we probably don't need to worry yet, but they wanted her admitted and on the monitor. In case there's some fetal distress."

"Who's the attending?"

"Your boy."

"Lazar?"

"Quite the charmer."

"Shit! Were you with her when her water broke?"

"Yes."

"Why didn't you call me?"

A blankness drifted across his face like ink from a squid, alerting her that the next words to issue from his lips were going to maintain a fraught if not adversarial relation to the truth. "I lost my phone," he said.

"Lost it where?"

He shrugged. "In the car."

She decided, whatever the lie, to let it go for now. "How is Gwen?" she said.

Since leaving the house to meet Rain and Audrey at the hospital, Aviva had been aware, a ground underlying the figure of every calm suggestion she made to Rain, every forbearing interaction she had with the staff, that the whole of her emotional capacity—carefully concealed from everyone around like the blacked-out windows of some wartime aircraft factory—had been shifted over to the production of anger; she was furious with Gwen.

No, it was something deeper and more selfish, more craven than fury, which had to Aviva's ear a notion of scourging, of refining fire. Aviva was hurt. And her anger was the especial, bitter anger of the indicted. Gwen was breaking their partnership, renouncing their shared calling, for reasons that Aviva could not dismiss without doing violence to certain inconvenient and embarrassing facts about the nature and demographics of their practice, about the paradoxical taint of the boutique that hung over modern midwifery, a profession that had at one time, not long ago, confined its ministrations to poor and to rural women. Aviva was annoyed—though this annoyance was also not uncontaminated by consciousness of those fucking *facts*—by the deft and ruthless mau-mauing to which Gwen had, with perfect justification, subjected the hapless review panel. And that in spite—or because—of Gwen having saved their asses by so doing.

"She is not happy," Nat said. "She doesn't know where Archy is, that's one. Two, no way is she ever letting that fuckhead Lazar lay one hand on her, quote unquote. Three, get your ass down there, please, as fast as you can. She needs you, Aviva. She says she's not going to have the baby without you there to catch it."

"How sweet."

"I'm just the messenger. And I better get back to her. I don't think Julie is a whole lot of support."

"Julie?"

"He's with us. He's kind of—"

"How did that happen?"

Again a mild facial paralysis, a narrative dystonia slackened his features. "I picked him up," he said. "Uh, on the way."

"What the fuck is going on, Nat? No, forget it. I'll kill you later."

"Okay."

"Okay?"

"Later works for me."

"Good. Now. Tell Gwen—"

"Aviva?"

It was Audrey, standing in the corridor making a tentative little handwringing gesture, her head inclined toward the door of Rain's LDR. "She says she wants to push."

"Ho-kay," Aviva said. She gave Nat a push of her own, fingers to his sternum, rocking him back a step or two. "Tell her I'll be there as *fast* as I can. You help her get settled, see her into a room, all right? Make yourself useful. Play the dad. Think you can do that?"

"I think I can fake it," Nat said.

"Meantime, where the fuck is Archy?"

"I've been trying him, he doesn't answer."

"Try sending one of those text-message things."

"What is that, I don't know what that is."

"I don't, either. Ask Julie."

"Aviva?" Audrey said, venturing closer in her tone toward accusatory.

"I have to get back to Rain," Aviva said. "Go. Tell Gwen I'll be there soon."

"What if you get hung up, though?" Nat said. "They send in Lazar, I think she's going to fucking bite his head off."

"It's a hospital," Aviva said. "They can sew it back on."

☉ . ☉   ☉

"I think I would have to say, 'Mirror, Mirror'," Julie said.

"The beard," Gwen agreed vaguely as another contraction gathered out there in the gulf of pain on whose shore she was planted like a low-lying town, levees buckling under the advancing wave. She had put Julie's hand against her stomach during the last one, let him feel the skin turn from upholstery to plate. "Spock with a beard."

"The beard is, like, even more stylish nowadays than it was back then," Julie said. "Goatees are in."

She had instructed him to distract her, though he suspected that she didn't mean it, that she was not capable of being distracted from her purpose today. The contractions took up all of Gwen's attention. Each one became, as it arose, the object of intense study. But Julie was trying his best, even though, for his part, he was feeling, if anything, *too* distracted. Knowing he ought to be there, totally there, for Gwen, at least until his father got back or, better, until his mother showed up. But he couldn't stop thinking about Titus, wondering where he was, where he might choose to run, if he was ever coming back. The elusive Titus, a cat burglar rappelling down the sheer wall of Julie's life. Fugitive as a passing aspiration, one of those daydreams that you knew, even as you daydreamed it, would take more money, more luck, more coolness than you could ever hope to have.

"Keep talking *Trek*," Gwen instructed him softly, holding herself still, her eyes closed, possibly keeping some kind of internal count, even though Julie, with his watch, was faithfully tracking the contractions' frequency and duration on the back of an envelope he had found in her car. "It's helping. Also I think it was more of a Van Dyck."

"Okay," Julie said, unsticking his legs from the vinyl seat of the LDR's armchair. He turned around to face Gwen, holding her moist left hand

in his right one. Gwen was lying on the bed in Archy's old Xavier Mc-
Daniel T-shirt and a clean pair of leggings she had sent Julie into her
house to retrieve on the way here. She had allowed herself to be hooked
to the fetal monitor, but she refused to change into a gown as a way of
proving her determination not to have this baby until Aviva was free
and there was no need for the nurses to page Paul Lazar. "Also, the Captain's Woman, on that one?"

"Oh, you like that." The soft voice, studious, a librarian of pain running her finger down some endless index of burning. "Do you."

"She's, I don't know. I guess she's pretty kick-ass."

Not saying that whenever he watched that episode, which he first
remembered seeing with Gwen the night his parents went out to see
Almost Famous, he liked to imagine that *he* was the Captain's Woman,
stalking the quarters of the evil Kirk with her bare midriff and her
Tantalus Field, waiting for the captain to return to her arms, her lips,
to the retro-future 1960s starship bed with the red sparkle-mesh bed-
sheets.

Forty-nine seconds went by in silence, and then she opened her eyes
again. Julie wrote down the time and duration on the back of the envelope, which had been sent to Gwen by the law firm of Leopold, Valsalva
& Rubin and which Gwen had not bothered to open. It bore a serious
and, Julie would have thought, urgent aspect.

"Over," she said, swallowing, licking her lips. A last little fizz of
pain in her eyes. Julie could see it dying away, like Sally Kellerman in
"Where No Man Has Gone Before" when the psionic fire went out of her.

"You okay?" he said.

"I am fine. If Lazar comes in here, I will not be fine. You will have to
kill him."

"I can do that."

"You will have to be my Captain's Woman, hit him with that Tantalus
Field."

"Dude is toast."

She took hold of his hands in hers. "You are a good boy, Julius Jaffe,"
she told him. "Your momma raised you right."

"Thank you."

"That must have been a weird, weird scene over there at that motel this morning."

"It was *insane*. I don't know *what* was happening. I don't get what the deal is."

"Who were the guys?"

"I don't know, they work for, you know, Mr. Flowers, they have the suits, so they look kind of like Black Muslims, only with bling, and neckties, not bow ties."

"Yes. Yeah."

"I don't know, it's some kind of *thing* between him and Luther. Mr. Flowers and Luther. From back a long time ago, when Archy was little."

"Archy didn't tell you what it's about?"

"No. He just said he would take care of it."

Gwen bit her lower lip, not in pain, and shook her head once turning away from Julie. He was about to reassure her that Archy was coming, that he would come as soon as he heard that she had gone into labor. It occurred to him, however, that this might not be true. Julie had no idea what kind of situation Archy had walked into. The dudes from the funeral home went around armed and were probably dangerous, even if the big one, Bank, had proved surprisingly vulnerable to assault with a wooden katana.

"Titus, he's the one ought to be in the emergency room," Gwen said. "He was hurt, huh? I did the wrong thing, I should not have let him go. That was wrong. I don't know where my head was. I guess I was feeling kind of crazy."

"He had a bloody nose, but he was okay. He is pretty, like, tough." Julie feeling a rush of gratitude toward Gwen for affording him an excuse to talk about Titus. "I think he lived in some pretty, you know, not so great places? Like where he was living here? Across the street from Mr. Jones."

"I heard about that."

"They treated him like shit."

"Language, Julius."

"It was a nightmare."

"You like him, don't you?"

"He's my friend."

Vulcan mind meld, Julie looking at her face could read her thought: *Something you never really had before.* "What did he ever say about me?"

"He . . . I don't know. Probably he's a little afraid of you. I know he, I mean, I could tell he was kind of, like, kind of excited about this."

"The baby."

"Yeah. His brother. He said you told him it was a boy."

"It is. He is."

"Yeah, he seemed excited. I bet if he knew you were going into labor, he wouldn't have run away."

"Huh," Gwen said, and at first Julius took it for an expression of mild interest, Gwen registering a minor gain in information on a subject she formerly had known little about. Then the sound deepened and transformed and drew itself into a moan, *huuuuuuuh*, and he saw that another contraction was coming on.

Julie heard the rattle of Gwen's file in the rack outside. He stood up just as the door opened and a lean, pale doctor with a stubbly scalp stuck his head into the room. He wore blue scrubs and a stethoscope necklace.

"Seven minutes apart!" Julie reported, holding up the envelope. "Seven minutes!"

"Seven minutes!" the doctor echoed. "Is that English time or metric?"

Julie lost himself in a fascinated confusion over this concept, the year divided into ten months, the month into ten weeks, the week into ten days. No, that would be too many days.

Gwen had closed her eyes; Julie was not even sure she had seen the doctor. "Not you," she said, her voice so soft it was barely audible. "No fucking way."

Lazar glanced at Julie, trying to enlist him with a look. Julie returned his most basilisk stare, willing it to vaporize the doctor into a shimmering Tantalus mist.

"Who's your friend, huh?" Lazar said to Gwen. He took a look at the fetal monitor, tried to take hold of Gwen's wrist. "You having one right now?"

She yanked her hand free. "No," Gwen said. "I'm fine. The baby's fine. There's no sign of distress. I can wait until Aviva gets here."

Then the contraction rolled in over Gwen, and she was swept up in it, swept away. Julie felt himself, Lazar, the hospital, vanish from her thoughts. Lazar stood there watching her. His eyes had looked dead before, exhausted, but now Julie saw a quickness there, an alertness, almost, Julie would have said, a sense of adventure. Lazar waited and waited, glancing at the monitor display. When Gwen opened her eyes again, he said, "Tell you what I'll do. And this is all I'll do. Ms. Shanks, you can wait for your partner, hang out here and labor, I'll be only too happy to stay out of your way. But the *instant* we see one little blip of what I feel to be evidence of fetal distress, I am going in and getting that baby. Period. Got it?"

Gwen only nodded.

Lazar seemed to hesitate, on the point of saying something more. But he just jotted a few notes in her file and walked out.

"I'm sorry," Julie said, "I didn't kill him."

"That's all right," Gwen said. "There's time. I think there's time. I wish my mom were here."

She started to cry about her mom a little bit. She said she missed her father and her brothers, all of them back in D.C. and Philly. Julie gave her a tissue, then a second. His father came in holding a rattling cup of ice.

"Aviva'll be here as soon as she can," he announced. "Probably any minute. Also, I brought ice."

"Bless you," Gwen said.

He handed her the plastic cup, and she crunched thoughtfully. Eyes aswim, staring at Julie in a way that made him worry he might start to cry, too. She was feeling sorry either for herself, having a baby three thousand miles from her family, or for him.

"You know where to look for Titus?" she said at last, around a mouthful of ice.

"Maybe," Julie said, drafting a thesis almost immediately. "Maybe I might."

"Go on and find him, then," she said. "This baby is going to want his brother."

⊙　　⊙　　⊙

"I don't know you," said the little old Chinese lady. "Why I would know your friend?"

"No reason," Julie said. "But—"

"He's my student?"

"No. But like I said. He keeps his bike here. So I—"

"You think I'm deaf?"

"No."

"Because you talking so loud."

"I—"

"Deaf, old, Chinese, and stupid. That what you think?"

"No." Julie took a deep breath. *Start again.* "Hello," he said. He held out his hand. "My name is Julius Jaffe." He took out the cards from his wallet, shuffled through them. Found one, an old one, that identified him as OCCULT RESEARCHER. Passed it to her. She read the proffered text, frowned, took another look at him, betraying neither skepticism nor interest.

"My friend Titus," he said, "hid his bicycle behind your Dumpster, in the, uh, honeysuckle bush? He has to hide it there because, okay, when he was living in Mrs. Wiggins's house? Around the corner on Forty-second? Stuff kept happening to his bike. I guess there's a lot of people living there?"

"Miss Wiggins." He could tell that she knew which house he meant. "Okay."

"Like one time somebody took it and, like, rode it. And they broke it. And another time somebody sold it to buy drugs, and Titus had to steal it back. So he started hiding it back there because, I mean, there's so much honeysuckle. You can't see it. And because I am *looking* for him, to tell him that his baby *brother* is being born right *now*—"

"Loudness," she cautioned him. "Volume."

"I was going to see if he's at Mrs. Wiggins's. So I looked, and his bike is in the bushes. But then I thought, I don't know. That maybe he might be here."

"Here?" She shook her head, looking closer to smiling than he had yet seen her. "Not here."

"I mean, you don't *know*. He could have sneaked in. Titus has skills."

"Look at me, occult investigator," she said. "You think because I am old, stupid, deaf, and Chinese, some boy can sneak and hide in my house and I don't know it?"

"No," he guessed.

"You must be a really lousy occult investigator."

"Kind of."

"I think ghosts are laughing at you."

"Probably."

"No ghost here," she said. "Your friend went to his house. Go look there, tell him, 'Little brother is coming.' "

"Yeah, but what about," lowering his voice, glancing up and down Telegraph, "that room you have?"

"No room."

"No, the, like, secret bedroom? The door that's hidden behind a poster of Bruce Lee? Where Gwen was staying. Gwen Shanks."

She blinked and handed him back his card. "No ghost. No ghost room. Good luck. Goodbye."

Julie thought about trying to slip past this annoying old person. Run upstairs, take a look for himself in the room that was behind the Bruce Lee door. He turned away, dropped his board to the sidewalk, stepped onto the deck. Hesitating, trying out a different kind of move.

"Oh, uh, you taught Luther Stallings, right?" he said. "From the movies. My friend, Titus? He's Luther Stallings's grandson."

She came out in her gray gi and black sandals, skinny and feather-weight with the walk of a younger person. "Let me see this ghost bicycle," she said.

Julie led her around the side of the building to the parking area. They crunched across the gravel over to the Dumpster. He pushed aside tangles of honeysuckle, covered in flowers like a scattering of buttered popcorn. The heavy fragrance of the flowers mingled with the rancid atmosphere of the Dumpster. Before Julie could help or prevent her, she grabbed the handlebars of Titus's bicycle, tugged it out of the tangling vines with surprising ease. She seemed to regard the bike's presence as something of an offense, but there was also, Julie thought, a touch of puzzlement; even, possibly, of wonder. She looked sidelong at a small, square window at the top of the building—it *was* open, though there was no obvious way to climb up to it—then back down at the bicycle.

"Weird bike," she said.

"It's called a fixie?" Julie said. "No brakes. No gears. You just pedal it. When you want to stop, you have to pedal the other way."

She climbed on the seat, gripping the handlebars, pedaled forward slushing through the gravel, fingers fluttering to find hand brakes that were not there. She slammed backward on the pedals, stopped, ground forward till she hit sidewalk. For three seconds she wobbled on the bike like a kid fresh from training wheels, a frail knot of bone, tendon, and gray silk. By the fourth second, she had figured out how to pedal backward, weaving away heedless down the sidewalk without looking over her shoulder. She disappeared behind a high fence. Ten seconds later, she reappeared, pedaling forward, and gestured curtly with one hand, master of the fixie now and for all time. "Come on," she said.

"Come on, where?"

"Miss Wiggins. Look for your friend. Mr. Occult Investigator, scared of ghost house. That's why you come here first. Talking about some lamebrain idea, a fourteen-year-old boy could sneak into the Bruce Lee Institute and I don't know about it. You came here because you are afraid to go there. Right or wrong?"

"Right," Julie said. "Basically. But seriously, Titus does have skills."

"Insult me one more time," she said, "I don't go with you."

He got on his skateboard and they set off, the lady tearing down the sidewalk with such impossible energy, such abandon, that Julie could not keep up. She stopped and waited for him, gesturing toward her shoulder with her chin. He took hold of it. It was rope and bone.

She towed him down to Forty-second Street and turned the corner. They rode past Mr. Jones's, the house looking empty and forlorn. On the porch stood the perch where Fifty-Eight used to sit, empty, abandoned.

She pedaled on, rolling toward the door of the house where Titus's auntie moldered like some ancient monarch whose kingdom had gone to lawlessness and ruin. The lady—she'd said to call her Mrs. Jew—hoisted the bike and rolled it up the crumbling front steps of the porch. She pounded on the door, bang! bang!

"Titus," she told the young man who opened the door, eighteen, nineteen, pop-eyed and heavy-jawed, with a frowsy tangle of chin beard. Shirtless, lean-bellied, his skin blotted with unreadable, uninterpretable tattoos. The elastic of his boxer shorts and an inch of dark blue lozenges on light blue background emerged from the waistband of his knee-length denim shorts.

"Titus," Mrs. Jew said again.

The young man gardened at his chin beard with two fingers. Julie lingered on the bottom step, feeling exposed and dangerously faggoty in his short shorts and his sleeveless T-shirt. From the open mouth of the house came a steady exhalation of marijuana and a low rumble of television, maybe a football game. There were voices, too. Not angry or hostile. Just voices. People talking, laughing.

"I teach kung fu," Mrs. Jew said.

"Kung *fu*?"

"Bruce Lee Institute. Around the corner."

Julie remembered his father telling him once about how when Julie was little and he would go around the neighborhood wearing his little Batman or Spider-Man costume year-round, people used to think he was cute and all. But when he went around the block dressed up like Superman, people would *light up*. Over and above the cuteness of some little dude masquerading around all solemn-face in the gaudy S-suit, there was something about the idea of Superman that made people happy. It was probably like that when you mentioned Bruce Lee.

"Bruce Lee," the young man said. "He really was a student there?"

"I was his teacher."

"For real? You?"

"I kick his ass," said Mrs. Jew. "On a daily basis. "

"Yo," the young man called, glancing over his shoulder into the house. "Where Titus at?"

Somebody said something, and the man stepped aside. It was easily accomplished, without violence, subterfuge, or even use of the word "please." Julie felt ashamed of his trepidation and anxiety, but he did not renounce them as he followed Mrs. Jew into the house. It was old and cramped, maybe kind of charming once upon a time. The fireplace mantel had that medieval feel you saw in a lot of little bungalows. Handsome columns of painted wood held up the ceiling here and there. The living room was all about the television, an old rear-projection number whose sun-dimmed display struggled to contend with the color palette of *The Fresh Prince of Bel-Air.* Three teenage boys and two girls on a sectional tartan-plaid sofa repaired with accumulated yards of silver duct tape. On the floor a girl about Julie's age, in a Catholic-school skirt, and four or five little kids. The girl looked more Latina than black to Julie, and one of the little kids was almost white, with drifts of reddish-brown curls. Across from the plaid sofa, a young man in a wheelchair breathed air from a green steel tank. He laughed into the plastic breathing mask. An empty bag of spicy Cheetos lay on the floor. On the coffee table stood two large bottles of Coke. A pizza box. A plastic tub that once held Trader Joe's animal crackers. It was messy, dirty, crowded, and there was a miasma of Cheetos, but mostly, it was a bunch of kids sitting around watching a show that Julie also enjoyed. He had been expecting strobe lights, peeling wallpaper, people passed out on the floor, the flash of crack pipes. Twenty-four-hour pounding of woofers. Baleful people, he thought, lurking in the corners of shadowy rooms.

He was such a racist.

The young man who had greeted them at the door led them all the way to the back of the house, down some ill-sorted steps to an addition. In one of the bunks, a boy not much younger than Julie lay cuddling a Game Boy.

"Titus?" Julie called.

It was a kind of bunkhouse, furnished with a variety of bunk beds of different periods and styles, some made of steel tubing, some of scuffed and gouged wood. Not much light. In the rear corner, on the bottom bunk, under a *Blue's Clues* sleeping bag, Julie found Titus. "Hey," he said.

"What are you doing here?" Titus said from under the comforter, voice muffled but sounding, to Julie's ear, roughened by weeping. "Man, get the fuck out."

"Okay," Julie said, and tears came to his own eyes. He started to turn away but then wiped his face with his arm. The little kid with the Game Boy was staring at him. "I just came to, uh, tell you that I thought you might want to know that Gwen is having the baby. About to. Right now. I mean, she's in labor. If you come now, you, you know, you could kind of like, be there, or whatever. When your brother's born."

Titus didn't move or speak.

"He got a brother?" said the boy, doubtful.

"Almost," said Julie. "Titus, come on. We got your bike. Let's go, don't miss this. It's really awesome. Brothers are cool. I wish I had one." He looked at the boy. "Right, brothers are cool?"

"Not really," the boy said.

"Could you, maybe, like, could we get a little privacy?"

"Why, so you can suck his dick?"

"Yes, totally," Julie said without missing a beat, exhilarated by his own daring. "Here." He took five dollars out of his wallet. "Go buy some candy or something."

The kid left. Julie sat down on the corner of the bed.

"I know, I mean, I get that you . . ." He took a breath, let it out. "I just wanted to say, if you came back here, you must have been feeling pretty lonely right then. Like, okay, Archy was being an ass and all. But, I mean, this is your brother, it's a, here's your chance, you know? To have somebody that loves you and looks up to you. Besides me, I mean, because I know that's, like, not really such a big deal."

"Get up," Mrs. Jew said. "Go to the hospital. Now. Or I will kick your butt. Do you believe me?"

Titus sat up, looked at Julie, then back at Mrs. Jew. Nodded yes.

☉   ☉   ☉

Over. A rest between measures scored for kettledrums. A patch of blue sky between two rolling thunderheads.

☉   ☉   ☉

Gwen in the birthing bed, between contractions, hating the only friend she had in the world. Hating his aftershave: a compound of unlit cherry cigar and the cardboard pine tree dangling from the rearview of a taxicab. Underneath that smell a deeper rancor, raw bacon gone soft in the heat. Hating the shine of his scalp through crosshatched hair. The whitehead at the wing of his right nostril. The fur on the backs of his fingers. Hating him for not being Archy.

Nat sat upright in a leatherette chair, chin raised, stiff-backed, looking like he was waiting for something freaky to happen, something that would demand more from him than he was prepared to deliver, like maybe any minute Nurse Sally was going to roll some weird Filipino piano into the room, made from sharks' teeth and tortoiseshells and coir, which he would be expected to play. The expression on his face saying, *Please, Lord, do not let this spectacle become any more revolting than it already is.* Eyelids half-lowered, widening, narrowing again, the poor man trying to find that sweet spot between shut-tight-in-horror and wide-eyed-attentiveness-to-the-miracle-of-birth. Jitter in his legs. Hunch of impatience in his shoulders. Considering that the man had been married to a midwife for seventeen years, Gwen considered it surprising how little he seemed to know, recollect, or be able to intuit about the needs of a woman in labor. The sum of all the birthing wisdom he had managed to acquire was compassed within a cup of ice and the area of the washcloth that he regularly returned to the bathroom to douse with water and wring out in the sink before returning it, blessedly cool, to her forehead.

"Thank you, Nat," she said, furious with gratitude.

Had to be a thousand degrees Kelvin in the LDR, Gwen feeling strangely but not pleasantly buoyant in the heat. Sweating, fouled, writhing. Hair like a gorgon's. The bed a swamp. Her skin in full rebellion, as if the baby were something not only to be expelled from her womb but shed from the outside, too; the hospital gown intolerable, abrasive, a crust of toast against the roof of the mouth. Gwen felt desperate, wild to labor naked. Wanted to rip off the gown, burst from it like the Hulk trashing one of his professor-dude lab coats. But here was this guy who was her only friend, wanting to see her naked even less than she wanted him to. His gaze already, every time Gwen rolled over or sat up, lashing around the room like a loose garden hose. The man appalled by the horror of it all, head down, cringing, a palace lackey sent into the foulness of the labyrinth to tend the roaring Minotaur. And humming. Running a metal key, a broken bottleneck, back and forth endlessly along a taut string of piano wire.

"Nat, boy, I beg you, you have to cut it out with the *god*damn humming."

"What humming?" Nat said.

He got up and opened Gwen's phone for the tenth time, trying to raise Archy. The gesture exhausted Gwen; she hated it more than all of the other incredibly annoying things that Nat was being, doing, and saying right now, put together.

"You might not want to do that. Archy Stallings comes through that door, Nat, swear to God, I'm going to call security on him."

She had caught him on the point of dialing the last digit, his finger hesitating over the nine. Eyebrows arched, looking at her, entertaining the remote possibility that he had misheard her.

"Put. The motherfucking phone. Away."

Nat nodded, lips pursed, eyes wide, his expression saying, O-*kay*. He snapped the phone shut. Sometime around the time that Gwen uttered the obscenity, Nurse Sally had come back into the room, or rather, she was simply there again. Endowed, Gwen noted, with her own combination of odors, almond extract and armpit and some inexcusable derivative of gardenia.

"Hi, Mom, we are fine?" Sally said in that mildly broken English, in that treacly little voice, with that unbearable giggle. "I think your wife, hee, she's still trapped," she told Nat. "That other mom, my goodness, she is taking her time."

"We're fine, Sally," Gwen said, working as much normal into her voice as she could manage. Tiring now. Needing to be done, with a longing that brought her—just when she hoped most to appear cheerful, fresh as a daisy, infinitely game to wait it out—to tears. "Just hanging."

"Totally," Nat agreed.

"How often?" Sally wanted to know. She went right to over to the heart monitor. "Huh," she said. "I'm sorry, Mom. Ms. Shanks, I'm so sorry. I have to get the doctor in here. I know you want it to be Ms. Jaffe. I heard you had, I don't know, some kind of problem with Dr. Lazar. But I think we can't wait anymore."

"What is it?"

"I think it's a deceleration. Just a little one, but. Time for doctor."

"Oh," Gwen said, watching Sally's flowered back as she race-walked out of the room. "Oh, no."

She was barely able to get the words out as another great slow umbrella of pain opened inside her. Combing her thoughts, yanking them into a pigtail. Everything fading but the pain: the room and its furnishings, the whispering of pumps and monitors, the circuit of the hours, daylight, the world. The husband who had abandoned her to bear their child into that world. Pain like a closing of the eyes.

"Hee breaths," Nat managed to dig up from somewhere.

"Shut the fuck up," Gwen countersuggested.

Paddling to stay on top of the wave as it broke, trying to ride it. A big one, really big, the biggest one yet, high, wide, deep, and rolling on and on like an earthquake. Impervious as an earthquake to her will, which amounted in the end to nothing more than the words "please be over" repeated for what felt like hours.

This time there was no rest between measures, no patch of blue. The flow of pain within her simply shifted, shunted by some switch in the rail yard of her nervous system, from the bands of steel that belted her abdomen to someplace lower and farther inside. To her horror, then, and as from a great distance, she heard her own voice blubbering, pleading with Nat, begging him to run and get Aviva, drag her ass *out* of that other room with that cupcake girl, that skinny little tattooed chicken wing, because the baby was coming *now*, and Aviva needed to be there to catch it. For so long Gwen had scorned, condescended to, or pitied, in varying measure, the doomed and futile dreams, the hopeful visions of soft light and ambient music and a kind of vaginal satori, that pregnant women were prone, in their birth plans, to fall to dreaming.

Now she saw that her own doomed birth plan, simple as it was, burned in her heart with a utopian fire. It comprised only one item, and that was Aviva, calm and crafty, without resort to knives, drugs, or synthesized hormones, smuggling the life of her man-child into the light. Any light, any child; let the only certainty be Aviva Roth-Jaffe. Gwen swore to Nat and to Sally, when the nurse came back in to announce that the doctor was on his way, that she would not permit this baby to exit her body, that she would hang on to him, that she would chew nails, lasso herself to granite boulders, fold space-time down to an endless single point, until Aviva could be fetched.

"Go!" she tried, and maybe, right about then, she went a little crazy. "Jesus Christ, Nat, you're so fucking *slow! Go get Aviva now!*"

And yet all the time that she raved, and fought, and swore to keep the baby clutched within the intricate and formidable musculature of her uterus, she felt, more powerfully than any sorrow over the spoiling of her birth plan or the latest and greatest failure of her husband to meet his obligations to her, an urge to push the baby out. She knew that it would be useless, too late, for anybody to run.

Nobody ran. Nat got to his feet. There was something weird in his expression, a stoniness, a condemned look, as if he had made up his mind to do something irretrievable. Looking back at this moment afterward, Gwen would see him stepping into a harsh shaft of light.

"A minute," Gwen said. "Just one. Oh, Nat, please. Let's wait for Aviva just one more minute."

"No fucking way," Nat said.

So she abandoned her modest dream of utopia, pushed it out of herself with the violence of disappointment.

"I am going to shit," she announced.

"Okay," Nat said. "Go for it."

"It's going to be so disgusting. I'm so disgusting."

"That reminds me," Nat said. He went into the bathroom and washed his hands, lathering them with a precision she found commendable from the standpoint of hygiene but questionable given the imminence of parturition and, given the size of the turd that she felt she was about to expel from her bowels, possibly premature.

"Oh my goodness," she said. "Oh, Nat, oh."

He hurried out of the bathroom, drying his hands on a towel. Without apparent hesitation, he directed his attention to her crotch and said, "Oh my God. Okay."

He leaned in, reaching toward her, hunching the way he hunched over the keys of a piano. With a sense of regret, Gwen forced herself to stop pushing. The irritation, the discontent verging on rage that had been flowing freely through her for the last hour backed up inside her, weighing like a dammed river against the floodgates. She balanced on a point between rage and its relief. Amid the layers of conscious thought and the involuntary actions of her body, Gwen found herself in possession, coolly palmed in her thoughts like a dollar coin, of the idea that she was about to bring another abandoned son into the world, the son of an abandoned son. The heir to a history of disappointment and betrayal, violence and loss. Centuries of loss, empires of disappointment. All the anger that Gwen had been feeling, not just today or over the past nine months but all her life—feeding on it like a sun, using it to power her engines, to fund her stake in the American dream—struck her for the first time as a liability. As purely tragic. There was no way to partake of it without handing it on down the generations.

Then Archy walked into the room in a yachting cap. Stood there gawping at her. He looked a mess, creased, untucked, his hair misshapen. In the instant before his new son tumbled, bawling and purple, into mortality and history, Gwen's heart was starred like a mirror by a stone. One day the feeling might come to resemble forgiveness, but for now it was only pity, for Archy, for his father and his sons, for all the men of whom he was the heir or the testator, from the Middle Passage, to the sleeper cars of the Union Pacific, to the seat of a fixie back-alleying down Telegraph Avenue in the middle of the night.

Then she was holding her own little man, with his smell like a hot penny and his milky blue eyes, and although she had taken no drugs and received no anesthesia, she thought she must be feeling kind of loopy nevertheless, because it seemed to her that a handsome black uniformed policewoman, whose name-badge read LESTER, had come into the LDR along with Nurse Sally and Dr. Lazar—brown cop, golden nurse, white doctor, all of a sudden it was like some kind of nightmarish version of *Sesame Street* in here—and was asking Nat Jaffe to come along with her. Nat washed his hands and then, exchanging a hangdog shrug with his partner, followed Officer Lester out of the room.

"What'd I miss?" said Archy.

⊙   ⊙   ⊙

A 2002 Subaru Outback station wagon, fatigues-green, pulled into the driveway of the house on Stonewall Road, over the blood-brown stain deposited five weeks earlier by the leaky gaskets of Aviva Roth-Jaffe's Volvo. The man of the house, red-bearded and slight, was in the carport, adrift on a floe of spread newspaper, painting a blue crib white. He worked his brush down one slat, finishing the stroke with a dainty twist of the wrist, laid the brush across the open mouth of his paint can, and rose to his feet, clad in a spattered pair of fawn Naot sandals. You could see from his diffident smile that neither the Subaru nor the occupants of its front seat, a hulking black man in a pumpkin beret and a black teenager who, even through the windshield, was visibly in the grip of an intense, perhaps fatal, spasm of embarrassment, meant anything to him.

"The plaintiff," said the occupant of the backseat, concealed from view by the driver and by the fact that she was canted over the car seat—duly faced to the rear—with her blouse unbuttoned, her bra cup unlatched, her nipple the sole joy and plaything of the car seat's occupant, whose parents had argued, though only briefly, over whether to name him Kudu (suggested by his father) or (in honor of his maternal grandfather) Clark. She was topping Clark off now, having restored him to sleep after he determined, for unknown reasons, to cause a disturbance midflight.

Just as she eased the cork of her nipple with a moist pop—a sound that never failed to densify the cloud of embarrassment around Clark's older brother—from the slumbering vessel into which two ounces of rich hindmilk had just been decanted, a second Outback rolled to a stop along the curb. From it emerged the cetacean form of Michael Oberstein, Esq., in a remarkably ugly taupe mohair suit whose construction, Archy thought, must have necessitated the cruel slaughter of dozens, possibly hundreds, of moes. It did not so much clothe as wad him.

Archy got out of the car to greet Moby, eager for the excuse to release himself from the cramped, styleless, and mildly punitive confines to which, once he had conceded that a '74 El Camino legendary for its unreliability might not be the most suitable car for a family man, fate had sentenced him. Selling the El Camino was only part of a diverse package of concessions, amendments, resolutions, and reparations that he had agreed to under the terms of his repatriation to the house on Sixty-first Street. One day, he hoped, this foreordained path would lead, amid countless chutes and precious few ladders, to the square of ultimate redemption—Forgiveness. Parts of the journey had been painful, and Archy rarely bothered to shield his wife and sons from awareness of this pain. But he had confessed to no one how bitterly he wept on the day when some dude from Livermore drove his El Camino away.

He raised a hand to Moby, who was molesting the knot of his necktie in the side mirror, then nodded to the plaintiff, Garth, standing by the half-white, half-blue crib looking wary, closed down, and as worn out and sleep-deprived as Archy.

"She'll be right out," Archy said. "Boy's just finishing his snack."

The plaintiff nodded, then turned back to the crib with an air of regret or longing, as if he would much rather continue with his brushwork than go through what Gwen had in mind.

At the back of the carport on a workbench, a radio reported on the count facing Miguel Tejada, and below the radio, strapped into a bouncy seat, busting out with some intricate mudras, lay the troublesome baby. Archy had forgotten its gender and name. The baby had something wrong with its skin, he noticed, some kind of weird blotches of discoloration on its fingers and face. A wire of panic lit up in Archy's chest; it had never occurred to him that Garth might have actual grounds for his lawsuit. Then he saw that the blotches appeared to be precisely the same shade as the blue stain on the half-painted crib.

"It didn't occur to me that she was going to lick it," Garth said.

"They will lick pretty much anything, is my understanding," Archy said.

"Yo, Arch," Moby said. "What up. Mr. Newgrange, Mike Oberstein. We spoke on the phone."

Moby skipped the hand theatrics for once and rolled on over to shake Garth Newgrange's straight. He turned back to the car as Gwen climbed out of the backseat, running a finger down the buttons of her blouse, tugging her skirt down over the dimples of her knees.

"Hey, Gwen."

"Hi, Moby. Hello, Garth."

Moby had spoken to the man, prearranged it for them to come over, but Garth looked ambushed. He folded his arms across his chest, took a deep breath. "Hello."

"This is my husband, Archy. Archy, this is Garth."

Archy got the man to unlatch one hand and offer it, small and freckled with melanin and white latex semigloss.

"That's, in the car, that's Titus, Archy's son. Titus, get out of the car and give this man a proper greeting."

Titus, operating under the terms of the more modest package that he had negotiated with Gwen, which included room, board, and at the end of his own Candy Land path, the ambiguous pink-frosting-roofed gingerbread house of a family to love him and fuck him up, instantly got out of the car, observed the agreed-upon conventions of civilized intercourse among strangers, and got back into the car. The boy was still visiting their planet from his own faraway home world, but Archy figured that with time, he would adjust to the local gravity and microbes. Keeping close to the baby most of the time, as if Clark were the object he had crossed the stellar void to study.

"And there she is," Gwen said, noticing the blue-stained baby in her seat. "Little Bella."

"There she is," Garth agreed, not saying *No thanks to you.*

An awkward silence ensued that Archy did not have the energy or the courage to break.

"Can we—Garth, I was hoping we, you and I, could talk?" Gwen said, gesturing to the stairs that must lead downslope to the house.

"Here's good," Garth said.

Gwen blinked, looked at Moby. "Okay," she said. "All right. I guess what I came here to say isn't going to take very long, anyway. It's really just two words long. I should have said them to you a long time ago, the day that Bella was born, right away. But they are not, they have never been, words that come very easily to me, I don't know why. Maybe because, I'm not making an excuse here, but maybe because, the way I was raised, you know. That, basically, I have nothing to apologize for. Almost as a matter of, I want to say, policy. Politics, if you will. But even if that's true in a broad, you know, like, historical sense. On the personal level—"

"You said tell you if you ran on at the mouth," Moby said.

"Two words," Gwen repeated, as though to herself.

Archy was enjoying this. He had been dwelling in a deep, capacious, and impregnable doghouse for weeks. He tried to remember if he had ever heard Gwen utter, in any but the most pro forma way, the phrase that came, halting but credible, to her lips.

"I'm sorry," she said.

When she seemed content to leave it at that, Garth cross-armed and frowning without much of an apparent rise in temperature, Moby lofted an eyebrow toward one of the upswept flukes of his bangs: *Go on.*

"I'm sorry that I lost my temper the way I did," she said. "With the doctor. I let my . . . my . . ."

"Self-righteousness?" Archy suggested helpfully.

Gwen nocked a scowl to her bowstring, aimed it at Archy, then lowered her bow and nodded. "Self-righteousness. My thin skin. Part of the same thing, I guess, that makes it so hard for me to apologize. But I do apologize, and I am sorry. My focus right then ought to have been on Lydia and the baby and nothing else. I failed them, and I failed you, and thank God that baby of yours is healthy and beautiful, because if anything had happened to her . . ."

She started to lose it, pulled herself together. Carried on. "I understand your anger. I accept it. But I'm hoping that you might find it in your heart to forgive me."

"Okay," Garth said.

"Okay, you forgive me?"

"Of course," he said. "Why not?"

"Does this mean—" Moby said. "I'm sorry, but, informally acting as Gwen's attorney, I have to ask. Are you dropping the lawsuit against her and Aviva?"

"No problem," Garth said.

When they got back in the car and drove away, Gwen let herself go. She cried until they got down to the lower gate of the Claremont Hotel, and then she stopped. "I think you ought to try it," she said.

"I already did," Archy said. "I got no traction."

"I wasn't ready then," Gwen said. "I didn't know how good it feels."

"Okay," Archy said. "I'm sorry, Gwen. I fucked up long and often, in all kinds of ways, and I'm just nothing but sorry about that. Do you think you could find it in your heart to forgive me?"

"No," Gwen said.

"What?"

"But almost."

He glanced over at the boy sitting beside him, staring out at the road, nothing much happening in his expression but a bright shine on the eye.

"Okay, then. Titus, you, too. I'm sorry I wasn't any kind of a father to you for the first fourteen years of your life. You are a fine young man, and I hope to do right by you from now on. Do you think maybe someday you could find it in your heart to forgive me?"

"Okay," Gwen said. "That's it. You're good."

Then they stopped for a red light, and the baby woke up again, disconsolate and hungry, and Archy stepped on the gas to get them home. It was weeks before he realized that he had never gotten an answer out of Titus, and by then the matter seemed to have lost its urgency.

⊙   ⊙   ⊙

Archy and Nat met at the property, an upstairs suite in a handsome commercial block of the 1920s, on the Berkeley-Oakland line. Red roof tiles, oak beams, stucco painted a Lena Horne shade of tan. The ground-floor tenants included a hardcore bike shop, an avant-garde knitting supply, and a dealer in vintage tube amplifiers.

"Already got that crank vibe going strong," Archy observed. "You're going to fit right in."

"Funny," Nat said. He was pacing off the larger of the suite's two rooms, laying out the shelving, stocking it with vinyl. Wall-to-wall, floor-to-ceiling. Satan architecting Pandemonium. "It doesn't make you nervous, three thousand pounds of records on the second floor."

"Building had a total retrofit," Archy said. "Two thousand one. Previous occupant was a Pilates. You know they have all those heavy-ass machines."

"I have spent surprisingly little time around Pilates machines."

"They are heavy," Archy said with a show of patience. "Mr. Singletary had the floor braced, cost like ten grand."

" 'Mr. Singletary,' " Nat said.

Archy put his hand to his chin, bunched up his shoulders, shook his head. Sheepish little smile on his face.

"Now the motherfucker's going to own the building *and* the stock," Nat said. "Doesn't even care for music."

"He likes Peabo."

"Peabo is actually quite underrated," Nat said.

"Not by Mr. Singletary."

"Huh."

The baby woke up and began to fuss. Archy took an Avent bottle from the hip pocket of his leather car coat, uncapped it, gave the nipple a sniff. Crouched down beside the car seat to urge the bottle on his son, fitted it to his lips, waited for him to resume his nap.

"Go to all that pain and trouble to have it," Archy said. "Then spend your life keeping the little fucker sedated."

"He doing okay?"

"Seems to be."

"That's formula?"

"Last of the frozen breast milk."

"The lactation consultant couldn't help you guys?"

"Nat, please."

"Sorry."

"Catch one baby, now you're the damn La Leche League."

"What's the rent again?"

"Eight hundred."

"Ouch."

"Includes water and trash. A third interest in a half-bathroom. I'd say that's low, for a building of this outstanding caliber."

"I imagine you would," Nat said. "That's just the kind of thing a real estate agent is supposed to say."

"Oh, I can definitely talk the talk," Archy said. "Alas, that ain't what's on the exam."

"Are you going to take it?"

"I'm still deciding."

"The baby is a great gimmick. Who's not going to want to buy a house from a giant-size cuddly black man with an achingly cute little baby?"

Archy pondered the question. "Almost no one," he said.

"I think you have to go for it."

"I think *you* do, too," Archy said. "Mr. Singletary—Garnet—you already gave him too much time, as it is, to reflect on his rash offer."

Nat looked around at the bare tile of the floor, black and glossy as a record, the freshly painted white walls, the three small windows that overlooked the alley behind the building. "Won't be a counter. Nobody coming here to hang out, shoot the shit," he said. "I thought that was all Garnet cared about at Brokeland."

"I guess something put him in a generous mood. Mr. Jones dying. Dogpile Thang going south on Chan Flowers. G Bad's moving the whole deal over to the city, going to put it in Hunters Point."

"I heard Visitacion Valley."

"But I'll tell you, Nat, I get the feeling his good mood's about to wear off. Chan Flowers is already back on his feet, brushing the dirt off his shoulder. Shifting the blame, pulling the levers. Got a guy in the economic development office fired because 'the city government lost Dogpile,' so on, so forth. The guy who got fired? Was Abreu's brother-in-law."

"No more counter," Nat said, resuming his previous train of thought.

"No more bins, writing up the little comments in Sharpie on the dividers. No more watching the world go by through the front window. That magic window. No more *customers*."

"You would have customers," Archy said. "All over the world. Every time zone, some Samoan, Madagascar motherfucker, hitting you up for a five-thousand-dollar original pressing of Blue Note 1568, deep groove, mono. Anyway, there's folks, I'm not saying who, but there is a general consensus at large, Nat, says you are not really a people person."

"I like people in theory," Nat said. "That's what was good about Brokeland. It was all just a theory we had."

"Turns out," Archy agreed.

"So now, you're saying, it's time to *get real*."

"Follow my helpful example."

"Selling *real* estate."

"That's only one of my many ways."

"And for me to *get real*, I need to start a website that will sell forty-year-old chunks of vinyl on consignment to invisible Samoans."

"I showed Mr. Singletary the books," Archy said.

"You what?"

"He went over them. Got way down deep inside."

Nat shuddered. "A man of courage."

"He asked me a lot of questions. Who did I know that was trying to make it online, how they handled it, did they go through eBay or have their own online store or what. I guess he even went and talked to some people, talked to the dude at the mailbox store about shipping costs. He thinks you could do it. Sell off all of Mr. Jones's wax. Make you *and* the estate some money. And Nat, if Garnet Singletary smells a profit, I think you got to take that shit seriously."

"Wait, I have to get real *and* take shit seriously?" Nat said. "At the same time?"

The empty bottle fell out of Clark's hands, startling him awake.

"Oh, shit," Archy said. "Okay, little man. All right." He unstrapped the baby and grabbed him, threaded him through the handle of the car seat. Cupped the baby's bottom in one palm while the other hand played triplets on his back. Clark was not impressed. Archy fished an enormous key ring out of the other pocket of his John Shaft car coat, barbed with dozens of keys, each one stamped DO NOT COPY, the green plastic fob bearing the legend SINGLETARY PROPERTY MANAGEMENT. He jangled the keys in front of Clark's face. Clark listened in apparent horror to their clangor. Archy tried to pass the key ring to the boy, let him jingle it for himself, and the keys clanged against the tile floor. At that Clark nearly jumped out of his OshKosh onesie.

"Wow," Nat said. "Quite a set of lungs."

"Sometimes you have to do this," Archy said, taking his son under the arms and subjecting him to a firm oscillation, his hands sweeping and rising, sweeping and rising, back and forth across his body, steady as the works of a clock. As he was synchronized to the rotation of the earth, or maybe just stunned by the sudden increase in velocity, Clark quieted down some. But he remained unwilling to commit fully to silence. So Archy added a complementary leg move to the pendulum swing, a simple harmonic motion, up and down.

Titus Joyner appeared in the doorway of the empty two-room suite. He watched his father's absurd dance routine with unfeigned, possibly good-natured scorn.

"What?" Archy said.

Titus held up Archy's cell phone. "You left it in the car," he said. "She called."

"What I tell you about that 'she' shit?"

"Gwen. She called."

"Yeah? Clark, man, come *on*. What'd she say?"

"Said don't forget she's working tonight. At the hospital."

"Shit, I did forget. I have to get dinner." He looked at Nat. "Gwen started in at Chimes, part-time LDR nurse."

"I heard. Aviva ran into her on the ward."

"Just to keep some money coming in."

"We figured. Medical school's going to be a stretch?"

"What do you suppose?"

"She can get help. Smart and experienced as she is. What school's not going to want her?"

"You are replete with rosy predictions today about our future."

"Just quoting Aviva."

"Gwen's worried Aviva's still mad at her."

"It was a blow. It was, you know."

"I know."

"Kind of like a divorce. You don't stop—I mean, you're mad, but. Let me try him?"

"No, man, I got it."

"You don't stop loving the person. You miss them."

"You do."

"Come on, give me little mister."

The partial charm of the pendulum treatment had long since worn off. Archy shrugged and handed over the baby, whose cries had taken on a feline rasp.

"Hey, hey, big boy. Okay, now. We're friends, aren't we? Oh, yeah, we go way back, Clark and I."

But Nat, though he broke out his most sonorous and somniferous material to hum, proved no more adept than Archy at quieting the baby.

"Give him," Titus said.

Archy okayed it with a nod, and Nat passed the baby to his older brother, who carried him out of the suite, along the hall, to the terracotta stairs of the old building. By the time he came out onto the sidewalk, Clark appeared to have run out of things to complain about. He lay supine in a crook of Titus's arm, hot and sweaty and smelling of clabber. The October sunshine was dusty and mild. Halloween a week off, here came Julie Jaffe, rolling up on his skateboard, ready a week ahead of time. All in black, blazer, pants, a black string tie like Val Kilmer's in *Tombstone*. Wearing a long, threadbare satin glove, purple and finned, on his right hand. Hair dyed a matte black. Stealth hair, absorbing all ambient light, reflecting nothing. Black hair, red freckles, kind of weird in combination, but somehow he made it work. He left his white earbuds buried in his ears. Stomped on the tail of the deck, flipped it up into his arms. "What's up?" he said.

"Yo, check it out," said Titus. "It's Johnny Cash."

Julie tugged out each earbud, pop, pop. He crossed his eyes at the baby, kissy-faced him. Reached out one finger, touched the tip of it to a teardrop that clung to Clark's cheek. "Why was he crying?"

"Boy don't really need a reason," Titus said.

"I saw you coming out of Fred's Deli, uh, yesterday."

"Yeah."

"With Kezia. She's pretty."

"She's all right."

"I knew her at Willard. Actually, I went to kindergarten with her. She was always really nice to me."

"She remembers you, too."

"And those guys, Darius and, um, Tariq, I know them, too. They're okay."

"Yeah."

"I mean, they aren't the worst. It's good you made friends or whatever."

"Julie."

"I'm sorry."

Titus looked away. Watched the traffic, lips compressed, an air of imposing patience on exasperation. "Everybody crying," he observed.

Without quite looking at Julie, he handed over the cloth diaper that had come along with his brother, stuck to his pj's by static electricity. Julie used the diaper to wipe his eyes. It came away bearing the calligraphy, painted in smeary guyliner, of his sadness.

"Sorry," Julie said. "I'm such a loser."

"Nah, whatever."

"I made a couple friends, too."

"I know."

They stood there along the shoulder of the street that had carried them, rolling, into the darkness of a few lost summer mornings.

"Oh, fuck, what time is it?" Julie said at last.

"Like around three?"

"Fuck. My dad can't be late. My mom sent me to get him, he must have his phone turned off. They upstairs?"

"Yeah. Can't be late for what?"

Julie waited before replying, took a deep breath. Rolled his eyes. "Picking up trash by Lake Merritt," he said.

"Ho."

"I know, right? How could I *not* be a loser?"

"Stealing a zeppelin, though. I mean, that's kind of badass."

"No, it isn't. He just *untied* it. It went up. It came down in Utah. I better get him."

After Julie went inside, Titus sat down outside, on the topmost step. He propped Clark next to him on the step, holding him up by the armpits, and they pretended for a minute that Clark knew how to sit. At this point, that was about as much fun as the boy knew how to have. A few minutes were lost to this pastime, and then Julie came back out of the building with Nat behind him. Titus returned Clark to the crook of his arm.

"Archy's just locking up," Nat told Titus. "He'll be right down."

"Okay."

"Say hi to your stepmom for me."

"All right."

Nat walked over to the Saab, which bore the marks of its cruel treatment at the hands of a hurricane fence, got in, and drove off to Lake Merritt to pay down his debt to society amid its eternal snows of goose shit.

Titus and Julie clasped fingertips—one bare-handed, one gloved—yanked loose, brought their fists together in a soft collision. Then Julie laid down his board.

"Yo, Artist Formerly Known as Julie," Titus said. Julie turned. "I'll probably be on tonight. Like around ten, all right? Meet me in Wakanda."

"If I get my homework done," Julie said. "Okay." Then he hopped onto the deck of his skateboard and pushed off, rumbling down the sidewalk away from Titus.

"Y'all not going to hang out?" Archy said, coming out of the building swinging the empty car seat, locking the front door with a key from the jingle-bell key ring.

"Maybe I'll see him on MTO. Here, you take him. Go on," Titus told Clark, turning custody of the baby over to their father. "Y'all smell like Monterey Jack."

Archy and Clark were reunited on friendlier terms than those under which they had last parted. "What'd you do?" Archy said to Titus.

"Nothing."

They watched Julie skate away into the late-October afternoon, looking back over his shoulder only once.

"He still play as a girl?"

"Yeah."

"What's his name?"

"Dezire. With a z."

Archy shook his head slowly, a gesture that put him somewhere between admiration and disdain. "That's how you friends now. In a game. With him being a girl and you being, what's it?"

"Black Answer."

"Right. Dezire and Black Answer, hanging out in downtown Wakanda."

"No, but we mostly meet up in the Blue Area of the Moon."

"Of course." Archy buckled Clark into the car seat, snapped the seat into its base in the back of the station wagon. "Right, shorty?" he said to the baby. "I mean, where else?"

Clark, as yet unfamiliar with the secret domed refuge postulated, in the pages of Marvel Comics, to lie forever hidden on the moon's far side, said nothing.

"That's pretty much the only place," Titus said.

He got into the backseat so that he could, when required, make faces at Clark or give him a bottle. Archy started for home along Telegraph, but then when they hit Sixty-first Street, he missed the turn.

"Where we going?" Titus said.

"To Wakanda," said Archy.

"Where?"

"The Blue Area of the Moon."

He didn't stop when they got there, though. Just slowed down, in his drag-ass, baby-smelling, style-free Subaru wagon, long enough to check out a banner announcing, in baseball-jersey script, the imminent opening for business, between the United Federation of Donuts and the King of Bling, of a trading card store called Mr. Nostalgia's

Neighborhood. Beyond the fourth grade or so, Archy had never taken much interest in baseball cards, but he could feel the underlying vibe of that particular madness. Although he knew he would never be able to set foot in that building again without breaking his heart, he understood that the new operation held promise, and in principle, at least, he approved. The merchandise was not the thing, and neither, for that matter, was the nostalgia. It was all about the neighborhood, that space where common sorrow could be drowned in common passion as the talk grew ever more scholarly and wild.

"I hope you make it," he said to Mr. Nostalgia, whoever the dude might be. "Truly, bro, I really hope you do."

He eased his foot off the brake, thinking as they rolled away that, after all, perhaps one day a few years from now, he might have recovered enough to feel like he was ready to stop in. Say hi, drop a little lore and history on the man, tell him all about Angelo's, and Spencer's, and the Brokeland Years. See how they put the world together, next time around.

Berkeley, California
September 30, 2011

Acknowledgments

T he following creditors, progenitors, enablers, verifiers, sustainers, readers, and supporters of this book are hereby indemnified against blame for its flaws:

The MacDowell Colony, Peterborough, New Hampshire; Dagmar and Ray Dolby; Steven Barclay and Garth Bixler; Philip Pavel and the staff of the Chateau Marmont, Los Angeles, California; the Headlands Institute, Sausalito, California; the Mesa Refuge, Point Reyes Station, California;

Zak Borovay (*Music*); Kent Randolph (*Vinyl*); Beah Haber and Nancy Bardacke (*Midwifery*); Adam Savage (*Dirigible Liberation*);

Ta-Nehisi Coates; Daniel Mendelsohn; Dave Eggers;

Jennifer Barth; Mary Evans; Amy Cray; David and Arla Manson; Jonathan Burnham; Michael McKenzie; Howie Sanders; David Colden; Scott Rudin; Sophie, Zeke (*MTO!*), Ida-Rose, and Abraham Chabon;

Wax Poetics magazine, Andre Torres, Editor-in-Chief; *Blaxploitation Cinema: The Essential Reference Guide*, Josiah Howard; *Women of Blaxploitation*, Yvonne D. Sims; *Will You Die with Me?: My Life and the Black Panther Party*, Flores Alexander Forbes; *The Death of Rhythm and Blues*, Nelson George;

Blaxploitation.com (www.blaxploitation.com); Oakland Geology (http://oaklandgeology.wordpress.com/);   Funky16Corners   (http://funky16corners.lunarpages.net/); Birth Stories Diaries (www.birth diaries.com);

and James Rouse, dreamer of the original Brokeland.

This novel was written using Scrivener on Macintosh computers.

About the Author

M ichael Chabon is the author of *The Mysteries of Pittsburgh*, *Wonder Boys*, *The Amazing Adventures of Kavalier & Clay*, *Summerland* (a novel for children), *The Final Solution*, *The Yiddish Policemen's Union*, and *Gentlemen of the Road*; as well as the short story collections *A Model World* and *Werewolves in Their Youth*; and the essay collections *Maps and Legends* and *Manhood for Amateurs*. He is the Chairman of the Board of the MacDowell Colony. He lives in Berkeley, California, with his wife, the novelist Ayelet Waldman, and their children.